TABITHA

FROM THE SAME AUTHOR

For Young Adults
The *Flip!* trilogy:
Flip! On the Edge
Flip! Beyond the Horizon
Flip! The Daisychain

The *White Gates* series:
The Kicking Tree
Ultimate Justice
Winds & Wonders
The Spark

Short Stories & Poems
Stardust

Non-Fiction
Adventures with God:
Exploring Faith & Intimacy with Infinite God
WYSIWYG Christianity:
Young People & Faith in the 21st Century

TABITHA

T.N.STUBBS

THE
LISTENING
PEOPLE

The Listening People
15 Cleeve Grove
Keynsham,
Bristol, BS31 2HF

Email: TLPpress@yahoo.com
Web: www.thelisteningpeople.co.uk

ISBN 978-1-915288-07-3
British Library Cataloguing in Publication Data.
A catalogue record for this book is available from the British Library.

THE
LISTENING
PEOPLE

*This book is dedicated to the wonderful people
who teach our teenagers.*

"Who in the world am I? Ah, that's the great puzzle."

Lewis Carroll – *Alice's Adventures in Wonderland*

PART ONE

1

1

*B*eattie's Bingo is packed. Some come to play, some to gamble and most to catch up on the gossip. It's the break after the second card.

"That Tabitha, she were no but eight year old, they say, when she started on walkin' into t'other folks' back gardens."

"Private back gardens?"

"Well, the back garden what belongs to the Old Lodge down by t'big gates, at any-road."

"Yer don't say, Cat. What were she up to?"

"Just sitting on t'grass, apparently. But I don't buy it."

"No, she's a rum 'un, that 'un, for sure."

"Bit of a liability, if you ask me. 'Eadstrong. 'Er's goin' to come a cropper one day if 'er mother don't rein 'er in."

"Who, Cindy? Hardly. Her's a proud 'un. Regular here at bingo, once, she were. You could guarantee on meeting her 'ere but now it's only every now and then. You can see where her daughter gets it from. That Cindy's got history. She i'nt from around here. Her girl must've had a black father, so where'd she find him? Not on Beck Ings that's for sure."

"She's in the same class as our Rosie."

"And our daughter's friend's girl, Amy. Yer know, the Lanes. She says they try to be friends but Tabs Johnson don't want to join in their games. Goes off on her own."

"Could be that's she meeting up with a boy. They're never too young these days."

"Maybe. Who'd you reckon?"

"Well, I've seen that Green lad following 'er around. He's the type. Up for it. 'T wouldn't surprise me..."

Bing-bong. The bingo caller chimes for attention through his loud, sexy speakers. "Yer third game, ladies. Prizes on this one for t'top row and full 'ouse... Eyes down, now. First out... Number twenty-one."

"Key o' the door," they all chorus.

2

Trotting to the end of a path through the houses one sunny day, eight-year-old Tabby found herself on the Puddleham Road, one of the roads that skirted the old council estate. She followed a bend opposite a high wall, an even older construction built to surround 'The Park' – a sixteenth-century 'big house'. The gentry folk who had once lived there had left many years ago – better-off people no longer liked draughty places run by servants, it seemed. The building was now a college, teaching some kind of engineering.

Tabby stared up at the ornamental iron gates that led into the grounds. She dappled her foot in the build-up of pebbles at their base – they didn't seem to be used much. The ironwork and the view of the great trees which lined the driveway were one of Tabitha's favourite places. She never came here with anyone else; she kept her visits secret. She had discovered the place in one of her early explorations. Here were gates for giants, the most enormous in the world, extending right up into the sky.

It was a place of great fascination to a little girl, especially one who had an affinity for nature, and she would often just stand there and gaze at the great trees, watching the way they changed with the seasons.

Some "nature", as she called it, often got taken home. Acorns, leaves, feathers, snail shells, pebbles and even the occasional dead spider. Although Cindy drew the line at things which were still alive, even the minibeasts were a great fascination. Little Tabby spent a long time crouched at the base of the wall watching them go about their business – ants, earwigs, woodlice and even big black beetles that scuttled along above ground in case it rained. Tabitha understood that if you saw a black beetle, then rain was on its way, and given the number of rainy days that occurred in West Yorkshire, it was often the case that she had had to run home quickly to avoid a soaking.

To the left of the gates was a smaller wall that met the high one at right angles. It enclosed a gatehouse. In it was a small

3

wooden door. This was magical and filled Tabby with curiosity. What lay beyond? The wooden door had a latch that could be lifted by pressing down with the thumb.

One sunny summer day, Tabby's curiosity overtook her. She reached above her head, pulled the little lever down and pushed. After a couple of tries, the gate had opened just enough for her to creep through. She found herself in a well-kept garden behind the small isolated gatehouse. At one time it had housed a busy gatekeeper but now the cottage was quite separate. It would be someone's home but little Tabby found the place deserted, so she took courage and ventured further. To her left was a kitchen garden and to her right, a high beech hedge with a small opening between it and the wall. Tabby wanted to know where that led.

What she found was beautiful – a tiny garden as if made for a small person. Something made Tabby feel that it had been put there just for her. In the centre of it, a small square flower bed surrounded a short plinth on which balanced a little forest nymph. Could it have been a girl who had been magicked? Her clothes seemed to be falling off. Maybe that was what happened to children who sneak into other people's gardens. Had this little lady been caught and turned into stone? Tabitha checked that her clothes were most firmly fastened – perhaps she would be safe if she kept herself properly dressed. But then, maybe, the stone figure hadn't been a person at all. Could it be a fairy? That was it. This little garden probably belonged to fairies – a real fairy garden.

Tabby crossed the secret garden and caressed the deep green shiny leaves of a line of laurels which joined the beech hedge. Behind the statue was more of the high wall. Tabby was drawn to a small iron gate. It was a little like the big ones across the drive in its design, only this was of normal size and locked with a large brass padlock. Through it, she could see woodland. She breathed in the scented red and white roses trained up and around it and peered at trunks of the big trees beyond. This was the way to a wonderland.

A stone bench with carved feet straddled the corner but she did not try to climb onto it; instead, she sat cross-legged on the short soft turf beneath her feet. It was springy and delicious. The smell of the grass filled her nostrils and its cool softness caressed her skin. Tilting her head back, she looked straight up into a blue sky splotched with little white clouds. From the other side of the wall, the vast trees sent up branches that seemed to go as high as the sky, itself. Birds, large and small, flitted across and filled the air with their song. On that first visit, Tabby had remained there a long time.

This was the most perfect place in the whole wide world; perhaps it was a bit of heaven itself. It *must* be a place where fairies lived. It was so different from any garden she had seen before. Fairies hide when people come, so, of course, you'd never see one unless you were really lucky.

Despite six years of frequent visits, Tabitha had never yet seen a soul – no fairies or people. Someone must have looked after the garden and cut the grass but no one had ever appeared. Surrounded by the turmoil of everyday life on a rundown estate as an only child in a hand-to-mouth single-parent family, her secret garden had become a sanctuary of peace and natural beauty. But it wasn't real life, was it?

3

Th-rump, th-rump, th-rump, th-rump. A loud and unrelenting beat filled Tabitha's head; the walls of the dark cavern pressed in; her nightmare was reaching a novel intensity. For the first time, the dream cave she was trying to get out of was reverberating with a heavy rhythmical pulse; it had never been accompanied by sound before. Crumpth, th-rump, th-rump, th-rump, th-rump. Urgh.... She struggled and, as consciousness returned, she screamed – a scream that broke through her lips into the waking world. She kicked off her duvet and sat up, sweat pouring down her face.

Now fully cognisant, Tabitha collapsed back onto the bed and rolled over – she hated that dream, all trapped in as she was. And it was getting worse. Sound was a new dimension and, even now, as she struggled to rid herself of the nightmare; the noise continued to blast her brain. She began to panic. Was she losing it? She had heard that if you were going to go mad it would most likely come out at puberty with everything else teenage hormones threw at you; the danger was upon her – she was four months away from her fourteenth birthday.

No matter what she did, Tabs could not stop the rhythmical thrump beating on her conscious world. She tumbled out of bed to get some air; she needed to break free. As she pushed open the double-glazed window, she realised, with immense relief, that the noise was not inside her head; it was coming from outside. It sounded like it was coming from all directions at the same time - she couldn't see anything in the street with its dim lighting. Th-rump, th-rump, th-rump. Tabs checked her phone; it was only just after midnight. She had been asleep for less than two hours. Th-rump, th-rump, th-rump.

Tabitha decided to take a grip; *be sensible*, she told herself. Whatever that noise was, it was outside and probably not malevolent. It was unlikely that she would be abducted by aliens, even if that is what happened in books or in the 18-rated films she shouldn't have been watching aged thirteen and three-quarters.

6

No, this wasn't necessarily the end of the world. She must stop reading so much in the horror department – at least not just before going to sleep. She had already given up on Instagram when she had inadvertently tumbled into a thread of dark posts.

Now the noise shifted slightly – it seemed to be coming from above the roof. That was OK – there were upstairs flats between her and it, so if anyone was going to be abducted, she wasn't in the front line. She and her mum lived in a downstairs flat – number 49 Ings View – on the Beck Ings Estate. It had once belonged to the local council but now they paid their rent to a housing association.

The whole place continued to shake. Tabs was not scared now but curious; she leaned of out the window and looked up to see... a helicopter, very low and directly overhead. She heard her mum stumble out of bed in the room next to hers and say something she wouldn't have done if she thought her daughter could hear her. Tabs left the window and went to open her bedroom door but before she got there—

Wham! The flat reverberated as the communal door that led to the street banged to, followed by heavy, noisy footsteps running up the concrete stairs which led to the upper flats. Bang. The front door to number 51 immediately above closed equally noisily. This was not unusual but not at ten minutes past midnight. The people upstairs had moved in less than six months ago and Tabitha and Cindy were still getting used to it. Before these tenants, they had had an elderly couple who you hardly knew were there. These new people went by the name of Brown – at least the mother did – Tabs had gathered they didn't all have that surname. They were a single-parent family like hers but there were more of them, a mother in her thirties, a son in his teens, a bit older than Tabs, and two younger children, one of primary school age, and one preschool.

"What the hell." The Browns had their window open and Mrs Brown's dulcet tones could be clearly heard screaming, "What yer bin up to? Where yer bin?"

"Shut up, Mum."

"Don't you shut up, me. What the 'ell's going on?"

The youngest began to cry.

"Look, now you've woken him. I'll never get him back down. What's that you've got?"

"Stop asking bleeding questions and hide this somewhere."

"Where on earth did yer get all that, Darren?"

"Shut up, Mum." The baby was now in full voice.

Tabs opened her door to find her mother in the hallway putting on her dressing gown.

"What's going on, Mum?"

"I don't know, but it don't sound very nice. Better look decent."

There was a banging on the front communal door.

"Open up, police."

Cindy stepped out of her front door and pulled open the communal door to be confronted by half a dozen policemen in body armour.

"Police." An officer thrust a badge in Cindy's face. "We're looking for a young man seen entering this building a few minutes ago." Cindy indicated the stairs.

"First floor, number 51."

Four of the policemen mounted the stairs two at a time and rapt on the door of number 51. Mrs Brown opened it a sliver.

"What—" but before she could say any more, the leading policeman forced the door open and the three others pushed in. The children screamed, and then Darren was heard shouting.

"Lay off me. I an't done nowt."

"What's this all about?" yelled his mother.

"Where is it?"

"Where's what?"

"You know what I'm talking about. Mrs, have you got a kitchen knife?"

"Course."

"Can you find it for me?"

"Why, what the bleeding hell yer goin' to do with it?"

"Just find it."

"OK, keep you're bleeding hair on."

At the bottom of the stairs, Tabitha and Cindy, now joined by Mrs Harris from number 50 across the passage, heard Mrs Brown rattle drawers in her kitchen. "It's not here."

The policemen's radio crackled.

"Good," said one, "bag it and bring it here ... number 51"

"Serge," said a policeman emerging from one of the bedrooms.

"Ah, good work, Geoff ... So, Darren, where did you get all this money from?"

"That's mine. I been saving it. Let me go, you're hurting me."

"OK. Let's all sit down." The voices then became more muffled.

Another policeman entered the building with what looked like a carving knife in a plastic bag. The ladies indicated the stairs and he climbed them more carefully than his colleagues had a few moments before.

Twenty minutes later, as Tabs, Cindy and Mrs Harris sat in Cindy's living room clutching mugs of tea, Darren from upstairs was led out in handcuffs followed by more policemen. Three of the four police cars parked outside drove off. The helicopter had already vanished and quietness fell once more on Ings View. It was only broken by the sounds of thumping and scraping from above and the whimpers of the children.

Half an hour after that, a car drove up, and a man got out and mounted the stairs. He came back down with a policeman – both were carrying cardboard boxes – and was followed by Mrs Brown clutching a toddler and a black plastic bin bag. A dishevelled child of about six years old trailed after them. Finally, Mrs Brown returned and banged the door of number 51 resolutely shut and left, ignoring the other residents in the block. The car drove off followed by the final police car. The silence was eerie.

Later, they learned that Darren had, allegedly, threatened the manager of Beattie's Bingo with a knife as he was locking up and leaving with the night's takings. The man had made no resistance but, as soon as Darren had legged it round the corner, he rang 999. The armed robbery was acted on without delay. Unluckily for Darren Brown, the helicopter was already in the area. A lone man running through the streets of a housing estate at midnight shows up bright and clear on the infrared camera and they simply followed him home. He had thrown the knife in a hedge but that

had also been spotted. The hedge was pinpointed by the
helicopter and the knife had soon been retrieved with the help of
a dog.

4

Sun streamed through a gap in the curtains waking Tabs from her fitful sleep. She stretched out her limbs – she was now tall enough to touch the foot of her bed without difficulty. *How much more will I grow?* Then she remembered the events of the night and wondered for a moment whether she had only imagined them. She wished she didn't have the kind of nasty dream it had begun with. In the bright sunlight, things seemed so normal – apart, that was, from the gathering of people in the street exchanging their own take on the incident of the hovering helicopter.

Tabs got dressed and stepped through into the kitchen where Cindy was filling the kettle, watching the gathering through the net curtains.

"Look at 'em. It'll keep them happy for a day or two. Something to gossip about. It's this sort of drama that keeps some people going. Life would be too boring without it. This time it's all too close for comfort, if you ask me. That manager at Beattie's is not the sort – too delicate. Wouldn't say boo to a goose."

"Pretty scary, though."

"Some of that money must've been mine."

"What would you have done, Mum? If you had been there."

"What *he* did with a knife in my face. Wouldn't you? No. Don't tell me you'd a shouted him down. It sounds easy when you're thirteen."

"Oh. Here comes Cat. Number one busybody."

"Like gossip makes life worthwhile. Why can't there be something nice to break the boredom?"

"Yeah, there is – if you can afford it."

"Surely, not everything nice costs money?"

"Well, if there is, I haven't found it yet."

The sun was inviting and Tabitha longed to get out; the world was full of interesting things if you bothered to look and none of them cost money. She liked the flowers that pushed through the

11

crevices in the paving slabs, against the walls and in the gutters, even the little tiny ones that lots of people miss. Since the summer school holidays had started, she had collected and pressed the different grasses that grew on the waste ground at the end of the street. Amongst the rubbish, she had discovered at least ten different varieties. Her mum thought it was a bit odd getting excited about grass, but at least it was safe. Now her once little Tabby was coming up fourteen, she dreaded the time when boys would come into the picture. She, herself, had taken an interest at that age and she had regretted it.

Tabs pocketed some of her spending money to go to the convenience store. Sweets were another thing she liked. It was only a block away but she decided to take the long way round beyond the estate to the edge of the old town with its stone-built houses put up in the days when the woollen mill was taking over what had been up to then a rural village surrounded by hay meadows.

On the way, she passed Ashol and her older brother, Deng. She smiled at them – she knew them from school but not to talk to. They had not long arrived in the area from an African country called South Sudan, which, by all accounts, was hot and war-ridden. Rumour had it that their family had had to run away and they had been taken into Britain as refugees. The interesting thing was that, although there was no shortage of black people in West Yorkshire, there were very few at Tabitha's school and none of them lived on Beck Ings – except her. Her mum was white but somehow she had met a dude from Nigeria and married him and little Tabby had been the result. But he was no longer in the picture and her mum kind of pretended that her daughter was as white as she was. But you can't pretend that as a kid – even if you were not as black as the Thomases with their strong African accents. The other kids – and sometimes even their parents – kept reminding her of it.

Tabitha left the road with its stone-walled front gardens and interesting flowers basking in the June sunshine and re-entered the red and yellow estate which climbed up past the row of three shops, one of which was a Spar convenience store. A Mars Bar and some liquorice laces in hand, Tabs was queueing behind an elderly lady when Gareth Green and his mates, Gary Smith, Shaun Robottom and Dean Slater – his 'disciples' as Tabs called them – poured into the shop.

Bother, she sighed to herself because she knew she wouldn't escape attention. Known to his associates as Griff, Green had been the bane of her life since they were both six. Mr Patel kept his eye on the CCTV screen as the boys circled the aisles, which only slowed him down but it was less than half a minute before Green came up behind her; she knew what he was going to do.

"Get your filthy mitts off me." Tabs glared at him, bravely, as he persisted with his large hand on her bottom. He had been bullying her one way or another forever.

He had been among the reasons she hadn't wanted to go to the comprehensive school which served the town but there had been no real choice. Now aged almost fourteen, Green's bullying had morphed into molesting her whenever he got a chance. Tabs had her own name for him; she called him 'Gross Griff' but not to his face – that would have been most inadvisable. At school, he was a real pain and had been suspended a couple of times. Why he was like this, Tabs couldn't imagine. Her mother simply said that some people were 'that way out' and it didn't need any further explanation. "Asking 'why' doesn't get you anywhere, lass," she had said, "some things you just accept. That's the way of it." In primary school, Tabs had wondered if he would eventually grow up to be nicer but it turned out the other way round – the older he got, the meaner he became. Her mother explained that 'them that are that way out' usually got into serious trouble when they got older. "He'll probably end up in prison, mark my words. Just you make sure you give him a wide berth."

There was nothing her daughter wanted more but it was easier said than done. And here she was in the shop where he and his stupid cronies had probably deliberately followed her. Gross was a pain to everyone but he seemed to have a 'thing' about her more than other girls. She didn't know why this was any more than the rest of the mystery. Griff, she concluded, was just a nutter.

"Get lost," she spat, forcing his hand away.

Mr Patel came to her rescue. "Leave the lass alone or leave

my shop," he commanded. He could do without this gang.

"Or what? You going to send for the fuzz? Keep your 'air on. Not my fault... accident." Green indicated that his mates snickering behind him had pushed him against the girl. But Tabs knew it had been deliberate – you don't put a hand where he had put his by accident. Growing into adolescence seemed to do things to some people and what it had done to him wasn't very nice.

Tabs bought her sweets and hurried out of the door of the Spar shop and concluded – not for the first time – that she didn't fit in on the Beck Ings estate even though she had grown up there. *One day I'll get away from this place – right away. I don't belong here. It in't just the colour of my skin. It's that loads of the kids have got grandmas and ancestors who have worked in the mills – me and me mam are off-comers. And, actually, I don't like people much at all. I don't truly fit into human stuff much – I like nature. Woods and gardens are where I belong. Better than people.*

Although Millheaton stands in the heart of the great West Yorkshire conurbation clustered around the cities of Bradford, Leeds, Halifax, Huddersfield and Wakefield, there are patches of green among the houses, factories, shops, churches and the complicated network of roads which join them. The local authority built the council estate on the meadows above the beck and called it, appropriately, Beck Ings. Since then, the industry had declined but most of the people on the estate, even then, were descended from those who had initially inhabited it... but not Tabitha or her mum.

It was on a day in nursery school when a child repeated a comment made by his parents about her skin colour, that Tabitha had first come to realise that most people were different from her. He followed the comment by saying his mum had told him to stay away from her. Had she known, Cindy would have sprung to her daughter's defence, but little Tabby – like most things – had kept it to herself.

Tabs cut down a snicket and rounded a corner before Green and his mates could see where she was going. Making sure she wasn't followed, she made her way towards the little garden.

Still breathing heavily from her extended detour to avoid Gross Griff and his cronies, she squeezed through the small door in the wall as she had done so many times before, lay on the turf of the secret garden and nibbled on her sweets. *One day, I'll escape Beck Ings completely and live forever in a magical place like this with nothing but nature and fairies. It'll be a safe place where the likes of Gross Griff – or anyone else – can never be. Just me and the fairies.*

All too soon, though, it was time to go home. Her mother had grown more anxious about her whereabouts these days than she had been when she was only eight. Perhaps times had changed or it may be that Cindy knew her daughter was of an age to attract unwanted attention. Tabs traced her way slowly back up from the beck towards her flat, hoping she would not encounter Gross and his crew on the way.

Growing up in Leeds in a mixed-race environment, Cindy had taken up with Tabitha's Nigerian father, Joshua Johnson, where he still lived and worked. They had been happy for a time, living in the multicultural Leeds suburb of Chapeltown, but the relationship had soon lost its appeal – somehow they had become bored with each other. Tabitha's mum left her husband and took the first offer of a council flat outside the city.

Joshua believed in naming children after the place where they were born, so Tabitha's middle name was Chapeltown – she had been registered as Tabitha Chapeltown Johnson. To his credit, he still owned her and she was supposed to spend one day a month with him. It didn't always happen and Cindy was not sad when he said he couldn't manage a particular Saturday. He had re-married – a black woman this time – and had three little black boys, who hadn't got to know their stepsister properly.

Tabs didn't know much about the history of the place she had grown up in – it wasn't something she was interested in. If she had listened to her teacher instead of daydreaming about her garden or avoiding Griff, she might have heard her explaining that the Beck Ings housing estate had been constructed in the 1930s. The planners had designed a carefully organised pattern of houses and flats with gardens surrounded by privet hedges. The streets did not go in straight lines; there were crescents, squares and triangles all to make the place more interesting and attractive.

All that Tabs noticed was that no one grew much in their gardens. Her mum had said that the more enterprising residents in the 1950s, who had decided to continue to grow vegetables even after the Second World War, had found their gardens raided by hungry children and so they had soon given up. An apple tree was deemed a legitimate target – scrumping was not regarded as a real crime – so most of the fruit trees had long since been chopped down to avoid the invasion of kids doing more damage to hedges and flower beds.

Downstream from the estate, the beck flowed between and under the remaining mill buildings which lined both sides of the valley bottom. Before the Industrial Revolution, the only mill had been a flour mill but in the eighteenth and nineteenth centuries, several woollen mills had sprung up with carding machines for combing the wool and spinning machines for making it into yarn. Then a dye factory had appeared, and finally, a four-floor brick monstrosity which housed giant looms where carpets had been woven for six generations. From the start, this had had to be steam-powered – the Mill Beck did not have the energy to turn machines on each of these floors. The furnaces had belched huge plumes of smoke which had blackened everything in the neighbourhood, including the elegant façade of The Park. There had also been a mill turning out shoddy stuffs – cloth made from recycled fibre. The carpet factory closed in the 1980s but it was when the shoddy mill closed that a lot of people on the estate, women in particular, lost their jobs. That was the time the estate had especially gone downhill.

5

In the weeks that followed, Gross Griff Green continued being a pest, albeit in a low-level kind of way. After the September return to school, he found a new distraction behind the bike sheds. The new Year 9 had been caught up in the latest craze – experimenting with vaping and then, for the more enterprising, smoking cannabis. Any kid who didn't want to be left out of the group was lured into trying it, and that was all but a few.

Once you showed an interest in vaping, you became a target for the drug pushers. They knew all about teenagers' fear of being marginalised and they preyed on it. Griff Green quickly made a bid for a leadership role in this trade, despite his lack of funds. Those who ran the drug business, or at least those at the dealing level who were targeting kids at Beckside Academy, quickly identified Green as a willing distributor. They provided him with a tiny cash return and a personal supply of cannabis but, most of all, the kudos that went with the job.

Tabs was not on his hit list but that didn't prevent her from getting invitations to share a spliff. As the opening term moved into its third week, nearly all of her fellow classmates with whom she had grown up were vaping and trying weed – some had even begun buying.

Rosie Peters went, "What you waiting for, Tabs? You coming through t'ginnel back o't'sheds dinner time?"

Amy Lane cajoled her. "Go on, Tabs, you need to try this. It's cool. I thought you were one of us. You gonna spend dinner break on yer own?"

Tabitha knew it was not only against school rules and illegal but her mum would be shocked if she knew she had even thought about trying a spliff. *Mum's so protective of me but she don't understand,* she told herself. *If there was any harm in it, then most of the kids would be spaced out most of the time and they aren't.*

Of course, there were all the lessons on the dangers of drugs and she knew the argument that soft drugs led to hard drugs but weed wasn't as harmful as tobacco, was it? It didn't give you cancer. So why all the fuss? *Anyway, one drag won't do me no harm,*

17

will it? she persuaded herself. She had a lot to lose; it was bad enough being different because of her skin colour without being abandoned because she was too scared to take a drag on a spliff.

"OK. I'm in. But I in't buying."

"Course. Yer poor, right?"

Tabs ignored the implied slight.

At midday, Tabs and the other girls made their way to the path which led behind the bike sheds and through a gap in the hedge into the lane outside the school boundary. The gap was being constantly repaired but because it was such a shortcut and obscured by the bikesheds it was regularly re-opened. They followed the lane along to a gate to a field where several distributors were operating. The air was powerful with the sickly smell of weed. Tabs reflected that here she didn't need to actually smoke any, all she needed to do was breathe – it didn't smell bad, though. She and some of the other girls from her class were just queuing for a spliff off some likely lad who was enjoying the female attention when the dealers – including Griff – just melted away. They had planned their getaway if authority should arrive, keeping the path from the school field in view. But Tabs and her mates had their back to it and they were caught before they knew what was happening.

A posse of teachers: Mr Frost, Miss Wright, Mr Kendall and Mademoiselle Gaudet – the French teacher – rounded up a dozen kids and they were marched off back into the main school building and made to sit on the hall stage behind the curtain. They were obliged to sit in silence awaiting the arrival of the head.

Tabs wasn't unduly worried about what any of the teachers would have to say and she wasn't scared of what the head would do. She didn't mind the idea of being suspended or even expelled but she knew she wouldn't be – it took more than being found out the back of school premises. Drugs were banned but she hadn't even taken a drag, had she? What she truly dreaded was the look of horror and disappointment on her mum's face when she found out what she was going to be accused of. Her mum hadn't a clue what actually went on in school; nor what it was like trying to fit in.

The head gave them a lecture – the usual 'it's stupid to do drugs' one.

"Marijuana rots your brain. Do you want to become a drooling lune?" he ranted.

Amy Lane claimed they hadn't known what was happening in the field – they had merely followed the crowd. "It were just, like, curiosity, sir."

It was clear that none of the captured party had taken any drugs, so all he could do was reprimand them for leaving school premises and issued the appropriate detention. His parting shot was that he was sick and tired of hearing other heads tell him Beckside Academy had got the nickname, Weedside Academy. One of the boys snickered. Fuming, the head pulled him out and dragged him off to his 'lair' - the kids' name for the head's office – while he handed over the rest into the hands of Jack Frost. "Mr Frost, I'll leave you to deal with the rest of these sad individuals."

"All right," called Jack, when he had gone. "The rest of you I want to see after school in the geography base. Now, get back out there and prepare for your afternoon studies."

At a quarter past three, Tabs and her friends reported to Jack along with some of the girls. Not all of them were there; Jack said he would deal with them later.

"We never took any," protested Rosie Peters.

"So what were you doing there, outside the grounds, then?"

"Just followed. Wondered what was, like, going off."

Tabs concurred, "We was just looking, sir. You in't going to tell on us to us parents, are you?"

"And why shouldn't I do that, Tabitha Johnson?"

"'Course we haven't done nothing, sir."

"You were there. Tabitha, I must say I'm surprised at you. What possessed you to go though a gap in the hedge?"

"I dunno, sir. It was, like, everyone were going." What was Tabs supposed to do? Ignore all the other kids?

"Who led this excursion?"

"It weren't us, sir," piped up Amy.

"I know that. Who was at the front of the queue?"

No one spoke.

"You know that if you suspect any dealing is going on anywhere, your job is to report it – not going yourself to see what's happening. OK? I don't suppose any of you know who it was who was dealing, do you?"

No one replied. Tabs had recognised Gross Griff as one of the distributors but if she dobbed him in, she'd never hear the end of it. He'd get his gang onto her and maybe even his cronies higher up the chain. The drugs scene was dangerous, wasn't it? The least she had to do with him and his gang, the better, so she kept mum.

On their way out of the classroom, Jack stopped and called Tabs over to him. "You know Tabitha, you're different from the rest."

"Different? I guess," she was immediately conscious of her colour. "I try to forget it – ignore it when people call me names."

"Oh. I don't mean in your appearance. I mean in the potential you have. There's a bright brain in there, Tabitha. You should use it."

"Sorry, sir. But that in't true."

"Isn't it? How long did it take you to do your geography homework last night? Ten minutes?"

"About that."

"And it's supposed to take at least twice that time. And unlike some, you never fail to do it."

"Me mum makes me."

"You're a fortunate girl. Not all mums care about their children that much." Tabs knew that was true. "I'll do a deal with you, Tabitha. Your mum has to be informed that you were in a field beyond the school boundary where drugs were being sold but I'll make it clear to her that you were not part of it. You are only guilty of being silly enough to be in the wrong place at the wrong time. In return I want you to have a go at this for me."

"What is it?" Mr Frost lifted his briefcase and pulled out two A4 closely typed sheets, stapled together. It bore the title 'Climate Change and Methods to Combat It'. "I want you to read this and then evaluate it for me in your own words – about three hundred." Tabs looked askance; how was she to begin to do that? A look of panic spread across her face. Mr Frost was ready for such a response. He continued, "Start by underlining the main points and then identify which three things you think are the most important for West Yorkshire and why."

"But I haven't done nothing like that before in geography."

"There always has to be a first time."

"But that's like what they do in the top set. I'm in set three."

"But what if you were in the top set? You know, Tabitha, I think you could be if you tried."

Tabs took the sheets and looked at them. "If I do this, you'll tell my mum that I weren't doing owt at lunchtime?" Mr Frost nodded. "That's, like, blackmail, sir."

Mr Frost's face broke out into a smile. "You're right. So no conditions; I'll make it clear to your mum you were not involved beyond being in the wrong place. But I would still like you to try and do this. Just do your best. Would you like to improve your set? If you earn a place in a higher set, that's something I would delight in telling your mum."

"And would you put me up a set if I do this?"

"Let's see how well you do it, eh? I'll give you until the end of the week."

Tabs didn't find Jack Frost's paper difficult. There was nothing in it she didn't already know – not if you followed the climate change debate, so she hadn't had to do any underlining. When she finished she counted her words and they came to three hundred and twenty-one. She was sure that Jack wouldn't count them too diligently.

The next lunchtime she took her work to the school library to type it up and do a spell-check. The library wasn't a place she frequented often. There was no one there from her sets but sitting opposite each other were Ashol and Deng. Ashol was in the top set for everything in her year.

"Hi Tabitha," she grinned. "Haven't seen you for ages. How's it going?"

"OK. Jack Frost has given me this geography stuff and I thought I should type it up to spell-check it."

"Let me see."

"Why? Nah. It's OK." But Ashol saw what it was.

"Oh, the climate change thing. If Jack gave you that, he believes in you."

"Believes in me? What do you mean?"

"Like, he thinks you're worth his time."

That figured. "That's what we got in the top set. Jack asked you to evaluate it?"

"Yeah. He reckons I could do top-set stuff. I said I'd have a go but I won't be doing no more when he sees this."

"Can I see what you've done?"

"Why?"

"I could tell you if it's what he wants."

"No harm you seeing it, I guess." Tabs found herself passing over her draft. Somehow she trusted Ashol not to mock her. She was different. Different like her? Maybe.

"Wow, Tabitha. This is good. How long did this take you?"

"Dunno. Less than half an hour. The thing to read wasn't that hard."

"If... *when* Jack puts you in the top set, I can help you with any catching up, if you want."

"Thanks. You reckon he will?"

"This is as good if not better than mine."

"You're only saying that."

"Hand it in. Let Jack be the judge."

"Just like it is."

"Just like it is – after you've done the spell-check. Have you got your own computer?"

"No. That's why I've come to the library."

"Look, that one's free over by the window. Grab it before anyone else does."

A week later Tabitha found herself in the second geography set. But it didn't end there. By her birthday on the 6th October, Jack Frost was offering to promote her to the top set if she was willing to do some extra catch-up work. But when she saw how much there was it took the wind out of her sails and she decided to be contented with the second set. After all, she wasn't that bright, was she?

"I'm not doing no more," she told Ashol. "He never said how

22

much I gotta do. And I'm not that good."

"But if he's asked you to, he thinks you're capable. Jack wouldn't ask you to do the impossible."

"Capable? Nah. I ain't."

"Look, girl. Don't give up before you've tried. Here, let me see what there is."

Tabs handed over Jack's list of pages she had to study.

"You can do this, Tabs. Look, what if you came to our house on Saturday? We could study together. There's room for both of us on the dining table. And I can help you if you get stuck."

The thought of going to Ashol's was inviting.

"Yeah. OK. I'll ask me mam."

Cindy had no objection and within a week, Tabs had produced all that Jack Frost had asked of her. Even he was astonished at how quickly she completed the catch-up. There was a problem, however – the top set period clashed with her English lessons. Mr Frost said he would have a word with her English teacher, Mr Kendall, and, to her amazement, she was bumped up a set in English, too. No questions asked. Now, she no longer found herself with the girls like Rosie and Amy she had needed to keep in with by exploring the weed scene.

Tabs took to Deng straight away. He was different – he didn't even try to fit in and she was intrigued. Deng was in the year above her and Ashol but had been put into her class to learn French because he hadn't done any in South Sudan. One day, Miss Chandler, the French teacher – the one before Mademoiselle Gaudet – had been banging on about the importance of learning French and not making much sense. Tabs had reckoned, like most of the kids, that so much of school was having to learn things that were useless. French, like history, was a good example. No one who spoke only French and not any English would come anywhere near Beck Ings, would they? So it was pointless, no matter how much Miss Chandler rabbited on about understanding other 'cultures', whatever that meant. The woman didn't give up, though, you had to credit her that. She kept saying things no one understood or wanted to, like *Taisez-vous* and *Écoutez*.

Anyway, one day, Gary made a funny noise and then everyone had laughed. Miss Chandler responded with a, "*Tais-toi, s'il te plaît, Gary.*" What made it worse was that she said, "Gar-ree", like it was French. Loads of kids then began to, kinda, hoot. Griff had gone, "Gar-ree." and other lads were following his lead. How Miss Chandler got the courage to stand there and defy him, Tabs did not know. She knew where this was leading, though; she'd seen teachers run out in tears. She liked her teacher but there wasn't anything she could do about it. She winced. Gross was in his element and was enjoying himself.

But then Deng stood up from his seat at the front – all six feet of him, even though he was only fifteen, and everyone fell silent. What was he about to do? Was he going to clock Griff? Never.

He must have smiled at Miss Chandler because she smiled back at him. He slowly turned round and addressed the class in a measured tone. "If you don't want to learn," he said, "that's up to you. But I do, so please be quiet." It was amazing. Deng was taller and stronger than either Griff or any of his gang but no one had ever seen him fight, probably because he didn't have to. Griff had been so shocked that he had stayed silent – for that lesson, at least. It didn't last, of course, but no one said anything to Deng. He was just too big and too much of an unknown quantity, especially for Griff who was only brave if people were slighter than him, which most kids were. Tabs was impressed. Deng was tall but he was soft-spoken and he didn't seem to care what anyone thought or said about him, he just wanted to learn.

Miss Chandler left at the end of that term and when Mademoiselle Gaudet took her place she continued to offer Deng extra French tuition at lunchtimes and because Tabs looked like she was interested in learning, she invited her along, too. She went – although it was definitely more to do with Deng being there than a burning desire to learn French.

Deng spoke three languages already and was lapping up the French. He explained that it was spoken a lot in Africa. Perhaps he would go back one day. But what he told Tabs about the country his family had left made the Beck Ings Estate sound like paradise. People, where he came from, he explained, didn't eat every day at the best of times, mothers were dying in childbirth all the time and people were getting sick with malaria, typhoid and things, and many people died before they were fifty of something you'd get better from in Britain – if you got it in the first place, which you probably wouldn't. Some of them lived in refugee camps and guns and bush knives were everywhere. Tabs frowned but listened and the more she listened, the more Deng talked. In school, he was quiet... kind of above all the stink, which was what had intrigued Tabitha in the first instance, but now he was opening up to her as if she was special. This was a new experience for Tabs. And he was so gentle and polite, it made her feel like a real lady. He was amazing.

***

Jack was true to his word. At the end of term parents' night, he made sure Tabs got her mother to come in and then told Cindy the good news. It was a good feeling. It bucked up her mum for Christmas which was always a difficult time. It was the time of the year that she missed being married the most – there was only she and Tabs on Christmas Day, and on Boxing Day, Tabs always went to Leeds to be with her dad and his growing family. To be honest, Tabs found it was much nicer and happier there than on Christmas Day with just her mum watching the telly most of the time. The awful thing was that on Boxing Day it meant her mum was completely on her own and, when Tabs got back, she knew her mum would have drunk too much and be in a rotten mood. She would also be horribly hung over on the twenty-seventh. But there was nothing Tabs could do about it – it was part of the divorce settlement and her mother never wavered in making her daughter go and see her dad. Apart from anything else, Cindy believed it was important that Tabs kept up with her father, even if he, himself, wasn't as diligent.

Before the holidays, Mademoiselle Gaudet set Tabs a pile of catch-up stuff in French. Her student's new reputation had inspired her to try and get her properly into the language. "One 'as to, 'ow do you say it? 'Strike while the iron is 'ot.'," she said. Clearly, she thought that Tabs was both up for it and capable. To tell the truth, her student was grateful to have something she had to do over the holidays and it gave her a reason to keep in touch with Ashol. Her mum wanted to know why her daughter had homework to do in the holidays but Tabs explained that that was what happened when you got into Year 9. It was – if you were in the top sets.

T. N. STUBBS

***

January was cold that year – the sun didn't come out for weeks. But Tabs struggled on, trying to keep her mum's spirits up. School was hard, though, because, apart from Ashol, she knew fewer people in the classes she now found herself in. But the consolation was that Gross and his gang were mostly elsewhere in class time. When it was cold and wet they didn't seem to spend much time on the streets, either. This was good news because Tabs could steal off to the garden feeling confident of not being seen.

The term led into March and the signs of spring were everywhere. The way the hedges and trees first came into bud and then full-leaf fascinated Tabitha. The conker trees came first – they had sticky buds which burst with pale green fresh leaves like a hand with five fingers. Then, gradually, the other trees followed. The cherry trees had masses of blossom almost before the leaves came out and the bees were having a heyday around the blackthorn bushes with their little white flowers.

7

The halcyon days were not to last. The warmth of the sun invited the bullies back out onto the streets with renewed vigour as they re-established their territories. Tabs had had to steer clear of Gross on several occasions now the weather was more inviting and one day he and his gang were laying in wait as Tabitha made her way back from the shops. Gross stepped forward and went to take her arm. She shrugged him off and gave him a sharp piece of her mind.

"Gerroff me. Get lost."

The lads just thought that was funny and Tabs was thinking how she might get away from four now quite large individuals – boys who had grown up to be bigger and stronger in the last year – when Rosie and Amy drifted along and joined in her defence.

"You 'eard 'er. Get lost."

As Griff and the boys sidled off, Rosie produced an enormous wolf whistle. Although she didn't fancy Griff, she rather liked one of the others. She and Amy began to giggle and sloped off after them without even saying goodbye to Tabitha. She watched them go and felt a pang of rejection. But she quickly decided that she could certainly do without the attention of stupid boys and she was bored with the frivolity of the girls and was glad she was alone again. That didn't stop her from feeling lonely, though.

Tabitha hurried the rest of the way home, dropped off the shopping and made her way down to the iron gates, the little cottage and the garden where, although she had always been quite alone, she never felt lonely. The fairies might remain unseen but that didn't mean they didn't welcome her. Somehow, although she had stopped believing in fairies a long time ago and had rightly identified the statue as a dryad of ancient Greek mythology, the sense of welcome had never left her. She had been visiting her 'secret garden' for the past six years now and she knew exactly what to expect at all seasons of the year. As she grew older, so the garden had seemed to reduce in size, and the sparsely clad nymph had gradually become less like a fairy.

Tabs lay as usual on the close-cropped lawn; it must have been cut only that morning. No, she didn't believe in fairies anymore, or wood nymphs, but someone was looking after things, weren't they? She had no idea who lived in the cottage and she did not want to know because she wanted to keep the magic of the garden to herself. However, each year that passed, it became harder – the magic became more difficult to maintain.

Over the years, she had adopted some of the pragmatism of her mother but also some of the cynicism of the women on the estate who felt that life was deliberately organised to be a burden to them. Some of it came from a dull and often ugly series of disappointments which were entirely expected. Any idea that there was anything beyond the everyday drudge was just poppycock – an unthought-through but persistent legacy of a European 'age of reason' that dismissed the world of myth, legend and spiritual things with the adage: 'If you can't see it, touch it or prove it, then it doesn't exist'. Parents on the Beck Ings Estate seemed to be just as determined that their children should *not* believe in Santa Claus after the age of eight, as they were adamant that their children *should* believe in him before that age. Add to all that, the gross behaviour of the teenagers who felt *they* should own the estate – or, at least, their bit of it – and there was little to encourage Tabitha's sense of magic. Her mother and the estate grown-ups hadn't much time for the things of nature, and her teachers, beset with the challenge of getting their pupils through the SATS and achieving a decent performance rating for their school, were more ready to explain and dissect the planet than marvel at it.

That spring, even more than before, Tabitha began to wonder what lay beyond the small iron gate in the garden that led into the woodland beyond. It had always been locked and, in any case, she had mostly been comfortable just to be in the garden, but now she felt a new growing desire to explore.

Now on this May morning, as she tiptoed across the fresh green grass, Tabs noticed something laid across the bench. She got up from the turf and took a step towards it. It looked like a large piece of colourful cloth, patterned with deep reds, greens, browns and splashes of orange. As she got closer, she saw that it was a long skirt with an elasticated waistband. The colours appealed to her, they were the colours of nature. Tabitha had never worn anything like this in her life – she had lived most of it in denim jeans and T-shirts or tank tops. Today she was wearing a pair of tightly-fitting cut-off jeans. Since the time she had grown out of wanting to dress up in party dresses – at the same time as she stopped believing in fairies – she had rarely dreamed of wearing anything out of the ordinary. Few of the girls she knew had anything else in their wardrobe unless it was for a Christening or a wedding – and even then it was usually rather revealing. Long skirts were for people who were different, a bit 'folksy' perhaps.

But, I suppose, I am different, thought Tabitha to herself. *I guess, if they were real, I would choose to be a dryad rather than a girl, sometimes. Still, I could not wear one of those. I like the colours, though,* she thought as she held the skirt against her waist. It wasn't too long; it came to her ankles without trailing on the floor – just where a full-length skirt should come.

"Goodness, and what's this?" she uttered to herself, out loud. On the bench lay something shiny and metallic; it had been hidden beneath the skirt. "Wow. It's a key. I wonder where it...? Could it be...? I think it is." she breathed as she picked up the key and took the few steps to the gate which led into the grounds of The Park. It fitted the padlock perfectly. She began to turn it, but then stopped. It might be the right key, but surely she shouldn't go through the gate. All these years she had simply gazed at the trees from behind its bars. The prospect of stepping through was daunting – even scary. And, anyway, she felt she mustn't, it would be wrong. Someone – clearly not a fairy but a person whose skirt this was – had inadvertently left it on the bench. But why that someone should forget a skirt, she could not think.

Tabs replaced the key on the bench, folded the skirt exactly as it had been, and laid it back as she had found it. She hoped that the owner would not notice. Then, suddenly, she became anxious about being in the garden; she had never been given permission to be there after all; the key and skirt brought home to her even stronger that for the past six years she had been an intruder. It

30

wasn't her place.

She hurriedly left the garden looking towards the cottage rather than the direction she was going. As she closed the little door behind her, Tabitha became overwhelmed by a sense of loss. As usual, there had been no one to be seen in the rest of the garden or the house but there was something final about this departure. The appearance of the key had frightened her – might now be the time to stop taking the risk of being caught. She couldn't be caught. A little shiver spread up her backbone. What if she was at that very moment being watched? She turned her face from the little wooden door and, *Yipes!* She was face-to-face, not with the owner, but with none other than Gross Griff and his cronies.

"We-ell, looky here? Look who's come to meet us." Green drawled to his disciples, a huge triumphant smirk on his face.

"Ugh. What you doin 'ere? I don't want nothing to do with you. Buzz off."

"What am I doin 'ere? Could ask you the same question."

"Mind yer own business."

"Now, no need to get tetchy."

"You followed me. Didn't you?"

"So, 'spose we did. What you doin' in that there garden?"

"Nothing that has anything to do with you."

"I like it when you spit fire – it adds spice." Griff leered at his victim.

"What you on about?" Inside her, despite her defiance, Tabitha was beginning to panic.

"Well, out here there in't a soul to be seen – apart from you, me and me mates, that is. I reckon this is a good place for you to give me that snog you've been promising me... Come to think of it, you might like to give us all one."

In obedience to their master, Griff's cronies began to lick their disgusting lips and make assenting noises.

"In your dreams." Tabitha turned her back and made to walk past them out onto the road. But Green grabbed her arm and pulled her back, and then pushed his ugly face towards hers close enough for her to smell his rancid breath. *Probably hadn't cleaned his teeth for a month.*

"Geroff me you vile monster." Tabs moved her head to avoid his puckered lips and sniggering nose.

"That's it. Go on shouting. I like it. Nobody'll hear you."

What happened next happened at the speed of light. Instinctively, Tabs kicked Griff in the leg with the point of her shoe – a blow that would have got her a red card on the football pitch – and, as he jumped upwards in surprise, she followed it up with a punch that landed fair and square in the middle of his fat, ugly, snotty nose. The result was amazing. He staggered backwards, doubled up, expelled a spurt of blood and made a hideous noise mixed with a variety of expletives. The blood continued to run and he sank down onto one knee clutching his face.

"You bitch."

Tabitha stood upright, walked past him head aloft, and made towards the road once more. Had Green been alone, she would have won. But he was not.

"Get 'er," he groaned to his henchmen. They were hesitant at first but then decided that loyalty was less risky than tackling a girl, even if she was wild, angry and dangerous. There followed an enormous fight with Tabs shouting and screaming at the top of her lungs. They had almost decided to let her go when Griff, having recovered himself, inadvisedly put his hand across her mouth to silence her. She bit on it as hard as she could. At first, she tasted sour sweat but that quickly turned to blood as she continued to bite down hard.

It was at this point that a car rounded the bend.

"Pigs." yelled Gary and was off in the opposite direction. Shaun was after him, vaulting the fence on the opposite side of the road. Dean let go as Tabitha began to kick more freely, and he somehow managed to reach and shin up the iron gates and drop down the other side and scarper, limping, through the trees.

The community policeman in the car which Gary had instantly recognised had seen it all and pulled up across the drive. Griff jumped onto the bonnet and over the car and charged down the road in the direction of the estate, blood dripping from his hand and his nose.

PC Brown got out of his vehicle and steadied Tabitha as she

reeled trying to get her balance. He caught her shoulders and looked into her eyes. "You OK, lass?"

She spat out Green's gross blood. "Yeah."

"They hurt you?" asked the policeman.

"Nah..." The brave girl wiped her mouth with the front of her T-Shirt and spat again. "His, not mine," she explained.

"Not yours? Not your blood?"

"Griff Green's. Got his fingers too near to my face."

"What happened?"

"Him and his gang wanted a snog and I weren't playing."

"So they decided to force you?" asked the officer, a concerned look on his face.

"That's about it. Got a lot they didn't want, though." Tabitha became aware of a sharp sting on her neck and put her hand to the place where someone's fingernails had grazed her skin. "Ouch."

"We'd better get that seen to," stated the policeman, checking it out.

"It's OK," protested Tabitha.

"No, it'll need some antiseptic. It might get infected." The policeman was firm.

"Green'll need some antiseptic too, then." said Tabitha, fiercely.

"Judging by the amount of blood he left behind on you, the road, and my car, I guess any infection has long been flushed away. But he'll probably need to be seen by a doctor to get patched up. I'll take you to the surgery before he gets there."

"No... I don't want to go to the doctor... I'll... I'll go to the pharmacy."

"OK. I guess that'll be good enough. I'll drop you off." She quite clearly had not suffered anything worse. "You know you could press charges for this? What if I had not come along?"

"You would've had four idiots lined up in casualty," replied the girl, defiantly.

"You've got guts, I see that. What're you doing out here alone anyway?" PC Brown ushered Tabitha into the front seat of the car. She chose not to say anything.

"You won't drive through the estate, will you? I can't be seen in a cop car – all heck will be let loose. Me mum will never let it rest for a start."

"I'm taking you into the town to the pharmacy. That's all."

"OK. But as you go past the bottom of the estate, I'll duck down."

"So, what were you doing out here?"

"Just going for a walk."

"Well, I suggest you walk with other people for the next week or two... and don't venture so far. Mr Green and his friends will not be too happy. They're already on a caution and they will expect me to follow this up."

"What will you do to them?"

"That rather depends on you."

"I just want to let it drop. It won't do no good – just make Gross more vile. And Mum'll ground me for sure... for, like, ages."

"What did you call him?"

"Oh. Gross? Gross Griff – it's my nickname for him. Don't go telling him I call him that, though."

"No, I won't. But I like it." He grinned. "He will have to be given another caution. But I doubt if it will be long before he does something that will result in some court action. I'll do my best to see if I can stop Gary, Dean and Shaun from following 'Gross'," he smiled.

"Yeah, they are not much of a problem without him. Dean's a bit thick in the head, and Shaun's mum really cares. Gary's an idiot because he has the brain to do something. He's good at mending things, like engines."

"You know them well."

"They're all in my year. Been to school with them since I was six."

8

Ten minutes later, Tabitha was in the pharmacy getting the right stuff for her neck. It hadn't occurred to her that she couldn't pay for it until the man asked her if she wanted a bag. Everything was still a bit of a blur; her peaceful morning in the garden had turned itself on its head.

"Oh. Sorry. I'll have to go home and get some money," she whispered, embarrassed.

"That's OK, dear. I'll pay for it," said an old lady with white hair and a big smile, who was standing behind her in the queue. "Your name is Tabitha, isn't it? Haven't I seen you in my shop? It's that one over the road, 'Friends of Africa'." Tabs remembered that she had indeed seen this old lady before. She and some of the other girls had occasionally browsed in the little charity shop, which sold second-hand stuff and trinkets from Africa.

"Y... yes, I'm Tabitha. B... but I couldn't let you do that. I... I'll go home and come back."

"It's all reet, lass," said the assistant, betraying his broad Yorkshire. He was conscious of the queue that was forming. "Just tek it and pay later."

"I... I...." Tabs protested. But the man slid it over and looked up at the next customer. She took it, embarrassed by the number of people watching her now. The lady from Friends of Africa left her place in the queue and walked with her to the door.

"Look, why don't you come to my shop for a cup of tea? Meet my assistant, and Lulu, our cat. And I've got a sink you can use to wash off some of that blood."

Tabs became conscious of the mess she was in and she felt even more abashed. What would people be thinking? Her top was stained with blood and dirt, both back and front. People were looking at her. And she couldn't be seen by her mum, that would beg far too many questions; she couldn't walk home like, like... what her mum would call, a 'sight for sore eyes.' Tabs considered the offer. *I would not normally accept an invitation like this but I have to get cleaned up and it's, like, a public shop, in't it?* And, anyway, the cuts were beginning to sting – a sure sign that the wound needed treating. *Got to get Gross's slime washed off and the stuff put on to kill his germs before they get inside me.*

Tabs was familiar with Friends of Africa. It had been the trinkets and dress jewellery as well as the second-hand clothes which had mostly attracted the girls. Tabs had never bought anything though; her mother always believed it was better to get something new, even if it was of lower quality. 'You never know where it has been,' was her mother's adage. Tabs wouldn't have cared about that – some of the stuff in charity shops looked hardly worn and she might have tried to persuade her mum if she'd been into lots of clothes like some of the others. When she had come in with them she had soon gravitated towards the books at the back of the shop. She wasn't a great reader but she liked the pictures and imagined the stories they contained but she never bought one – most of her pocket money went on sweets and the like.

As they entered through the front door, a big bell jangled and the old lady smiled a thank you to a gentleman sitting by the till. "Thanks for minding the shop, Bill."

"Honoured, Mary," he said, standing to greet her. "Only one customer. A book by Barbara Cartland. Oh, and someone came in with a pile of Elizabeth Goudge. I accepted them. I hope I did right.

"Excellent," responded the old lady, "Elizabeth Goudge is always popular."

"Only got a quid for the Barbara Cartland, though."

"That's good. It went for 50p last time round." Many of Mary's customers brought the books back again once they had read them.

"Bill, this is Tabitha."

"*Enchanté*," he said with a smile in passable French, making a theatrical bow. Then changed his expression to one of concern. "My, you look as if you've been in the wars." Tabs blushed and put her head down.

Mary scolded him. "Enough said, Bill. Can you mind the shop

a bit longer while I see to Tabitha?

"*No problema,*" this time in doubtful Italian. His eyes twinkled as he winked.

"Don't mind him," said Mary when they had passed through to a stock room piled high with half-sorted clothes. "Bill is the kindest man you could wish for, but, like a lot of men, he has an odd way of charming the ladies. And he thinks with his tongue. But he's right, you do look in need of a bit of a clean-up. There is a sink in there." She indicated a second door. "Look you'd better change that top; it's got rather a lot of blood on it. I'll see what I can find." Tabitha opened the door and groped for a light switch while Mary returned to the shop and disappeared behind a rail of second-hand tops.

Tabs tugged at a pull cord switch that illuminated a large bulb above her and became face to face with herself in a mirror. *Ugh! Yuk!* She couldn't blame Bill for his insensitive remark.

Mary returned with a loose T-shirt with a light green leafy pattern. "How about this one?" Tabs couldn't protest; the green shirt was definitely the better option. She smiled an embarrassed thank you, took the proffered garment and a towel and closed the door. She tugged the neck of her tank top to get it over her head without dragging it across her face, threading through her hair and threw it in the sink.

Yuk. She took another look at herself in the mirror and the blood spattered tank top and decided to chuck it. No point in trying to wash it – it would never be free of that boy's foul spit and blood. *What if I've caught something nasty from him. If I have, I'll murder him.* She was distracted from thinking about the top when she noticed more damage – a blackening bruise coming up on her upper arm where someone had restrained her. That was the worst of it, as they had grown up the boys had got stronger and she softer. She wondered if Gross's face was damaged much, she'd certainly landed an accurate one there but it was probably just a nosebleed. He hadn't liked it at the time, though, had he? It had caught him unawares and his pride would definitely be dented. It did something to lessen her anger when she thought of him doubled up, groaning in pain and surprise, though.

9

As Tabitha bathed her face and neck, the sounds of African music playing in the background caused her to think of Deng and his sister Ashol. At one time, Tabitha thought that all the business of girl-boy attraction was going to leave her out – boys were all to be despised, not just Griff and his cronies. How could anyone be attracted to the lads she went to school with? If they weren't downright revolting, they were gross, or drips – or just dull. But that was before she met Deng Thomas. For some reason he was different.

Deng was really black, not even dark brown like her father, and tall and good-looking. But it wasn't those things that set him apart for Tabitha – it was the way he wasn't part of the ordinary. He was deep – mysterious even. Exotic? No, he wasn't that. He was kind and quietly thoughtful. Intelligent? Certainly that. And wise. That was it. She could imagine him being one of the Wise Men from the East who had followed the Star to find the baby Jesus.

The Thomases did not live on the estate but in one of the knocked-through back-to-backs by the old mills. His dad, Mr Garang Thomas, worked for the local authority in an office in the town. It wasn't a very grand job but it was one he had got after he had learned to speak, read and write English better than most of the people in Millheaton.

Ashol and Deng applied themselves at school. Ashol had told the class that many people from her country did not get to go to school at all and a secondary school education was special. A lot of the local kids found it strange that anyone would want to go to school and do the work the teachers demanded. After all, what difference did it make? The kind of things you might want to do when you left school – work in a mill, or more likely these days, in a supermarket, a shop or a pub didn't require you to have passed any GCSEs. If you aspired to anything more, you would have to leave the town and all that that implied. Parents expected their children to marry local people and stay within easy walking distance.

But the Thomases were ambitious for their children. In South Sudan, they had been among the group of people who saw education as a way to make something of your life – to escape the poverty that pervaded so much of the community. Ashol had told her friend that in South Sudan you'd never ask the question, "Why am I bothering to learn to read or discover the ways the planet works?" It was dead obvious.

Tabs tried to understand when Ashol spoke like that but, to be honest, it wasn't that 'dead obvious' to her. Certainly, the kids who grafted were the ones who might manage to leave the estate but, in the end, most of them didn't; it took more than a few GCSEs to escape the constraints of the pervading culture. Millheaton people were 'normal' and why people elsewhere wanted to be different they couldn't imagine. In truth, they wouldn't know how to live in a world beyond their patch and they dared not venture. Escape? It might be what Tabs would love to do sometimes because she didn't fit in but it wasn't that simple – nothing was. She recalled one day waking up with the intention of actually trying to pay attention to the lessons but the following history lesson had changed her mind; it had been deadly dull and something about the First World War that seemed to have no bearing on what kind of job you might do in today's world. And, anyway, so many of the kids were mucking around in class that there was no hope of learning enough to pass an exam, so Tabs had given up. Now, however, she was being offered a second chance. Jack Frost seemed to think she was worth it. Was she?

The African music soothed her as she studied herself in the mirror. Who was she? Could she 'escape'? Should she? Where would she go? Leeds? To do what? But, then there was her mum – there was no way she could leave her. Tabitha Chapeltown Johnson was not going to go anywhere, was she? Not even Chapeltown.

Tabitha pulled herself back to the present. If Deng had been around when Griff had tried it on, he would have stepped in but she wouldn't have wanted that. He was above that kind of thing.

She washed her face and arms thoroughly in the sink. Her neck stung when the scratch got wet and she swore again out loud. "If that slug, Gross, comes near me again, I'll kill him." She dried herself and put on the loose green T-shirt which seemed to be three sizes too big. Apart from her school uniform, since she had developed a bust she'd never worn anything that didn't fit tightly. All of the girls in her year did the same. But now Tabitha was glad of the long sleeves that covered her bruise. She wanted to brush her hair but there was nothing to do it with.

When she went back into the shop, Mary expressed her delight.

"You look as pretty as a picture. The shirt suits you."

"I'll wash it and bring it back tomorrow."

"You'll do nothing of the sort. It's yours to keep. If you don't want to wear it out and about you can sleep in it. Now let me see to that neck."

Tabitha sat on a chair while Mary applied the antiseptic. It stung even worse than the water, but Tabitha thought that that was good because it would be killing all the bugs Gross had left under her skin.

"Now that looks clean enough but do put some more on when you get home. Do you want to tell me what happened? I won't mind if you don't."

"Some idiot boy scratched me."

"I rather gathered that. And you drew blood from him."

"Yeah. His nose got too near my first and his hand got too near my mouth." Tabitha's face creased in a faint smile.

"That explains all the blood on your top."

"Sure does. You can chuck it out. It's contaminated."

"If you want. I doubt it'll wash out clean. I'll see to it."

"Thanks. I'd better be getting home now. Thanks."

"It's been a pleasure. Always wanted a daughter but never had one. Come in any time. People come in here just to pass the time of day, you don't have to buy anything."

"Can I... can I buy a book to read? I haven't got no money now, but I'll come back tomorrow and I'll pay for it then."

"Of course. What sort of book would you like?"

"I dunno. Not something with words that are too big."

Mary scanned the young adults' shelves. "How about this one? *The Curious Incident of the Dog in the Night-time*? It's one of my favourites. Have you read it?"

Tabs took the proffered book. "No, I haven't seen this one. Thanks. How much is it?"

"50p. to you."

"OK. I'll bring it tomorrow... Where does the money go from the things you sell?"

"The profit all goes to help displaced people in Africa, refugees, who have been driven from their homes because of war or famine. We help provide food, water, medicine, and even schools in the camps. Some of them have been there over a generation."

"How do you get the money there?"

"Mostly through people who help coordinate the care. That's a challenge. Most of the money is spent on buying supplies and getting them to the people."

"How poor are they?"

"A difficult question to answer. Money-wise they have nothing, but sometimes they feel more blessed than most of us with all our things – especially when they get food every day, or we start a clinic or a school."

"My mum says she's always been poor. But I've never had to go without food."

"But food is just one thing. When it comes to opportunities, I guess, your mum hasn't had much of them. How many of you are there at home?"

"Just Mum and me. What sort of opportunities?"

"Well, choice of job, choice of where to live, choice of holiday. That sort of thing."

"We've never had a holiday away. My mum always says the best place is 'Argate'."

"Argate? Oh, I see. Your own front gate."

Tabs grinned. "Yeah. Except our flats don't have gates."

"So no holidays. But you have enough to eat, things to wear, a TV to watch and free schools to go to. That's very important. The kids in the refugee camps clamour to get to school."

"Because they want to escape. Find opportunities?"

"Exactly. I can see you'd like to escape sometimes - from the bullying. You feel a bit trapped?"

"Nah... not really," Tabs coloured. *Can this woman read minds?* "I... I... I'd better be getting back. I gotta go before—"

"Before 'Gross' is back on the street."

"Yeah... How do you know...?"

"How do I know your nickname for him? You spat it out a couple of times when you were in the bathroom. The door isn't sound-proof."

"Yeah, well thanks..." And Tabitha backed out of the shop and ran off in the direction of the estate up the back road that didn't pass the place Gareth Green lived, and where she was less likely to be spotted by any other young people. She liked Mary but she seemed to know a lot about her. It was a bit weird.

When she got home, Tabs went straight to her room with nothing but a, "Hi, Mum." Fifteen minutes later she had showered, washed her hair and pulled on something with long sleeves she had been bought for a party but had never worn since. "Felt like something special," she muttered.

"You look great." said her mother, "What you been up to, today?"

"Nothing much. Met the lady from the Friends of Africa shop. She was telling me about people not having opportunities."

"Yeah? Well, they could do with giving a few of them out here."

"That's what she said. She said we might have food every day – even if some have to use the foodbank – but we can be less than happy because we don't have opportunities."

"So what sort of opportunities is she going to give you?"

"None, I guess. She can't do that. She in't no fairy godmother. She gave me a T-shirt to sleep in, though."

"What. Does she think we need her charity?"

"Nah. It was a present. She likes me, I think. And I bought a book for 50p."

"50p? What's she after? You be careful."

"Mum. She's ancient. She's been in that shop for a hundred years. Everybody knows her."

"So, you know all about her. Where does she live, then?"

"I don't know. I didn't ask. But it in't the Planet of the Apes.

42

People know where she lives, I expect."

"Well, you just be careful."

"Would you like it better if I was going out with a boy?"

"What?" Cindy panicked. "A boy. Tabitha, you're far too young.... You aren't...? You haven't...?"

"Mum. I were only *saying*. Don't worry, I'm not. But you're, like, not thinking I can look after myself."

"You've no idea what this world can be like, my girl. I'm doing my bit as a caring mother." Cindy sighed. "Bringing up a teenager is hellishly difficult."

"Trust me, Mum. I've got a good idea what you wouldn't want me to do by now. And most of it makes sense."

"*Most* of it!"

"Well, all of it actually... most of the time. Look, Mum, if I wanted to do something that I knew you wouldn't like, I'd tell you about it. I wouldn't just do it. You tell me to do things because you care... because you love me. And lots of people's mums keep changing their minds about what's OK or not, depending on the mood they're in. Not everyone has a mum who really cares."

"That's the nicest thing you've said to me all week. You truly appreciate your mum?"

"Cause I do... And, Mum, you needn't worry about boys. They're a pain. I'm not going to get near 'em."

"Glad to hear it. So what're you going to do the rest of this afternoon?"

"I got this book to read, haven't I?"

"What's it about?"

"A boy and a dead dog..." Cindy's expression darkened. "It's just a story. It's called The Curious Incident of the Dog in the Night-time."

"I've heard about it. It was mentioned on the telly. It sounds like nothing much actually happens."

"That sounds just like the kind of book I want to read.... I've had enough of adventures today."

Her mum, of course, thought she was talking about books. If she had only known the half of it...

***

For the rest of that summer, Tabitha steered clear of the garden. In truth, being nervous of Gross Griff looking for an occasion when he might get his revenge kept her inside a lot of the time, and, in any case, going back to the garden along the quiet lane was decidedly out of the question. The last thing she wanted to do was lead Gross into the garden – that would be the ultimate violation. And the curious appearance of the skirt and the key worried her, too.

Anyway, Tabs had found a new interest to keep her busy – she had taken up reading in a big way. When she got to the end of *The Curious Incident* she delighted in her achievement: she had read that book all by herself from cover to cover. Then Mary managed to find her *The Lion, the Witch and the Wardrobe* by C. S. Lewis and she was hooked. Mary said she knew she could be a great reader and was ready with more books and an offer to accompany her to the town library if she liked.

10

It took until the end of the summer for Tabs to summon up the courage to be seen in the library. Her mum was not opposed, even if it had never occurred to her to use it herself. The English teacher, Mr Kendall, was astonished. Tabitha had read Thomas Hardy's *Far from the Madding Crowd*, the set book, and he moved her up to the top set. In the set to which Tabs had previously belonged, two of the girls had managed only part of the first chapter and the others hadn't even got started but Tabitha had been caught up in Bathsheba Everdene's tragedy and couldn't put it down. She actually wept at Fanny's fate and decided that most of the males sucked – except Gabriel Oak, of course.

One of the benefits of being in the highest set was that she got to know Ashol better. While her newfound love of literature may not yet have extended to other subjects, she realised that it was a bit of dedication that had succeeded in getting her out of a set that contained people of which she was not very fond. Currently, she was still in the same set for maths. Perhaps, if she worked at it, she might get out of this set too.

Amazingly, it proved much easier than she had imagined. After just one week, she managed a perfect score. Who was the most surprised – her or Mr Parks, the maths teacher – she did not know. And it wasn't a one-off because she did it again. Mr Parks was suspicious, so he asked her to talk through her workings with him. She did. It appeared she had mastered it. He was so pleased he offered her some catch-up stuff and, to his astonishment, she accepted it.

"If I do it, sir, would that mean I can move up to the next set?" she asked.

"Maybe. You'll need to learn how to do equations, though."

"How? What do I have to do?"

"You're determined, aren't you? Is that set so bad? Let me guess: Gareth Green." Tabs' expression showed that he had guessed right. The teacher sighed. "If he motivates you into doing your best, he will have achieved more than I have managed in the last two years."

"Sorry, sir."

"Tabitha Johnson, you and I know that you are not as slow as you – or I – once thought you were. However it has come about, I'm glad that the proverbial penny has dropped. And you're lucky because it's not too late. Go get your lunch, then come back here and I'll show you what you need to do."

Tabitha was surprised at just how many people were spending some of their lunch hour doing catch-up in the maths room. How come so many people wanted extra work? Both Ashol and her brother were there. Deng was tackling some advanced-looking stuff with graphs and things, which he called vectors. They both smiled and waved at Tabitha as she listened to Mr Parks explaining the rules of simple equations. How could maths be about letters like 'x'? How could she take away '2 xes' from '4 xes' if you didn't know what 'x' was?

It was Ashol who helped her get it. "Just think of 'x' like a banana," she said. That made sense. Four bananas take away two bananas.

"Two," answered Tabs.

"Two what?" persisted Ashol.

"Two what? Two bananas, of course," laughed Tabs.

"So what is the answer to your sum with 'xes'?"

"Two." Ashol waited, urging her to expand her answer. "Two bana... two 'xes'. Two times 'x'."

"Right. You don't have to know what 'x' is at this stage, just how many there are. Just put '2x' or '3x' whatever the answer is."

"Got it. Thanks."

That evening, Tabitha's phone played its generic ringtone. It was Ashol.

"My mum and dad say would you like to come for dinner tomorrow?"

"Dinner? Oh, you mean tea... tomorrow? Well, I'll have to ask Mum... OK?... Mu-um," she called out, "Ashol is asking me if I would like to go for tea tomorrow, round her house. She says her dad will walk me home afterwards since it will be getting dark. Can I go?"

"Well, I suppose so. Where does she live?"

"In the old houses by Firth's Mill. She's in my new English set at school..." Cindy nodded.

"OK. Mum says yes. I'll come after school then... Thanks."

"Ash – ol." Her mother sounded out the name she had heard Tabitha say. "That sounds African but I don't know where."

"It's Sudanese."

"So how does she come to be here in our town?"

"She came with her family. There was a war and they had to run away."

"There is always a war. Half of Africa would live here if they got the chance. Just ask your father."

"There was a real war, Mum. She says millions of people have died, lots of them children. She says they want to go back if things improve. It could be a long time, though."

"They'll not do that. Look at your father. He will never go back."

"But they're different. Ashol says her mum and dad want to go back."

"I don't doubt it. But whether they will is another question. Sudan. They'll be Arabs, then?"

"No, that's the problem. Ashol's family are from South Sudan. They're really black. That's some of what the war was about, I think."

"Well, you certainly know something about it. Then you'd better go. But mind you behave yourself."

"Of course, Mum." Tabs sighed, wistfully. "Why wouldn't I?"

"Well, to tell the truth, you've not been bad lately. You seem to be a lot more cheerful too. School always got you down, but it doesn't seem to so much these days. Perhaps, this Ashol's a good friend to have."

"She's helping me not to miss out like some. I have to take my opportunities."

"Opportunities again. You sound more grown-up all the time. Sounds like Africa's doing you good. 'Opportunities'," Cindy repeated slowly. "Well, you make me proud of you, and I'll be a happy woman."

"I will, Mum. And, Mum, I'm fifteen in a few days – that's

47

getting pretty near to being grown up."

"Fifteen. Hark at you. You've nowt but begun at that age, lass. Get on with you. You've become wise above your age, I'll grant you. I like that but don't let it go to your head. Now get along with you and let me get on here. I have some letters to write."

And after that, Tabitha often found herself around the Thomas's working on catching up on the maths she hadn't done over the past two years.

It took three weeks of counting bananas and then apples – 'ys' – but, eventually, she found herself moving to a higher maths set. She no longer needed to share any class with Gareth Green, or see him at all. But best of all, she liked the way she felt when Mr Parks smiled at her. Not only was she a rising star in English and was making progress in French, but she was also actually achieving in maths. She told her mum but Cindy wasn't aware of the full nature of the change nor the part a bully had played in it.

As Tabs was moving upwards, Griff was, sadly, sliding in the opposite direction. He did not stay in Millheaton long after Tabs' promotion. He was arrested after a series of warnings for antisocial behaviour and petty theft and then one day at the end of September, he disappeared. They learned that he had been up before the court and they had temporarily 'relocated' him in a juvenile correction unit – 'kiddy clink' as Tabitha's school mates were inclined to call it.

***

On Saturday, 6th October, Tabs' birthday, the sun was bright from the moment it rose. The dew soon evaporated and she could not stay in; she should catch up on her assignments and read some more of the adventures in Narnia but it might come on to rain later. This sun could not last but while it did, she was going to take advantage of it.

The joy of the day overcame her previous inhibitions and

Tabs covered the distance to her 'secret garden' in good time. By half past ten, she was pushing her way past the beech hedge whose leaves were turning a glorious golden hue. The bench was bathed in bright sunlight and on it lay the same full-length skirt she had encountered all those months before. She now saw it with new eyes – it was a wonderful combination of autumn colours. There was the deep crimson of the hydrangea blossoms set against the paler colours of autumn leaves ranging from yellow through copper and bronze, the dark browns of bark and soil, the rich green of wet grass, and the darker greens of holly, ivy, fir and the other trees which would retain their leaves throughout the winter. The pattern was as if all these things were laid on top of one another, randomly. It was simply the most beautiful skirt Tabitha had ever seen. It was so simple. It just flared out from an elasticated waistband and yet it was extraordinary – extravagant.

Tabs stepped forward and stroked the smooth warm cloth. She glided her hand along its length and then gathered up the hem a little. She discovered it was lined with a rich-brown silken underskirt. She lifted it and weighed it in her hands. She could not resist. Gathering up the hem, she slid her arms through and put it on over her head, pulling down the waistband until the hem swung free and brushed her ankles; it was exactly the right length as if it had been measured for her.

Tabitha glanced down to where her legs should have been. She would have liked to look at herself in a mirror – not something she was much in the habit of doing. She did a little hop and felt the skirt swing, and then she spun to make it fan out and lift in a colourful cone around her. She had hardly ever worn a skirt before, and certainly not one like this. This was a 'grown-up' skirt. At that moment on her fifteenth birthday, she gloried in her femininity – girls' clothes, it seemed, could be so exciting. But, then, when could she ever wear a skirt like this in real life? Like the garden, it was for a fairytale – a fairytale that wasn't a dream because it was real but it was a place quite different from the rest of her world. Apart from a few weeks when her shorts came out, most of the girls she knew wore jeans or tights all the time; there was no way anyone would be seen wearing a skirt in public unless it was something special like a prom ball, a wedding or a christening – and not even then, when complicated dresses seemed to be in fashion. The style of this skirt was too simple for that but, here on her own in this alternative world, she delighted in the moment as she danced around like a ballerina.

It was when she bent forward in a grand arabesque that Tabs noticed the key. It was on the bench beneath where the skirt had lain. Now that she had abandoned all reticence towards one offering, resistance towards the second was seriously weakened. If the skirt was hers to wear, the key was also there for her, wasn't it? She was caught up in this fairy story. This was her world, this was where she truly belonged.

Tabitha grasped the key and stepped over to the gate in the outer wall. She slowly inserted it into the lock and pushed it home. It fitted perfectly, sliding in smoothly as if the lock was in regular use. She turned it and it moved remarkably easily and the hasp of the padlock swung open without a sound. This gate, which had seemed firmly locked for so long, was now giving in so readily it was as if it had been waiting for *her*, rather than she waiting for *it*. She made to remove the hasp from the bolt but before she could, suddenly, almost gently but firmly, it began to rain. Tabitha watched the raindrops dance on the leaves and plop onto the ground. The sunshine still bathed the garden and Tabs looked for a rainbow but the massive trees beyond the gate blocked her view of the sky. Wet leaves began falling all around her, clinging to her hair and face and the magic strengthened its hold, taking her deeper into its thrall.

"Bleep, bleep."

Tabs was brought to by her phone in her jeans pocket. Shaking off the reverie, she reached towards it but, of course, it was under the skirt. She gathered up the hem and eventually pulled out the phone. It was a text from her mum. Where was she? Whoops. She had spent longer than she had realised in this place. "On way back," she texted, "caught in rain. C u soon. X".

Tabs locked the gate and replaced the key on the bench. The skirt was now getting heavy with the rainwater. She stepped out of it, shook it and put it back on the bench over the key as she had found it. It was as if she caused it to rain by turning the key in the lock. It was like being in the midst of a true fairytale – like being a kind of Alice in a wonderland.

"Rubbish," she muttered to herself. "That would be ridiculous magic. The world doesn't work like that, the world isn't magic – that was all in my head." Whatever the explanation of the skirt and the key, though, that wasn't supernatural – someone had put them there. *Get real. Those things don't belong to me even if I had a feeling, like, of welcome – that's a little girl thing and I am no longer a little girl. I'm grown-up. I'm* fifteen.

Sometimes, though, deep down, Tabs knew she wanted to be eight again – sometimes. But that was silly. The real world was about helping her mother make the money last the week, keeping the authorities off her back and avoiding the likes of Griff and his cronies.

Tabitha hurried back home, back into the real world.

11

As the nights became longer, the thought of the appearance of the skirt and key continued to intrigue Tabs. She had got into the habit of paying more frequent visits to the garden – the autumn was so beautiful – but there had been nothing on the bench. Halloween was approaching but despite the tales of weird happenings, the garden didn't feel at all spooky. The season of ghoulies and ghosts had always been a scary time for Tabs – the cave dream was intensified by a kind of fear of something bad lurking around the corner. Adults are not always aware of how frightening Halloween can be for some children.

On Beck Ings, it wasn't a ghost that appeared, however. On 31st October, Gareth Green reappeared to haunt the estate once more – the return of a dreaded all too material a malevolence.

No one knew exactly where Griff had been – he didn't let on and nobody dared to ask him. But Tabitha was no longer in any of the classes he was supposed to attend and he often bunked off, so it was not so difficult to avoid him. In fact, most people tried to keep out of his way – including, at first, his erstwhile disciples but within days, Dean, Gary and Shaun were following him around once more.

It didn't take long after that for tragedy to strike. According to Dean and Gary, it happened like this. Griff and the others had bunked off school and gone round to Shaun's house. Shaun's older brother and mother were both out at work. The brother had turned seventeen and had just got a motorbike. It wasn't a big one but it was a proper motorbike that required a person to pass a test to ride on the road. It had become his pride and joy and he spent more time cleaning and polishing it than he did riding it. He had a provisional licence, but whilst he was still learning, he continued to go to work on the bus. The bike was parked in the out-house, lovingly bound in its special cover.

When Griff and his cronies rocked up at Shaun's, they soon spotted the bike. Despite Shaun's protestations, Griff pulled off the cover and sat astride it. At first, they larked about a bit, then they wheeled it out onto the road. But that didn't satisfy Griff; he demanded Shaun went to find the key. Shaun was much more scared of Griff than he was of his brother, so he went back into his house, found the key in his brother's bedroom and gave it to Griff.

Even though he was only fifteen, Gareth had ridden a bike before, of course. He took it to the top of the street and began rolling down the hill on it. On the third attempt, he managed to start it, rev it and get it in gear. He stalled it and Shaun pleaded with him to give it up. Griff wouldn't stop until he had done some damage, his brother would be angry and so would his mother. Not only that but the noise was attracting the attention of the neighbours and they might already be calling the fuzz. Griff ignored him, calling him a 'wimp' and 'useless'. He got it going again and rode it back up the hill while his cronies stayed down at the bottom. At the top Griff turned, gave it full revs, and began racing back down the hill, tipping it up onto its back wheel to show off. He soon lost control; the bike reared up and tumbled him off the back. It careered forward, rolled over and slid fast down the hill, a screeching bundle of hot, heavy metal. Shaun's gang were not the fastest of kids and as it scythed through them, it took Shaun with it and, pinioning him beneath its wheels, it hurtled into a brick wall and burst into flames. Shaun's head hit the wall hard; he didn't stand a chance.

The fire brigade was there within minutes and an ambulance took the boys off to the hospital. Remarkably, Griff received nothing but a bruised ankle and Dean and Gary got away with a few scrapes and a couple of burns but Shaun was pronounced dead on arrival.

That was the last anybody saw of Griff on the estate and his mother left the area soon after. Nobody knew where she went.

A week after the accident, the school held a special assembly in which the vicar, Rev. Mike, and the Methodist minister were both present. Prayers were said, a hymn was sung and everyone kept a very long silence. Tuck, the headteacher, made a speech saying that now he did not have to remind the school of the dangers of motorcycles – he only wished he had done it before. He recalled that Shaun had been a better pupil of late, and, despite the sad way he had died, his family should remember him as someone who had been trying to make something of his life. He had been a victim of 'evil circumstances'. He then said that if anyone wished to attend the funeral in the local church and represent the school, he would be pleased to hear from them.

Tabitha had been sitting alongside Ashol as she had often done in the last few weeks. As they left the hall, she volunteered that if Tuck had mentioned the dangers of motorbikes, Gross would most probably have not been there to hear it, anyway. Not that he was likely to have heeded anything Tuck had to say.

"Yeah," agreed Ashol, "and it's him who Tuck means by 'evil circumstances', I guess... Do you want to go to the funeral?" She added.

"What? Who? Me? Why?" Tabitha was astonished. It had never occurred to her that she should attend.

"Well, you've known Shaun since nursery school... I'm going, and Danielle, Rev Mike's daughter. Rev. Mike has already asked at the school and Tuck has agreed to us going."

"How come the vicar asked you?"

"Because we go to church, I expect. He rang Mum and asked if we were planning to go, and we said we hadn't thought about it. Then he said that it would be nice to have a few young people there who knew how church services worked. So we said yes if we could get off school. He rang Tuck this morning and he said we could go."

"Well, if you're going..." Then she thought again and said, "Do you think it will be all right? I mean I've never been to a funeral before. What do they do? Isn't it a bit creepy? You know, the coffin and all... and the singing and chanting. Kinda Halloween for real."

"We don't do Halloween; we have a Light Party which is all about heaven and being loved forever. The coffin will be there, I suppose. But the singing will be fine. The prayers will be all about being with Jesus and resurrection and all that, Rev Mike said."

"What's resurrection?"

"Rising to new life with Jesus in heaven. You know, like at Easter. Jesus said that where he was going, he will make a place for us. Like, in heaven. God will make Shaun whole again in his heavenly home."

"But Shaun's dead."

"Yeah, his body is. But he's not going to need that in heaven, is he? God will give his spirit a new heavenly body. That's what a funeral is saying."

"You believe in ghosts?"

"Well, I believe our spirit – that's the bit that makes us, us – doesn't die when our bodies do."

"So it's not all about talking about dying then?"

"No. Just the opposite. I went to a funeral last year of an old man who was our friend. He had been a church member for most of his life. The service was a great celebration of his life and rejoicing that he'd gone to glory. It wasn't sad at all. We were told to put on our brightest clothes."

Agh. Clothes. Tabs knew there was no way she should be going to Shaun's funeral. You have to dress up for a funeral, don't you? And she had not got anything suitable.

"I can't go. I got nothing special to wear – whatever they want for Shaun. What will you wear?"

"No problem. School uniform. Tuck has said we are to represent the school. All you need is what you're wearing now."

Tabs was running out of reasons not to go; perhaps she should. She felt sorry for Shaun's family. Tuck was right; he wasn't bad. He'd never been a bully. The truth was that he was probably more scared of Griff than anyone and couldn't stand up to him. Tabs liked the idea that people would stick up for him and his mum would appreciate it if some kids turned up.

"OK. I'll come with you. If Tuck and my mum let me."

Tabs wasn't sure about the heaven stuff – it sounded too far-fetched – but she was sure that there was far more to life than the Beck Ings Estate and the familiar world she knew.

12

Tabitha's mum was amazed that her daughter wanted to go to a funeral and she had not heard her say anything positive about Shaun in all the years she had known him. She knew the idea had come from Ashol but she was happy to let her go if she was going with Ashol and Danielle – they were decent friends to have and Cindy was proud of her daughter.

The headteacher was more than pleased to consent to Tabs going; he had not had many pupils express an interest.

The day of the funeral was cold but bright. Everything looked more cheerful than the previous days since the accident. When Tabitha, Danielle and Ashol arrived at the church, some of Shaun's family were standing outside, all of them dressed in black. The three young people stepped through them, sheepishly, and made their way to the south door of the church where Tuck and two other teachers were waiting for them.

When they got through the glass door, they were given a service sheet and shown to a seat halfway down the church. Ashol waved to a few people she knew as she passed, all of them church members. As they sat down, a pleasant smiley lady came over and said how good it was to see them.

"Hello, Miss Spinks. This is Tabitha," Ashol introduced her friend.

"Pleased to meet you," the woman said, taking Tabs' right hand. "You a friend of Shaun Smith?" Tabitha nodded but said nothing. It was all very overawing – the church was so old and so big and mostly empty. And, anyway, she didn't know what to say. Ashol replied for her.

"Tabitha's known him since they were at nursery school together." The smiley lady nodded and seemed happy with the reply.

Then someone came into the church that Tabitha did know. Mary from the Friends of Africa shop. Tabitha was really pleased to see her – a familiar face in this very unfamiliar place.

"Room for a little one?" she asked, squeezing in next to Tabs.

Now being a bit squashed between two people she knew made her feel safer.

After a while, Rev Mike arrived at the main doors wearing a big white robe with a colourful scarf around his neck and a book in his hand. Everybody stood up. Behind him, four men in dark suits with tails carried a coffin down the aisle and put it on some trestles in front of the altar. They were followed by the family headed by Mrs Smith, Shaun's Mum, who could hardly stand up. She was upset and was being held by her elder son. When they had sat in the front pew, Rev Mike said a prayer and announced a hymn. To her amazement, Tabitha knew it. It was one they had sung in primary school, *One more step along the world I go*. Ashol, Danielle and Mary sang it out loud, as did some of the others who were clearly church members. By the end of it, Tabitha was singing too.

The vicar said some things about Shaun's short life – the things he liked, his favourite music, and the things he had achieved. They were not very many, but apparently, he had won a relay race when he was ten and still had the medal on the wall above his bed. The vicar didn't mention the years Shaun spent in Gross Griff's gang, but he did say something about the way he died. He said it was a tragic accident that could have been avoided. He hoped that his friends had learned that motorbikes could be dangerous, and urged people to pray for those who were there when Shaun died. He added, quietly, that they must be feeling very mixed up at that moment. Dean, Gary and, of course, Griff were not there.

Then Rev Mike went on to talk about the hope of heaven and the strength that God would give his family and friends when they called upon Him. He explained that Shaun was deeply loved and read a passage from the Bible about God wiping away everyone's tears and making everything new.

At the end of the service, some of Shaun's favourite music was played through a loudspeaker system. It was heavy metal stuff that sounded dreadful in the church, Tabitha thought. It was the kind of music she didn't care for, anyway. The coffin was carried out and the family all followed it outside.

Teachers joined a line of people waiting to shake hands with

Mrs Smith. When they had gone, Mary shouted above the music.

"Let's stay here a bit. Let them leave for the crematorium. Then would you youngsters like to come with me and get some lunch in town? We can get chips and ice cream?"

Chips and ice cream. On a school day.

"Great." said Ashol.

"You'll need to clear it with your people. We have to take the safeguarding rules seriously."

"Have you got your phone, Tabs?" Ashol produced her mobile. "Why don't you ring your mum and ask her if that's all right?"

When Mrs Thomas and Danielle's mum had given their consent, Tabs turned on her phone to tell her mum where she was going and who she was with. It occurred to her that she wouldn't have normally done that and her mum was very pleased she had.

"Let's assist Harriett Spinks to tidy up and then we can be off." Ashol and Tabs began to help the cheerful lady collect up some of the service sheets. Tabs spotted a handbag left under one of the seats and pulled it out.

"Well done," said Miss Spinks. "It's Tabitha, isn't it?" Tabs nodded. "You can call me Harriett." The lady was definitely old enough to be Tabs' grandmother and she would never dream of calling someone that age by her Christian name. Mary noticed Tabs' confusion.

"It's all right. Here in church, we don't worry about 'Mr' and 'Mrs' much. Harriett won't think you rude if you call her by her name. She likes it." Harriett laughed. "Getting called Miss Spinks reminds me of school. And besides, this young lady is taller than I am." It was true.

As soon as the last of the mourners had left the church, the music was turned off abruptly and the gentle hiss of the wind from the organ sounded like a sigh of relief. The organist emerged from under his pipes and called out to them, "That, he said, is the worst cacophony of noise I have heard this year." He seemed angry. Mary laughed. "Takes all to make a world."

"Seems so...", he muttered and shambled off.

"He's upset about Shaun, not just the music," said Mary, "he has a heart for young people, although it doesn't always show.

Come on, let's go to Bella's Fish Bar."

As they reached the door, they were approached by an anxious woman tottering forward trying to balance on her very high heels.

"Excuse me," she breathed. "Have you seen a handbag? I think I may have left it in the church..."

"Yeah. I gave it to Harriett," replied Tabs.

"Harriett is still inside," smiled Mary, "If you don't see her, she'll be in the vestry."

"Oh, thank you."

"I'll go and find her," shot back Ashol as she ran into the church. The lady staggered forward a little but there was no way she was going anywhere fast.

"Are you part of the family?" asked Mary.

"Yes... They're waiting for me."

"She'll be quick. Our hearts are with you."

"Thank you. It is good to see Shaun had kind friends. His mum was so pleased to see you, girls."

Ashol bounced back up the aisle with the handbag and got called an angel before the lady tottered back to the waiting car waving her handbag.

"Job well done, girls. Quick, let's escape while we can." Mary laughed.

Mary took them back to her shop and told Bill – who it seemed to Tabs did most of the work – that they were all going to Bella's.

"No problem," he smiled. "Hi Tabitha, Ashol, Danielle."

"Hi," said the girls together.

"Now we celebrate," said Mary. "The first thing that happens when you get to heaven is a party, so let's join in."

"But, chips for all of us?" protested Tabs, "That'll cost a bomb."

"No buts. I never had children. Today you three can be my daughters."

They ate huge plate-fulls of cod, chips and peas, and bread and butter with a pot of tea. Then followed it with ice cream. Bella's was famous locally for its speciality ice cream. Tabitha hadn't realised just how hungry she was.

59

"Good," said Mary when they couldn't possibly eat any more. "Now come back to the shop. I've got something for you, Tabitha."

When they got back, Bill was busy with a short queue of customers. Mary presented Tabitha with a carrier bag. "For you," she smiled.

Tabs was taken aback. "What is it?"

"Open it."

She opened it and pulled out a long skirt. It was full-length with an elasticated waistband like the one she had seen in the garden.

"I gather you like long skirts but you probably don't own any of your own. This is for you if you like it."

"F... for me? Why I... How do you—"

"Do you like it?"

"Y...yes, it's... beautiful."

"Then it's yours. Take it... no arguing. Today, I am spoiling you like a daughter. It makes me happy. It's not new of course. I've put something into Friends of Africa for it." And she went off to help Bill with the queue.

"She does this all the time," explained Danielle. "Mary's quite safe. She likes giving us things. When we first came she gave our family lots and lots. And she sends all her profits to Africa. She lives to give. Don't argue, take it and make her happy."

"When you put it on, you will make Deng happy," laughed Ashol. "He likes it when you dress in pretty things." Tabitha went a distinct shade darker. She was quite embarrassed. *Deng looks at me?* She stifled her confusion by shaking out the skirt. It was indeed lovely.

When Mary came back after helping the last customer buy a Joanna Trollope, Tabs announced, "Thanks, Mary. I will wear it, even if only at home. I don't know how to thank you, properly. I don't deserve it."

"You do and you can thank me by wearing it. I hope it suits you." Without more ado, Tabitha pulled it on over her school uniform.

"There." she exclaimed.

"Give us a twirl," said Mary. Tabs obliged. "Just the right

length, I think. Glad you like it."

Tabitha was almost home before she remembered that it hadn't been long before she had been at a funeral. Mary was brilliant, she decided. She knew just what to do to make people feel OK, even when it might seem impossible. She told her mum about the funeral, Bella's, Mary and the Thomases, and ended by showing her the skirt.

"Wherever will you wear that?" mumbled her Mum, dismissively.

Tabs reflected. She didn't have to wear jeans all the time. She would wear it when she went to Leeds next – when she wouldn't be seen in the town. People wore all sorts of colourful things in Chapeltown.

"I can wear it when I go to Leeds to see Dad at the weekend. Mum, can I take Ashol and Deng when I next go? He might like to meet them."

"You'll have to ask your father that. Why would they want to meet him?"

"I dunno... he comes from Africa... and, well, we're friends."

"Well, I can't see what harm it'll do. If you really want to take them, you'll have to ask him... Can't imagine how he and... and his family will cope with you all, though... Tabitha, you are becoming a girl with too many surprises. First, you want to go to a funeral, then you come back with a hippie skirt, and now you want to take your friends to Leeds. You amaze me. Go easy on your poor mum."

"Thanks, Mum. I amaze myself sometimes." Tabitha smiled with her tongue in her cheek and a sparkle in her eye. "I reckon I'm just amazing."

"Oh, you do, do you? Mind you don't let things go to your head, my girl." she reproved. But she recognised that Tabitha was growing in genuine confidence, not just in some kind of superficial arrogance and she liked it.

13

Now Gross had gone, Tabitha's dream became less threatening. She even went a week without dreaming it at all. Her thoughts turned to the garden.

The last Sunday of November was a beautiful day and she set out with excitement but some trepidation too as she skipped down the lane. Few people were about on a Sunday morning and she had the world to herself. Until, however, she bumped into Mary on her way to church.

"And where are you off to in such a hurry?" Mary inquired.

"Oh. Just a walk. Nowhere special," she said, instinctively.

"Is that so? Well, you be careful, my girl. You know what can happen when you're out and about on your own."

"Oh, Gareth Green has been shut away. It's OK now. And besides, I got the better of him, didn't I?"

"If you mean you can look after yourself, I don't doubt it. Nevertheless, take care. I'm off to church and I mustn't be late – I'm giving out the books at the door today and my little car is in dock." And she took off at a fair lick towards the town.

I wonder where she lives? thought Tabitha. It occurred to her that that was something she had never known other than it was not 'the Planet of the Apes'. What was Mary doing here? Her mum had suggested she might come from some rabbit hole that led into a strange and different world. Indeed, anyone who lived off the estate was rather mysterious. She could have walked for miles.

Thinking of different worlds, Tabs continued on to the gate in the wall. She looked around but there was no one to be seen. For six and a half years she had kind of imagined that the Old Lodge was not occupied by real people. It didn't cross her mind that it could be Mary who lived there – the garden cottage and Mary belonged to different worlds.

Tabitha slipped through the door and into the little garden. Its grass was still covered by the late autumn dew that the sun had not got high enough to evaporate, except in one corner. There wasn't any dry grass to lay down flat on, so Tabitha took off her Parka jacket and, choosing the sunny corner, laid it down and sat cross-legged on it. The happenings of her visit with the skirt and the key came flooding back. Now, she had a skirt of her own. It wasn't quite so wonderful but it was amazing that Mary should have thought to give her one.

Then she found herself contemplating the peril she was in again and she shivered. It was only a matter of time before she was caught, wasn't it? She must seriously make this the last time. A wave of sadness spread itself over her.

But as the sunshine spread back across the grass and the little nymph changed from grey to creamy yellow, the little garden began working its wonders. Perhaps fifteen was not too old, after all. Perhaps the 'fairies' knew all along of her coming and kept her safe, out of sight. And if she was caught, she could meekly express her delight at the place and take whatever was said.

Fairies. For goodness sake, they in't real. But what is real and what is not? Narnia wasn't a real place – it was all made up by C. S. Lewis – but it told you about things that are true, about people and how they work together. Real life. How life works anywhere – that's what Lewis was trying to say. Tumnus, for example, wasn't real but you could meet people just like him in the town. They didn't quite look like him, of course... yet in some way they kind of did.

She may not believe in real fairies any more but that did not stop her from thinking that somewhere deep down there was more to things than met the eye. There was mystery in the world. *There in't fairies but there might still be something beyond what I can see. Like Ashol were on about – spirits, not ghosts floating about but... I can't put it into words.* Mary had been going to church, so she must believe there was a God too.

At last, as the sunshine crept up the beech hedge and bathed it in sunlight, Tabitha grew hungry; it was time she headed home – her mum would be wondering where she was. On a Sunday, the only people that seemed to be about were the few on their way to worship, and the football club yelling instructions to each other across the pitch but being heard in the next street. Neither activity appealed to her. At one o'clock her mother would be up, but still in her dressing gown. Tabs came home after a whole morning of inner wonderings.

"Where have you been?" Cindy demanded as she closed the door. Cindy's wonderings were waking and finding her daughter gone.

"Oh. Just a walk."

"Where? Where did you go?"

"Across by the football pitches and onto the lane. I saw Mary from Friends of Africa on her way to church. Look, Mum, I need some exercise. I feel all cooped up inside, especially on nice days like today. People walk to church safely enough on their own. Mary was."

"Well, OK. But—"

Before Cindy could say any more, Tabitha's phone bleeped a text. Ashol was asking if Tabs would like to come to tea at her house. It seemed that the Thomases made a special thing of eating together and they could dress up. Tabs could wear her new skirt.

"Ashol is inviting me round for yea? Can I go?"

Things were changing for Cindy. She was having to let her daughter go. It was bitter-sweet. Cindy went to get dressed – she didn't want her daughter see the tear in her eye.

Tabs arrived at the Thomas's at the given time to find great preparations were underway to receive her. As soon as she arrived, Tabitha opened the plastic carrier bag and took out her new skirt. When she had got it home, she had washed it at her mother's insistence. Now she admired it anew. Now she could put it on for her new friend to see.

Ashol was duly impressed. "This so suits you. You like long skirts?"

"This is the first one I've owned. I haven't worn one before..." That wasn't entirely true, was it? "We-ell," she faltered, "not properly, not of my own. I've always worn jeans or leggings from being quite little."

"Not properly? You have had one on, then... before?"

"Well, yeah... but not really. Just tried one on," Tabs added. Should she tell Ashol about the skirt in the garden? No. The garden had to be kept secret – from everyone.

"I have some long skirts. Come and see."

They scuttled up the stairs to Ashol's small bedroom where

she opened her wardrobe to reveal, among her everyday clothes, three colourful skirts and an African lady's 'twin set'. This last consisted of a top and bottom made of the same flower-patterned material in which the top was a shaped blouse with puff sleeves which zipped down the back, and the bottom a skirt that hugged the hips and thighs but flared around the calves to finish at the ankles with a deep frill. It was made of cotton with splashes of bright blue and green that reminded Tabitha of a parrot she had seen in an aviary on a school outing. The skirts were equally bright colours, and one was almost as full as Tabitha's.

"Wow. Wonderful." Tabs was truly amazed. "You never see colours like that in this country."

"Well maybe not in this town, but you do in Leeds sometimes where many of the black people live. We Africans like colour. Don't we?"

We Africans. Tabitha had never thought of herself as African. But now Ashol had said it, she *was* half Nigerian; her father was properly Nigerian – born there – even if he'd moved away, so she did have true African genes.

"I think I must have some of that in me. I mean the love of bright colours. I love all these."

"Let's dress up for dinner. You put on your skirt, and... let's see... this white blouse that will set it, and you, off." She produced a pure white cotton blouse that had a draw string neckline and short puffy sleeves with red-brown trimmings that complemented the skirt. Tabitha hesitated – for all of five seconds. She took her skirt and held it up. Now she was actually going to wear it for real and not just for Ashol in the privacy of her room.

"You have definitely worn a skirt like this before." exclaimed Ashol, as Tabitha pulled it purposefully over her head and down to her waist.

Should she tell? No. "As I said, not really. Only tried one on with my jeans still on underneath. No one saw."

"When was that? In Friends of Africa?"

She could tell. If she could entrust anyone with her secret – if anyone would understand – it would be Ashol.

"No. I was somewhere where there just was one laying there

65

and I tried it on."

This was too much for Ashol. "Just laying where?"

"Oh. In a garden... somewhere."

"*Tell me, Tabs.* You're hiding something from me."

"It's a secret. It's been a secret since I was eight... OK. But you must promise never, ever, to tell anyone else. Not even my mum... especially my mum."

Ashol stood silent, a cloud of guilt passing across her features. "Sorry, I should not have asked. Don't say any more. Keep your secret."

"No. I want to tell you, Ashol. I trust you. You're the best friend I've ever had. I know you will not laugh at me or say I'm silly or anything. It began when I was eight." And Tabs poured out everything about the garden and the skirt... but not about the key, though. Not yet.

Ashol was brilliant. "Your secret is safe with me, Tabs. If it is the fairies, they have good taste," she added. Ashol didn't ask where the garden might be found – that would not be fair. But she could guess. She thought she knew. It sounded familiar. Perhaps she had seen it, herself, but she didn't say.

The drawstring blouse was the most dressed up top Tabitha had ever worn and she felt fantastic in it. Ashol put on a full-length yellow-flowered skirt and a cream top with a boat neck.

"Let's make an entrance." she proclaimed, checking herself in her long mirror. "Can you pass me that hair clip, the gold one? Thanks." She dexterously turned up the ends of her plaited extensions and put in the clip. Tabitha decided to let her own hair go loose. She had dark brown hair with a natural wave which came to the middle of her back. Gathering it up in her hand, Ashol brushed it for her. "You have beautiful hair," she commented, "I wish I had long hair like this."

"But yours is great. You do it well."

"It takes ages at the hairdresser's, though. To put it all in can be a pain, and it needs to be done at least every three weeks. And it took ages to get the teachers to agree to me having the braiding in for school. Rev Mike brought it to the governors' meeting and they had to make a policy decision."

"A policy decision. That's ridiculous."

"They didn't want to make a precedent for the girls who wanted to put in blue extensions and that sort of thing, I guess. So they made an exception for people belonging to ethnic minorities. I love your natural long hair."

"Ethnic minorities. I could do what I like then. I never thought of dying it but I'm not sure about blue. Perhaps bright red," laughed Tabitha. "I could say that they should let me because I'm black."

"I don't think that would work. They don't do that in Africa or the Caribbean or anywhere and it would be cheating."

"I could say it was my religion."

"What religion? It would look as if you were supporting Millheaton Town FC."

"Really? Oh no. I'd better stick to my natural brown," she giggled. "You know, I think I like the African way of dressing best, though." She looked at herself in Ashol's mirror and swished the skirt. It's like, like, kinda being free. Mum's always wanting to blend in. But she's white. I can't."

"And so embrace it. If you're gonna be different, go for it, is what I say. That skirt and that top suit you."

"Thanks for lending me it. I really like it."

"It's yours, girl. It's found its home. Keep it."

"What. I can't..."

"Yeah, you can."

"I... thanks, Ashol." They hugged.

"Ready? Come on let's wow them."

The girls descended the stairs and swished into the living room. Tabs thought Deng's jaw had come loose as his eyes feasted on her. He was a young man of few words but his expression said it all. Tabs lowered her eyes.

"Now, that's how girls should look," said Mr Thomas, light-heartedly, relieving the tension.

"Don't be sexist," chided his wife. "Young women are not just here to please you men, you know."

"I know, but I do think that when something can be beautiful it should be. Come on, Deng, let's put on our finery too."

"Don't be too long about it," called Mama Sarah after them. "You know, Tabitha, I believe African men are the vainest in the world."

14

Under orders and hungry, the boys weren't long. Here were the two Sudanese gentlemen in their Sunday best. Father and son both sported smart ironed shirts with cuff links, colourful ties and jackets with matching trousers and polished shoes. Tabitha was impressed and returned Deng's smile as she took him in. Could any guy look like that except on TV?

"So let's eat," proclaimed Mama Sarah. "We're going to eat Sudanese this evening." They all went to the sink and washed their hands, just like Tabitha had been taught as a little girl. She quickly learned that regular washing is all part of being South Sudanese.

Tabs feasted her eyes on chunks of meat in a rich spicy gravy with tomato and onion, cabbage, and a heap of rice in a bowl which Mama Sarah and Ashol placed in the centre of the table. Mr Thomas said grace and Deng handed Tabs a large ladle for her to help herself to a portion to put on the plate in front of her. The only piece of cutlery was a spoon – for Tabs; the family all ate with their fingers.

"You can use the spoon," smiled Mama Sarah.

"Or you can do it the Sudanese way, if you like," challenged Ashol.

"Yeah. We like to use God's original," explained Deng. "You won't think us rude, will you?" he added, worried what Tabs might feel.

"No of course not," said Tabs, embarrassed at her own surprise. She picked up a piece of cabbage. Eating chunks of meat and gravy with the fingers should have looked gross but somehow it didn't. It was not what you did, but how you did it that seemed to matter. She tried to emulate them but the delicious gravy defeated her – how do you eat gravy with your fingers? She took up the spoon for that.

After fishing in the pot three times, Tabitha had eaten enough. But three helpings delighted the hosts.

"So now we eat Yorkshire," announced Mama Sarah. And she produced a bowl of tinned peach slices in syrup and a block of ice cream.

"This," explained Mr Thomas, "you cannot get in South Sudan. Well, at least not in the shops we used."

"How can someone live without peaches in syrup?" exclaimed Ashol.

"Very well," said Tabitha. "I cannot recall when I last had them. But no ice cream in South Sudan? However, do you manage without that?"

"Oh, we have it but you have to be very special to have electricity 24/7. Most people don't."

"And no chocolate either," moaned Deng. "You'd need a fridge and for that you need electricity, and for that, you have to have a generator..."

"So, for most people, it can't be done," summed up Mama Sarah.

"Not even for chocolate," smiled Tabs. *Oops,* she thought, *was that joke insensitive?* But she needn't have worried because they all laughed. Tabs couldn't imagine a world without chocolate or ice cream. Even the poorest family in Britain didn't go entirely without them, did they?

"Not even for chocolate," replied Mr Thomas, "but to purchase a generator and a fridge for a supply of chocolate... it is a close thing," he chuckled. "So we have to choose between our own lovely homeland with real free sunshine without chocolate and ice-cream or a cloudy cold place with both. A difficult choice."

"You miss South Sudan, don't you?" ventured Tabitha.

"It is our home, our own true home in this world. Don't get us wrong. We are grateful to Britain for taking us in. We have jobs and a free education for our children and we don't have to pay the doctor when we are sick. Your NHS is the best thing. You have lots of good things."

"Including chocolate," chimed in Ashol, definitely a chocolate devotee.

"Including chocolate," agreed her mother, "but Britain isn't home."

Tabs felt her pain. "So, you plan to go back?"

"Oh yes, of course, as soon as we can."

"And Ashol and," she looked up at the smart young man seated opposite her, "Deng, too?"

"Of course," said their mother but Tabs detected a slight diffidence in Ashol's expression that the others might not have noticed.

"I was born in Yorkshire but I don't feel at home here in this town," mused Tabitha, quietly.

"We know," replied Deng. "You're like us."

"But I don't have any other home to want to go to. And Mum is happy here, I think, as much as anyone is."

"But you don't have white skin," said Mama Sarah. "You might feel happier in the city where there are more black people."

"Maybe. But it's more than just colour. I don't exactly know what. Other kids don't seem to see the things I see. Notice what I notice."

"Like what?"

"Nature. The trees. The environment, I suppose you might call it. I think that the world is a..." she sought for the word, a word they would understand. She was going to say 'magical' but she thought that might mean something different in Africa, "the world has a deeper something. There's something beyond what you can see. I feel it – but I don't know what to call it."

That evening, as the November night with its wisps of fog enveloped the path, Tabs was walked home by Deng. It was the first time she had been escorted anywhere. She hadn't changed out of her skirt and top beneath her Parka and she felt like a real lady being looked after by the most wonderful boy she could have dreamed of – only it wasn't a dream.

At her front door, he looked into her eyes and half asked, half stated, "You will come and eat with us, again?" And he handed her her carrier bag with her jeans and shirt.

"Course."

15

Buoyed up by the knowledge that Ashol had talked her into revealing the secret of the garden and hadn't laughed at her, Tabs couldn't resist going back there, despite her fears. Ashol was wise, she had learned her secret and had understood. Tabs felt good.

When she got there, there was the beautiful skirt again. Should she...? She ignored both skirt and key for five whole minutes. *No more magic.* But she had been emboldened by Ashol and her evening with the Thomases, so despite the December chill, she pulled off her jeans and shoes and picked up the skirt. And beneath it, there was the key. Wow. She donned the skirt and danced on the damp, cool grass, swinging its fullness about her, feeling its tug on her waist and then the way it continued swirling, hugging around her calves and thighs when she stopped.

What about the gate? Could she enter into the park beyond? She hadn't touched the key, yet. She looked at it, sitting alone, waiting patiently on the bench. Tabs strode across the grass, took it into her hand and felt the cold metal. It wasn't really magical... was it? Just a key. She approached the gate and put her finger on the keyhole of the lock. Then, thoughtfully, carefully, inserted the key into it. Then took it out again.

No, I mustn't. Should I? Could I? Might I?

Slowly she put the key back into the lock and turned it. There was a little resistance but not much and suddenly, with a click, the padlock opened. She lifted the hasp clear and slid back the bolt and the gate swung open a little. It did not rain this time – there was no bolt of lightning or anything to indicate Nature's displeasure. It was as though the woodland was saying, "Welcome, special one, to the place where you belong."

Was all this a delusion? The thought struck her that this was too easy. Who was she, dressed in borrowed – stolen(?) – clothes, entering onto sacred ground? But, even as the thought came into her head, the place issued a renewed welcome and seemed to draw her in, dispelling all misgivings.

Tabitha stepped forward onto a narrow path which led into the heart of the wood, to a glade that was hidden from the gate. Here she was completely secluded. All around her was Nature in grand abundance. Trees, tall and short, grasses, bushes, mushrooms and toadstools, including a large one with a red top with white spots straight out of the storybooks. She had no idea these existed in real life. All of this was within half a mile of her run-down estate and she had not known just how rich it was. Her classmates somehow had missed it altogether.

Part of Tabs was glad she had not beheld this until that moment because she would not have appreciated its true magic as a young child when everything was magical anyway. Now she did not have to believe in fairies, because this reality was more glorious than she had ever imagined in the fairy tales.

She gasped. There beneath a tree was a big hole in the bank. It was just like the badger's house in *The Seasons in Fern Hollow* – a kids' picture book that had turned up in the Friends of Africa shop. *Can there be real badgers here?* Then, in the centre of the glade, she saw a rabbit, then another, and another. They didn't seem to be worried that this stranger had appeared in their midst. *Real wild rabbits. Wow.* The rabbits she had seen along the lane always ran away if you got anywhere near them, but these were different. She was 'Alice' again on the edge of a wonderland. She explored, stood, listened and drank in this place for what must have been an hour and a half; yet Tabitha had lost all sense of time.

At last, reluctantly, she trotted back down the track feeling the mud ooze between her toes. It might have been late in the year but in the sunshine the ground was soft and Tabs wasn't aware of the increasing chill creeping into the afternoon.

Still half in a dream, she forgot that she was still wearing the skirt as she passed through the garden and began to walk down the Puddleham Road just as the Thomas family were passing in their old car. The car pulled up and Deng lent out the window and shouted. "Tabitha, get in we'll give you a lift."

Tabitha ran to the car and Deng got out and opened the back door for her to get in. It was only then that she realised she had still got the skirt on and had left her jeans, her shoes and her phone on the bench. Too late.

"Wow. Love the skirt," whistled Deng.

"Oh, er. Just borrowed," explained Tabitha. "I... I left my jeans in... back up there. I must go back and get them."

"That's OK," said Mr Thomas, "we'll wait for you."

"No. That's OK."

But, of course, they waited.

Tabitha scuttled up the road as Deng watched. He couldn't help noticing her bare feet and smiled broadly. *There's nothing for it*, she thought, *they're going to see where I turn in but they won't know about the garden. Only Ashol knows.*

Inside the garden, Tabs changed quickly and laid the skirt back on the bench over the key where she had found it. With her trainers back on and phone in her pocket, she ran down the road to where Mr Thomas and Deng were waiting for her. Deng and Mr Thomas were real gentlemen and didn't ask questions. All Deng said was, "You looked great in that skirt, you know."

16

Tabs arranged to visit Leeds with Ashol and Deng two weekends before Christmas. Introducing them to her father felt really cool. Her dad said he would be delighted to greet her new friends, especially when he discovered they were African.

As they walked out of Beckside Academy the day before the trip, Ashol suggested they take their colourful skirts. Tabitha thought this was a wonderful idea; it would make the trip even more exciting.

They took an early bus and were in Leeds bus station by nine o'clock where Mr Johnson met them.

"Hey, Dad." Tabitha rushed to hug him. Their relationship had not always been so warm but had improved so much of late – especially after she began coming by herself. At first, when she was too young to go alone her mother had brought her and there had often been a tense handover; Cindy felt it was an imposition and had made no secret of it. And Tabitha recalled it all being arranged without anyone asking her what she wanted. The agreement had been that her father would have her one weekend a month.

Once she was there, Tabs hadn't missed her mother – her dad worked hard to entertain her, so much so that after a short while when she got used to it, she began to think of Leeds as a treat rather than a thing she had to do. In some ways, it was. At least, it was a break from Beck Ings and the people she had to put up with all week.

When she had turned fourteen, Tabs had demanded to be allowed to go by herself. Her mum took little persuading if her former husband promised to be at the bus station to collect her, which he always was.

On one occasion, there had been some event on at school on the given weekend, so Tabs got to choose an alternative and from then on she exercised more control. Sometimes she went more often than once a month, which pleased her dad and didn't

75

appear to bother her mum so much; it made the visits seem something different from an enforced requirement. In the past few months, since she got the desire to 'take her opportunities', she had been a lot nicer to know and things were more relaxed between her and the step-family – she had begun to understand her dad really loved her and enjoyed being with her.

"Dad, this is Ashol and this is Deng." Tabs smiled as she introduced her friends to her father for the first time.

"Pleased to meet you. I've heard so much about you," enthused Mr Johnson in return.

"Pleased to meet you, too," said Ashol, extending a hand. She had been very curious to meet him. Deng said nothing but just shook hands, too. In Sudan you can't shake hands often enough – maybe it was the same in Nigeria. With an air of shyness, Deng looked down at Tabs' dad; at sixteen, he was taller, albeit much slimmer than the older man.

"You are very welcome to come to our little house. It isn't a mansion, I'm afraid, but Tabitha says you won't mind sleeping on the floor."

"No problem," affirmed Ashol, confidently.

Mr Johnson took his daughter's backpack and led them through the indoor market.

"Cool," whistled Deng, awed by the huge Victorian architecture – the high roof, the pillars and the ironwork. "Supposed to be the largest indoor market in Europe," he mumbled, mostly to himself.

"You've done your research," laughed Joshua. Deng shrugged a smile while he looked up and around. The smells and sounds were unlike any he had experienced in their small town; here there was a faint echo of South Sudan – the colourful stalls, the milling crowds, the scents of fruit and spices, perfumes and incense and the subtle smell of bolts of cotton cloth offered for sale by traders with Asian faces, even the grimy damp floor with scattered rubbish was reminiscent. Somehow Deng felt more at home here than in Millheaton with only the convenience shop and ethnic food restaurants and take-away owners the chief exception to the white Yorkshire working-class culture.

"How d'you know that?" questioned Ashol.

"Know what?" responded Deng, lost in his thought.

"That this market is the largest market in the world?"

"Not the largest market in the world. The largest indoor market in Europe."

"OK," persisted Ashol. "So how do you know?"

"Internet. It's all on the Internet. I Googled Leeds when I knew we were coming here."

"That's clever of you," said Joshua.

"No, not really. The really cool thing would be to have a smartphone and look things up on the go."

"But you don't have one of those?"

"Wish I did," he sighed.

"So would I." exclaimed Ashol. "I would love one. I'm about the only kid in my year not to have one. But Mum and Dad aren't that rich."

"You can't have everything, I guess," smiled Joshua.

"Dad bought me my phone," explained Tabitha. "Guess it's OK." She slid her hand into a pocket in her jeans and took out a slim device.

"OK?" laughed her father. "That's an expensive bit of equipment that comes with a contract that charges my credit card every month."

"Dad, it's 'OK'. 'OK' means it's cool, these days. It isn't 5G but I don't care. I like it."

"It's ten times better than my old thing," moaned Ashol. "It only does texting and actual voice – which no one does these days, do they? It's positively ancient. The man in the phone shop said it was, like, 'out of the ark' – years out of date. And that was last year."

"Out of the ark," mocked Deng, playfully. "Noah would have been amazed if he had found any digital technology on the ark. Keep it safe, though, because next year it might be worth money as an antique."

"I must apologise for my brother. He's—"

"Your brother," laughed Joshua. "I like your choice of friends, Tab. They're... 'OK'."

"Thanks, Dad."

But Deng was no longer listening – he was back delighting in the architecture. "Like, this market is really old, guys. It's so cool."

Joshua took them to a pie stall selling all kinds of different sorts of pastries and he bought a large home-baked stand pie with golden pastry and a delicious savour. They continued past stalls selling all kinds of produce before they found one which smelled of a whole mixture of spices. Here, they bought lentils, cumin seeds and coriander powder.

Ashol noticed that there seemed to be people from every corner of the world in Leeds – literally. A woman in a burka followed a man with a heavy beard. He was doing the shopping while she lugged two heavy bags one pace behind. It was as if she were a kind of prisoner tied to him with an invisible rope. Ashol tried not to stare.

"Bet that's uncomfortable," she whispered.

"Perhaps not for her," said Deng. "You never know, she might have all her favourite kit on underneath including the latest smartphone."

"Stop teasing your sister," commanded Tabitha, giving him a look.

Leaving the market at the opposite end, they emerged onto New Market Street which was packed with slow-moving traffic, stationary buses and hundreds of people bustling about doing their Christmas shopping. They waited for the lights to turn green for pedestrians. Mr Johnson escorted Ashol by the elbow and ushered her across through the mêlée and Deng took Tabitha by the hand to guide her. Her first reaction was to shrug him off – she was not a child that needed looking after. Ashol didn't know this road, while she did and Deng had never been here. But then she decided she liked the sensation of her hand in Deng's strong grasp and so said nothing. When they reached the pavement opposite they followed Mr Johnson down a side street into a pedestrian precinct.

"We're meeting up with Georgina and the children at twelve. Would you like to go round the shops until then?"

Ashol's face glowed. This was a fabulous surprise. All these wonderful stores. She set off and they pursued her into Mark's and Spencer's. Somehow Deng forgot to let go of Tabitha's hand,

and he was still holding it when they reached a rack of colourful skirts.

"You see." exclaimed Ashol. "There are lots of people who wear these. Not all girls wear jeans all of the time." Then she caught sight of her brother and Tabs holding hands and her face broke into a wide animated smile. Tabitha's face went hot and she quickly detached herself and, pretending nothing had happened, mumbled, "They do on Beck Ings."

"But we are not on Beck Ings now. Look there are people here from all over the world."

Tabitha spotted a girl that looked Chinese, and another like herself that may have been mixed race. Could be Indian, though, she decided. The wonderful thing was that they all looked at home in that store.

"I want to buy Mum a new top for Christmas," pronounced Ashol.

"Goodness. Where do you start?" wondered Deng. Markets were one thing but department stores were quite another.

"Here. Then we can go to the other stores, there are lots of them around here... I mean, if that's all right Mr Johnson."

"Who's been doing the research now?" chuntered Deng. Ashol pulled a face at him.

"Perfectly fine with me," answered Joshua.

"Whatever," said Tabitha, who wasn't keen on shopping – she had never had much to spend – but was pleased to give Ashol the opportunity. The only person Tabitha had bought a present for in the past was her mother. This year she thought she might get one for her Dad and his family too.

"Yeah, whatever," echoed Deng. Ashol moved over to a group of rails displaying tops, and Deng grasped Tabs' hand once more.

"I won't get lost," she whispered. Deng dropped her hand as if it were red hot. Tabitha looked up and smiled at him in his confusion. "But *you* might," she laughed, taking his arm, and leading him across the aisle to stand by a pillar and watch Ashol look around, pulling out clothes here and there. "Are you going to do any shopping?"

"Hate it. I mean I don't like buying things with other people around. And it all takes such a long time. I get all my presents online."

"That's a good idea. How do you pay for it all?"

"With Dad's debit card. He trusts me. I pay him back when the bill comes in."

At last, they moved on from M & S and crossed into the Bond Street centre, and then up Lands Lane. All the while Tabs holding on to Deng. "You do hate shopping don't you?"

"I don't mind. Really I don't mind but I'm not that interested in the stuff that Ashol wants to buy. I am a bloke after all."

Tabs giggled, "You're so patient."

"If you say so."

By then it was a quarter to twelve. The time had passed much quicker than Tabitha had realised, and Ashol simply couldn't believe it when Mr Johnson gathered them up to take them to where they were to meet Georgina. "We've only been into four stores," moaned Ashol. "Where has the time gone?"

"No idea," mumbled Tabs.

"It was when he was out shopping with his wife that Einstein got the idea for his theory of relativity," said Deng.

"Really?" said Ashol. "How does that...?" she trailed off, seeing the look of triumph on her brother's face. She swung her shopping at him and told him to give over teasing her. "Brothers."

"Come on," urged Mr Johnson laughing, "before some innocent shopper gets caught in the crossfire." He took Tabs in charge, completed the final stretch of Lands Lane and rounded the corner onto the Headrow and then Tabs knew where she was. They were heading for MacDonald's on Albion Street.

They arrived outside just as Georgina was crossing the road.

"Hi," called Tabs. Georgina was delighted to see her stepdaughter. Ashol and Deng were introduced.

Inside the warm restaurant, seated together, Tabs reflected to herself that she was the only one of the group who had any non-African blood in her. But in this company she was to be black – and she was surprised just how comfortable she felt about it. These people seemed more content with their lives than most of the residents on her home estate. At least, when she met them they didn't moan about much. There was always lots of laughter.

It never occurred to her that she might be part of the reason for that – because they were clearly enjoying her company. She did remark to herself that indeed they had little to complain about, they came from two happy families – more people than just two – and it was an absolute delight to be among them. Certainly, in one way she was the odd one out – the stepdaughter. But today she was also the link between her friends and her father's family. And as they sat eating burgers and fries followed by blueberry muffins, Ashol and Deng were getting on well with her dad and Georgina. And that made her feel good.

"Where to next?" asked Joshua when they had finished eating. "We have all afternoon."

"Let's go see the butterflies," responded Tabitha, immediately, "Unless you—"

"Such enthusiasm," laughed her father, "and a brilliant idea."

"Butterflies?" wondered Ashol. "Is that art or something?"

"No. Real ones. From all over the world." Georgina explained about the butterfly house in the Canal Gardens, *Tropical World*.

"Sounds cool," said Ashol.

"Great," added Deng, genuinely interested. No more shops.

"Well, it's nice and warm and reminds me of Africa," said Joshua. "and Tab loves it. It's not just the butterflies but the tropical plants that don't grow in this cold country. You know how she loves natural things."

"I do," declared his daughter, delighted her suggestion was to be taken up.

17

They had to fight their way back to Vicar Lane against a strong, cold easterly breeze but they were fortunate to step straight onto a bus and headed up the stairs. Soon they were riding past the playing fields of Roundhay Park. At the terminus, they all tumbled down the stairs and strode towards the walled gardens in which the tropical houses were situated.

When they got inside past the tropical fish tanks into the heated glass houses it was like entering a different world. Ashol was transfixed. They not only had some of the most beautiful butterflies and moths in the world, but jungle trees and bushes among waterfalls. Great big flowers hung from the roof and there were giant water lilies in the ponds. In stark contrast to the bitter east wind outside, the atmosphere was hot and steamy. It reminded Deng of what his parents kept calling 'home'.

"Would you ever go home?" Deng asked Joshua, "I mean, to Africa?"

"No, not now. Sure, there's lots I miss and things I might like there, but it's been too long. It will have changed and so have I. There would be more I would miss here now. I am settled in Leeds... I couldn't live where you and Tabitha do, though," he added. "But I like our multicultural city." He turned and looked at his daughter with a mixture of shame, and even regret. "I don't visit Tab at home. I just couldn't—"

"I know," interrupted Tabitha. "I do understand. I really do.... and I like coming to Leeds. You belong here. I can't think of you anywhere else."

"Yeah. It's a real OK place," broke in Ashol. OK was fast becoming the theme of the day for Ashol. "I wouldn't mind living here. There is a uni, isn't there? Lots of cool students."

"Our Mum and Dad keep talking of going back to Juba, though," added Deng, "that's where their hearts truly are."

"Would you like that?" asked Tabs. "I mean if they left England and went to Juba? From what I hear it's not very nice at the moment."

"What's nice for you depends on how you feel about things. It would be better than where we are now because Mum and Dad would be happy. They keep saying they want to be able to help South Sudan grow. If the war is properly ended, they want to be part of the regeneration. There Dad could get a big important job; here he just works to keep the money coming in."

"And what about you? Would you be, like, better off in South Sudan?" Tabitha felt she had a vested interest now their friendship was deepening.

"It does sound exciting. So yes, I would give it a shot."

"Mum has taught us to speak Dinka, our tribal language," added Ashol. "It would be great to have other people to talk it with... And I do like it hot." And to prove the fact she took off her coat and spun around on the walkway as the heat of the tropical house began to soak in.

"Do you have an idea of when? I mean of going to Juba?" asked Georgina.

"Dad says he's started looking for ways to get back there as soon as possible."

Going back to Africa. Tabitha became alarmed. The thought of losing her friends was the first cloud on this wonderful day.

"But it'll probably be years before we know how things will turn out, or we could afford to go."

"Oh... yeah." Tabitha felt relieved. *Not so soon, then,* she assured herself. When she was older she would definitely try to move to Leeds. But, then, she thought of her little secret garden and the woods beyond the gate and wondered whether the trees in Roundhay Park were a place where she could be alone with Nature, too. From what she had seen, Leeds all looked rather full of people.

That evening in Chapeltown after a proper Nigerian supper, they gathered in the sitting room. One of Tabitha's father's hobbies was keeping tropical fish like in the entrance to the butterfly house. Ashol and Deng showed great interest because this was something new to them. Mr Johnson began to answer their questions and soon they were deeply absorbed in the intricacies of the different varieties and how to keep them. Tabs, who had heard it all before, sat with Georgina over her embroidery. She showed her some of the different stitches and Tabs tried a few herself.

"Are there woods in Roundhay Park where you can be completely surrounded by trees and listen to the birds and things?"

"Well, yes. But you're never far from anywhere. The Ring Road goes round the north side of the park, so you can always hear the traffic wherever you are."

"Are they big enough so that you could be all on your own? I mean the woods."

"Tab. You must never go there alone. It's too dangerous – even in the daytime."

"But I like to be alone with trees and nature and things. Where could I go?"

"That's lovely. But I would not go on my own in any of the lonely places in Leeds," frowned her stepmother. This girl was deep and different but not very streetwise. "I go walk in the park on my own sometimes but keep to the public bits. Do you go out alone in Beck Ings? Is it safe there?"

"Well, sort of. I know most of the kids, and I know which ones to watch out for." Tabs had not told them about her secret garden, of course. One day she might, but it would have to be someone who would understand, and not think she was mad... or urge her to give it up because they didn't think it was safe.

"What about strangers?"

"Never thought about it. I don't think outsiders come to

Millheaton much."

"But in Leeds it's different. There are hundreds of thousands of people who live here, and new people coming and going all the time... and there are lots of funny ones among them. The neighbours here are always changing. Two doors up there was a police raid and they took a guy off in handcuffs. I hadn't seen him before and I guess we won't again."

"There was a guy in our block who tried to nick the takings at the bingo but they got him with a helicopter. He wouldn't have done anything to us girls, though. Well, no one said he did. He didn't seem the type."

"How'd you know?"

"He wasn't very old – lived with his mum. Still in his teens, I guess. And I in't heard of anyone going for *people* – it's mostly breaking into houses." Georgina felt troubled. Tabs was still too innocent. Her mother had done a good job of protecting her. She was frightened that she might do something silly one day.

"You need to be careful, Tab. The world is not a safe place."

"Don't worry," chuckled Tabs seeing Georgina's lined forehead, "I shan't go off anywhere alone here. I come to Leeds to be with Dad, and you. I can be alone any time I like at home but I can't see you everyday. While I'm in Leeds, I want to be with you."

"And we both like you coming here," Georgina's face relaxed. "And your Dad is so pleased that you wanted to bring your friends. Look at him, he approves of your choice. He's proud of you. He likes the way you've turned out."

The rest of the weekend went far too quickly. Tabitha could not remember being happier. Deng and Ashol had enjoyed the Nigerian food, lots of African stories had been shared, and they clearly liked meeting other people they had something in common with.

When they got to the bus stop in Beck Ings it had been dark for a couple of hours. Mr and Mrs Thomas were waiting for them and they walked Tabitha home. She gave them all a hug before she went inside – inside to her Mum who would be watching the telly and probably be grumpy. Tabs had learned not to be too effusive when she came back from Leeds because she knew it upset her. She would have been lonely while her daughter was having a fun time.

She opened the door and shouted. "Hey, Mum."

Cindy was watching *Strictly* for the second time. Tabitha sat down and watched, saying nothing. She hadn't watched a telly programme at all over the weekend. The Thomases hadn't seen *The Matrix* and so they had watched the DVD and then talked about whether or not what we see is real, or whether there might be a greater reality beyond. And, if so, whether it was good or evil.

"Had a good time?" asked Cindy.

"Yeah. OK." Tabs kept her voice neutral.

"Your Dad well?"

"Yeah."

"Go all right with the Thomases?"

"Yeah. We talked a lot about Africa."

"Good. There's some shepherd's pie for you on the side you can put in the microwave."

"Thanks, Mum, want a cup of tea?" Tabs got up to put the kettle on. She was home... but she had been experimenting with foreign cuisine and had got a taste for it, so she sneaked some extra pepper under the potato of the pie while her mum wasn't looking.

18

Leading up to Christmas, Tabitha was having the time of her life, and Christmas Day hadn't even arrived. Being friends with the Thomases was great. They seemed to have lots of Christmas traditions that started before December had hardly begun.

The first thing was they kept the season of Advent. In their living room they had an Advent wreath in the middle of the dining table, whilst in the kitchen there were five Advent calendars, one for each person and one they all shared. They had lit the first candle of the wreath on Advent Sunday – that year the last Sunday in November – with a prayer for hope for the future, even asking Jesus to come again and wind up the world so they could all go to heaven. They said the prayer together every day for seven days, and then they moved on to the second candle with a prayer for justice in the world.

"Is this what everyone does in South Sudan?" inquired Tabitha.

"No, it's a European custom. We learned it a few years ago from a church Garang happened to attend during Advent. He thought it was a great idea, so we adopted it," explained Mama Sarah.

"And I looked it up in a book of Christmas customs which told us how to make the wreath," added Deng.

"In Juba, we're good at picking up new ideas for worshipping God," went on Mr Thomas. "We like ceremonies and things. We don't have holly in South Sudan, of course, so when we're back there, we'll use something else."

"But this year we're in Britain and we've got real holly," said Ashol, excitedly. "Mary from church gave us some from her garden." She watched Tabs closely. Not a flicker. She clearly hadn't linked her secret garden with Mary but Ashol felt sure she was onto the right place.

"*We* generally put up a Christmas tree when December starts," said Tabitha, not wanting to feel they had no customs at their house.

"The third candle is for peace, and the fourth for love," explained Mama Sarah. "Jesus coming into the world is our only hope. We all have to follow him, together, for there to be any hope of peace."

Tabitha could see how important this wreath was to the Thomases and why things mattered so much. She was used to Christmas being about pretending things were OK, whilst secretly knowing – but not admitting – that, in fact, they weren't. It was supposed to be about families coming together, yet so many of them were broken and more people seemed to fall out at Christmas than at any other time of the year.

For Tabitha, there had always been the sadness of a failed marriage. The neighbours at 57 refused to have their family for Christmas anymore because several years ago their son-in-law got drunk and said some nasty things. But the Thomases truly believed that Jesus was with them still.

"Yes. The world is a very dark place," said Mr Thomas, "but God has come into it and shines in the darkness." That was what the candles were all about. *Cool*, thought Tabitha.

"What are you and your mum doing at Christmas this year?" asked Mama Sarah, breaking into her reverie.

"Oh. It's just Mum and me on Christmas Day. The only thing that I have to do is go to Dad's on Boxing Day. He's coming for me in the morning and I'll go for the day. He has to fetch me on Boxing Day because the buses don't run the same. Mum hates it because she has to be on her own and there is nothing to do except watch telly."

"Would you like to come to us on Christmas Day?"

Tabitha was shocked. Christmas was when you *didn't* see your friends, only your family. "Th... thanks but I mustn't leave my mum any more than I have to... But thanks, it would have been great." How wonderful it would be to be with these people but no way could she, or would she, leave her mum. She was all Cindy had.

"No, I mean both of you," emphasised Mama Sarah. "Why don't you both come on Christmas Day and then your mum can spend the day with us on Boxing Day while you're in Leeds."

"And then you could come and sleepover," said Ashol, excitedly. "They *can* come and sleep over can't they, Mum?"

All this was happening too fast for Tabitha. Mrs Thomas detected her slight panic.

"Well... I'm not sure Ashol. We couldn't ask Tabitha's mum to sleep in the sitting room. You can't put a lady like her on the sofa bed."

"She can have my room," interjected Deng. "I can use the sofa bed. I don't mind."

"No.... no. We couldn't do that," objected Tabitha.

"Yes we could," insisted Ashol, bubbling over.

Mr Thomas held up his hand. Everyone fell silent. "My family seem to have decided on this. Now I think it is my turn to say something. Now I will agree to—"

"Yes, yes...." exploded Ashol.

Mr Thomas held up his right hand again and Ashol clamped her mouth shut, "I will agree to this so long as both Tabitha and her mother want to come and, more especially, Mrs Johnson. She must be truly happy about it."

"Oh, she will be, won't she?" persisted Ashol.

"I don't know," answered Tabitha, doubtfully, "She's never done a sleepover anywhere ever that I know of."

"But you *will* ask her?" asked Ashol, anxiously. "You want to come?..."

"Course. I'd love to. But I don't know if Mum would sleep away from home. And I don't think she would want to stay here without me on Boxing Day. And... and I couldn't ask her, anyway. She wouldn't believe you would actually want her... She'd think I was not saying it right. It's not what most people do at Christmas, is it? I mean in England."

"Don't worry. Don't you say anything. We'll write a proper invitation," said Mrs Thomas.

Two weeks before Christmas, Saturday was a bright cold snowy day. It had snowed heavily overnight but now the sun was out and Tabitha trudged through the snow towards her garden. She doubted whether she would get into it but at least she could look up the drive through the big iron gates. When she got there, she saw a set of footsteps in the snow by the front gate of the cottage. They were small, like a child's or perhaps a lady's. They led from the gate and into the road, in the direction of the town. In all the years Tabs had been visiting the garden, this was the first solid evidence of anyone living at the cottage that she had had – other than the mysterious someone doing the mowing and hedge-trimming, of course. She approached the wooden door in the wall. It was a little ajar and jammed up by the snow. She pushed it and it creaked open.

With all this snow it'll be obvious I've been here, I'd better not go in. But the garden and the sunshine looked so irresistible. They'd know but she wouldn't get caught – she never had. And those footsteps were leaving through the snow, going away from the house and garden. But if *she* could interpret footprints, so could someone else. Tabitha shuffled her feet in the snow to make it difficult to see how big her feet were.

Inside the garden, the snow was pristine. There was no way Tabitha could advance further. The last thing she wanted to do was to damage the perfection of this place. The pure white snow covered the whole of it except just under the wall on the far side. The scantily clad nymph looked colder than she had ever seen her; frozen in her dance. There were five centimetres of snow piled up on her head. The bench emerged from the snow as if covered with a thick white duvet with Christmas card sparkle and the evergreen leaves on the hedges bent under the weight of their individual burdens. But the general impression of the garden – a quarter of it sparkling in the bright but low sunshine – was of the purest and most perfect corner in all the world. Tabitha had never imagined it like this – and its sheer beauty spoke to her of the things you could only think possible in another world. Had she seen it like this when she had been only eight it would have confirmed her deep belief that it was cared for by light, bright fairies with gossamer wings and wands with magic coming out of them. But to this fifteen-year-old it was not just the wonder of the garden that impressed her, it made her reflect on her own imperfection. To enter it, would be to pollute it. Not just on this beautiful snow-covered, sun-bathed day but anytime, ever.

In that moment, Tabitha conceived of another reason never

to enter the garden again; it was too pure for her. The sheer magical wonder of the garden was something beyond which her base imagination could only dimly grasp. It spoke of depths and heights way beyond human reach and she not only felt small but soiled. It was enough to have been granted a glimpse of this marvel.

She whispered a thank you. And then tiptoed back out of the garden door following the same trail she had made through the snow on her way in. When she got to the road she turned left away from the town. She walked as quickly as she could and took the first footpath on the right opposite the end of the wall. It was deep in driven snow, but it was off the road. She did not want to be seen in case the owner came back and suspected her. The snicket was totally covered by snow and suddenly it came right up to the top of her legs as she lunged forward. This changed Tabitha's mood; her sense of unworthiness left her and was replaced by a feeling of being set free. This was fun. She ploughed on through the drifts, her jeans saturated. Eventually, the path came to a gate into a snow-covered field which seemed to go on forever up towards the horizon. Tabitha became aware that it was getting dusk even though it was long before teatime– it was time to retrace her steps if she wanted to get back before it was fully dark.

By the time she got to Ings View, the street lamps were lit. She was very cold but very happy.

"Where on Earth have you been my girl?" exclaimed her mother seeing her so wet but with a bright glowing face.

"I've been in heaven," laughed Tabitha scattering snow as she headed for the bathroom.

While her daughter had been out, the post had arrived with a card in an envelope addressed to Cindy. It was a hand-written invitation from Mama Sarah. When Cindy had read it she had been both surprised and horrified. She waited until Tabs emerged from the bathroom.

"Tabitha. What's all this about Christmas with the Thomases? What have you been doing behind my back?"

"What's up, Mum? What have I supposed to have done?"

"Don't come the all innocent with me, girl," she raised her voice as she pushed herself into Tabs' room. Something which she rarely did, anymore. She thrust the card at her daughter. "You can't be inviting yourself to people for Christmas. And certainly not without saying anything to me, first."

"I haven't, Mum, honest," said Tabitha trying not to sound upset. She had known this was how her mother would react. "It was Ashol's idea. Mr Thomas and Mama Sarah want us to come but I told them no. I did. Honest, Mum. I said you wouldn't want to go."

"And I expect, you also told them that you would."

"Of course not. I told them I wouldn't even ask you. That's why Mrs Thomas said she would write."

"But didn't you tell her, no?"

"I did. I *would* like to go, of course, but I wouldn't go if you weren't happy, too, would I?" Cindy kept silent. Then tears came into her eyes.

"That's great. So you will be here but want to be there. That would be worse than not being here at all. No, you go. I won't stop you."

"No, Mum. Not without you. Not if you forced me. Get real, Mum. I'd never leave you on your own at Christmas, would I? And Mr Thomas said they wouldn't have me without you, anyway... I have to go to Dad on Boxing Day because he's my dad, but I hate leaving you. I always have. That's bad enough."

Cindy streamed with tears. She had heard her daughter, despite the 'Get real' bit. Tab did love her it seemed, more than she deserved. And the Thomases were sensitive to the situation. Maybe they did care. They seemed to be genuine people and she was pleased with Tabitha's choice of friends.

"And you want me to go?"

"I know they're my friends but they want you, too."

"So it depends on me saying yes?"

"I guess so if you want to put it like that. They want you to stay with them on Boxing Day without me. They wouldn't ask that if it was all about me, would they? They know I have to go to Dad's."

"You shouldn't go round telling people our business."

"It's not like that, Mum. What should I tell my friends when they ask me what I'm doing at Christmas or anything? Tell them I'm not allowed to talk about it? Tell 'em it's a state secret? Lie?" Tabitha was letting her voice get too high.

"Don't you take that attitude with me, my lady."

"Sorry, Mum..." Tabs knew she had overstepped the mark, and lowered her head. "But Mum, they just care. They really care."

"And who asked them to? I didn't." Now it was Cindy who was getting too loud.

"Nobody asked them to," murmured Tabs, quietly. "They just do. They're like that." She felt bad about getting cross with her mum.

"So why do they want us?"

Tabs shrugged. "I'm their friend, I suppose. They seem to like me. They seem to want me."

"They won't like me."

"Mum. Just say thank you for the invite but no. I already told them no."

As Tabs walked to school in the dusk of the following Monday, she made a decision. *I won't go to Leeds on Boxing Day. Dad'll understand. I'll ask if I can go on New Year's Day or something instead.*

That evening, as soon as Tabs got in, Cindy told her that OK, they would go to the Thomases for Christmas Day, but she was not sleeping over and certainly wouldn't stay with them when Tabs was in Leeds.

"I've thought about that and I've decided I won't go to Leeds. Dad's got his other children. He'll understand. I'll see if they will have me in the New Year or something... Want a cuppa? I'll put the kettle on." She divested herself of her coat and began to fill the kettle and put it on the hob.

"But you have to go. That's what we agreed when you were little."

"But I'm no longer little – I'm taller than you. It's not fair that you should spend Boxing Day all on your own. I'll tell Dad."

Tabs made the tea and brought it through.

Cindy sighed. "You are hard work, young lady. What if I insist that you go?"

"You won't, Mum."

"You mean that, don't you? You really mean you would stay here with me all through Christmas."

"Yes. Are you going to write to say we'll go to the Thomases for Christmas Day?"

"I'll ring them. I don't do notes... Come here." Cindy took her daughter in her arms, and despite Tabitha being taller than her mum she sat her on her lap and hugged her.

"Thanks, Mum."

Things were soon arranged. Joshua was disappointed Tabitha was not going to come over for Boxing Day; he had planned an outing. But he respected his daughter's care for her mother and it was soon arranged for her to go on New Year's Eve and see in the new year with them. Cindy was never one for caring much about New Year things but if she wanted to, there was a Bingo Bash on in the Community Centre. Cindy found herself promising to go to church for the Christmas morning service in St Chad's where they would meet up with the Thomases.

And Tabitha and Ashol had agreed that it would be a long skirt occasion.

19

On Christmas morning, it was treacherous. For the first time Cindy could ever remember, it had snowed on Christmas Day itself; the weather was extremely cold. There was an eerie silence in the air and the white cold blanket brought a kind of hush over everything. The treated roads that led out of the estate were dirty gashes on the surface of an otherwise pristine landscape. Only the bus routes had been salted and somehow the whiteness everywhere else had covered all the normal scruffiness.

The snow had turned to ice on many of the pavements and Cindy and Tabitha hung on to each other as they gingerly trudged in their welly boots with their shoes in a shopping bag to the end of Ings View. Tabs had to hitch up her skirt to keep the hem out of the wet snow. They turned into Arnolds Place where, on a normal Saturday, the 76 came every hour. But there were no buses today, and they would have to walk to the town. The couple saw no one else. Nothing was stirring outside at nine o'clock on Christmas morning on Beck Ings. Inside the houses and flats, there would have been excited children opening presents, but the snow and ice had even prevented those with new bikes from venturing forth. No one else, thought Tabitha, would be going to church from their roads, but it didn't bother her in the least that she was different. At that moment she wouldn't have swapped with anyone else in the world, let alone on the estate.

On Arnolds Place they stepped out onto the salted tarmac and walked right down the middle of it. Tabitha had never done that before and it was exciting; it lent her a glorious sense of freedom. If there had been any cars about, they would have heard them long before they needed to get to the side. They even traversed the roundabout at the entrance to the estate as if they owned it. When they got to the main Puddleham Road the pavement on one side was cleared and now they were passed by a stream of cars behind a white van with, "*AAA Plumbing. All your Plumbing and Central Heating Needs,*" painted on the side. Someone was working on Christmas Day – and some poor person had need of a plumber. Tabitha felt sorry for both the customer and the workman.

They got to St Chad's earlier than they thought they would but the place was a hive of activity nonetheless. The music group were humping equipment into the church from the car park. One of the musicians – a guy in his late teens dressed in a denim jacket over a Christmassy T-shirt and jeans – recognised Tabitha.

"Hi, there. Merry Crimbo. Tabitha isn't it? You going in? Can you carry this box for me?" and he dumped a cardboard box of assorted electrical leads into her arms before retreating back to his van.

"Yeah, sure," said Tabs calling after him. She was forced to follow two similarly-laden young people into the church right up to the platform the singing group were going to use. Cindy crept into the church and slunk into the shadows casting about for the Thomases.

"Hello, Tabitha, Merry Christmas." It was Rev Mike, the vicar.

"Merry—" she began but Mike was already looking away. "No... excuse me...," he was saying, turning to a man dressed in black and white robes who was looking a bit fraught, "... there's no collection this morning so *It Came Upon a Midnight Clear* will be quite long enough at the offertory." He turned back to Tabs. "Our choirmaster," he explained as the man made his way back up the aisle, "Poor man was up till 1.30 this morning after the Midnight Communion... Ah, Danielle, yes just like a usual Sunday. Just put them on the altar... excuse me," he said again, smiling, "it'll be all right on the night, as they say..." and stumbled off after Danielle in the direction of a table that stood in the centre at the base of a step beside the musicians' platform.

Tabs retraced her steps back down the aisle after the two young people and found herself helping with more equipment. She was rewarded by a big smile from the denim-clad guy who turned out to be the drummer as he began bolting his kit together.

"Thanks, Tabitha. What name do you normally go by?"

"Tabs. The kids call me Tabs, mostly."

"Thanks, Tabs. Do you play?" She shook her head, looking a little abashed.

"Hey, Merry Chrissy." Ashol came bounding up looking the picture of loveliness in her floaty skirt.

"Hi Ashol," They kissed and hugged.

"I see you've become acquainted with Dave. Made an impression already. He's already nineteen – a bit old for you, though."

"N... no, I was just helping with lugging in their gear."

Deng and his parents met them halfway down the church having already rescued Cindy from her corner. Mama Sarah, as she asked to be called, hugged Tabs and then Cindy who was taken quite off-guard. But Mama Sarah was so full of beans she hadn't the chance to feel awkward. Mr Thomas then took Tabs' hand and kissed her cheek and was doing the same to Cindy just as she saw Tabitha take Deng in her arms and give him the biggest of Christmas hugs.

As they went and sat in a pew, Cindy found herself on the end next to Mama Sarah with the entire Thomas family between her and her daughter who was on the other end in rapt conversation with Ashol.

"So glad your mum agreed to come," she whispered.

Tabs was amazed at how friendly the service turned out to be. It was not like what she expected – all serious and austere holiness. The holiness was in the joy. The worship bounced along like Ashol.

After the service, Mama Sarah asked, "Did you like the service?"

"I must say, it's very different from what it used to be when I was young," said Cindy.

"I think it was cool, especially when Danielle gave her dad that present," giggled Tabs.

"She's not shy, is she?"

"Danielle gets a lot of teasing at school at times," said Deng. "It's not easy being a church-goer, but being a vicar's kid is kind of extra hard, I guess."

"If your father was a vicar—" began Mr Thomas.

"I'd hate it," exclaimed Deng.

"But Deng, you would be quite good at being a vicar," Tabs found herself saying to him. "You care about people..."

"And be a pain to my kids?"

"Danielle seems to cope very well," said Mama Sarah as the very girl approached them.

"Hi." greeted Danielle, "did I hear my name?"

"Ah. A girl with long ears," smiled Mr Thomas.

"We were just saying that it must be hard to be the vicar's daughter at times," explained Mama Sarah. "You know Tabitha's mum?"

"No. Hi. Pleased to meet you... Happy Christmas. Yeah, sometimes it sucks, like when teachers expect you to behave, like, real special. Like last week, Jack Frost – he teaches us geography – went, 'I'm surprised at you knowing that word, Danielle,' like I live in some place where I only hear the King's English. But sometimes it has its advantages, like, you can just rock up to things because they know my dad. That's how I got into the school choir. Farty-Doh just says, 'Of course Miss Buckley. I expect you sing a lot in church,' when everyone else has to do an audition."

Cindy looked both shocked and puzzled all at the same time.

Tabs thought she'd better explain. "Farr-Te-Doh. She's the music teacher, Mum, Mrs Farr. That's her nickname." Her mother looked rather doubtful. "Farr—"

"Tabitha. You don't have to repeat it again," admonished Cindy. Turning to Danielle, she asked, "But don't you get teased a lot by the other children?"

"Yeah. Like, all the time by some people like... like Gareth Green and his gang. Loads of people do. Tabs gets it too from him, don't you?"

"Yeah. But he's left now – after the accident."

"Yep. Banged up for Britain. Hope he's got life." Danielle caught sight of another friend.

"Hi Adele, you know Tabitha?" A girl a bit younger than Tabs came over with a boy in tow.

"Hi." said Adele. "Xmas merry and all that. Yeah. We know each other. *This*," she indicated the good-looking boy of her own age, "is my cousin Clint from, guess where?"

"Hey, hi ladies," he drawled before turning to Deng, "Bro." He and Adele didn't seem to notice the adults present. It was obvious that he was American after the first "Hey."

"The States," volunteered Ashol.

"California." exulted Adele. "How cool is that?"

"Los Angeles?" asked Ashol.

"Close. I live near Santa Barbara."

"I've heard of that," said Tabs, "it's by the sea, isn't it?"

"It is so." Clint gave her a broad smile that seems to affect her knees.

"And, guess what. It's just been decided that I am going out to stay with them in the summer," bounced Adele.

"Cool," said Danielle. "Can I come, too?"

"Yeah. Can we all come?" laughed Ashol.

"I know," laughed Danielle. "We'll make it a church trip and get the bishop to pay." Then, without any embarrassment, she called across the church to her dad. "Dad, we're having a church trip for young people to Santa Barbara next summer, OK? And you're asking Bishop Stephen to give us the money."

Rev Mike excused himself from a deep pastoral conversation. "Excuse, me, Mrs Timms, I think I'd better deal with my daughter before she bankrupts the diocese."

Balancing a cup of coffee and a mince pie in one hand and a couple of Christmas cards in the other, he moved over to them. "Am I indeed? We might get as far as Haworth. So, hello. You're Adele's cousin, I gather." He made as if to take Clint's hand but gave up when all he could offer was a hand clutching a half-eaten mince pie.

"Clinton, sir."

"Welcome to our humble Yorkshire Christmas, Clinton. Looking forward to Christmas dinner?"

"Yes, sir."

"I know I am," said the Rev Mike looking suddenly quite tired. He had led five services in the past twenty-four hours including the one at midnight.

"And now we must get back to check on ours," broke in Mama Sarah. "Sorry to break you young people apart, but we adults are ready to move." Tabs' mum was beginning to look more tired than the vicar. All this was so new.

The adults rode in the Thomases' car while the young people put their wellies back on and picked their way through the ice and snow, skirts pulled up, anticipating the rest of an exciting day.

"California," sighed Tabitha, dreamily. "I'd love to travel."

"You must come to South Sudan," said Deng.

"Deng," said Ashol. "Leave her be. Juba doesn't quite have the same attractions as LA, or, where did he say he lived, Santa Deborah?..."

"Santa Barbara," corrected Deng.

Tabs said, cheerily, "I bet Danielle does get to America. She's got what it takes to blague herself into anything. She's right, being a parson's kid gives you a start that you don't get if... well if your dad's not even around."

"But," stated Ashol, emphatically, "I reckon Tabitha Chapeltown Johnson will accomplish all she sets out to do, no matter how ambitious. I mean that."

"Thanks, Ashol. It's nice to have someone who believes in me. I'll remember you when I become prime minister."

"No. You won't ever want to be prime minister. You'll do better than that. You'll do something much more cool."

"Like what?"

"Oh. I don't know... yet."

"Well, tell me when you know. I don't think I could ever have the brains to be a doctor like you, Deng."

Deng kicked at a clump of ice. "You're cleverer than me, Tabs. I find studying hard." He looked down at his feet again on the slushy road.

"Oh, come on Deng," goaded Ashol, "Don't be so gloomy. You put in too much work if you ask me. Besides, it's Christmas, and Tabs has put on her special skirt for you which she has had to tuck up so high to keep it out of the snow that it's almost a miniskirt." She lunged into some soft snow, scooped up a handful and lobbed it at her brother. Soon the snow was flying everywhere, long skirts or not.

"I bet it doesn't snow in Santa Barbara." shouted Tabitha through the mêlée, "I bet Clint's having a great time here."

"... and all his bored friends on their surfboards are envying him," cackled Ashol.

It's odd that, mused Tabitha. *Everyone seems to want to be somewhere else, from where they are. I mean, everyone reckons that they hate Beck Ings. The Thomases want to be in South Sudan. Danielle wants to go to California. I don't know what I want but I do know I want to see somewhere else. And I don't want to stay here all my life... I am so glad I met you two,* she thought watching Ashol and Deng try to stuff snow down each others' necks.

They passed a house where an extractor fan sent out a flurry of the rich aroma of Christmas food.

"Come on, I'm hungry." yelled Ashol. And they ploughed on as fast as they could the rest of the way to the Thomases' house.

By the evening, Cindy was feeling quite exhausted. She had never had such a lively Christmas, not even as a child. She had laughed and sang, played games, watched 'Wallace and Gromit' and helped in the kitchen. She was, however, forbidden to assist with the washing up which was allocated to Mr Thomas and the young people. The Thomases never drank alcohol and it was the driest Christmas Cindy had ever known, but somehow that did not take anything away from it.

At the end of a long evening, Mr Thomas drove Cindy and Tabitha back to Ings View. It was now freezing, so he had to take extra special care. As they waved him off and the sound of the engine faded, Cindy searched for her key and the silence settled on them so profoundly that it was as if *Star Trek* had suddenly "beamed them down" into another world.

As sleep crept upon her, Tabitha sang in her head, *Joy to the World... Let every heart prepare Him room... And Heaven and Nature sing, And Heaven and Nature sing, And Heaven, and Heaven and Nature sing.*

20

Tabitha discovered she was quite looking forward to spending New Year's Eve in Leeds. Going to Leeds now after a happy Christmas seemed a bonus. Life had become rich with adventure. Her father had promised to take her out with some of the young people from his street who were going to a down-town venue. How wicked was that? Her mum had had a great few days and was now ready for a bit of space, so she knew she would not be missed so much. Anyway, Mary had arranged for Cindy to join a group of ladies on a jaunt to the local garden centre where there was a sale on. Not that they meant to do any serious shopping; it was to be more of a day out.

New Year's Eve in Leeds promised to be a real education for Tabitha. She found herself at a city-centre gig chosen by some teenage neighbours in Chapeltown. Joshua and Georgina were anxious that Tabitha's New Year should not be dull. A kind old lady had consented to babysit her young step-siblings, so Tab was swept up by a group of teenagers and her dad and step-mum were left to tag along.

The venue was not officially geared to fifteen-year-olds but their age wasn't questioned, so they felt quite grown-up. There turned out to be plenty of alcohol, which legally neither Tabitha nor her new friends were supposed to taste but no one was taking much notice of the law, it seemed. Soon, more people joined the party and Tabitha took to the dance floor and became surrounded by people she hadn't come with. Some boisterous lads forced something what looked like fizzy pop into her hand. They were loud but then the music was too, and they didn't seem to be much older than her. They seemed kinda nice. Nobody had ever bought Tabitha a drink before. They didn't look bad; she thought they were quite fit actually. They were a bit rough and ready but quite different from Griff and his gang in Beck Ings. One guy in particular took her fancy and she liked the feeling. She was almost grown up now, wasn't she? She was no longer a kid. She was as tall as most women – taller than some. She rather liked the idea that this guy might come on to her like some of the lads were doing, smooching with sophisticated girls – she could handle that. It would be a new experience. She sipped the drink – it tasted surprisingly pleasant. It was nothing like wine or beer, but oranges, sweet and light, so she guessed it must be OK. This was all rather exciting.

The guy she liked began to dance in front of her. Great. Tabs attempted to move to the beat of the music, trying not to spill her drink. Then, after a few minutes, she quite suddenly began to feel a bit woozy and the music seemed to get louder and yet more distant at the same time. Whoops. The floor became, like, soft.

She excused herself and moved to the side to hold on to a rail. The boy kept dancing – he didn't seem to miss her. Then she spotted some of the others behaving oddly – *everything* seemed kinda odd. At that point, alarm bells rang. The drink. She decided to drink no more of the orange stuff.

Tabs made her way to the toilets. She took her drink with her with the intention of replacing the contents with water so that she still had a glass in hand and didn't have to accept a new one. Inside the ladies' was a different world. She was shocked to see one girl with her head down a loo, vomiting, and a second sitting on the pan with the lid down, shaking.

"You OK?" she asked.

"What does it effing look like?" was the gasped reply.

"You look as if you need some help."

"Eff off. Mind your own effing business." The girl continued shaking.

Tabitha went to the basin, poured out her drink, refilled the glass with water and took it to the girl.

"Here. Drink this," she insisted, quietly.

The girl took the glass and drank. Then wiped her mouth with the back of her hand smudging her lipstick. "Thanks," she spluttered. "Now eff off."

The girl in the other cubicle had finished throwing up and was leaning over the sinks washing her face. She looked terrible with her make-up spattered everywhere and her eyes bloodshot. Tabitha decided she was beyond the kind of help she could administer. Perhaps living in Leeds had its downside after all, she thought. She washed her glass and refilled it and made her way back to the dance floor. She tried to find the teenagers she had come with but under the strobe lighting, couldn't make anything out properly.

It was coming up to midnight and the music was turned off and a countdown began. At the stroke of twelve, a large wide-screen TV showed fireworks emanating from the London Eye and the South Bank of the Thames. The boy that had bought Tabs the drink came up from behind her and grabbed her in a tight clinch, planting his lips firmly on hers and filling her nostrils with the taste of hops and tobacco. Her first instinct was to lay him out, but she was still level-headed enough to disentangle herself without doing him any harm, and to her surprise, he slipped to his knees. Yuk. The taste of him in her mouth was foul. She took a gulp of water, swilled it around her mouth and spat it back into her glass, all while the boy was trying to get up. Before he could get his feet under him again, Tabs simply pushed down on the top of his head with her free hand and he sprawled full length at her feet. She stepped over him and made her way back to where she saw some older people but before she reached them, there was her father. He came over to her and asked if she was ready to go home.

"Too right I am." She thumped her glass down on a table.

"Are you OK, Tab?"

"*I* am," she yelled as the music began to blare out again, "but that lot aren't," she indicated the guy still trying to find his feet.

"Come on, let's get you home."

"What about the people we came with?"

"All outside. They decided things were getting out of hand when they spotted some boys spiking drinks."

"So they left me, inside?"

"They couldn't find you."

"I guess I must have been in the loo."

"Then they spotted you at the midnight countdown. Come on, your carriage awaits you."

A large cheer sounded as she emerged from the hall with her father.

"What happened?" they demanded. Tabitha said nothing.

"All I saw was Tabitha floor a guy that came onto her, just, like – amazing," said one of them.

"Ooo. Tell us about it. Will he live?"

"He was already dead from the neck up," stated Tabitha, baldly.

More cries of, "Oooo..."

"... and what about the rest of him?" Asked a girl, mischievously.

"Dissolving fast," she said disdainfully, making everyone laugh. On the way back, their laughter began to brighten her mood.

Tab's dad put his arm around her.

"Cheer up, girl," he said. "I am quite proud of the way you dealt with that boy." Tabs thought that that was not the way she wanted to be kissed. First Gross Griff, now this. She hated boys.

"Yeah," said one of the others, "tell us how you did it?"

Tabitha decided to lighten up. No need getting down about it. These kids were an all-right bunch and were restoring her impression of humanity.

"Oh, it was my Kung-Fu training," she joked.

"Really? You do Kung-Fu?"

"Nah. He was just drunk and couldn't stand up. I must admit I thought of flattening him, but I didn't have to. You should have seen what I did to a kid at home who was not drunk and who thought he could try and kiss me."

"Ooo. What happened?"

"I hit him on the conk and then bit his hand. He had to go to the hospital."

"I bet he steers clear of you now," chortled a girl with blonde hair, a white sparkly top and shocking pink trousers.

"He would do if he were still about, but he's in clink."

"He's in prison? Wow."

"Well, some kind of young offenders' place, I think."

The group were hanging onto Tabs every word, now. Her status had risen high. "Because of what he tried to do to you?"

"Nah. Nothing to do with me," she dismissed. "He got one of his mates killed by mucking about with a motorbike, among other things."

"Whoa," roared the sparkly blonde girl.

"What you going to do when you leave school?" demanded another. "Become a personal bodyguard? Join the army?"

Tabs shrugged her shoulders.

"She's clever, she is," proclaimed another of the girls wearing a peaked cap. "This girl's not goin' to do some ord'nary job. You'll do sommut well 'ard, won't ya? I mean, wiv yer brain."

"No idea," dismissed Tabitha. It was time to change the subject away from herself. "What're *you* going to do? When you leave school?" she asked the blonde girl.

"Me? I want to be a nurse."

"Some hope," mocked a boy. "You couldn't even stick a band-aid on my hand the other day. You got the sticky bit on the cut."

"Get lost, Darren. It stopped it bleeding, didn't it?"

"Just tell me which hospital you're goin' to learn to nurse at, and I'll be especially careful when I go near it," laughed the boy.

As the banter flowed back and forth, a sad Tabitha texted Ashol: *HNY. Mis u lots. Luv :)*

Joshua took his sad exhausted daughter back to her bed in Chapeltown saying that she would feel better in the morning. All Tabs wanted was her own bed but she collapsed into the one she used in Leeds and fell into a troubled sleep. In the dark small hours of the new year, she reflected on the contrast between the teetotal Christmas she had had at the Thomases and the New Year's Eve event. Christmas Day had been truly special – an entirely different world from the one in the club. Apart from the excess alcohol and the drugs, it was the absence of any sense of meaning or purpose, a dark chasm, like a big black hole that struck her – everything designed for the moment with nothing left at the end of the day. It freaked her. She just couldn't imagine how those people felt about themselves. The realities of the next day were bound to kick in with a complete emptiness, on top of the physical pain of the drug and alcohol abuse. It was all so depressing.

Tabs woke at 10 am with a headache. She got up and struggled to dress. She wanted to get home but the buses were few on New Year's Day. Her dad suggested she stay another night but she told him she had too much schoolwork to do – she had made a new year's resolution to apply herself to her studies, and this included a lot of catching up. So despite his urging to at least stay for some dinner, she got him to drop her off at the bus station at 11.30 am. That morning she had checked the times of the buses but when she looked for the departure bay, she discovered that it had been cancelled. There would not be another until 2 pm. The place was draughty and her feet were cold. Tabs wished she had brought a book to read but amid the Christmas euphoria, she hadn't imagined she would have much time on her own. She walked up and down, and sat occasionally but was soon jumping and skipping to keep warm. It was a gloomy first day of the year. Only one or two other buses came and went – she had never seen the place so bleak and deserted. She was torn between calling her dad and braving it out. *I am fifteen for goodness sake. I'm not a kid. I should be able to handle this.* So where was the fear coming from? Her mum, probably. She'd always been over-protective, hadn't she? What was there to be frightened of? *That's stupid. I in't scared.*

At half past one, the notice above the bus stand changed from 14.00 to 55 mins. The bus was running twenty-five minutes late. Tabs felt the cold up to her knees – her feet were numb and her fingers freezing despite her mittens. She was hungry but had nothing to eat.

It was then that she noticed a couple of vagrants sheltering under a heap of cardboard. How could they survive this weather? Earlier, there had been a van serving hot soup which they had stood around but now it had moved off. Eventually, one of the men got to his feet began to shuffle around – in her direction. Panic rose into her throat and she shivered and moved back towards the edge of the bus station. He didn't follow her.

At 2.45 pm. Tabs was considering getting on any bus just to get away. She had her phone – she could call her dad but she didn't want to do that; she'd look weak, *and* foolish for insisting on going home straight away.

At last, the bus came. Tabs never thought she would ever be so grateful to see a bus as she was then. When she got some life back into her fingers she texted her mum to say she was on the bus. It was another half an hour before they set off and for the first part of the journey she was the only passenger. It was well and truly dark when she eventually got home.

The next day, 2nd January, was no more cheerful; cold, wet and grey summed it up. She couldn't get the thought of the vagrants out of her mind. What must it feel like to have no place to stay? Apart from the soup van guys, everyone else just gave them a wide berth. A sense of guilt rose in her – even she had backed off. What did this say about the world? All the excitement of Christmas had been great but in the cold gloom of January, was that only hype – a cosy lie to cover up the reality of things? In truth, the world was a dark and friendless place for the most part. There were so many wars, so many kids starving, and so many girls and women raped in what the news called 'gender-based violence'. Another politician had been called on to resign over the latest scandal in parliament and the popular singer she admired turned out to be someone who abused children – the sentiments of his songs were not something he believed in. Another lie. Was Christmas a lie? If God had come into his world because he 'so loved it' why was it still so bleak?

Ashol was a shaft of light, though. She would cheer her up. But when Tabs texted them she discovered the Thomases had all gone down with the flu. So more gloom. Cindy made them a shepherd's pie and took it round to them – leaving it at the door as they were isolating. Tabs Whatsapped Ashol. Her light had dimmed because all she got in reply was, "Feel grots".

Tabs decided she did not like this new year and disappeared into her room with a pile of homework. She never imagined maths would lighten her mood. It did. But then she got onto Macbeth and understood it like from the inside – the whole play was about foul being fair and fair, foul and a world in which, "good men's lives expire before the flowers in their caps". She committed Ross's lines to her memory: "Alas poor country. Almost afraid to know itself... where violent sorrow seems a modern ecstasy."

21

Tabitha was grateful that school was to begin before the end of the week. She found Mlle Gaudet not there, though – she was stuck somewhere mid-Channel, caught up in a French strike – or was it British? And Jack Frost had succumbed to the weather like Ashol. Deng eventually rolled up but he wasn't cheerful. He was struggling with some elements of his maths course and was finding the demands of his GCSE year hard. They agreed that they would meet in the library to study. Being together helped to make the work less lonely and it enabled Deng to concentrate. Although he was a quiet kind of boy, he still seemed to need company and somehow he couldn't get caught up with his work in the same way Tabs discovered she could. He perked up a bit when he was doing humanities stuff – especially history which he enjoyed – but, he told her, maths and physics were essential if you wanted to be a doctor. And he needed to be a doctor so that he could make a difference in South Sudan.

The news coming out of Juba, though, was not good. Stories of killings and raids by independent militias rumbled on. Few international reporters were anxious to visit the country following a succession of attacks and kidnappings of journalists and the country's woes did not seem to hit the headlines. But the Thomases were being kept up to date through their personal contacts, most of whom were telling them that now was not the time to return.

***

As January turned into February, Tabitha got to feel better. Her schoolwork was smoothing over some of the sadness that had overtaken her. She never imagined that work could do that. Ashol told her again that it was because she was clever – seriously clever. But she had never thought of herself as at all gifted. Different, maybe, but not particularly bright. Nevertheless, she enjoyed doing her homework – something she never thought possible before. She even did extra research on the Internet and read chapters that were not part of the set work. The history teacher told her it showed.

"Reading as much as you can around the subject is what marks out an excellent pupil from a good one," she explained. It made Tabitha feel good that teachers were taking a new interest in her; she had been the subject of discussion in the staff room, it appeared.

It helped as well that, since the accident and the second disappearance of Griff Green, the annoying pestering had come to an end. Without Green, the others had turned their attention away from her and were just kind of floating around aimlessly, smoking and snogging stupid girls behind the bike sheds and doing bits of vandalism here and there as the whim took them, but mostly doing nothing. It was too cold to roam as they were wont.

Tabitha had ventured once to her garden but the outdoors was so cold and damp. The snow had long since been replaced with grey splodges, the dryad was streaked and stained and looked utterly down-hearted and the grass was water-logged, so Tabs decided not to return until the spring. Had she but known of the beautiful winter world beyond the wall, she would have been more cheerful. She would have been enthralled by the rich display of moses, liverworts and even lychens, which had taken a hold in the woods since the chimneys had stopped belching the smoke they had been inflicting on the landscape for more than a century.

On the bright side, Cindy developed a real friendship with Mama Sarah and, although not going to church on Sundays, she had begun joining in with some of the church weekday activities. Because of the new study drive, Tabitha hadn't gone with her to Beattie's bingo for ages. And it seemed that Cindy had become bored with it, too. Rather than go on her own, she had joined St Chad's women's evening group. It had once been called, "Young Wives" but the members had decided to change their name when the youngest of them turned forty-five and some of them were no longer wives or never had been. It now had a few new members at the younger end and Cindy fitted in well. She also volunteered to help out with the old people's lunch club that the church put on once a fortnight. She occasionally had also put in time at Friends of Africa. It had begun by her covering for Tabitha on Saturdays when she had too much homework to do but now seemed to involve her more than her daughter. Cindy found she liked Mary – even though she would insist on treating her to the most peculiar teas like Earl Grey and Jasmine. She admired her determination to help people she hadn't even met.

Then, at last, it was March. On the first day of the new month, the world was everywhere yellow and bright green. Early daffodils and celandine basked in the bright morning sunshine. Dandelions were driving through the cracks and crevices and along the margins of the snickets. The winter grey concrete of the Beck Ings Estate was imbued with the colour of fresh cream once more and yellow, purple and mauve crocuses provided an eye-catching contrast in the middle of the roundabout on the way into town. During the previous year, there had been a big row about some drink-related vandalism in which these flowers had been damaged but so far this year they seemed to have survived without anyone crossing through the traffic to the little island. Beauty had won the battle over disorder this time.

It's wonderful just how Nature comes back again and again and never stops, thought Tabs. It seemed that Nature sprang up, and out, with every opportunity. Her life-force was not going to be easily held back by being overlooked, taken for granted or persecuted by human beings. It might be damaged or constricted but was not overcome – not even with the widespread use of concrete. Tabitha felt that same spring inside herself; somehow the life-force of Nature was in her too, and now she recognised it and loved it, tended and treasured it – her life was full of spring, even if she, herself, was less than perfect. Nevertheless, she was wary of being caught up in the moment. She had done that at Christmas only to discover that a lot of it was just made-up hype – in reality underneath there was a lot of sad emptiness. How many new springs would there be if humanity continued to pour fossil carbon into the atmosphere and species were becoming extinct in their thousands every year? The beauty of spring was a temporary phenomenon – how much of its destruction would she witness in her lifetime?

Tabs had come to realise that she seemed to see what others in her year at school never saw. How many of her companions in primary school would have sensed any magic in the little garden at all? For them, if fairies had existed they would not have had any more attention than they gave to the flowers and the trees. Her imagination had set her apart and still did.

But now, with Ashol and Deng, she had friends who would recognise the wonder of her secret garden and the great woods beyond. But it had always been a *secret* garden and there was no way she could share it with anyone – not even them.

So on a blustery but bright March morning, Tabitha set off for school looking forward to another promising day; it was geography first lesson and she would be with Mr Frost. Maybe, just maybe beneath the surface, life was good deep down and the badness was the stuff on the top, rather than the other way up. 'God was in his creation and all would be well.' She wasn't sure which was true. Was the creation fundamentally light or darkness? Could anyone actually know?

***

The day was not to remain bright. As the morning progressed, clouds covered the sun and the wind veered towards the northeast, the kind that seemed to penetrate the thickest of coats. At Beckside Academy, Tabitha was settling into learning about climate patterns in sub-Saharan Africa. She imagined stepping off a plane into the tropical heat and the thought warmed her up.

At the beginning of morning break, she realised she had left her English coursework at home. Cindy would be out shopping like she always was on a Tuesday, so there was no point in phoning her. Had she time to nip home to get it? Perhaps, if she ran.

Meanwhile, unbeknown to Tabitha or her mother, a plain white van drew up outside number 49 Ings View. A young man in a peaked cap, with his collar turned up against the wind and the prying eyes of neighbours, got out, entered the hallway of the block of flats and rang the doorbell.

As he expected, there was no answer. He bent down and lifted the flower pot on the right side of the inside front door. Underneath it was the key he knew would be there – Cindy had been putting it there for years. He opened the door and stepped back a pace so he could see the driver in the van, and signalled to him. He and two others equipped with tool bags got out of it and followed the first into the flat. Half an hour later they left the flat and drove off.

Betty Achroyd at number 43 watched the van leave and muttered to herself, "Cindy must be having some work done. She should have told me and I'd have seen they got offered a cuppa."

Cindy, as she often did on a Tuesday, treated herself to a meal in the supermarket café. She bumped into Cat who was, as always, loaded with the gossip of the day. She just plonked herself down at Cindy's table.

"I 'ear that the Browns are back," she began.

"The Browns?"

"Yeah. You know. The family that were above you with t'boy who nicked the bingo takings. You can't tell me you've forgotten about the 'elicopter and all."

"Oh. Yes."

"They're back on t'estate. Somewhere in t'Royds – Royd Close." Cindy did not doubt that Cat's 'somewhere' was a precise address. She knew where Royds Close was and it was far enough away from Ings View for her to be quite satisfied she'd not have to meet them.

"Lad's with 'em, too. Trial's taking too long and they've let 'im out."

"That doesn't sound wise."

"Innocent until proved guilty," said Cat. "Unless yer knows anythin' diff'rent." Cindy did know different; she'd heard every word shouted by him and his mother but she was not going to tell Cat.

"They say 'e's out to shut up anyone who might testify agin 'im."

"Is that right? Not my business."

"We've missed you at bingo," Cat changed the subject. "Thought sommut might be up."

Cindy remained tight-lipped, knowing that anything she said would be around the neighbourhood at the speed of sound if not light.

"No. Nothing. No reason."

"I 'eard," continued Cat, undaunted, "that you've taken up goin' t'church things instead."

"What things?"

"St Chad's Women's Fellowship, for one. A bit posh for you, in't it?"

"Who told you that?"

"Oh. Everybody knows."

"I mean, who told you it was posh?" Cindy had to admit that most of the members of St Chad's came from the private houses in Millheaton but she had never exactly thought of them as posh.

"En't they? Aimin' 'igh, in't ya Cindy? In't we good enough for you at Beattie's Bingo, no more?"

"Cut it out Cat. You're a troublemaker. Nothing makes you happier than spreading rumours."

"It in't me, Cindy. Like them rumours that you're best friends with them black people supposed to be refugees but really only 'ere to take our jobs. You always 'ave been partial to them sort. Like black men, don't you? That's why your Tabs is black."

"Like I said. You're a troublemaker, Cat. I don't rate people on where they come from – black, white or sky blue they're all the same to me. You can tell them, I'll come back to Beattie's when I'm ready. I'm due for a win. But no one's to say I can't go to St Chad's if I choose. At least, they don't spread rumours and gossip."

"'Ark who's talking. I know things about you that—"

"I dare say you know more about me, Cat, than I do, myself. Now, I must be getting home."

"See you." Cat was already eyeing up someone else to talk to.

Cindy breathed a sigh of relief. On her way out of the

supermarket, however, she bumped into none other than Mrs Brown – literally. "Sorry," she said. "Mind elsewhere." Mrs Brown grunted, glared at her and pushed on into the shop.

When Cindy got home, she knew something was wrong – the plant pot had been disturbed and the key was still in the door. *No!* she panicked. *Ruddy thieves.* She gingerly opened the door a little and called. All was silent. She breathed a sigh of relief – even if she had been robbed she wasn't going to find them still in the place. But what she saw was beyond her imagination. The intruders had not come primarily to steal, it seemed, but to destroy. The room had been trashed with broken furniture strewn across the floor, all the pictures ripped from the walls and on the far wall of the living room, daubed in bright red paint were the words, "W*gs and w*g lovers f*** off back home.". It was then she caught sight of what appeared to be a horribly mutilated body in the middle of the floor, mostly covered by the upturned settee. There was blood, too.

Cindy let out an ear-splitting scream and staggered backwards into the hallway, her lunch rising into her throat. Fleeing out of the outside door, she tripped on the step and fell headlong into a stack of recycling bins. Betty saw her fall and came rushing out to pick her up. At first, she thought she had suffered a heart attack but as she got to her feet, Cindy gestured, mute with shock, towards the flat.

Seeing that it was what was inside that was the problem, Betty popped her head around the door and shrieked.

"Bloody heck! God almighty!"

The story continues on page 135

'WHO AM I?' and 'WHERE AM I HEADED?'

Thoughts on Paper from the Pens of Young People

The following pages are contributions from some very brave teenagers. They give us an insight into what occupies their minds.

We cannot listen too closely when they speak.

For very good reasons, young people are often reticent, self-conscious and reluctant to open up to adults or each other.

Bullying is common, as some - their self-esteem rocky - are desperate not to find themselves at the bottom of the pecking order. Online, teens can be abused everywhere they go - there is no safe place.

Some adults fail to understand teenagers or appear not to, sometimes dismissing them, sometimes teasing them. Others put them down because they are no longer cute children and not yet adults. They are seen as 'difficult' and the expression 'behaving like teenagers' is a form of ageism.

I am enormously grateful to those who have expressed themselves here and also those whose work has not made the final selection. I have offered to give young people an opportunity to appear in print and the right place to do so is, surely, within the pages of a coming-of-age novel.

T. N. Stubbs

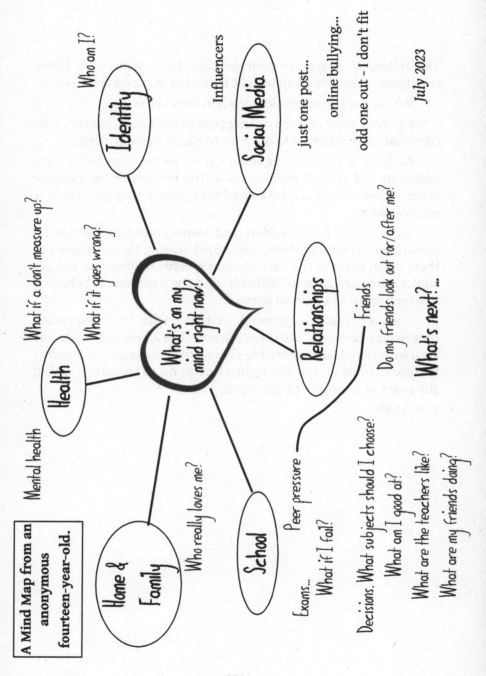

A Mind Map from an anonymous fourteen-year-old.

What's on my mind right now?

Identity
Who am I?

Social Media
Influencers
just one post...
online bullying...
odd one out - I don't fit

Health
What if a don't measure up?
What if it goes wrong?
Mental health

Home & Family
Who really loves me?

School
Peer pressure
Exams... What if I fail?
Decisions. What subjects should I choose?
What am I good at?
What are the teachers like?
What are my friends doing?

Relationships
Friends
Do my friends look out for/after me?

What's next?...

July 2023

I Don't Know How I Look

I don't know how I look
but I know that I am blonde.
If I go another colour
I might be gone.
I need to wear polkadots,
gogos, berets and cardigans.
I need more shoes
before life gets hard again.

I once heard Ed Sheeran.
I haven't listened to him since.
I like Blondie, New Order,
Billy Idol and Prince.
If I could live anywhere
I'd live on Neptune
It's blue and serene
like a ghost in bloom.

But Earth is all right
There's women and there's trees
And England has teacakes
and crackers and cheese.

I have a blemished nose
that's always in a book.
I like to be around people
but I don't know know how I look.

Mini

Young people are fixated on the imminent collapse of our planet. They recognise that humanity needs to change the way we live or they will lose the wonderful world we enjoy. Concern over climate change is one of the underlying factors in young people's mental health. Robyn lives in South Africa.

Robyn writes:

I have drawn a picture of a bee carrying the world on its back for social commentary. I think these are incredible, and absolutely underrated animals, and that the world is so dependent on them for survival. :)

At the heart of the things Rosie enjoys, we find a beautiful prominant dog. Pets are nearly always seen as full members of the family and often play a positive role in helping youngsters form relationships. If anything should happen to them, children and young people need special care.

Hi!!! My name is Rosie and I live with my mum, dad and dog. Recently, I wrote a letter to a famous person and I am hoping that I will get a reply back.

Celebrtities take note :)

Too Late

Create, crack, crunch.
The trees groaned loudly.
All I could hear was the
Thump, Thump, Thump
of my pounding heart
as I ran
from it.

I could hear it
getting closer.
Its loud breath burning
Its roar screeching.

Crash.

I fell. Hard
rocks digging into my knees
I scrambled to my feet.
Too late.
It was on me,
claws digging,
mouth snarling.
Blood pouring.
Too late
Too slow.

Alexandros :)

122

Life is good for Mia.

My Unusual Self

1. The sun rises.
The sun sets.
It's warm and sunny,
Then it's wet.

2. I go to school.
I come back home.
I'm an only child,
so I'm all alone.

3. I've a unicycle
But no TVs.
Few online games
Yet a trapeze.

4. A spinning plate.
A diabolo.
A fireman's pole
down which to go.

5. Juggling clubs
and balls and rings
And monkey bars
on which to swing.

6. I learn piano
and flute too.
A variety of choices
of things to do.

7. Guides on Thursday
Church on Sunday
And then back to school
on a Monday.

8. My life
you could say
is unusual
in a way.

9. Quite a lot
of circus things.
An absence of
normal things.

10. But I like it like that
- it's much more fun
And I'm totally different
to everyone.

Esther

by Toby

I count myself lucky

As I sit here waiting for my turn on the stage,
I count myself lucky for the nerves and the knot
Playing its paradiddles in my stomach.
For not everyone has a passion
that gets them through the stress.
I am lucky because when I am overwhelmed
I have my garage and I have my drums.
That's my holy place.
Would I cope without it?

Leo

A snapshot of Charles' mind as the end of term approaches.

July 2023

What's Next?

What's next in my life?
To be honest, I don't know.
I'm looking at universities...
I'm not sure where to go.

I want to be creative.
I want to have more choice.
I want to be an artist
and I want to use my voice.
I want to be an actor with a spotlight on the stage
I want to paint and illustrate
like pictures on a page.

It isn't realistic
and I might not have a chance
But I think I'm going to try
Even if they say I can't.

Anna

By Grace. Notice the emphasis on 'doing' contrasted with 'being'.

I would like to do sixth form and go to uni.

When Im older I would like to be something to do with design

I like doing art and being creative

Who am I?

I love baking and art with my mum

I play badminton and I do ballet

my favourite school subject are Drama and art

DESign

By Abigail

The sums (and life) get harder for a teenager!

Voice of vulnerable children

 My name is Silvia Kubana from South Sudan. I am in first year of secondary school and I want to talk about children and their vulnerability. To me, vulnerable children are the voiceless children, the orphans, children born to poor parents, children of single parents and those who are rejected by their parents. Children born in war zone community, they are those who have no access to good medication, nutrition or those affected with chronic diseases like HIV/AIDS. These children are at risk because most of have no hope for the future, some lack shelters, food and education. Poverty, war and hunger are the three greatest enemies to millions of children not only in South Sudan, but also in Africa and in the world. These enemies make it hard for children to study, to play and live a joyful life as children. In my country, there are many children dying because of war, hunger and extreme poverty and my question is that "Is there hope for vulnerable children?" who will rescue these children from poverty, hunger and from war caused by adults. In the cities, millions of children are drawn into sex industry every day, most of them walk by the roadside hawking for trade. Boys are recruited as soldiers to fight evil war caused by evil politicians. Other children can be trafficked from country to country.

In Juba, thousands of children aged 14-17 are nickname as criminals, thieves and drug users, they cause violence for food in the slums and in the market places, the grab phones and money from people, their future is doom and no one think of how to set such children free from such life. Some of these situation put children at risk and cause vulnerability in our community and in the world but who will be the voice of these voiceless children to set them free and lead them to the promise land (this promise land is hope and bright future for every child in South Sudan).

Vulnerability of children in our community

When war occurs, among its most hapless victims are millions of children who are born into miserable situation, they are impoverished during childhood owing to events outside their control. It is not just that children find their own fate being shaped by life's chances rather than themselves. Children also are poverty's innocent victims because their voice is rarely counted in community and are too often discounted. We need to act and advocate for children, the church supposed to be the voice for these voiceless children. Children from zero to three years also are at high risk of vulnerability. They can't do anything for themselves, at least in the earliest stages. They must be fed, or they will quickly weaken and die. They are prone to sickness, injury, and disease. The extra layers of vulnerability upon some children may be consequences of cumulative effects of chronic circumstances or of a single catastrophic events such as, hunger, poverty, natural disasters, political or family conflict, exploitive labor and HIV infection.

What is God's heart for the little one?

This theme could be a focal discussion for our community where most children are at risks. Children somehow are abandon, forsaken and reject. Sometime they are not consider as part of the community, they are the first victims when adults cause troubles. But what does God think about children and their place at home, in the church and in the market places?

"What is God's heart for children?" God's heart for children is a heart fully of compassion and love. He hates unjust and partiality done to children or to those who are weak (Psalm 82:2-4). God sees the affliction and grief of children, he cares for the fatherless and defend them in all circumstance (Psalm 10:14-15, Prov 12:31). God wants us to defend and care for children as well as we teach them godliness. Jesus stated that "unless you turn and become like children, you will never enter the kingdom of heaven" (Mathew 18:3). The kingdom of heaven belong to little children but here in this world many adults do block these children from the gate of heaven. "Fear not little flock, for it is your Father's good pleasure to give you the kingdom" (Luke 12:32). The little flock mention in Luke 12:32, is about a young person not a very big adult.

In a biblical context, children are gift of God and sources of joy, they are sinful creatures and moral agents, children are developing beings who need instruction and guidance, they are fully human and are made in the image and likeness of God, they are models of faith and sources or vehicles of revelation and final children are orphans, neighbors, and strangers who need support, protection, justice and compassion. God's heart for children is that we take good care of them, protect them and instruct them in the ways of the Lord.

God wants us to protect and defend children from any kind of injustice, partiality, war, trafficking and harm (Isaiah 1:17, James 1:27). The church must speak out the need to nurture faithful children in the communities. It takes both the community, church and the government to supervisory, nurture and raise up godly children who in turn will also do the same to their children, parents need to exercise integrity and godliness because children's lives can only be inspire when they see their parents, church leaders and the whole community living out their faith and trusting in God" (Deut 6:5-7).

We should know that children are blessings, we should not provoke them or kidnap them, and they may fulfill different needs within the families and in the communities and in the church. They may fulfill a strategic purpose for evangelism and for the future of the church, so the church should not keep quite when children are recruited into army.

God's heart for children is that "He want every child to know Him as the Lord Almighty, He want every child to be protected, loved and surrounded by a lovely and godly family" (Deut 6:6-9). We should not neglect children in our midst because they are created in the image of God and should participate in our daily gathering as we gather to worship the Lord our God. The bible tells us that

God's heart is full of compassion, love and cares for children, the bible also noted that children are vulnerable, they need to be loved and cared for. Apostle James stated that "true religion (church) is the one that visit orphans and widows in their affliction" (James 1:27). In every circumstance, children are innocent and they need our care and supports, they look unto us for help and direction both in the things of God and in the things of daily lives. We need to spend our time with children as Christ himself loved to be with them, He cares for them and they were in his daily teaching.

The voice of children in my community

1 I am a child not a soldier, I need peace, security and prosperity

2 We need education to brighten our future

3 You need to see us as individuals with their selves valued, worth and recognized because we are humans and our rights must be valued. Do not force me to get marriage, I am still a child.

4 Why is it that those concerning the welfare of children cannot come done to us and spent at least few time with us so that they may know our situation.

5 Sometime in the church when seats are not enough for people then they will start removing us (Children) from the seats so that adults may sit, the worse is that even when we were the first people who keep time and arrived very early. Are we not equal before God? So we are tired of being abused and rejected everywhere.

Thanks
Silvia Kubana
(Story recorded by Rev. Remigio Raphael
Children ministry's worker.)

PART TWO

1

Within minutes, most of the street was gathered outside. A neighbour opposite phoned the police and an ambulance. "I think it's just shock," said Betty Ackroyd. "Help me get her into my place." Cindy was unable to walk and a group of ladies picked her up and sat her down in Betty's downstairs flat. A kettle was soon steaming. "'Ot sweet tea. That's what she needs."

The police arrived. The Beck Ings Estate was alive with gossip and the news spread rapidly. Knots of neighbours from several streets away gathered up and down Ings View and the police taped off the area around the door.

At Beckies, Tabitha had decided she hadn't had time to run home and back in the morning break for her missing book. But at the end of the school day, she elected not to hang around. She trotted out of the school gate at half past three just as the head was receiving a call from the police.

The word had travelled faster than the police, however, and one of the residents opposite the school was on the phone and, looking out of her window, she spotted Tabitha. So the body wasn't hers but she was clearly unaware of the news. The woman, dripping with excitement to be the first to break the news to her, ran out of her front door and bounded up and yelled, "'Av ya 'eard? Yer flat's bin trashed.... And someone's bin murdered in it."

"What?!"

"Dead body in t'livin room. Writ all sorts of disgustin' things on t'walls, I 'eard."

"What? When?"

"Yer mum found it this ah'ternoon."

"Mum. Where's Mum?"

Just then, a second neighbour, this one of a more sensitive nature, puffed up. "Yer mum's OK, Tabs." She gave the gossip-laden neighbour a reproachful glare. "Get yerself inside, Maisie. If ya can't be 'elpful, make yerself scarce." Maisie was about to protest but thought better of it. The girl looked fit to collapse.

"Yer mum's safe, Tabs," continued the kind neighbour. "She were out at t'shops when it 'appened. She's in Betty Ackroyd's – number 43."

Without saying anything and before the woman could stop her, Tabitha panicked and took off in the direction of home, dashing out into the road. Mr Frost had to apply his breaks hard. He lowered his window and leaned out. "Tabitha Johnson." he called. "You'll get yourself killed. Where are you off to so fast?" Tabs stopped. She had to – Mr Frost's car was in her way.

"Got to get home.... Mum's in trouble. There's a dead body in the flat," she puffed.

"What? Hang on. I'm coming with you." He swung his car onto the side of the road and jumped out at the same time as calling over to Miss King who was walking on the opposite pavement.

"Miss King. Are you free for half an hour or so?" Miss King stopped and crossed the road with a look of concern following Mr Frost's apparent urgency. "Tabitha's mum's in trouble. Something seems to have happened in their flat. I think it would be best if someone goes home with her. Will you walk with us?"

Miss King immediately agreed and fell in beside Tabs as she walked as fast as she could without actually running. Miss King pulled out her mobile and called someone to say she would be delayed, clearly alarming the recipient. "No, I'm perfectly OK. It's a matter of caring for a student. Bye..." She sighed.

Through all of this, Tabs said nothing. She didn't dispute the uninvited attention – the teachers might be useful.

"What's wrong at home, Tabitha?" puffed Miss King.

"A woman in a house next to the school – I think her name's Maisie or something like that – just told me someone's been killed in our living room. Mum's in one of the neighbour's. Got to get home." Tabs put on a spurt.

The presence of the teachers was definitely for the best because they protected Tabs as she ran through the people that crowded her street, gawping at all the police cars, the ambulance and the blue and white no-go tapes around her flat. Mr Frost pushed forward authoritatively and people stepped aside. As soon as she got close enough, Tabitha lunged forward, ducking under the tapes.

"Whoa, steady there, young lady," shouted a policeman who came across and grabbed her arm. She swung around, yelling. "I live there. Where's Mum?"

"What's your name?"

"Tabitha Johnson. I live there with my mum." She gestured towards No. 49.

Attracted by the disturbance, an inspector came across. "What seems to be the problem?"

"Says she lives at 49," reported the officer.

"Tabitha Johnson?" asked the inspector. Tabitha nodded, vigorously. "We've been looking for you. Your mother's safe. She's with a neighbour at number 43. We'll take you to her."

"The flat?" demanded Tabs. "What's happened? Someone said someone's been murdered."

"Sorry, can't say any more yet, Miss." The inspector summoned a woman police officer. "Take her to number 43 to join her mum, would you? I'll come and talk to them both in a few moments."

Suddenly, Tab's adrenalin levels crashed and she hunched her shoulders and began to cry.

The friendly police officer put her arm around her and led her to the neighbour's flat. Tabitha kept her head down as she was led through the crowd.

Inside No. 43, Tabitha saw her mother huddled up with a cup of tea being tended to by two neighbours and a police officer.

"Mum. Are you OK? What's happened?"

"Tabitha! You're all right. Thank God!" She put down her cup and gathered up her daughter. Tears flowed. "When I saw..."

"What did you see, Mum?"

"It was awful. Blood everywhere, and I thought..."

"Oh. Mum. Who's been murdered?"

The doorbell rang and the police inspector was ushered in.

"Who is it?" demanded Cindy. "Who's been killed?"

"No one," he said, reassuringly. "It appears someone has put part of a recently slaughtered pig in your living room."

"Oh. That's good... I mean no one's been killed."

"Can we go home, now then?" asked Tabs. "I mean when

they've taken the pig away?"

"Tabitha," said her mother, "you've no idea; you haven't seen it."

"No one's to go in for the moment, Miss." The inspector turned to Cindy. "What can you tell me about who might have done this to you?"

"No idea."

"None? You did see the racist comments on the walls? Anyone with things against you?"

"Oh. People gossip. My husband's – was – black. Tabitha's father."

"Racist?" demanded Tabs. "What's racist?"

"They've scrawled some stupid stuff on the sitting room wall... in red paint," answered Cindy.

"Is it about me being black?"

"Far too early to say," replied the inspector.

"When can we go home?" asked Tabs.

"I'm afraid it will be some time."

"It's a mess, love," Cindy put her arm around her daughter. "The things they wrote on the walls... bad things. Tabitha, promise me you won't go in there until I can clean it up."

"That's silly, Mum. Whatever needs to be done, I am going to help. How bad is it?"

"Bad. Horrible. I haven't seen all of it. I only got as far as the sitting room. I backed out into the hallway and tripped over the front door and fell into the bins. I must have made a noise because, by the time I got my bearings, neighbours were coming from all directions."

"Only three," put in Mrs Ackroyd. "We thought she'd hurt herself but the bins saved her from what could have been a nasty fall."

"But, Tabitha. You MUST NOT go in there."

"Rubbish, Mum. Where am I going to sleep? It's my home."

"But there are things young girls shouldn't see."

"Mum, we live in the days of mass media. We see things on the TV and in films all the time."

"*You* don't. This would be rated 18 if it were in a film."

"That bad? But Mum an 18 rating is to warn over 18s they wouldn't like it. It's OK if you're under 18."

"You know that's not true. Anyway, you haven't seen an 18 film, so you don't know."

"Mum. Which planet are you living on? Everyone's seen 18 films."

"Tabitha." Cindy glanced towards her doting neighbour. Soon, all the estate would know her daughter watched 18 films. This was going from bad to worse. She would have to take this up with Tabitha later. She fell silent.

"Mum, It's OK. I can face what's there. If you have to, I have to."

The inspector smiled and departed.

Outside the house, Charlie Frost approached a policeman and asked in an authoritative tone, "May I ask what's happened here, officer?"

"... And you are?"

"Charles Frost, one of Tabitha Johnson's teachers from Beckside Academy. She was told there has been some kind of crime at her flat."

"I'm afraid I can't discuss the details with you, sir."

"May I see Tabitha? I believe she's in that flat next door."

The officer inquired of the inspector on his radio and permission was given him to join them in No 43 if the Johnsons allowed it and Mrs Ackroyd didn't have any objection.

A policeman accompanied Mr Frost to the door and knocked. Mrs Ackroyd opened it.

"A visitor for you ma'am. Is it all right for him to come in?"

As Mr Frost was introducing himself, Tabs heard him and called out, "Mr Frost. Sorry, I forgot you were outside." Mrs Ackroyd beckoned him in.

Charlie Frost saw himself reflected in a large mirror that hung over the old-fashioned fireplace that housed an electric bar fire, beside which Cindy and Tabitha were huddled.

"Mr Frost," said Tabs. "Mum, you know Mr Frost from Beckies."

"Mr Frost. Yes. We met at the end of last term, I believe. I'm sorry I'm not sorted for entertaining visitors."

"No, of course not Mrs Johnson. I just wanted to make sure

you and Tabitha were all right and ask if there is anything I can do?"

"Thanks. But nothing thank you. I'm just waiting to be able to get back into the flat and then I'll be OK."

"Can I fetch you anything? Do you need anything from the shops?"

"No. I just got back from shopping, thanks." Cindy was overtaken by a real urge to go home, whatever it was like. "I just want to get back."

"But, Mum. You heard them. It'll be ages."

"That's correct, sir," confirmed the police officer. "As a crime scene, I'm afraid it's off-limits until forensics have finished."

Mr Frost was offered a cup of tea. He hadn't intended to stay, but he felt he should wait a bit. It had occurred to him that the Johnsons might need somewhere to stay for at least one night and perhaps he could find somewhere, and the more he heard, the more he realised that the damage to the flat was too extensive for it to be habitable. It was going to take at least a couple of days to clean up after forensics had finished with it and who knew when that would be.

"Have you got anywhere to stay for the time being?" he asked.

"Well, no. But we'll be OK. We'll manage."

"Mrs Johnson, I—"

Tabs interrupted. Her mum had always been doggedly independent but they had to sleep somewhere, didn't they? They couldn't stay all night with Mrs Ackroyd. "Mum. You said it was a real mess. What are we going to do?" she turned to the officer. "What about the bedrooms?"

"I gather they are rather disturbed, too, miss. I haven't been in, myself."

It was at that moment that the intent of the crime finally seeped into Mrs Johnson's mind. It had been a deliberate attack on her and Tabitha to try and drive them off the estate. Things would never be the same again. Anger gripped her and she seethed. "The vile, wicked, brainless... evil..."

Cindy ran out of adjectives she could use in front of the people around her and could not think of a noun. There were no polite words in her vocabulary that fitted the way she felt at that moment.

No one said anything. Tabitha cuddled her mum.

It was Mr Frost who broke the silence. "I'm sure we can find somewhere for you and Tabitha to stay a couple of nights, Mrs Johnson."

"Thank you, er... Mr... er..."

"Frost," reminded Tabitha.

"You must excuse me, Mr Frost, I'm not exactly myself at the moment... Thank you but we couldn't put you to the trouble—"

"It's no trouble."

"I think ya should tek 'im up," said Betty, who was wondering just how long she was going to have to look after the Johnsons herself.

"Give me an hour," replied Mr Frost, handing his empty cup and saucer back with a smile and a thank you.

2

As Mr Frost left number 43, his mind was racing. He must tell his wife why he was delayed and find some way of securing accommodation for Tabitha and her mum. When he got back to his car he rang home.

"Where have you been, Charlie? I was just about to ring you. Have you forgotten your parents are here? They arrived an hour ago."

"Good Lord. I'd forgotten they were coming to stay. Look, there has been a crisis with one of the kids. I'll be home as soon as I can." The incidents of the afternoon had quite banished from his mind the fact that his parents were coming to stay for three nights. So they had no spare room at his home. His brain whirled and his heart uttered a silent prayer. The vicar, he whispered to himself, I'll ask Mike. I hope he's in.

The phone in the vicarage rang. The vicar was indeed out but not his wife, who put the hospitality wheels in motion. Ten minutes later he got a phone call from Mary in the charity shop.

"Tell me what's happened, Charlie," she demanded. Charlie did his best to explain. "Give me a few ticks to get home and put a meal on and then bring them down to the Old Lodge." Dear Bill was to be left in charge of the shop yet again.

"Thanks, Mary. You're an angel."

"Always pleased to oblige. I can't do everything, but this is something I can do."

Charlie Frost returned to number 43 and told them that Mary had volunteered to look after them for the night.

"I took the liberty of asking at the vicarage and they suggested Mary. Mary from the charity shop. She says you know each other. I hope that's OK."

Tabs jumped with delight. Mary. She was the safest person she could think of. "That would be fantastic. Mary. You know Mary, Mum. From Friends of Africa. She's ace."

Cindy by contrast was horrified. The lady was a complete

stranger and you didn't air your dirty linen with strangers. This teacher had indeed taken liberties. "I couldn't possibly—"

"Yes, we can, Mum. Mary's lovely. She's always looking after people. And, Mum, where else are we going to go? Thanks very much, Mr Frost."

Betty Ackroyd smiled – a smile of relief, perhaps. "That's very good of you, Mr Frost. It seems teachers do more than teach kids things. What do you teach?"

"It's more about who I teach rather than what," he replied.

"Jack..." Tabs began and then went a dark red. "I... I mean, Mr Frost teaches humanities." Her teacher grinned. Compared to some, his nickname wasn't bad, especially as meteorology was one of his subjects.

Mrs Ackroyd had no idea what humanities were but she made a pretence of knowing. "A labour of love."

"It is. I need to go home and greet my parents and then I'll come straight back to take you to Mary's."

Cindy was not happy; she needed some control. "You may know all these people but I don't. I don't care what state the flat's in, I'm staying in it."

"But Mum, you heard the policeman. We can't. They won't let us."

"They're going to have to let us. They can't stop us."

"Mum," pleaded Tabs. "I want to go to Mary's. I'm not staying here."

Cindy looked out of the window. There were three police cars and no-go tape all around beyond which were several layers of interested onlookers. She relented. Her daughter needed protecting from everything. She mustn't go into the flat and see what she had. "I know this Mary sounds kind but I think we would be better in a hotel... or—"

"Mum. That would mean going away from Millheaton and it would cost loads. And, anyway, how would we get there? A taxi? How are we going to pay for all that? Sometimes, Mum, we just have to let people help us. No one can do it all on their own every time. People want to help because ... because they think we're worth it and they can. If it was the other way round, you would do it, wouldn't you? And if people went off to a hotel they couldn't afford in another town, you'd be upset."

Cindy welled up with uncontrollable tears. "We'll need night things - washing kit, pyjamas... They have to let me in to get them." She edged forward in her chair. "Just give me a mo—"

"I'll go." Tabs called out to the police officer still guarding the door. "We need to collect some night things. Can I be allowed in just to do that?"

Her mum protested. "Tabitha. You can't—"

"I can. If the police let me in." She looked at the officer again. "Can we, sir?"

"I don't know. I'll ask the inspector."

He came back a few moments later to say that one person could enter to collect some night things, so long as they touched nothing else. He also asked if they could give them a sample of their DNA for purposes of elimination. They both nodded and the officer ushered in a man dressed in white overalls armed with the equipment for taking the samples. After he had departed, Cindy stood up. She was determined to keep Tabs away from the flat. "I'll..." She wobbled and collapsed back into the chair. There was no way she was going to be able to walk, let alone enter the flat.

"Careful, Mrs Johnson. The police constable checked Cindy's pulse. It's the shock. I don't think you should try to go back in just yet."

Cindy was too weak to protest.

"I'll go. I said I would." Tabs sprang up and made for the door.

"Tabitha." But her mother's weak call was in vain; her daughter was already outside approaching the inspector.

"Come with me," he commanded. "Don't touch anything. Nothing at all. Tell me the things you absolutely need, and I'll hand them to you."

When she got inside it was indeed like something out of a horror movie. The butchered pig had been covered with a sheet but blood had seeped through it. She hadn't anticipated the graffiti with its racial message. No wonder her mother was trying to be so protective. But it was far worse than even her mother had imagined; Cindy had only managed a few steps.

Nearly every surface was covered in insults and obscenities. Some had to do with race, others were telling them where they could get themselves lost and some were just rude. There was one that threatened them with worse if they were "stupid enouf to ang arownd". They had found Mum's lipstick and had used Tabitha's felt-tip pens. The intruders had hung a cheap St George's flag on the mirror above the mantlepiece on which were scrawled the words, "England for the English – foreners go home" in what looked like paint. Ornaments and pictures were thrown onto the floor and some of them were smashed. The contents of the kitchen cupboards – flour, oil, vinegar, tomato ketchup and the rest had been emptied over the furniture and carpets. Some of the more valuable things – electrical items and Cindy's jewellery, it later turned out – had been stolen. They hadn't wanted the old TV. It was no longer state-of-the-art and had simply been pushed over. It was lying on its front on top of a broken vase of crushed daffodils that had once stood on the hearth.

In the other rooms, the intruders had tipped all the drawers out and scattered the contents, torn up magazines, pulled off the bedsheets and dragged clothes out of the wardrobes. In the middle of Tabs' bedroom lay the long skirt Mary had given her. It had been badly torn and on it was a note attached with a cheap but treasured souvenir paper knife that she had got on a rare day out to Blackpool. "This is wot apens to them wot think there i and mitey."

Tabitha stood in her bedroom having no idea where she was going to begin.

"What do you need?" ordered the inspector. "Please don't touch anything."

"Er ... night clothes, and clean things for tomorrow... And some washing stuff out of the bathroom. Mum'll want a bath."

The inspector summoned a forensic officer clad in a white suit. "Everything here belong to you, miss?" he asked.

"Yeah, I... er, think so – it's such a mess."

"Sorry, miss. What do you need, here? We're not finished in the bathroom yet – can you manage for tonight?" he spoke with a matter-of-fact but kind voice.

Tabitha didn't know what to say. Nothing was where it should have been. Eventually, she spotted some clean pyjamas underneath her dressing table. She pointed them out, and a pair of jeans together with a top from beside the bed – and some underwear that the forensic officer just picked up and put into a plastic bag. She had no idea how she was going to begin putting everything back. She was not the tidiest of people, and dirty things were all mixed up with those which had been in the drawers and wardrobe. The inspector stepped over a mug which had once contained half a cup of cold tea.

They went next into her mother's bedroom. Tabitha felt sick. Her mother treasured lots of things – they had memories. She wanted to take the photos in their frames but the forensic officer insisted she left them.

Tabitha indicated some things for her mum. For the first time, she was choosing what her mum should wear instead of the other way round. It was a funny feeling. The bathroom was out of bounds. "Sorry, miss. We don't want you in the bathroom for the moment. Tell the officer with your mother and she'll get you taken to the shop."

"Why? Can I just look in? ... I won't touch anything."

"No, miss. This crime is of a very personal nature. I need a lot more answers before I let you go further. I'm making an officer available to guard you overnight. I'd rather like to see you when you're settled. There are a lot of things I need to ask."

"Like, who might have done this?"

"Have you any idea?"

"None. It looks like a racist attack, doesn't it? Those horrible words. I don't know anyone who would do this. I've lived here most of my life. I've always got called racist stuff at school but it's never been like this. No one at school would, like, write this sort of stuff. I have made new black friends in the last couple of months, though. Me and mum. But they don't live on the estate."

"We'll talk about it later. Now, have you got what you need?"

"I think so. I can't think of anything else if I can't get anything from the bathroom." The inspector escorted her across the hallway and gave her the plastic bag with her selection of clothes in it. Her mother met her with an angry, "I told you not to go in. You shouldn't have just rushed off like that."

"Mum, it's OK. I can cope with things. Probably better than you. It isn't right to protect me anymore. I'm nearly sixteen. I've got a few things. I'm sorry if they're not right but everything was scattered about everywhere."

"You're not sixteen for another six months, my girl."

Tabs let the reproof go. This was March and her birthday was October. That made it seven months, so she'd got away with a month.

Cindy rummaged through the bag.

"They wouldn't let me get anything from the bathroom. The inspector said they would take me into the shop."

Cindy sighed. "I just want to go home."

"Yeah..." she knelt beside her chair. "But, Mum. They're giving us a protection officer for tonight. I think they think we're still in some kind of danger. Even if we could go home, it may not be safe. They wouldn't even let me look into the bathroom – said what was in there was of a 'personal nature', whatever that means. The inspector said he wanted to talk to us when we get to Mary's. Fill us in and ask more questions. I told him we had no idea who could have done this. We've been in the flat since I was six – I can't see why it's suddenly all about me having a black father or being friends with the Thomases. No one's done anything to *them*."

"What do they want to talk to us for? Why can't they just get on with catching whoever did this? Tell them I'm not ready to talk to them."

"Mum. We have to talk to them. They're on our side," said Tabs, slightly exasperated. Why was her mum being so difficult? Surely she was stronger than this.

"Tabitha. Don't be rude. They can wait."

"Well, I said it would be all right."

"And who are you to say what's all right and what isn't?"

Betty Ackroyd shifted in her chair.

"Mum, we have no choice. You want them to catch these people, don't you? Look... I'm sorry if I sounded rude," she added. "It's just—"

"OK, OK.... we'd better get going then." Her mum made to get up again but Tabitha laid her hand on her arm.

"Mum. We must wait for when Mr Frost says."

"Oh. I don't know whether I'm coming or going," sighed

148

Cindy. "I need the lav."

"Of course," said Betty. Tabitha held her mum as she got to her feet. This time, she got her balance and felt her way across the room. She was still in the bathroom when Charlie Frost returned.

"Mary Macey says she has everything ready for you."

"Thanks, sir... Mum, we're ready to go when you are," she called.

"These your things?" Charlie asked as he picked up the plastic see-through bag.

Mrs Ackroyd found him a cardboard box to put it in to keep their personal items from the public gaze. "And this is 'er shoppin'," she added, picking up the two bags of groceries and Cindy's handbag.

Mr Frost took everything to his car while Cindy reappeared. She was walking a little more freely. "Where does she live, this Mary?"

"I don't know, Mum. Millheaton somewhere. I told you, it isn't the Planet of the Apes. But it isn't Beck Ings. At least I don't think so."

"So, you've never been to hers?"

"No, Mum. You know I haven't. I've always met her in her shop."

Cindy put her hand to her head. For a moment, Tabs thought she was going to faint. She'd never seen her so weak. It was scary; she wasn't old enough to have to be a carer.

She helped her mum to the outside door. "Thank you," she said to Betty over her shoulder. "Sorry to be—"

"You're welcome," smiled the neighbour. "There's no need to apologise, I'm sure. Hope it all works out for you."

Tabs thought the lady must be glad to get her flat back to herself at last. What Tabs didn't know was that after they had gone, Betty went to the kitchen and found a large knife to put under her bed in case the attackers decided she was next.

Mr Frost explained that Mary Macey was ready for them but he was to say her little cottage had not had anyone but herself in it for ages. She would, however, be very happy to look after Cindy and Tabitha.

"Where is it she lives?" asked Cindy.

"It's by the old gates to The Park on the Puddleham Road. It's the Old Lodge."

Woah! Tabs took a sharp intake of breath. Had she heard him right? She opened her mouth but no sound came out of it.

"Tabitha, you OK?" he teacher asked. "Shock comes in waves. Come on, let's get you both in the car. It won't take us long."

"We need to go to the shop and get toothbrushes and toothpaste and stuff."

"Let's get you straight to Mary's. I can nip to the shop for you for your bathroom things afterwards."

"Th... Thanks."

"No problem. Any particular flavour toothpaste?"

Tabs shook her head. "No, whatever's on offer if there is one... the cheapest."

3

On arrival at the cottage, the policeman escorted the two refugees to the front waist-high deep-red gate, overhung by a lilac tree which Tabitha remembered would be covered in white flowers later in the spring. Mary opened the small wooden front door to welcome them. Tabitha had never seen it open before and it felt strange – for years it had seemed like it was only ornamental and not meant to open.

"Mrs Macey?" said the constable. "You are expecting these two ladies?"

"Yes. Indeed. Welcome," she smiled holding out her hand which Cindy took with an embarrassed stiffness.

The air was filled with the scents of spring given off by a plethora of pot plants. In the front garden, Tabs was attracted by a little border that now contained pansies of a variety of colours, yellow, purple, blue, orange, red and black, and a clump of wallflowers with a hint of colour in their buds about to burst. In the far corner was a flowering cherry showing the beginnings of little yellow-green shoots as it was getting ready to become a mass of white blossom and below the window a shrub covered in tiny leaves gave the little garden a pleasant living backdrop which blended well with the dull red bricks discoloured by the former decades of West Riding smoke.

"Thank you, Mrs Macey—" continued the policeman.

"Miss. Never met Mr Right... Mary Macey."

"Er, Miss Macey. Can I give your details to the inspector – including a telephone number?" He turned to Tabs, "We have your mobile number don't we, Miss Johnson?"

"Yes, I already give it to the policeman in charge – the one in plain clothes."

Cindy again felt sidelined and spoke up.

"And I don't possess one. At least, not after they put up the charges." Not having a mobile hadn't really bothered her since a landline came with the TV package.

"I doubt it'd still work, anyway, Mum. It was G2."

Cindy glared at her daughter.

"Sorry, Mum. Just saying."

Mary cleared the air with a quick, "Come in. I'll get the kettle on."

Tabs smiled. *Mary's answer to a crisis is always to make tea.*

"Come," Mary beckoned. "You look cold."

Mr Frost followed them carrying their things. "Here's your stuff. I'll pop to the shop now and get your toiletries. A couple of toothbrushes and some toothpaste – whatever's on offer. Yes?"

"Perhaps some soap and—"

"No need," interrupted Mary. "You use everything I have."

"But, we can't—"

"Yes, you can."

"I'll not be long," said Charlie.

Cindy felt for her handbag to give him some money but before she could open it, he was gone.

"Don't worry," smiled Mary. "You can settle up with him, later. Now then Tabitha, you may be surprised at where you are. I have to confess that I have deceived you over rather too many years. I know you have been visiting me, or rather my garden for a long time. I had decided I would wait until your sixteenth birthday and then invite you round for a party."

Tabs didn't know how to respond. She felt a mixture of guilt and embarrassment – a new sensation she couldn't put into words.

"Oh dear. I fear I should have said something, shouldn't I? I loved it when you came... and didn't want to spoil it. You and I have been the only human beings who have entered my garden these past six years."

"And the skirt... and the key..."

"Yes. I have to confess that it was I who put them there for you."

"For me?"

"Who else? As I said, apart from me, you're the only one who has ever visited the garden."

Tabitha froze and then murmured, "I used to think it was looked after by fairies."

"A rather ancient fairy with garden clippers and a mower, I'm afraid. But I used to delight in it being visited by a little girl. You were part of the spirit of the garden. I've been a rather naughty old spinster, haven't I? To tell you the truth, I have been feeling a bit awkward about it, recently. When you keep something a secret a long time – a secret that should be told, it gets a bit... well, difficult to know how to tell it."

Cindy at last found the breath to speak. "Excuse me, what's all this about? Secrets... More secrets. Someone's turned the ruddy world over. What have you been up to, this time, my girl? There are so many things – too many things – you keep from me. I don't need no more flummoxing."

"Don't be cross with her, Mrs Johnson. A lot of this is my fault, I fear. It's a long story. Come into my little sitting room and I'll let Tabitha tell you, while I put the kettle on."

"Your fault?" Now Cindy was properly confused. She felt she couldn't cope with much more.

"Well, yes. But I don't think any harm has been done. Just the opposite. That's why I let it happen. Come and sit down. Tea?" And she disappeared through into what must have been the kitchen.

Cindy collapsed into a large comfortable armchair while Tabs explained in as few words as possible about her venturing into the garden.

"Fancy going into someone else's garden aged only eight. You shouldn't have done that." Cindy was very conscious of intruding on another's domain, there was everything wrong with it and she was highly embarrassed by her daughter's lack of reticence.

Alongside the hearth, there was an old-fashioned rocking chair with tapestry cushions. As Mary brought the conversation to a halt by appearing at the door with a tea trolley, Tabs went to explore it.

"Tabitha. That's Mary's chair." reprimanded Cindy. Her daughter had just far too much off and it must stop.

"You go for it." exclaimed, Mary. "Feel free to have a good rock in it." She pushed the gold-toned metal trolley loaded with a teapot, cups and saucers and a large cake into the centre of the room. "Make yourself right at home. I don't get to share my house with many people and it is a delight to have you here."

Lowering herself onto a settee, she explained to Cindy how delighted she had been to see a pretty little girl aged about eight trot into her garden. She had been aware that she had had a visitor – there had been little telltale clues – but she had not known who it was for a week or two. When she eventually saw her, the little girl had looked so at home there. Mary felt it was as if she was being visited by a real live fairy, one who had a very special affinity with the garden. She had thought that if she let her know she had seen her, it would have put her off coming. "And I didn't want to do that," she added. "It was so magical having her there. I'm afraid I didn't try and find out where she came from... That only came to light when the boys attacked her over there by the gates and a policeman brought her into the pharmacy... Now, sugar Mrs Johnson?"

"Please. Er... you can call me Cindy."

"Cindy. Nice name."

"What did you do in this... garden?" her mother looked intently at her daughter. How many more shocks was she going to have to endure?

"Nothing ..."

"Don't tell me nothing," spat her mother, angrily. "You keep telling me that. 'Nothing'. It's 'nothing' every time. But you are always up to something. You're not like other kids. You've got a good idea of what they're up to. But my Tabitha Chapeltown Johnson? Oh, no."

"Please don't get cross, Mrs Johnson," pleaded Mary again, gently. "I should have said something to her... to you. But I just delighted in her visits and left her to it. But keeping out of the way rather encouraged her, I'm afraid. She's telling the truth when she says 'nothing'. She would just lay on the grass staring at the clouds or sit cross-legged watching the birds in the trees over the wall. She allowed the garden to speak to her." Cindy looked puzzled. "Gardens, Nature, *can* speak, you know."

"I don't know what you're talking about..." began Cindy, but then broke down in tears. There had been far too much drama for one day.

"You must be exhausted," whispered Mary. "Come on, drink up, then I'll show you to your bedrooms. You've had a horrendous day."

"Oh dear," sighed Cindy, "I am fair done in. We won't need to stay more than tonight, though. I'm sure. We'll get the flat cleaned up tomorrow and get ourselves home."

"Well, good luck with that. But you can stay as long as you need to. *Mia casa, tua casa* as they say in Mexico. My house is your house."

But before they could budge, there was a knock on the door. It was the inspector who introduced himself as DI Gillespie.

Tabs and Cindy told them all they could but it didn't amount to much at all. Neither of them had felt they had any particular enemies that would do such a thing.

The DI arranged a time the next morning when they would be allowed back into the flat and check if anything was missing.

"Good. Sleep well, if you can. I will see that the road outside is regularly patrolled tonight. But if there is anything untoward, ring 999 immediately mentioning my name, DI Gillespie."

After he had gone, Tabs went to turn on her phone which had been off since she was in school. Somehow, it had not occurred to her to do so before – a measure of the extreme circumstances. Almost immediately it began to bleep. Message after message popped up. Most of them seemed to be from the Thomases and a couple were from Danielle at the vicarage. When she tried to respond, the battery gave out. And her charger was, of course, at home in the flat.

"They'll all be worried about me. And I can't even text them to say I'm all right. It's not fair. No one should be forced out of where they live with all their stuff still inside." She looked up at Mary. "I guess that's what it's like in Africa?"

"It can be, yes. But not just in Africa. War and fighting happen all over the world. We're very lucky here in Britain. Refugees need friends. That's why I call the shop Friends of Africa."

"And why you're being a friend to us, too?"

"Exactly. And one day it might be your turn to befriend someone. No one can predict the future."

Cindy dropped off in her chair.

She woke to the rattling of pots and pans and her daughter's voice in the kitchen. *What's she up to now?* She dreaded finding Tabs exploring again without leave. But she needn't have worried because Tabs was in the throws of cutting potatoes into chips while Mary was setting a pan of oil on the stove.

"Good evening, Cindy," smiled Mary. "You have had a good nap. You must be hungry. Your daughter is. Apparently, you normally eat around five and it's now gone seven. And," she continued, quickly, "don't worry, it was I who asked Tabitha. She was a model of patience. I inquired what you normally ate and she told me that tonight it was egg, chips and beans and that I have in. Tabs said you don't always have oven chips. And I have a willing volunteer... Tabitha can cut the chips to the thickness you are used to – it's not something I get round to doing for myself much."

Cindy shrugged. The smell of heated vegetable oil did arouse some kind of hunger. "Not too many for me, Tab. I... I'm not that hungry."

"That is quite to be expected. But my experience of these things is that when you start, you are hungrier than you thought."

And so it turned out. It was a good thing that her daughter had just made the usual amount. With two hours of sleep and a full stomach, Cindy began to feel as if the world was beginning to come somewhere to becoming the right way up again.

It was as Tabs was moving to help with the washing up that she thought about her dead phone. Could she ask Mary if she could borrow hers? Had she got a phone – other than the ancient-looking landline by the front door? She began, "Mary. Maybe. I should—" but she was cut short by the sound of the doorbell. Mary went to see who it was and a moment later ushered in a concerned-looking Danielle and her dad.

"Danielle," yelled Tabs. "I just got that you were sending a text and then my phone went dead... battery..." Danielle rushed over to her and gave her a squeeze.

"You're OK? Er, you're both OK?"

"Yeah. Just can't go inside the flat."

"And no phone. You poor thing. Ashol and Deng have been frantic but I told them you're here with Mary and they send their love."

Mary shooed them out of her small kitchen while she put the kettle back on. The vicar sat in the rocking chair opposite Cindy and began to listen to her while Danielle and Tabs chatted noisily on the settee. Danielle listened to Tabs saying what she had seen and kept going, "Wow!" at every new revelation.

"The girls seem to be getting on well together," said Mike.

"Yes," agreed Cindy. "It's what Tabitha needs right now. Thank you for coming."

"No trouble. I'm glad Mary's been able to help. If there is anything else we can help with, please don't be afraid to ask."

When Mary wheeled in the trolley once again she asked Tabs if she would find two more cups in the dresser by the door. She got up and found them and Mary checked them over.

"Be a dear," she smiled, "and swill them out, will you? I don't think they have been used for ten years." Tabs trotted into the kitchen, which she was quickly becoming familiar with, accompanied by Danielle as Mary settled on the settee and stirred the pot. Danielle and Tabs found themselves employed in taking round tea and offering the biscuits and topping up the pot with more boiling water as the adults engaged in earnest talk. Tabs took Danielle back into the kitchen and they completed the washing up together.

"I never knew Mary lived here," said Tabs.

"I kind of did. But I've never been in before. It's cool, isn't it? I guess it's got an oldy-worldy garden to go with it. You'll see that in the morning."

Tabs giggled and told Danielle her secret. Ashol knew and now her mother did, too – so it was no longer a secret to keep. Danielle contributed even more wows. "Tabitha Johnson, you really are a deep one." She laughed.

4

It was about 4 a.m. as she lay awake in the silence and darkness of that night when all Tabs' outward calm and bravado completely dissolved. The realisation of what had happened tore into her. She had been determined to be strong for her mother – had to be. If she hadn't faced up to things when her mum wasn't coping, it would have been worse – much worse. But in the stillness of the night in a strange bed, she couldn't get the scene of the destruction of the flat out of her mind. The pig thing was foul but the worst bit was the violence – the upturned furniture, the smashed telly lying on top of crushed daffodils, her ripped skirt with its note pinned to it with her paper-knife from Blackpool... and the messages painted onto the wall. That could only have been directed at her. *I'm the black one – not my mum. If it weren't for me, it wouldn't have happened, would it?* And hadn't the policeman said she wasn't allowed into the bathroom because of the *personal nature* of what was in there? Whatever could that be? What could be more personal than having your favourite skirt ripped, being told you weren't wanted and threatened if you didn't pack up and leave the only home you had known?

Tabitha got up and walked to the window. It was dark – too dark to make anything out. The sky was shrouded with cloud and there were neither moon nor stars and, unlike on the estate, no street lights out here to pierce the gloom. It made her feel even more trapped. She wished she'd brought her doll, Minnie, along with her night things so she could cuddle her under the duvet. She hadn't taken her doll to bed with her for years but now she felt vulnerable and a little frightened in a strange bed. Come to think of it, she hadn't seen Minnie about anywhere in her room; she was no longer on the shelf but then nothing was. She was a distinctive doll – made of black felt with braided black hair. When they got back she would make sure she found her and rescue her – almost as soon as she retrieved her phone charger.

It took a long time but eventually sleep overcame her; she was more tired than she could ever remember.

But her sleep was not peaceful. Trapped in the cave, she was backed against the wall while a faceless brute of a man was engaged in trashing everything around her. No. He mustn't find Minnie. No. "No," she screamed as he lifted her discarded bedding – Minnie was in amongst it. She must be and he mustn't find her. *No.*

Tabs awoke, sweat pouring off her, and then she shivered – her duvet was missing. Exposed and frightened, she sat up. It was pitch black. She groped around for something to cover herself with and then found the duvet on the floor and realised she must have shaken it off while caught up in her nightmare. Had she screamed out loud? She had in the dream. But all was still and she could hear her mother gently snoring in a room not far away. At least she was sleeping peacefully. Tabs relaxed, got up and slid her hands along the wall until she found the door and then a light switch. Trying to be as quiet as she could, she tiptoed to the bathroom where she washed her face and tried to rid herself of the dream fug, returned to her room and got back onto the bed leaving the light on. Then somehow – she didn't quite know how – she went back to sleep.

Tabitha opened her eyes the next morning to the sound of rich birdsong. It was loud and it took her a moment or two to remember where she was. She rolled out onto the floor, stood up and drew back a curtain. She found herself looking down on the back garden – the vegetable beds in front and, behind them, a glimpse of her secret garden. It made her feel a little better; nature was strong, wasn't it?

The Old Lodge turned out to be rather good – better than she had expected. Being in the West Riding, it wasn't a classic storybook cottage with timber, mud and thatch, of course, but this was still the most unusual house she had ever been in. It had character. The windows were smaller than in modern houses. In the bedroom, there was a small 'period' fireplace made of cast iron and colourful tiles. The gold and brown chintz curtains, supported by wooden rings, were heavy and snug. In the centre of the room were a matching carpet square and an upholstered chair in plain autumn gold.

Tabs couldn't quite take it all in. *So, I find myself homeless and taken to a fairy cottage.* She picked up the poker and examined the blackened end. *Does Mary have real fires in this grate?* Hung beside the fire surround, there was a big brass fork with a long handle. *I know what this is for. I saw it on the telly in some programme set in the old days. You're supposed to stick bread and stuff on the end and toast it over the fire.* She wished she had noticed them earlier – they might seem innocent but they were the devil's tools, weren't they? He used them for stirring up the fire of hell and stabbing people for being bad. She had seen pictures of the devil with horns and a pointed tail poking frightened naked people with a fork like this. *If the devil can use them, so can I. I can protect myself from evil men who put dead pigs into people's houses,* she thought.

Tabs put on her school uniform. It was going to be a lot farther to walk, so she'd have to make an early start. And it was going to be a difficult day with everyone now aware of what had happened in her flat. But Danielle – and no doubt Ashol, too – would stick with her and help her get through it.

Downstairs, Tabs found Mary already up, dressed in an ancient housecoat. It wasn't worn or anything, just old-fashioned.

"Sleep well?"

"Yeah," she lied. "I love your house. It's full of old things. Like this rocking chair." She plonked herself down and rocked it as far as it would go. "And the big bread fork beside the fireplace in my bedroom."

"Ah. Crumpets," grinned Mary. "Crumpets. I haven't tasted crumpets for years and years," she mused with a little involuntary excitement.

"Crumpets? I've never had them."

"You might call them pikelets?"

"Yeah. Never tasted one. Could we have some and cook them using the fork?"

"Hmm. That would be absolutely delightful. It'll take a trip to the supermarket on the Leeds Road, though you'll have to stay another night, then."

She was still speaking when Cindy appeared in the doorway, bleary-eyed.

"Another night. Nonsense. We'll get cleaned up today and not impose on you further, Mary."

"Sleep well, Cindy?"

"No, not really, despite your very comfortable bed and those sleeping pills."

"Look, Cindy. Seriously. Listening to the police, it may take more than a day," said Mary, in a business-like tone. "It will be a privilege to look after you both as long as it takes. I mean that. We'll go along to Morrison's and get enough stuff in to feed us for a week, including some crumpets. I haven't had any for years. Although we'll do them under the grill since there is no need to light a fire. That OK, Tabitha?"

"Mary, I—"

"No, I insist. I absolutely insist. It's very good to have someone to share my little house with – it makes a change."

"Great," cheered Tabitha, before her mother could raise any further objections.

"Now what would you like for breakfast? I don't have the usual things and there isn't much bread to share between three. I've got some ice cream but someone will have to help me to scoop it out. I usually soften it a little, but I haven't thought about it, I'm afraid."

"I'll do it." Tabitha catapulted out of the rocking chair and was already on her way to the kitchen. Mary followed hard on her heels, laughing.

Cindy just sighed, defeated. Things were out of her hands. She was outnumbered. Well, she sighed to herself, if you can't change things, you might as well go with the flow. I can't remember when I last had pikelets. Then, she checked to see that Mary and Tabitha were safely in the kitchen and moved across to try the rocking chair. She had read somewhere that rocking chairs are enjoyed by the young and the old. She wondered which she was. Was she getting old prematurely, or had she still got something of the child in her? In many ways, Mary herself was young at heart, that was probably why she seemed to get on so well with Tabitha.

In the outhouse, Mary dived into her freezer and produced some ice cream and some rhubarb she had blanched the previous summer. "Fancy some rhubarb with it?" Tabitha's nose betrayed her reaction. "Don't worry I'll put in plenty of sugar."

"Don't think I have tasted rhubarb since I was a kid," she explained.

"Then you have a great treat in store."

For one short moment, surrounded by the comfort of the cottage, the food, and Mary's clear delight in having them as guests, the horrors of the previous day became eclipsed. The trashed flat, if not out of mind, was out of sight.

Then the phone rang. It was Inspector Gillespie. Could he meet Mrs and Miss Johnson at their flat at nine o'clock? Tabitha said about school; it was a Friday.

"I'd rather Tabitha didn't go in today," said the inspector. "There are a few things we need to clear up before she gets talking to anyone else."

"I've already talked to Danielle and, apart from Ashol and Deng, I'm not going to say anything to anybody, ever."

"I don't think it will be so easy," replied the policeman, diffidently. "I have to say, Mrs Johnson, that although Beck Ings doesn't win any awards for the purest of estates, this is very out of the ordinary. I need to see you both in the flat and get you to tell me what's missing and, if you can, give us any other clues. We need to find who's behind this as quickly as possible."

"You've no idea yet who did this, then?"

"Mrs Johnson, this does not have the hallmarks of a local job; it's not something we can associate with any of our regulars. I'll see you at nine."

"I understand inspector. We'll be there."

Tabs wasn't surprised at how relieved she felt. School wouldn't be a normal day, would it? And now she could concentrate on being strong for her mother.

"Can I...? May I just go into the garden and say hi to the fairy?"

"Of course, you may. We should leave by ten to nine, though."

Cindy watched her daughter follow the narrow garden path to the gate in the side wall and then cross to the hedge which divided off a small area beyond. Then she retreated back upstairs to the bedroom to ready herself to go and, looking out of the window, saw Tabs just standing still on the dewy grass looking up at the huge trees that rose above the end of the garden. She wasn't getting up to anything; in everyday terms, she was doing nothing but, at some deeper level, she was alive with the possibility of doing all kinds of things.

But it wasn't as positive as that for Tabitha. The garden was soggy and forlorn that morning. The nymph and bench were stained green and looked drab and sad, while the grass was long and lank – it was too soon for its first cut – and the trees were bare and damp. Tabitha felt empty, the garden seemed like it was struggling to stay alive. *It's just my mood*, she told herself. But then she shuddered – what had happened yesterday wasn't just in her head, it was real. It was not like a sad thought or even a dread that could be addressed by thinking cheerful things and dismissing it as a made-up nightmare. The reality was that they – she – had been the target of a hate crime and nature was not doing very much to help her, the sun was hiding behind a plain white blanket of cloud. Everything was dull, damp and depressing. *That's what's truly real. There is no magic in this place – there never has been.* That's *what has been inside my head – the illusion. Real things are not like that. Kids make up fairy stories in their heads and I'm not a kid no more. Not since yesterday.* Reality was stark and grim. A robin hopped across the grass only to be chased away by a bully of a blackbird. All their singing was simply to tell other birds to get lost, wasn't it? It might sound sweet and melodic but its message was far from gentle.

Tabs retreated from the garden feeling worse than ever. All that silly banter about the toasting fork when actually one of her first thoughts was to use it as a weapon. Mary was great. She was bending over backwards to help them and Tabs told herself she had to be strong for her mum. *All this is my fault for being who I am. Come to think of it, who really am I? What am I?* But her mum loved her and she owed it to her to keep up the cheerfulness – even if it was a sham. *Behave yourself, Tabitha Johnson. Be strong.*

"You can ring me on my mobile if there is anything you need," said Mary, as they prepared to leave. "Here's the number. I'm going to Morrison's. Anything you want?"

"You could get me a couple of boxes of tissues? Here," Cindy pulled out her purse and took out a ten-pound note.

"There's really no need—"

"Take it. I agreed to stay the weekend for Tabitha's sake, but I'm not taking anything else from you."

Mary knew she must allow the lady at least some dignity, so she took the note. "You know, Cindy, I haven't had anyone to look after for years, you must make allowances for an old lady indulging herself. I am delighted to be around for you. Anything you would like, Tabitha?"

Tabitha gave her a gentle hug. "Crumpets." She ignored her mum's look. "Thanks. You've been a kind of fairy godmother to me all along – ever since I was eight, although I never knew it."

"And now you do, and that's the silver lining to this dreadful business for me."

"Would you call the school – make it kind of official-sounding, like?"

"Of course. When I've done that I'll drive you to your flat."

5

As they drove into the estate, they noticed clusters of people chatting on several corners. People had clearly turned out to gossip. Two police cars stood outside the flat. The front door to the block – still the other side of a blue and white 'do not cross' tape – stood open, a constable on guard. Tabs and her mother ducked beneath the tape and introduced themselves to him and he escorted them into their own home as if they were visitors.

"The ladies are here, sir." The inspector was waiting for them. He was standing beside the now righted sofa. The pig parts had been removed but there were dark burgundy stains on the carpet.

The DI murmured, softly. "Good morning. I hope you didn't have too many nightmares."

"We managed," responded Cindy.

"Good. You have a kind lady in Mary Macey..." He indicated the walls. "First, can you tell me if you recognise any of the handwriting... and if you can identify anyone you might know who may have used these insults against you before? Take your time."

Cindy studied her walls. It was frightening. It was meant to make her run away and protect her daughter. "I've not stopped thinking about this, inspector. It's a total surprise to me. We've been here more than twelve years and some people have remarked that my daughter has a black father, but it's never been any more than gossip. People have all kinds of histories, don't they? No one's any different. There's never been any real hatred before – not like this. This hasn't been done by anyone I know. And I know a few people, the neighbours, in the shops, at the bingo..."

"And what about you, Miss?"

"Same," replied Tabitha, blankly. "Sometimes when people have tried to bully me they might have called me a rude name for black, but that hasn't happened for ages."

"Do you get much bullying?"

"Not as much as I used to. I don't let them."

"But you have been bullied in the past?"

165

"Well, mostly because I wouldn't join in. Like, just hanging about doing boring things. But that was not about having a black father, just not wanting to be part of their stupid gangs. The only people who have met Dad are Ashol and Deng."

"Who are themselves black?"

"Yeah. Nothing bad has happened to them. I mean, not like this."

"You were bullied in the past. I need to know who did the bullying."

"But it's different now. Some of the worst have moved out."

"Who are we talking about, here?"

"Well, there was Griff – Gareth Green – but he's been gone some time. Disappeared after Shaun got killed." The DI nodded to a uniformed policewoman with a tablet who noted it down.

"Have you had any other trouble at school lately? Fallen out with any friends or anything?"

"Nah. I haven't hung out with some of them like I used to since I've become friends with Ashol and Deng."

"Anyone resentful of this new friendship?"

"No, not really. Nothing that'd make anyone act like this."

"Constable Brooks tells me you had a run-in with a boy some months back." DI Gillespie checked a pocketbook. "Ah, the Gareth Green you mentioned."

"Oh, that was ages ago. I blooded his nose when he tried it on."

"Tried it on?"

"He tried to kiss me. But that was months and months ago. Not long after that, he disappeared. Apparently, he got into serious trouble somewhere else and got taken into some kind of youth prison. Then he came back and his friend, Shaun, was killed with a motorbike that he was riding. He wasn't at the funeral; he went away again. But I haven't seen him since he went away the first time."

"And do you know where he is now?"

"As far as I know, he's back in the prison. He's never reappeared at school. He is, isn't he? I mean in clink?"

"Mr Green was released a month ago and has been living with his mother."

166

"Oh. But she moved away, didn't she? I don't know where. I've never seen him. Do you think he done this? It's not like him. I mean, he never hated me. Just fancied me when he got, like, fourteen. He was, like, being an annoying pest. But, like I said, that was ages ago. You don't think..."

"We have to follow up on all leads. At the moment we don't think anything. Forensics tells us there are three hands here. The scrawling in this room and in the hall is one person, the bathroom a second and then there is the note on your bed and on your mirror," said Inspector Gillespie, addressing Tabitha.

"Note, what note?" panicked Cindy.

"This note, Mrs Johnson. This is why we think the raid has something to do with Tabitha in particular."

"You knew about this, Tabitha. You didn't tell me."

"You were out of it, Mum. I weren't going to upset you more."

"Let me see it. Tabitha, what have you done? You know who wrote this."

"No, Mum. Wish I did. I don't know. Some people are just idiots."

"There are a few damaged people, Mrs Johnson, that go around with chips on their shoulders. I gather your daughter is quite a clever girl – working well at school. Getting on with the teachers. That sort of thing can be enough to trigger resentment in some."

"Well, I must say her attitude has changed over the last few months, certainly." Cindy struck a proud pose.

"For the better, would you say?"

"Definitely. She's a special girl who has begun to realise how special she is."

"A girl who dares to be different and distances herself from those who want to draw her into their gangs."

"I don't make enemies, though," added Tabs. "I don't tell on anybody or anything. I can't imagine who would feel like that about me... and do this. I never ratted on anybody over the weed. We all knew to keep mum about that."

The inspector's eyebrows lifted. "Tell me more. Cannabis?"

"Well, yeah. It was a long time ago now, though."

"When?"

"Oh. Ages ago. Just before I were fourteen, I think."

"And that was?"

"Eighteen months ago," supplied Cindy.

"And who did you not rat on?"

"Well, it were mainly Griff and his cronies but not only them."

"Ah. Green again."

"But he never knew I saw him. And, like I said, we never said nothing and he didn't get into any trouble for it that I know of. After that, it weren't safe for them in the lane behind the bike sheds, so it stopped. It didn't happen at school no more."

The DI nodded to his colleague who made another note. Then said, "Whoever wrote this had help. What do you make of the bathroom?"

"The bathroom?" breathed Cindy. "I never got that far. Tab what's in the bathroom?"

"Dunno. They wouldn't let me in," she mumbled. "They said it was too personal."

"It's not nice." said the DI, "They do know your name but I wouldn't take it as personal, exactly. These people are rather screwed up."

The DI led them through into the bathroom. On the mirror, drawn in lipstick was a lewd picture that might have featured on the wall of a public toilet with 'Tabs Jonson' scrawled beneath it and more vile words. Tabs couldn't quite make out what the picture was supposed to depict except it was gross and seemed to suggest some sort of sexual activity, and the words weren't commonly used among kids her age. She didn't know what some of them meant. She didn't want to.

"Yuk," spat Tabs. "That's sick." She looked away.

"That weren't done by someone Tabitha's age," stated Cindy. "That's by someone much older."

"We think so, too," agreed the inspector. "But, like I said, we don't think what has been done in your flat was the work of one person. I'm sorry you had to see this, ladies. You can't think of anyone you know who might express themselves in this way?" They both shook their heads. "I'll get someone to clean it off for you."

While an unfortunate policewoman set about cleaning the depravities off the bathroom mirror, Cindy and Tabitha moved on to her room and studied the message on the mirror there. It was written in red felt-tip pen. This time, Tabs knew the meaning of the words although they were badly misspelt.

"You sure this wasn't written by Gareth Green?" asked Cindy.

Tabs' mind reverted to the image in the bathroom. No way would Gross have done that – he didn't have the artistic ability let alone the imagination. And the dead pig... He'd never have come up with that idea, would he? It couldn't be him. Besides, it was ages since he'd seen her.

"I dunno. I can never remember seeing anything he'd written. He didn't like writing and in the end, he spent more time away from school than in it. And I made sure he never sat near me, anyway. The spelling is not very good, though, is it? Definitely by someone who can't spell."

"Or someone pretending they can't to put us off the scent," added Cindy.

"Maybe. But I wouldn't give them so much credit," smiled the DI.

They moved around, examining the wreckage. Cindy's bedroom, which was not so disturbed, gave them no further clues as to who might have done it. The kitchen was the least messed up and Cindy found the kettle and set it to boil. Remarkably, the perpetrators hadn't looked in the cupboard with the mugs and tea.

"Can I make you a cup of tea?" Cindy asked the officers. She was taking charge of her own home again. The woman police officer who had attended to the bathroom mirror was grateful but the DI declined.

"There is one more thing I need to tell you," he said. "We've released a statement to the press. We—"

"The press? Why? Why should we air our dirty linen more than we already have?"

"Because the gossip is out of hand. It's all over social media and it's the talk of the estate. Most of the rumours talk about murder. The press will be told what has happened – without the nature of the graffiti – and stop the untruths. It will also be an opportunity for us to ask if anyone has any idea who might be behind this. Someone knows."

"What about DNA?" asked Tabs. "Can't you find DNA evidence? That's why you wanted ours yesterday, wasn't it? To eliminate it?"

"Yes. That's true but it looks like they seem to have been wearing overalls and gloves and the footmarks are consistent with standard Wellington boots. They were pretty careful."

"Can we begin tidying up, now?" asked Cindy.

"Yes, you may. And please try and tell me if you find that anything is missing."

Tabitha started on her room. She put all the scattered clothing in a heap in one corner. It all had to be washed now, even if it had started out clean and, to be honest, she couldn't be sure which had been worn and which hadn't. She replaced the drawers into their slots. Her dressing table set was nowhere to be found and a little box in which she kept small pieces of costume jewellery and a few other treasures was also missing.

Some of her underwear had been scattered around the room in strange places but all of her clothes, as far as she could see, were still there. The skirt that Mary had given her, the one which had born the note, had been torn, but nothing else. Tabitha found a box of tissues and cleaned off the obscenities written on her mirror. It was in the same hand as the note on her skirt. Could Gross have written them? They were certainly gross enough but not too gross like the mirror in the bathroom, which had been done with her mother's lipstick. She gathered together her scattered make-up stuff. Some of it she had had a long time, the stuff of Christmas presents hardly used. Then she found Ted, her childhood teddy bear, under the bed and there were toys that she hadn't seen for a long time pulled out of the back of the cupboard. She put them carefully back into their box. She unearthed her phone charger and put her mobile on to charge.

But she couldn't find Minnie. Minnie was homemade – a cloth doll with sewn-on features which included a big smile and round eyes. She wore a colourful dress and sported braided black woolly hair. She had been a gift from Tabitha's father after one of his visits to Nigeria when she was two. She checked under the bed, behind the dressing table, everywhere, but she wasn't in the room. Why would they steal Minnie? She would have no value to a thief.

Tabs longed for a cuddle. Her mum was not a cuddler, though. And, anyway, that would be giving one not getting one. She texted Ashol. She would be in lessons, of course, but she told her where she was and asked her to call her at lunchtime. Then she wiped away a tear – just in time. Cindy came in.

"Missing much?"

"My trinket box and dressing table set – and Minnie. At least, I can't find her anywhere."

"Your doll? She wouldn't have much value would she?"

"None at all. But it isn't just about nicking things, is it? Have you lost anything?"

"All my rings and the pearls that belonged to your grandmother."

"Oh, Mum."

"... and, the... a tin containing a bit of money I had put some savings in."

"How much, Mum?"

"About two hundred quid. I was saving up to help you go to college one day."

"Oh, Mum. That's dreadful. You shouldn't have done that."

"Obviously." Cindy broke down crying, and Tabitha took her into her arms.

"I'm sorry, Mum." Then Tabs let go and wept.

"You. Sorry. What for?"

"If it weren't for me, this wouldn't have happened. I'm the black girl. And it was my name in the bathroom and my skirt that was torn... and the note."

"Don't say that. It's me. They're getting at me through you. Whoever's done this just wants me – us – off the estate. And they'll get what they want. We'll go right away... Scotland; I like Scotland."

"Scotland. Mum, we'd stick out like sore thumbs up there. We'd be invading Sassenachs or whatever they call us. I was born in Yorkshire. And Dad's in Leeds. He wouldn't want us to go away. If we're going anywhere, it should be Chapeltown. It's me they're getting at and they in't going to drive me to Scotland."

"You're brave, I have to say that of you. But there are times when running away from bear-infested territory is the wisest thing. And if you want to go down the line that it's all about you, the reason you're here in this world is because I gave birth to you, I wanted you. And I was the one who married a black man. It didn't work out but not because of his colour. That's just silly talk... The people who did this make me so angry." Her tears were replaced with defiance. "I'd do it again. Give me a nice black man who loves me and I wouldn't hesitate."

"Really, Mum? That would be fantastic."

"In your dreams, baby. There wouldn't be one nice enough who would want to marry me, so forget what I just said. Now, let's get something for dinner."

"If you're serious about flitting, we could go to Chapeltown. It's where I was born. It's in my name."

"No. Not Chapeltown. You wouldn't like it. There's no countryside for miles. The only green space anywhere near is Roundhay Park and that's a bus journey. And they're all posh up there. Believe me, Chapeltown isn't for you. There might be black people but not all of them are nice."

Would I miss the green things? Perhaps I need a break from them? And I wouldn't be got at for being black... But the problem is that Mum is white. And I'm half white, so where do I belong? It's, like, 'Who am I?' again.

They found a tin of spaghetti and defrosted some bread from the freezer and toasted it.

"The kitchen hasn't faired too badly. They haven't taken much from here?"

"No, just emptied flour and eggs all over the place and scattered the cutlery."

They sat on stools that Cindy had set upright again and ate at the counter staring at another choice bit of graffiti. "Certainly got a way with words."

"Or not. It's boring," complained Tabs. These people were not nightmare monsters. Just thick idiots. "And they can't spell it properly, either. I don't think the people who done this were very clever." Tabs laughed. "I feel like correcting the spelling for them."

"Tabitha. You don't know what half the words mean."

"Don't I? That one, there. They got the wrong word, haven't they? What they really meant to write was *****—"

"Tabitha!"

Cindy tried to look shocked. It didn't work because Tabs' mood had lifted. *Thick idiots.* She wore a playful expression and giggled which made her mother laugh, too.

Tabs managed to nibble another bit of toast. "They're real idiots because they done such a thorough job it's stirred up all the boys and girls in blue... who are going to catch them for sure."

"I hope so... How are we going to get all the stuff off the walls?"

"It looks like paint in here. It won't wash off. We're going to have to paint it over."

"That'll mean redecorating." Cindy's mood sank again. "How can we ever afford that? It's in every room."

Tabs had to go to the bathroom. The lewd stuff had been cleaned off but there were still lipstick stains on the paintwork. It smelled all wrong, too. As she sat, the tears welled up from deep down. She mustn't make any noise, though. Perhaps if she took a shower she could have a good cry. But the bath was cluttered with the contents of the bathroom cupboard – bottles of cleaning stuff piled in with toilet rolls and a bar of soap still in its wrapper all lying in a pool of what looked like shampoo – and there were no towels, anyway. So she grabbed a handful of tissue and wept as silently as she could. After a few minutes, she shook herself and washed her face, thoroughly in the basin. No towel. *No stupid towel. No Minnie. No nothing. Perhaps, if I fill my head with the worst swear words I can think of, it will help.* But then she couldn't think of any that didn't sound, like, just ridiculous. They weren't her. But who was she?

"You OK, Tab? You've been in there a long time."

Mum, can't you leave me be just five minutes? "There in't no towel."

"Oh. Hang on."

Cindy rummaged in the washing pile she'd accumulated. "No. I wouldn't use this one. Look, use a pillowcase for now." She pushed open the door and put one into her daughter's outstretched hand.

6

They had just put the kettle on again when there was a tap on the kitchen door. "Mrs Johnson," announced a policeman. "A lady called Mary to see you."

"Come in Mary, you smelled it. Please ignore the artwork."

"Thanks. I could do with a cup of tea." She took in the scene. "It's just appalling. These must have been done by some quite sick individuals." Mary checked out how the graffiti had been applied. She rubbed at it without success. "Some kind of paint. You're going to have to redecorate aren't you?"

Cindy groaned. "Cannot see any alternative. Tabitha thinks everything should be bright yellow."

Mary winked at her. "I have some magnolia. Not much, but enough to paint over the 'artwork'. And then we can get some fresh paint of your choice."

"Thank you. I should tell you that you shouldn't do this but I know what you would say... and that Tab would contradict me. The complete makeover will not be soon, though. They took all the savings I had," sighed Cindy.

"Oh no. Have you lost much?"

"No. Not really. The irreplaceable stuff like rings and things and me savings." Cindy indicated the place where the tin lay open and empty.

"They left your TV?"

"Yes, all wrecked, though. They smashed it against the hearth."

"And they took my Minnie," added Tabitha.

"Minnie?"

"My African doll. She was a present from Dad."

"Was she valuable?"

"Not at all... only to me."

"Oh, Tabitha. What I have got, you can have. I'll fetch the paint and we'll deal with these... erm... "

"Thanks," said Tabitha. "I'm itching to do it. The spelling's driving me bonkers."

175

"Right away, madam," smiled Mary, quickly finished her tea and headed for the door. "I'll be back *tout de suite*."

After she'd gone, Cindy said, "Tabitha, we mustn't take advantage of Mary. She's too good. She's a nice lady, but we can't keep taking from her."

"I know, Mum. But she's kinda lonely. She's having, like, fun... well, sort of. You know what I mean..."

"What's 'fun' got to do with it?"

"Well, not exactly 'fun', but she has a big heart and no one to share it with. That's why she spends so much time in Friends of Africa. It's not that she needs love, but someone to love."

"OK, give up getting deep on me, and let's get ready to slop her paint on, then."

They moved the furniture away from the walls in the sitting room, bedrooms and kitchen, and then began scrubbing in the bathroom. It was not easy, but with the elbow grease, the stuff was beginning to come off the tiles. Eventually, the doorbell rang and Mary came in with paintbrushes and a pile of plastic dust sheets, followed by the constable with a tub of emulsion.

"Right," she sighed. "Let's get started. I see you've got the furniture out of the way."

"Me first," volunteered Tabitha, excitedly.

Mary prised the lid off the paint and stirred it vigorously. Tabitha dipped the biggest brush.

"Gently," urged her mother. But Tabitha was impatient to paint over the obscenities, to reclaim her world. She painted a stroke across the letters. When the brush was empty, she stopped and pondered.

"These people are truly sick."

"Too right," agreed her mother, readily.

"No, I mean. Actually sick. Like, ill. That just felt like I was obliterating them, wiping them out with the graffiti."

"So what's wrong with that? They're a blot on humanity."

"It's just that their minds must be, like, kinda damaged. They like to hate, don't they? They can't be happy."

"They don't deserve to be."

"But what made them like that? Perhaps they never stood a chance."

"I think..." Mary hesitated. "I think some people have a rotten childhood and it is not easy for them. But, in the end, for the most part, they know what's right and wrong and they still have the power to choose and, however hard it is, they don't have to do wicked things."

"No, I s'pose not. But it would never occur to most people to do them. They're, like... well, sick. It's insane. There's no other word for it."

"Maybe that's true," retorted Cindy, "but they'd better darn well go to prison when they're caught. For a long time."

"Yeah. I hope they get them, and soon," agreed, Tabitha, "before they do anything to anyone else."

The graffiti was very soon painted over. The insults were obliterated, but the resulting splotches of magnolia were unsightly; the walls were begging to be painted anew. They invited the constable in for yet another cup of tea. He was admiring their handiwork when the doorbell rang. The policeman answered it, hoping it wouldn't be anyone difficult. He had already repulsed two lots of journalists during the course of the day – he knew Cindy was in no mood for an interview. But it wasn't someone unwelcome.

"It's the vicar," the officer announced. "Can he come in?" Cindy nodded.

"Do come in, Mike," shouted Mary. "I'm afraid you've missed the fun. We've been painting over the bad words."

"Good. By all accounts, the writing on the wall was not pleasant."

"You could say that," stated Cindy. "Cup of tea, vicar? Sorry, we've only got mugs."

"Perfect," he grinned. "To tell you the truth, I am rather thirsty. I've just come from the hospital; three parishioners in Jimmy's in three different wards a quarter of a mile apart. Well, you ladies have been rather through the mill, it seems."

"You can say that, again." replied Cindy. "Milk?"

"Please. No sugar."

"Sweet enough, then?"

"Definitely."

177

Mike was in his forties, fair-haired and clean-shaven. He had been vicar of Millheaton for two years. He had also taken on Thorpe Top which until then had been a separate parish. For the past hundred years, the two parishes had had their own vicars and even a curate. The last curate had left twenty years ago.

"It's really good of you to call," said Cindy. "You have so much to do, these days."

"Oh. I don't do it all like my predecessors. These days we have a very effective pastoral team – which includes Mary, here. And it's not every day that two such nice ladies find themselves in your situation. Besides, I'm here for the tea – same as this handsome policeman you've got."

"Handsome? Tell that to me wife," he chortled before his radio squawked again. "Thanks for the tea ladies. I'd better resume my place guarding the palace."

After the constable had left, Mike asked, "Seriously, is there anything I can do to help?"

"Thanks but I don't think so. It's just cleaning up and we can do that," replied Cindy.

Mike gazed around. "And redecorating, I think. What are the bedrooms like?"

"The same," volunteered Mary. "Kitchen as well. What about the team that decorated the church hall loos? Would they come out and help? I mean, if Cindy and Tabitha are happy about them doing it."

"We could certainly ask them," enthused Mike. "Fred wouldn't mind being asked. He's the kind to say no if he can't."

"What do you say, Cindy? If we got Fred and his team – four men from church just retired – they could do all of this in no time."

"No, I couldn't—"

"Mum, why not? It'd take us ages and we haven't—"

"Have you no dignity, young lady?"

"Mum, dignity doesn't always go with being, like... independent."

"It does. And don't be so impertinent... I must apologise for my daughter; she doesn't understand. We could never repay them – we'd be forever in their debt. And I don't just mean money debt."

"You would not mind if it was professional decorators doing the job?" asked Mary.

"No of course not. But I would be paying them, wouldn't I?"

"But we can't afford—" began Tabitha.

"Tabitha, enough. Of course, we can't... yet. I'm sorry vicar but I just don't think it would be right."

"I do understand, Mrs Johnson. May I call you Cynthia?"

"Cindy. You can call me Cindy."

"Fred wouldn't take it on if he hadn't time or didn't want to. I've not seen him happier than when he and his team were doing up the hall. I'm sure he would not mind being asked... I'm not saying he will, of course, but just being asked to help will be a blessing – for him. Being thought to be useful is a reward in itself."

Cindy remained looking diffident.

"Come on, Mum, say yes," muttered Tabs from behind her hand.

"Well, all right then. But..." Cindy could say no more as tears welled up and flowed.

Tabs just couldn't keep quiet, though. "Mum, you've never had friends, real friends. Not since I can remember. But now it's different. When something bad happens, you find all sorts of people who want to be your friends."

"That's true," agreed Mike. "It happens like that all of the time. Real friendship prospers in adversity."

"How can people give so much – be so generous?" Cindy wondered.

"Because they have received much, Cindy," said Mike. "And if you let Mary and Fred and others look after you and Tabitha, here, and love them for it, you will make them even richer."

"I get that," said Tabs. "It's cool."

"More visitors," announced the constable, putting his head around the door once more. "One Ash-ol and, what did you say your name was?"

"Deng."

Tabs screamed in delight and ran to the door. She and Ashol hugged each other and, then, after a split second of hesitation, she caught up the shy Deng with the same enthusiasm. She felt him encircle her meaningfully with his strong arms. As they pulled apart, their eyes met just for an instant. She conducted them into the sitting room where they shook hands with everyone. Tabs took them off into her bedroom and talked and talked and cried and talked some more. Ashol admired Ted, and Tabitha wept a bit more over her loss of Minnie. Deng vowed to annihilate whoever had done this to her and her mother but she told him they weren't worth it – they were sick, and probably unhappy, not like her, who, at that moment, was with her two favourite people.

"They may be sick, but that doesn't mean they're not dangerous," said Deng with a worried expression.

"They're gonna be caught, aren't they? Besides, until then, with all the boys and girls in blue on the case, they're probably keeping their heads down," reassured Tabs.

"Have they any leads?" Ashol wanted to know.

"Not yet. They think that they're from outside the estate. 'Not typical of Beck Ings'... You know what the graffiti said?"

"No. No one told us."

"No. Guess not. Good."

"Well," asked Ashol, full of curiosity, "what did it say?"

"You're too young and innocent to know," joked Tabitha. Deng continued to look shocked and concerned, so Tabitha went on, "OK. I'll tell you but you have to promise to keep it mum."

"Course."

"It was racial stuff mixed in with vile pictures and stuff like you get inside some public lavs. Most of it was telling me to 'go home', only in not such a polite fashion. Trying to scare us off the estate... And the spelling was, like, awful."

"Go home!" exclaimed Ashol. "Go home where?"

"Africa, I suppose."

"But you're British. You were born here – in Leeds."

"They in't interested in that. I guess they just want to get rid of all black people... and me mum too for being a black lover."

"That's disgusting," spat Ashol.

"What're you going to do?" asked Deng, calmly.

"Do? The vicar knows some people who might help us

redecorate. When we've saved up for the paint. That'll be a start."

"But, I mean, until they're caught?"

"If they dare to come round here again while I'm here, I promise you, they won't leave in one piece. But they wouldn't dare anyway. Look, don't worry about me. OK? Stop looking so worried, Deng, or... or I'll tickle you."

"Great idea," laughed Ashol and jabbed her brother in the side. Deng was very ticklish. He jumped and yelled, "Stop it." Ashol persisted. "Look, lay off." But he was laughing, despite himself.

"Ah. So we have discovered the Achilles heel," said Tabs, joining it. The noise of Deng's molestation quickly extended to the sitting room and the ladies went to see what all the noise was about.

"What on Earth is going on here?" said Cindy, amazed to see a six-foot male curled up into a ball on Tabs' bed under a pile of girls.

"He's being annoying," said Ashol.

"Looks more like he's the one who's being tormented," commented Mary. "Now, if you have finished your horseplay, would you all like to join us at my house for tea this evening?"

"Wicked," said Ashol, leaving her brother to get up off the bed.

"Sorry, Mrs Johnson. My sister's violent."

"So I see."

"Thanks for wanting to look after me," whispered Tabs in Deng's ear, "but I'm OK."

"Honestly?"

"Yeah. Sort of... with you and Ashol..."

That evening, Tabitha was to recall in later years, was great. They all sat toasting crumpets around an open fire. It was colder than on previous days and Mary couldn't resist the temptation to toast the crumpets properly on an open fire. She knew it would delight the teenagers.

At 10 o'clock Mrs Thomas came in her car to take her children home.

"Would you two like to sleep over tomorrow night?" asked

Mary. Deng could sleep in the spare room where Tabitha now is, and Tabitha, you and Ashol can sleep in here. That sofa by the wall converts into a bed. This house has never been full for years. I want it as full as can be."

"That would be lovely," enthused Tabs.

"Well, yes. All right," agreed Mama Sarah. "As long as you help take care of your sister and these ladies properly, Deng." Sarah Thomas was rather old-fashioned, sometimes. Or perhaps it was the lingering South Sudanese patriarchal culture.

"Of course," Deng replied with a serious expression. Despite her passionate belief in gender equality, Tabs didn't feel any resentment. It was nice to be cared for by Deng. She knew he wasn't looking after her just because she was female. He cared about her – as a person.

***

On Sunday, after Mary returned from church, they all went round to No. 49 to prepare everything ready to begin decorating. Mary explained that Fred, Harry and Dave had accepted the invitation to do the redecorating with enthusiasm. Fred had phoned to ask if he could come around and do an assessment of the job. Cindy rang him to say yes but warned him it would be a few weeks before she would have enough put by to get the paint. He announced he would "be there in fifteen."

"Eager," she breathed.

A policeman no longer guarded the door. The inspector had told them they could move back in but, at the first hint of any trouble, they were to call 999. They were no further forward with an arrest, so if they came up with any clues, anything that could help, they were to let him know immediately and he gave them a phone number.

The neighbours now started to arrive. Cindy had decided she must call at No 43 to thank Betty Ackroyd for taking her in but she beat her to it.

"Thanks for looking after me last Thursday, Betty."

"No problem. Are you OK now?" She noticed Deng and Ashol. "These your friends, Tabitha?"

"Yes. These are Tabitha's friends," replied Cindy, and she added to herself, *I know what you're thinking, and don't you dare to talk about race.*

She didn't. "I came to see if you needed any help."

"Thanks, Betty. But I've got people all lined up."

"Got good friends then?"

"Yup." She wasn't going to give her all the low-down.

"So... have they caught them yet?"

"Not yet, but I don't suppose it will be long."

The doorbell rang again. This time it was the press – a young woman in her twenties in a red miniskirt and clutching a tablet. She introduced herself as Sharon Pinkett, from *The Thursday Chronicle*. She had a photographer in tow who was craning his neck, trying to look inside. Cindy thought the time had come to get it over with and this slip of a girl was not so scary. Scanning the room with the furniture neatly piled up and dust sheets at the ready, the photographer's expression was one of disappointment. The pictures from the previous week of the flat surrounded by police would have to do. Pity they wouldn't let him in *then* – but that was usual.

Inside, Cindy hesitated. The room was crowded with the young people sitting on the floor and Mrs Ackroyd occupying the only usable armchair. She scouted around for a stool. "Sorry, Miss... er... let me find you somewhere to sit..."

But before she found a stool from the kitchen, Fred arrived with a handful of paint colour cards. "Come in," said Cindy, glad of the distraction. "You must be Fred."

"I am."

"Come in and join the party. This is Miss... er... from the *Green 'un.*"

Fred proffered his hand.

"Sharon Pinkett. You're Fred...?"

"Sorry," said Cindy again. "It's a bit rather... crowded. What do you want to know, Miss Pinkett?"

"Have—"

But before she could say anything else, Rev. Mike arrived. Betty Ackroyd decided she was not needed and it was time she went.

"Well, I'll be off. Let me know if there is anything else I can do."

"I will," said Cindy. "Thanks."

"I bear an invitation from my wife," announced Rev Mike. "She knows you're upside down and says she will put some soup on for lunch. Ready about 12.30 or whenever it suits you. Hello Deng, Ashol. You're invited too, Fred." Turning to the reporter. "Er... sorry, have we met?"

"Sharon Pinkett, *Thursday Chronicle.*"

"Ah, yes. You were the reporter who wrote the article on the lead that got stolen off the roof of St Paul's, Thorpe Top."

"Have they got anyone for it?"

"Not yet. So you're here about the Johnson's sad business?"

"Yes. Mrs Johnson, just a few details, if I may. It's Cynthia Johnson, 49 Ings View?"

"Cindy."

"Cindy," she wrote, "... and, er... and how old shall we tell the readers you are?"

"Why? Why do they need to know?"

"It's a convention. It helps when people want to research the history of a place in the future."

"And would they get an accurate record from your newspaper?" asked Tabs, who had been learning in history about the Second World War German propaganda machine at the same time as being warned in PSHE of the misinformation to be had on social media. So where did the *Green 'Un* rate?

"Well, we do our best. So you are..."

"Tabitha, and I'm nearly sixteen and Mum's thirty-eight."

"Fifteen." corrected her mother. "Can't have the *Green 'Un* publishing untruths."

"And who else have we got?"

"Friends, lots of them," replied Cindy.

"But it's just you and your daughter who live here?"

"Yes. Look, where's all this leading?"

"Just making sure we have everything correct. So would you like to make a statement about what happened?"

"Just say we were broken into and they did some damage but lots of people have come to help."

"Fine. Have the police any idea why they broke in?"

"To nick things."

"What did they take?"

"Some old jewellery. Mostly of sentimental value."

"And Minnie, my doll," added Tabs.

"I'm sorry. That's sad," but she was keen to get to the juicy bit. "I heard they did other damage as well?"

"I think you have all you need on that, Miss Pinkett," broke in the vicar. "The police will tell you what you can report on that."

"Thank you, vicar," replied Miss Pinkett, trying not to sound peeved.

"So, are they near to catching anybody?"

"Another question for the police," said Mike, calmly.

The photographer started to get restless. "Er... can I have a picture of you?"

"Why not?" said Cindy, glad to avoid any more questions. "Me and Tabitha and all my friends. And Miss... er... you write that we have real friends and we're not going anywhere."

"Better delete that last bit," interjected Rev. Mike. "OK, get your photo. We've work to do, haven't we, Fred?"

The photographer arranged everyone around Cindy and Tabitha with the vicar and Fred propping up each end like bookends. He took two photos and then asked everyone's name for the caption.

"Do you want all our ages, asked Ashol?"

"No. Pictures speak for themselves," he smiled and showed a picture of the sitting room crowded with smiling people – friends together who obscured the scars of where the graffiti had been.

Tabitha chose bright lemon yellow for her bedroom, but Cindy was happy with the same colours that she had had for the past ten years – only perhaps a bit lighter.

"But I'm afraid I can't pay you for it yet," protested Cindy.

"Ah, yes," said Mike, "I forgot." He pulled out an envelope. "There's £205, fifteen euros and twenty American dollars in there. From well-wishers."

"Dollars!" reacted Tabs, "from the CIA?"

Mike laughed. "No. A family in the congregation have some

Californian connections. Maybe from them. As for the euros, I've no idea. Left over from someone's holiday, I guess."

"But. I can't," spluttered Cindy.

"I can't give it back. It's anonymous. A lot of different people..."

"However will I thank them all?"

"That's easy. Just look happy in a clean, fresh, flat. Shall I give it to Fred?"

"That'll about cover it," said Fred.

7

On the Monday morning, Fred, Harry and Dave arrived on schedule, having bought all the paint and stuff on the way. They started washing down the walls in the kitchen and were soon into the bedrooms. Before lunchtime, they had chased Cindy out of the sitting room and she went off to the shops, where she pretended nothing was any different from normal, and returned with a feast for them; they had brought sandwiches but Cindy was hearing no excuses. By the middle of the afternoon, the first coat was on the kitchen walls and Fred was undercoating the woodwork around the windows.

"I thought you were just painting the walls?" exclaimed Cindy.

"No sense in doing half a job."

Meanwhile, Tabs had ventured back to school. Ashol and Danielle glued themselves to her at every break time on that Monday. Kids were kind. Some asked questions but Tabs just said things such as, "It's all, like, in the papers in't it?" and "No. We don't know who done it. Do you? Have you heard sommut?" Nobody had, of course. *Maybe someone knows*, thought Tabs, *but they're not going to split on them to me.*

Mr Frost and Miss Wright were especially attentive. The head of year asked her if she had all she needed.

"Can I stay behind and use the library computer after school to do my assignments? I can't do the stuff that I need a computer for at home. Mine got broke."

"Of course, you can," she said. "I'm glad you are wanting to get on with studying. From what Mr Frost told me, it appears you have rather been through it."

"He said he wouldn't let on," protested Tabs, feeling betrayed.

"Oh. Mr Frost hasn't told me anything other than that when you came back, you may be suffering from a bit of PTSD. All your details are safe with him."

Tabs felt relieved and then bad about doubting him. "It's OK.

I'm OK... I'm not distracted that easily," she insisted.

Tabs got home after five. She had done the stuff which required the computer but then more that didn't need a computer, too. She also found herself looking up things in the library, which was brilliant but took up time. She wanted it to. She wanted to think about anything else other than the horrors of the past few days. Plus, she wanted to make sure everyone else had left before she went out into the estate. She didn't want Ashol or Danielle, or Deng, to walk her home – they lived in the opposite direction, after all. And it wasn't that far. It was coming dark when she, at last, got in. The flat stank of emulsion. The blood-soaked carpet had been removed and replaced by a couple of old rugs.

Her mum was anxious. "Where have you been?"

"Doing stuff in the library. Needed a computer." Her mum caught her up in her arms.

"Fred and the other's gone?"

"Just. Five minutes ago. Look we can't stay here. The only room that isn't upside down is the bathroom. Mary's called and we are to go round to hers and spend another night with her. I didn't argue. No point, is there?"

"No, Mum. Being in her warm comfy house is like, well, restful. What I need right now."

"How was it at school?"

"Good. Ashol and Danielle looked after me. By lunchtime, most people were bored with the news and in the afternoon things were, like, more normal. Some kids were a bit scared that something like this could happen on Beck Ings but I told 'em that if someone wanted to give us free pork for a year, we weren't, like, going to argue. Made 'em laugh."

***

Tabs and her mum ended up spending the rest of the week at the Old Lodge. Fred and his chums were having a great time and were delighted to have Cindy come and make them some lunch each day but happy they could leave everything overnight. They said they expected to be finished by Friday.

At school, Tabs was grateful she had had her flash drive in her bag when her bedroom had been ransacked. At least she hadn't lost her work; Mr Frost's mantra of "back it up and when you've backed it up, back up the back up" had proved a good one. She had her long essay to be handed in before the Easter break.

By the following weekend, all was finished. On the Saturday, Cindy and Tabitha held a little party to say thank you. Fred, Harry and Dave brought their wives and Rose, the vicar's wife came with Mary. The Thomases all turned up too, and so did Mrs Ackroyd, but DI Gillespie declined the invitation. "Perhaps after we've got them," he said. Rev Mike came in at the end; he'd been busy arranging a christening. When everyone was leaving, he took Cindy aside and thrust another envelope into her hand. "More gifts," he said, "it keeps coming." Cindy open her mouth to speak, but Mike just put his finger to his lips and turned his attention to Tabitha.

"So, how's it been at school?" he asked.

"Getting back to normal. Jack has reminded everyone about the long essay he expects in two weeks' time, so everyone – everyone who cares – is all worked up about it."

"And you are among those who care?"

"Yeah. I am this year."

"Good. Who's Jack?"

"Oh sorry. Mr Frost. Like, 'Jack Frost'," Tabitha explained.

"Ah yes, Mr Frost. Thought his name was Charlie?"

"Ye-ah," she went with a raised inflexion. Like, the vicar didn't get it?

"Oh." The penny dropped. "Got it. Jack Frost. Should have guessed. Brain not working – must be the cold, freezing," he joked.

"Urghh," groaned Tabitha.

Mike laughed. "I'm off. Bye Cindy, bye everyone."

"Last to arrive, first to leave," said Mary.

"Must have another important visit to make," said Cindy.

"No. Boat Race," explained Rose. "He's a Cambridge fan."

After everyone had gone, Cindy pulled out the envelope. *He was making a getaway so I couldn't say anything. It weren't just the Boat Race,* she thought. They counted out the notes, it came to £245. Plus they had got fifteen pounds change from the decorating.

"So, we've 60 pounds more cash than before the break-in, and have a newly painted flat," said Cindy. "I can't believe it."

"If you don't count the jewellery, the telly or my laptop," said Tabitha... *or Minnie,* she added to herself but then she wasn't worth money.

"You haven't seen what Dave's wife brought, yet" said Cindy, "Go and look in the kitchen. It's not new but she said she didn't use it any more and would you like it? I said you would be delighted."

Tabitha dived into the kitchen and there on the side was a small red laptop in a plastic bag. She squealed in delight. She pulled it out, placed it on the side and plugged in the lead. It lit up.

"It works, Mum."

"I don't understand. What have we done to deserve all this? I just don't know what to make of it."

"I know what we can do with the money, Mum. Get a new telly."

"But I was saving it for your education."

"Don't worry about that Mum. £200 won't go anywhere. It costs thousands and thousands. You have to borrow it. Every student does."

"How do you begin to pay it all back? That frightens me."

"When you get a job. A bit at a time. You get a good job and earn more than you would if you hadn't been to college, so you can afford it... But that's only if you go to college. There are other ways to get a good job. Look, let's get a telly. You like to watch the news and stuff and Corrie."

"Corrie. I've had enough drama in my own home to last a lifetime. I don't need to import others', even if it's just all made up. No, Tabitha. I know what I'm going to do. I'm going to give some of it back."

"But you can't, Mum. People will get upset."

190

"No. I mean not back to them. I'm going to give ten per cent to Friends of Africa. What's that work out at?"

Tabs wrote it down. 245 plus fifteen made 260. She thought about how you got percentages – divide it by a hundred, then multiply it by what percentage you wanted. "Twenty-six pounds," she said. That sounds right, she thought.

"Right. I'll give twenty-six pounds to Mary. Then I'm going to get some insurance. And the rest will be for you when you're eighteen. No arguments. Now go and put the kettle on."

Tabitha knew her Mum was right. They could watch the TV on her new laptop if they wanted. When she started earning, *she* would buy her Mum a new telly, a really good one.

***

That coming Sunday, Tabitha and Cindy, Ashol and Deng went with Mary to church. The young people had not gone to sleep early but they had slept well when they did. There were too many of them for the car and they decided to walk; it was a bright spring day.

After the service, Rev Mike dashed off to St Paul's, Thorpe Top, while Cindy and Tabitha were surrounded by people all commiserating with them and hoping that things would soon get better for them. Tabitha chatted with some of the young people she had met at Christmas. Charlie, like Danielle, was a server, which meant putting on white robes. Tabs thought he was on the quiet side and wondered how he felt about dressing up in front of everyone. It didn't bother him in the church, he said.

"Got caught on film last Remembrance Sunday, though," he informed them, "and found myself in a picture on the front page of the *Green 'Un* next to the vicar. Suffered for that at school that week."

Tabitha pulled a face. She could just imagine it. "Why are people so cruel?"

Danielle spotted Tabitha with the Thomases and came over. "Hi. What gives? What smells?" she asked, looking at Tabitha's grimace.

Charlie explained.

191

"It's always been like that," she shrugged. "My dad said it was the same when he was at school. Some of them think we reckon we're better than them. Holy and all that."

Tabitha reacted: "But you're not!" Danielle laughed.

"I... I... er... I don't mean... er..."

"I'd stop while you're ahead."

"I mean, you don't go around saying that, do you?"

"Nah," said Charlie. "But it's not what you say, is it? They just think we're different, I suppose."

"Yeah, I guess." Tabs was fully aware of the implications of being different. "Does that bother you?"

"Sometimes," said Danielle. "It can get a pain at times. You know more than anyone what it's like... But I wouldn't want to be like them anyway, so I just brave it out. I'm sorry about what happened to you, Tabs. I mean they even tore your skirt. How sick is that?"

"Yeah, sick," agreed Tabitha.

"Why do people *do* that?" despaired Danielle.

"Mum says that some people are just that way out. They're just made that way."

"I don't believe that," said Charlie. "Like, God didn't create them to be like that, did he?"

"I reckon maybe they're kind of jealous," suggested Danielle.

"How do you make that out?" asked Tabitha.

"Well, like we're happy most of the time. Adults like us. We seem to have things they don't. We don't try too hard to blend in – try to conform. All sorts of things."

When everyone had finished their after-church coffee and biscuits – in Tabs' case, just the biscuits – she and her mother went to Sunday dinner at the Thomases.

They were all crowded around Sarah's dining room table – it had been extended by the addition of a second table from the sitting room – when Mr Thomas called for attention. "Before we eat, I have an announcement to make. I'm pleased you are here, Cindy and Tabitha. I have some news to tell you. I'm finishing my job with the council in June and going out to live in Juba."

Tabitha looked up, stunned. "But what about Ashol and

Deng?" she blurted. Her mother grabbed her arm. Why did her daughter have to speak up so quickly, especially when it wasn't her place?

"They will stay here," continued Garang. "At least for another year with their mother. I'm going out to get a job and find somewhere to live. I want to be in my country to help it grow. Then, when all is settled, my family can join me in their native land."

Despite her mother's tight grip on her arm, Tabs was undeterred. "But who's going to look after your family while you're away?" She just couldn't imagine Mr and Mrs Thomas being apart. It didn't seem right. Ashol and Deng needed a father, too; she knew what it was like not having one around.

Mr Thomas was a little taken aback. His own children would not be so outspoken; it was unseemly to argue with your elders but he answered her, nevertheless. "Deng is old enough to take care of his mother and sister. And Mama has got a job in the old people's care home. They won't be rich, but they will manage. When I get settled out in Juba, I shall be earning a good salary. And when Deng has finished his A levels, we can see where he will go to university. Maybe in this country, maybe in Africa."

Tabitha felt herself getting upset – even angry. How could he go off and leave them? And then dispatch Deng off to some medical college thousands of miles away and send for Ashol to be with him. And what about *her* education? And they had gotten so close and now this family were going to split up and go off in different directions and leave her. It all seemed so sudden. It hurt. She said no more.

During the meal, Mr Thomas went on to explain the politics and the situation in Juba and the rest of the country. He was clearly excited by the prospect of returning to his homeland.

The meal over, Tabs and Ashol went to her bedroom. Ashol read the sadness in Tabitha and said, "You have to understand. My dad and my mum, they don't feel they should be here. They ran away – had to leave their families, their friends... never said goodbye. They're lucky still to be together at all. Most of us South Sudanese are scattered. We have family in Juba, Nairobi, Kampala, Khartoum, Port Sudan, America, Australia and even Norway –

Mum has just found a cousin in Oslo. We don't know who is still alive and who isn't. When they left they always meant to go back. Imagine an army coming through Millheaton, planes shooting at you from the air and dropping bombs, soldiers that beat you up, and rape you, and kill you. You just have to run. Dad saw what was happening and he and Mum gathered up Deng and ran. They were lucky. They got to Kenya and I was born there. I've never seen my grandparents and Mum and Dad haven't seen them since then, either. Dad's father died five years ago. We know that his Mum is sick. He has to go, even if only to see her."

"I... I just didn't understand. Sorry if I was rude. It just... your family is, like, dependable. You love each other so much." Her eyes filled up and then overflowed. Tear-stained, she murmured, "Someone tried to wreck our home and I thought that was bad enough. But we'll be back in it tonight. And nobody died or got hurt. They nicked Minnie but losing you would be like... You're the best friends I ever had. Yours is a different world to ours."

"I get that, Tabs. But in South Sudan families are much bigger than just four people. There'd be none with just two like you. Nobody in England truly understands what it's like when people have to run away as Mum and Dad did. Not even me." She hugged her friend. "But Dad's happier today than he has been for ages. And so is Mum, a bit. She doesn't want to let him go, but it'll only be for a year. You know what finally decided it? Mum had been saying how Juba wasn't safe and Millheaton was. Then you got raided. So Dad said that nowhere was safe, really, was it? If they didn't like you being black, being British with your Yorkshire accent and everything, what about us? This gang could come to us next."

"Not if the police get them."

"No, but you know what he means. You can't do anything if you're not prepared to take risks. He keeps saying, '*The person who risks nothing, does nothing, has nothing, is nothing, becomes nothing. Only the person who risks is truly free.*'

"Wow. So, like, if you don't ever dare face up to things, you'll never do or be anything, and always have other people decide things for you."

"Exactly. So you see, he's got to go."

"And you too, and Deng, when the time comes?"

"When the time comes... Look, Tabs, I know you like Deng but don't give him your heart. All he wants to do is study medicine and go to South Sudan. He won't give that up for anything."

"I know. Don't worry... And all *I* have to do is find out what *I* should be. Who *I* am."

"Me too. But no doubt we'll find out soon enough."

"I guess so."

8

Mothering Sunday was late that year. Tabitha was determined to make up for the years she'd not done anything special for her mum. She bought her a box of chocolates and a card. At church, all the children were called out to get bunches of daffodils to give their mothers, even adults who had mothers, so Tabitha went out for Cindy.

They went home happy. Cindy found a jar to put the daffodils from church in. They kind of made up for the ones destroyed in the raid. Then they made a Sunday lunch which, although it may not have been as gorgeous as Mary's, was great because they were home again. Normal was good.

As the sun set that evening, they drew the curtains and Cindy settled down in the sitting room by the fire with a book while Tabitha set about backing up her essay onto her flash drive in the bedroom. She had her phone plugged into her ear thumping out her favourite songs.

Through the beat of the music, Tabitha gradually became aware of her mother shouting at someone. She was in the act of getting off the bed when, "Wham!" A large man, his face covered in some kind of mask, burst into her room and grabbed her up by the arm. As he pulled her off the bed, he put a gloved hand over her mouth. The computer slid onto the floor with a thump. It all happened so quickly that she just froze in shock. He stank of a revolting combination of tobacco smoke, alcohol and putrid sweat amid a plethora of other rancid odours. She fought to free herself using as much foul language as she knew but the monster was strong and he swung her around and grabbing her other arm, pulled it behind her back. She squealed in pain. It felt that her arm was about to break away from her shoulder. With both her arms behind her back and yelling oaths, the masked monster pushed and half carried her roughly into the sitting room and threw her at the wall. Her forehead struck the plaster and the assailant held it there while another man stuck some kind of tape over her mouth and then, with his knee against her bottom

196

forcing her into the wall, he bound her wrists with the same stuff.

Inside her head, Tabitha seethed. She fought with all her strength but she was no match for the huge man who thrust her face hard against the new paint. The smell of it mixed with the monster's into a putrid stink. Tabs' arms and face were pinned but her legs were still free and she back-heeled her assailant as hard as she could. She connected with his shin, but to no avail. She hadn't her shoes on, and even a well-aimed kick made no impression on a trousered leg. She couldn't even spit, let alone bite or shout. Then the man turned her and forced her down to sit on the floor. She saw her mother also in the process of being gagged by a similarly dressed man. Tabitha counted four of them.

Then one of them spoke in a gruff voice.

"You was WARNED. *We* don't like to be ignored. If you don't take a gentle 'int, then take a big one. YOU IN'T WELCOME HERE. Get the message? Buzz off 'ome. Wherever that is, it in't 'ere. If you don't, NEXT TIME you won't be needing any f***ing flat. Get it?" And he emphasised his point by smashing the crowbar he was holding through the kitchen door. Tabs flinched. He nodded to his gang. "OK. Let's show 'em we mean business."

While the leader proceeded to trash the sitting room with his crowbar, Tabitha and her mum could hear the others in the other rooms. "Don't be so bleedin' gentle," growled one. "Do a proper job. That's what you're 'ere for, in't it?" Tabs heard a noise from her bedroom.

After what seemed like an eternity but which couldn't have been more than a few minutes, the men reassembled in the sitting room. "Don't forget," the leader menaced, "if yer don't want to see us again...." He brandished his crowbar in Cindy's face.

As he moved forward, Tabitha noticed one of the thugs properly for the first time. He had been partly hidden behind the others before. She instantly recognised him. He was masked too, of course, but she had known him for so long that even the way he held his shoulders gave him away. Gross Griff Green. There was no mistaking him. She glared into his ugly grey eyes with as much venom as she could muster. But what she saw there was pain, and deep sadness. Was he pleading with her? Without wanting to, Tabs' defiant stare softened into one of 'why?' He knew she knew who he was and he made no attempt to hide himself. In the midst of *her* pain, Tabitha was arrested by *his*. He was crying out for help. The anguish in those desperate eyes hit her with force. In stark contrast, the clear exhilaration of the gang leader rippled through his body. But, for Tabitha, all this noise and vitriol receded in the realisation of the depths of Griff's misery. It was only an instant, then he looked down, in stark contrast to the others fired up with adrenalin and untamed energy. He was not party to this – not really. Tabs was sure of that. And then, almost as suddenly as they had come, they left.

The silence that followed after their van roared off around the corner was almost deafening. Tabitha and Cindy began to struggle against their bonds but they hadn't made much progress before, in less than two minutes, the silence was again shattered. This time by the police arriving, sirens blaring, pulling up with a squeal of brakes.

The policemen managed to get in just ahead of Betty Ackroyd. As they took in the scene, the older of the two went up to the mother and daughter while the other guarded the door.

"Thank you, Madam, we'll look after this," the guard said, making sure Betty didn't manage to get even a peak in.

"Nah then," said the older officer, in a broad friendly Yorkshire voice. "We're in a bit of a pickle 'ere en't we? Bit of a to-do. Mind if I begin with getting the young lady free first, madam?" he asked. "Her bit of sticky is a bit easier than yours. Now, this could hurt a bit," he smiled. And before Tabitha could take it in, he had ripped the tape off her mouth in a single jerk.

"Ow." she yelped.

"Sorry, miss. It's all off. A tiny bit of blood but no lasting damage."

Tabitha mumbled, "Grabbed my face before they put the stuff on."

"How long they been gone?" he asked.

"Not long. A couple of minutes. No more."

"Pity we were not here quicker. I should like to have caught them red-handed."

"In't the first time. They've been before. Inspector Gillespie—

"

"Is on his way. Now then, Mrs. Sorry, this one is going to be a bit more tricky..."

"Ambulance has arrived," stated his partner from the door.

"Good. Send them in." Two paramedics lugging large green bags stepped smartly in, not quite knowing what to expect but finding two conscious but frightened individuals, got to work.

"Anyone else?" asked one of the paramedics indicating the door into the rest of the flat.

"No," breathed Tabitha. "Just us."

"Good. We'll soon get you free, lady. Don't worry. Just relax," she said, seeing Cindy's panicked look. She got out a pair of scissors and she and her colleague made short work of Cindy's gag and the rest of the tape binding both their hands.

"Any damage?" she asked. "Can you walk?"

"Yep," said Tabitha, taking her Mum in her arms. "Just a bit sore... Did they hit you, Mum?"

"No, not exactly," she breathed.

The policeman now turned his attention to the crime scene.

"Can you get these ladies into your ambulance?" he asked. "I want to make sure we can preserve as much as possible for forensics."

Mother and daughter, accompanied by the paramedics, walked out to the ambulance. Once again the neighbours had gathered, several deep this time.

"I en't goin' to no hospital," protested Cindy. "There's nowt wrong with me that needs A&E."

The kind paramedic said she understood. They'd see. She asked if they had any other injuries. Tabitha told her her arm was sore. They carefully examined her head and then each limb in turn, manipulating them. It seemed nothing was broken or dislocated but they diagnosed a possible torn muscle and the bruising was already coming out. Tabs felt more delicate than she thought she was – up until now, she hadn't thought of herself as so fragile. The paramedic wrapped her up against shock and sat her down.

"I can't find anything serious but I dare say you will be quite sore and the bruises might come out rather blue for a day or two. But you'll soon mend. They... er," she whispered, "didn't take any, er... personal liberties?"

"No," she said.

"Wounded your dignity, though?"

"Dignity? It was so sudden. They enjoyed smashing stuff the most."

"They seem to have done a thorough job of that," said the other paramedic.

One of the policemen popped his head around the door and asked if they were going on to the hospital. "I'm not sure that that is going to be necessary but we do need to counteract the shock. They need hot sweet tea and blankets. Have you got your phones, with you ladies?" Tabs felt her pocket – it was still there and she drew it out. "To help with the long-term trauma," explained the paramedic, "it might help to play a game on it. Tetris, perhaps? Have you got that?"

"Tetris? What's that?" Cindy looked confused – even distressed.

"I have," replied Tabs. "I get it. Good for calming things down inside my head."

"Exactly. I'll play you a game, Mum."

"You won't. That's the last thing I want. Electronic games? Whatever are we coming to? Addles the brain, I reckon, at the best of times."

The paramedic ignored Cindy's protestations and affirmed Tabs' willingness. "But I guess you're going to have to do something else for the minute," she added. "Here's a plain clothes police officer."

"Hello, ladies. Can I come in?" It was Inspector Gillespie.

"Not too long," said the paramedic, protectively. "They are still in shock."

"I'm sorry, ladies," he said. "I was afraid this might happen. But we'll get 'em," he said defiantly. "You saw them?"

"They were masked," replied Cindy. "Big men, all of them. Only two on 'em spoke and they were definitely from Yorkshire. The leader said the same things that were on the walls. Warned us to leave the estate or we wouldn't need no 'ome."

"How many?"

"Four."

"Anything else you want to tell me that I can't see for myself?"

"The one that grabbed me stank of baccy, booze and I dunno, it might have been some kinda weed – apart from the fact that he hadn't had a bath for a year." He took a note.

"Anything else?"

Cindy grunted and Tabs shook her head and looked down.

"Fine. I'll get the details later. I hope you don't mind. I've sent for Mary Macey. You can't stay here and I guess you'd be happier with her than hospital."

"Thanks," groaned Tabs.

The DI nodded and stepped down from the ambulance. They heard him addressing the crowd.

"OK, everyone. The show's over. The ladies are fine. Nothing to concern yourselves about, unless anyone saw who it was who broke in?"

One or two shouted out that they had seen the van.

"It was me that rung yer," said one, "I seen it looked like the same van as before."

"Good work. Thank you. Did anyone get the registration?" There was silence. "Never mind. Give your name and address to my colleague here and he will arrange for you to make a statement."

"There was loads on 'em," shouted one girl, "I seen 'em. They was dressed in blue boilersuits with black balaclavas like in the army with just their eyes peeping out."

"Thank you. Speak to DC Biggins here, please. Now may I suggest, unless you have anything to share, you all move away. Come on now. If you have something to say, names and addresses to my officer, otherwise go home and make yourselves a pot of tea."

"Never seen so many people in our street," mumbled Cindy.

"It's like that all the time if you are a celebrity. But worse 'cause of the paparazzi," said Tabs.

"I don't care to be no celebrity," sobbed Cindy.

"OK, Mum. It'll be OK." Remarkably, Tabitha found herself

coming to terms with what had happened. Now she knew from where the evil had sprung, it made it far less threatening. But what stayed with her, more than anything, was the pain she saw in Griff's eyes. She'd never seen that before.

As the crowd was dispersing, Mary drove up and was ushered into the ambulance. She found Tabitha showing her mother how to play Tetris under the watchful eye of the paramedic.

A few minutes later, she got out of the ambulance and into her car and followed the ambulance to the hospital. The paramedics had insisted that they be checked out.

A few hours later, they emerged feeling reassured that there was no long-term physical harm. Paracetamol and sleeping pills in hand, Mary drove them back to Old Lodge

No one went to bed that night and two policemen stood guard until sunrise.

At half past ten Inspector Gillespie turned up. They told him what had happened in as much detail as they could. But, Tabitha, to her own amazement, could not mention Griff. He had not wanted to be there, she told herself. How he came to be involved she had no idea but she was sure he had not wanted to be part of it.

At lunchtime, Cindy and Tabitha went to bed, partly out of sheer exhaustion, and partly because of the medication, which was, at last, kicking in.

Harriett Spinks came and sat with Mary but neither of them knew what best to say. After a while, Harriett broke the silence.

"It's evil, isn't it? Where's God when you want him? That's what I want to know."

"With us," answered Mary. "I don't doubt it. But if you're asking why all this—"

"No. I know. No one knows why. Perhaps there is not a why at all."

"But whatever anyone says, I don't think it's God's fault. Not unless you blame him for creating us humans in the first place. He knows it's not perfect, that's why he goes round healing everywhere... but, I have to admit, sometimes you can't help feeling he's fighting a losing battle."

"Don't say that, Mary. In the end, he'll win. But when he does it will be the end, the end of creation as we know it. And we've no idea when that will be."

"A new Heaven and a new Earth."

"And in the meantime—"

"He says, 'I am with you always, to the end of time.' The last words of Jesus in Matthew's Gospel."

As Cindy and Tabitha slept their fitful sleep, Mary and Harriett prayed together. What anyone was going to do next, they had no idea.

9

Two days later the door knocker banged authoritatively – the person outside had a distinct purpose. Mary got up and left the sitting room where they were gathered drinking tea out of her china cups. It was Inspector Gillespie.

"Come in, Inspector. Tea?"

He beamed, ignoring the question, "I have news of an arrest."

"Come in, come in." Mary ushered him through to the sitting room. "It's Inspector Gillespie with some good news. Do sit down." Mary directed him to an upholstered chair. "Some tea?" Mary and tea were determined to be inseparable.

"Er, thank you. I will. If it's no trouble?" It would take her into the kitchen and make his job easier.

"I'll refresh the pot. I could do with another myself." Mary put the matching china pot on the hostess trolley and pushed it out of the room.

"I have something for you, Tabitha." The inspector drew a black doll in a plastic bag from his briefcase. "I believe this may be yours."

"Minnie!" exclaimed Tabitha with real delight. She jumped up to take her. She reached to get her out of the bag and cuddle her but the inspector shook his head.

"Later. She's evidence for now. Thank you for identifying her." He returned her to his case. "I'm afraid you'll have to wait until after the trial to get her back. She's important evidence; you reported this doll as one of the items missing from your bedroom."

"Where did you find her?"

"We found her, together with a black balaclava, in a drawer at the home of one of your erstwhile school chums."

"Oh, not Gross?" blurted Tabitha, without thinking.

Cindy was confused. "Who? What?"

"'Gross' being your daughter's pet name for Gareth Green," explained the inspector. "If I might ask, Tabitha, how did you know she might be there?"

A balaclava. Tabitha recalled the look in Griff's frightened grey eyes on that terrifying evening. And then what Tabitha heard herself saying was almost as much of a surprise to her as it was to the other people in the room.

"I know Minnie was on the list of the missing items but now I remember how Griff got her. I had taken her to school as part of a project I was doing and he grabbed her and made me chase him for her. He wouldn't give her back. I had decided to go round his house when his mum was there and get her back. Mrs Green – she's a nice lady really. But then before I could do it, Griff – I mean Gareth – and his mother disappeared. The word was that he had gone forever, off to some correctional place. I was so relieved... but I couldn't get Minnie... then I must have forgot."

"Now let's get this right, Tabitha. You're now telling me that she was *not* stolen from your house in the first raid."

"No, she was not stolen then. He got her earlier." Why was she saying this? Why was she lying to protect Gross Griff? She knew he must have taken her on that first raid. She knew he was there on the second occasion – and she had not told anyone she knew. Why? Griff had given her years of hell which had not let up but rather got worse. He and his gang had spoiled a lot of her happiness as a child. And it must have been him who had led that gang to her house. He had not only nicked Minnie but had invaded her very bedroom and gone through all her private personal drawers, not once but twice. That made her cringe, and her anger rose in her breast. Why should she not want him to be charged and sentenced for this? Was it only because of the look in those ugly grey eyes? Why had he looked at her like that? Was it that he knew he was going to get caught and so had tried to make her do exactly what she was doing now? Was this just an extension of his manipulation? Tabitha felt trapped. She had already kept back vital information from the police for days. If she changed her mind now and said what she knew, she wondered whether that meant she could be charged with – what was it in the TV dramas? – 'obstructing the police in their inquiries,' or some sort of thing. Panic rose within her; she fought to control it. *Should I say something? How much? Everything? But I'm sure Griff has got in deeper than he had intended. He might have started it but he's no longer in control of the evil, is he? I'm sure his look was a*

real genuine plea for help. And from now on, all he needs is a fresh start.
This might be when he eventually begins to change...

Everyone seemed to be waiting on her to say more. The DI
was looking almost angry. Was he? He had achieved a result only
to be told that part of his evidence was no longer evidence? He
had a right to be disappointed, perhaps even angry.

"Er," Tabitha faltered, "... was there anything else in his
house that belonged to us?" she asked, eventually.

"Not that we have found. It isn't usual for thieves to take stuff
home – especially if they have mothers who don't approve of
their actions. Most of the stuff would have been fenced
immediately, I expect. You're lucky to get Minnie back. But, as
you say, she may not have been part of the loot. But I think it is
fair to assume," he continued, "that we are pretty sure Green is
involved in this somewhere. He knows too much. We pulled him
in because we knew of the problems you have had with him in the
past, and the sort of thing that happened to you has to have had a
local connection. Someone local wanted this to happen, I'm sure
of that. It is very unlikely to have been initiated by strangers,
even if strangers carried it out. It has been too precisely
targeted."

"The men all wore balaclavas and it was impossible to see
them properly," recalled Cindy. "But just now you say Green had
a black balaclava, too? There's your evidence."

"Yes, indeed. But, sadly, it isn't sufficient evidence to put him
at the scene by itself."

"Lots of us have balaclavas in our year," broke in Tabitha,
suddenly. "I got one. We did an outward-bound week and it was
on our kit list. Not that we ever used them."

"Yes, I remember that," recalled her mum, "but, if I
remember correctly, you were relieved that Gareth didn't go on
the trip."

"No, he didn't go. Miss Dukes banned him because of bad
behaviour in class. But he was going to go. He could have begun
getting the kit. And, anyway, he could have got it from nearly
anyone in our year. Not from me, though. I ditched mine ages,
ago."

"So, you're telling me that if I searched the rooms of all your classmates, I might come up with a dozen or more with balaclavas stashed away in their drawers?"

"More like twenty-four than twelve," stated Tabitha.

"It seems we will have to do a lot more if we are to implicate Green, then. I know I have asked this before many times, but can you call to mind anyone else who would want to do this to you?"

"I have been getting a lot of stick recently for being black. Especially since I became friends with Ashol and Deng."

"You didn't tell me it like that," said her mother.

"No point talking about it, were there? Wouldn't change anything, would it? And going to church has made things worse because some of the girls think I have decided that I am, like, holier than they are."

"I can understand that. Being black, or the daughter of a black man and going to church makes you out as doubly different," volunteered the inspector. "But that's not what you told me when I asked that before. I must confess that your statements today are rather confusing. Who in particular has been a problem?"

Tabitha stiffened. "Well, no one person in particular. It's just there. I can't help it if I am different. I don't care. Even if people do horrible things to you, it's them that have the problem."

"Well said." exclaimed Mary, pushing her trolley into the room. "She's a tough young lady this one. Do you take sugar inspector?"

"I can see that... er, yes please, just one. What horrible things, Tabitha?"

"Just their general attitude. I mean people – everyone – kind of turns their back."

The DI sighed. "I'm afraid I'm going to be leaving with fewer leads than I came with. I thought we were onto something. You know," he added, gravely, looking Tabitha straight in the eye, "it isn't the likes of Green that I am most worried about. If he is implicated in this, he is merely the apprentice. The thugs that committed this crime need to be apprehended, not only for your safety but everyone else's."

Tabitha examined her feet, avoiding the eyes of everyone which must be fixed on her. Mary broke the silence. "You are absolutely right inspector. Biscuit?" And soon she was talking about how difficult it must be for the police force when threatened with funding cuts, how wonderful the specials were to do their job for nothing and finished by congratulating the British detectives, saying they were the best in the world – especially when you saw how they went on in America if the Hollywood films were anything to go by.

The tea drunk, the inspector left with a stern face that broke into a slight smile when he saw Tabitha eyeing his briefcase.

"Well, at least we got your doll back for you."

"Can I—?"

"No. Sorry. She might still be important for now. I'll make sure she's kept safe."

"OK. Thanks. And tell Gross, I mean Griff... I mean Gareth when you see him that it is lucky for him I remembered when he took her."

"I will, indeed, you can be sure of that. Oh... and, er... I am asking the Victims' Support Officer to call if that's all right?"

"If you think—" began Cindy.

"I do," he affirmed in a voice that brooked no argument.

"Well, fine then."

"Good. Thank you for the tea, Miss Macey. I will be back in touch."

When he had gone Mary sat down and poured herself yet another cup of tea. They sat in silence for a minute or two ."I am glad you have your doll back safe," said Mary. "Why are you protecting Gareth?" Tabitha blushed.

"Protecting Griff. Why should I do that?"

"That's what I was asking myself. It was clear to me that you were telling the inspector porkies, and almost certainly to him too. You can't lie to the police you know. They have a sixth sense for untruths. Within the hour, he will be asking Griff how he came to have your Minnie in his room, and it is highly unlikely that his story will be the same as yours. And his story won't be half as convincing, either, because he hasn't got the same imagination."

Tabitha sighed heavily. "I... I..." she stammered. Then she went for it. "I did know Griff was there – I recognised him under

208

his balaclava," she blurted.

All was still. The only thing to be heard was a robin through the slightly-open window. Her mother was too shocked for words. Mary looked at her, waiting for more while Tabitha became a mixture of shame, fear and confusion. All she could think about was becoming small enough to fall through a crack in the floor and disappear. She was amazed at herself – she couldn't truly understand why she had behaved the way she had. At last she found some words.

"I... I guess... I felt sorry for him... I recognised him immediately. You can't be in the same class with someone for so long and not recognise everything about them – just the way he held himself. And he knew I would recognise him. He looked at me... and he were, like, real scared. He didn't have to look like that. He wasn't staring me out like he used to. He just looked so horribly sad... He was kind of like... asking me to help him. *He* looked more much more scared than *I* was and it was me that was tied up... He looked so like, so full of pain like I have never seen before. He didn't want to do what was happening, I'm sure. He was saying sorry and asking for help at the same time...

"I reckon he kept Minnie because he knew how much I would love her. They didn't find anything else in his house, did they? I reckon he, kind of, rescued her."

At last, Cindy found her voice and she exploded, "You read all that in his look behind the balaclava. I don't believe it."

"Eyes can tell much," said Mary, quietly. "I hope Tabitha has read them correctly and that it is true that his heart is still safe. He is a very young man who has found himself in league with some quite wicked people. Whatever is in his heart, he has certainly unleashed evil beyond his control..."

There was more silence as Cindy was trying to come to terms with all this. Mary seemed so calm. Cindy glared at her daughter who was looking firmly at the floor. *Why have I been so stupid?* Tabitha kept asking herself.

But before Cindy or Tabs could say anything more, Mary began, "I think I agree with Tabitha. Gareth has to be protected somehow – from himself and most of all from the dangerous men he has found himself with. But how we go about it, is the question. I think the time has come for a strategic plan."

"A strategic plan. You make it sound like a military campaign," retorted Cindy. "Tabitha has just to own up. She's in enough trouble as it is. That boy deserves all that they will do to him and more they won't."

"No, not exactly a military campaign, more a campaign for peaceful change. Let's see what we need..."

Tabitha was now all ears. Mary was wonderful. She seemed to understand her better than she understood herself. She was so sensible, so clever. She had *agreed* with her – even when she was finding it hard to agree with herself. Well, at least with what she thought about Griff, if not what she had done. She began to feel better than she had for days. Just keeping Griff's presence at the flat secret had caused her a lot of underlying anxiety. The weight of that kind of guilt was something new for her. Now the secret was out and a dam burst somewhere deep inside and all the bad stuff began draining away in a series of sobs. *I'll never lie again,* she told herself. It was awful. Would her mum ever understand? Would she ever be truly forgiven? *Perhaps I should go to prison for telling the police lies. If I did, it might help me feel better. I'll tell Inspector Gillespie I want to go to jail.*

But Mary continued thinking out a strategy.

"The immediate problem is somewhere safe for you both to stay. That comes first – you can't go back to that flat, not just yet. Until Gareth tells the police who the gang members are at any rate. You can stay here. Then your long-term safety and that of the neighbours must be considered – at least until these perpetrators of terror are taken out of circulation... Then comes Griff. Tabitha has made a plea for him. What else do we need to consider...?"

"Tabitha has to call the police and change her story, so these men can be caught," asserted Cindy, and looking directly at her sobbing child, added, "Don't you?"

Tabs nodded. *But Mary has a plan,* she wanted to cry. But said nothing.

"You've got spunk, lass, I'll give you that," said Mary, "but whatever you believe about Griff, that clearly doesn't go for the rest of them. Next time they come they could get even more

210

violent; they may not just be content with wrecking things. And they *will* come back as long as you are there. You said how much some of them seemed to be enjoying themselves. Even if the police get Griff to open up, he may not be able to tell them enough to catch them, and I doubt whether they can guard your place 24/7 for many more days."

"So where are we going to go?" protested Cindy. "We can't stay with you forever. And what if they come *here*? You have some lovely things and this house is miles from anywhere else. It'll be too easy for them if they decide to follow us."

"Not exactly miles. But I think I might invite some men to join us for a holiday?"

"Men. You have men you can call on?"

"Oh, there's a few from the church. Someone might like to get in on the action. One is a retired copper. I think we can arrange a few to come in turns."

"But we can't do that. This is your home. It will be like an invasion."

"Oh. This is quite all right. I hate living alone. I spend as much time out of the house as I can – as your Tabitha can testify. She's been coming here for years and never knew it was me who lived here. In fact, you've probably spent as much time in the garden as I have. Tabitha's been my guest for many years. I have watched her grow. Having her come has given me so much pleasure. But she hasn't so often of late."

Tabs blushed for a second time. All her secrets were no longer secrets. Mary knew them all.

"I used to think the garden belonged to fairies but as I grew older and stopped believing in fairies, I still liked to come. You saw me all the time but you never came out."

"I didn't want you to think the fairies were as ordinary as me. I feared that if you met me, you would not come again. No, it was you who brought the fairy magic to that garden, you brought a little girl's wonder and that's exactly what the garden needed. You were the fairy. And now you bring your blessing to this house, too. I am not just offering you a port in a storm – I want you to stay. This place is your place, too."

"Thanks. You're just too nice. Griff led them to our flat

because of me and when they find out where I am, they'll trash this place, too. We can't—"

"So, let's hope they get them soon," said Mary, "Griff will eventually spill all his beans. That's for sure."

"So you think there is hope for Griff?"

"Well, I wouldn't have believed it until now. But, well, perhaps we could say you have spotted a lost sheep."

"Thanks." Maybe there was something good in what she had done.

Cindy was confused, again. What was she on about? "A lost sheep?" she queried. "What has that got to do with it?" Tabitha caught her look, and then realised what her mum was thinking and began to giggle. As soon as the giggling started, it welled up and took her over. The guilt of being caught out and embarrassed piled on top of weeks of anxiety – maybe even years worth – all came pouring out as she giggled uncontrollably. Her giggling made Mary smile. This girl would survive.

"I don't get it." complained her mum, after Tabs had regained a little control. "What's up?"

"You." spluttered Tabitha. "I know what you're thinking. You're thinking, 'Little Bo Peep'."

"So...?"

"Little Bo Peep? What's she got to do with it?" smiled Mary.

"Everything isn't it, Mum? *You're* thinking Little Bo Peep lost her sheep but *Mary's* thinking that *God* has. Isn't that right, Mum? Mum always told me that one. It's one of her favourites."

"God ...?" puzzled Cindy? "Now I'm totally lost. I'm going mad."

"Mary was talking of *Jesus'* story not the nursery rhyme. The lost sheep who allowed himself to be rescued. It means that God doesn't give up on sinners."

It took a while but Cindy eventually gave up feeling angry, just confused. She was happy that Mary was laughing too as Tabitha continued to giggle. As long as it was doing her daft girl good. She might be fifteen and bigger than her and had experienced so much dreadful stuff of late but she was still very much a kid – she hadn't lost it. Cindy liked that.

"You're such a caution at times, my girl."

"But to be serious," said Mary when the storm had abated, "you'll have to tell the Inspector..."

Tabs nodded. "Will you help me?"

"Of course."

At that moment, someone tapped on the front door. Sensitively. Not like the DI. They knocked again, more insistently but still carefully. Mary glanced out the window and saw a lady she did not know. "I wonder who this is?" she queried.

"Little Bo Peep," joked Tabitha.

She struggled to pull herselves together to receive the stranger. She introduced herself.

"Hello," she said solemnly, "I'm from Victims' Support. DI Gillespie has asked me to call on you. My name's Miss Little." At that, Tabs completely cracked up and despite the lady's shocked look, they all collapsed into uncontrollable giggles.

"Please excuse us," explained Mary, between outbursts. "We are treating ourselves to some therapeutic laughter. You don't have anything to do with sheep do you?"

"No. ... sorry."

"We were just talking of looking after a lost sheep who might be ready to repent and come home."

"Bringing his tail behind him," added Tabitha.

"Tabitha," shrieked her mother. "Stop it."

Three-quarters of an hour later, full of tea and cake, Miss Little had recovered from the unexpected introduction and left relieved that the little family had met Mary who was going to take them in. She would have much less to do because of Mary's excellent care. If only everyone had friends as good as her. The Johnsons were going to be all right. She also left with a message for DI Gillespie. Tabitha had something to tell him about Gareth Green.

***

Tabs, Cindy and Mary sat at a table in an interview room at Millheaton police station.

"So now you are telling me you recognised young Green sporting a balaclava when your flat was broken into?"

"Yes, that's right, Inspector," sighed Tabitha.

"Why didn't you tell us this before? It would have saved us a lot of trouble." The inspector looked cross.

Tabitha hung her head and took some time to answer. She had thought about how she was going to do this all the previous night; she had not slept above an hour of it. The previous evening she had tried to explain to her mother who still failed to understand how her daughter could have any sympathy with a boy who had bullied, tormented and teased her for the past nearly nine years. Her mother would have to know everything now because it would almost certainly come up at the police station; the time had come to confess to all her secrets – including Griff's following her to the garden. Mary knew all about the incident outside the Old Lodge, of course, and she waited patiently while Tabitha eventually confessed to her mum that she had put Griff into A&E before he had been officially cautioned. Griff could have harboured a grudge – probably did – and this and the other times she had confronted and frustrated him could form the motivation for the crime. Griff was in the habit of getting everything he wanted but he had never triumphed with Tabs. He'd not even secured a single snog. Other girls were a push over but Tabs had defied him – made him feel small, even got him into having stitches in his hand, and then arrested – even if she had not grassed on him on any amount of other occasions.

Tabs went bravely through with what she had resolved to say, "I am convinced he didn't want to be there, he was scared. He didn't like what was happening. I think he took Minnie home so he could bring her back sometime. I... if he goes back into prison again, he might never have a chance to make anything of his life... and... I... I think he wants to... wants to change."

"What makes you so sure?" asked the policeman. "With a previous record like his he is unlikely to have just reformed, especially in the course of a despicable crime. Presumably he and the others were also responsible for the first attack on your flat?"

"They were," interjected Cindy, "they admitted it at the time when they threatened to come back if we stayed there. And that's when he took Minnie isn't it, Tabitha?"

"Yes. I'm sorry I lied. I didn't want him to take the blame for it all. I don't know how he felt the first time but he certainly did not want to be there the second time. He were sad, scared, and sorry all at the same time."

"All in a look?" questioned the inspector.

"Yes."

"That's a lot to read into just a glance."

"It weren't a glance. We... he looked right into my eyes. He wanted me to see."

"So, you will make a statement to say you know he was one of them. Even though you couldn't see his face properly, you recognised him?" confirmed the DI.

"If I have to. Do I have to make a statement?"

"Yes. It's how this works."

"But if I do that he will get into so much trouble... And... and I won't stand up in court. I won't testify to him being there. I won't. I'm... sorry." Tabitha hung her head. The inspector looked extremely cross. So did Cindy. Despite everything, her Tabitha was continuing to be totally unreasonable. But Tabs hung on to her belief in what she was doing. She had no idea why – except Griff needed to know that someone thought he had already learned his lesson. *I'm not goin' to rat on him in court. He didn't want to be there, in our flat.* "Maybe if he thinks someone is on his side, he might not feel any loyalty to these evil people and tell you what you need."

There was a moment's silence before Mary said, quietly, "I know this young lady. I don't think she'll change her mind. If she thinks Gareth is repentant and is asking her to give him a chance, she'll fight to give him that chance." The inspector's expression slowly softened. He had to respect Tabitha Johnson; she had her principles and she had spunk, and he liked that. And, anyway, he knew Mary was right – Mary was nearly always right.

The DI addressed Tabitha with all the authority he could muster. "Young lady. You know I could charge you with wasting police time?" Tabitha nodded. "That may give you a criminal record. Are you willing to risk that to defend this boy who has tormented you for years and has now led an evil gang into your home?"

Cindy was horrified and was about to order her daughter not to be so stupid and stubborn but Mary caught her eye and she waited.

"Yes," said Tabitha, firmly.

The inspector sighed. He could not charge this girl. Now they knew the truth, Green would spill the beans and it was the others who he really wanted. "All right, we'll tell Green what we know. If it turns out that you are right and he's genuinely sorry for this, it will help his case. He will not get off scot-free, of course, but we will see that the others get the chief blame, as they deserve. But I have to have it from him. He has to convince me with more than a 'pleading look'. If he confesses to being there and tells me who the others are, and where I might find them, I'll go easy on him. Does that satisfy you, lass?" The inspector wore a hard expression. Then, after what seemed to Tabs like an age, he relaxed and there was a flicker of a smile on his face. "Agreed?"

Tabitha nodded, "OK. Tell him I know he is sorry. And... and thank him for looking after Minnie."

"You drive a hard bargain, young lady. Let's hope I don't get a denial and a lot of abuse because if I do, he'll leave me no choice, and, believe me, I'll give him no quarter... so let's hope you're right."

"If he gets cross, it'll be because he's scared, or I'm wrong. But I don't think I am," murmured Tabitha, quietly.

Cindy marvelled at her daughter's power. She had defied the inspector just as she had defied Gareth Green. She had no idea where she got the courage from.

Back at Mary's when Tabitha had taken a trip to the bathroom, Cindy muttered, "However did I get such a daughter?"

"You are a very lucky woman," said Mary. "I'd give anything to have a daughter like her."

"Like share your garden with her for six years?"

"Nearly seven now... Sorry... You don't mind, do you? I never approached her. Perhaps I should have said."

"No. It was a good place for her – a piece of heaven on what can be a bleak council estate. You understand her better than I do

216

sometimes. You have been so good to her... to us. I'm glad you think so much of her."

Two hours later, Gareth Green sat in his usual seat in the interview room at the police station. The inspector welcomed him back. After the standard introductions for the recording, he began, "So, Gareth, let me tell you what we know. You were in the Johnson's flat as one of the gang on the day of the second raid. We know because Tabitha Johnson recognised you. You were wearing a balaclava but it doesn't take a genius to recognise someone that you've gone to school with for years."

"You can't prove that. Er... no comment."

"Gareth, you were there. Let's be honest with each other. Amazing as it may sound, I want to help you, and do you want to know why I would want to help the likes of you? Because Tabitha Johnson, who is worth a hundred of you, thinks you are sorry for being there and wants me to take pity on you. And you know what, Green, soft as I am, I promised her I would. But only on one condition – you cooperate."

"Cooperate?"

"If you tell me you were there against your will, I will make sure the magistrates hear that. If you plead guilty it may not even get as far as crown court. I can't promise that because it's up to the magistrates but it could result in a lesser sentence. In mitigation, we could say that your school friend thinks you are a victim like she is, and that will go a long way to helping your defence. But all that requires you to come clean. Any refusal to tell me the whole truth will count against you. Now, you tell me who is responsible for all this."

What happened next actually surprised the inspector. Gareth Green, Griff the hard case, actually broke down in tears. They weren't put on. It wasn't in Griff's nature to do that. "D-do you b-believe her?" he stammered.

"Convince me, Gareth, Convince me."

Tabitha had been right, of course – but not completely. Griff was scared, and his old resentment for authority was still there. Yet the extent of the crime – the violence and the hatred – had shocked him. He had resented Tabs' rejection of him but he didn't hate her. She simply frustrated him, and he was jealous. She seemed to have what he didn't have but he couldn't quite say what. Her situation was no different from his. Yes, he had wanted to get back at her. He had seen her defiance; her being so kinda 'superior', so confident and so different had been a challenge. And now she was fifteen, he fancied her – she turned him on. She had never shown any fear of him like most of the other kids. He wanted to break her down. But the 'mates' he had called in to help – connections he had made through others in the detention centre – were evil in a way he had not come across in his small town. He had unleashed something that was beyond his control. He wasn't racist like they were – he didn't hate Tabitha for being black. For him, it was simply personal. He had not anticipated a second raid – and he had not actually intended to drive Tabitha and her mother off the estate.

Later, as he lay in the police cell, there were still moments when he was angry with her. If it had not been for her defying him, making a fool of him in front of Dean, Shaun and Gary nothing of this would have happened... perhaps. And had Tabs truly said those things about going easy on him? It was the sort of thing she might do. Her very goodness infuriated him.

But, in the end, he came clean about everything.

It was true that most of the damage was done by the others. It transpired that he could not even spell some of the words scrawled on the walls, anyway. He gave names for the perpetrators and their contacts. He was terrified of grassing on them but they were out to get him anyway – he wasn't one of them and he knew too much. As soon as the fuzz had knocked on his door, he knew that they would try and silence him.

When they had finished, Griff asked the inspector if he could see Tabitha.

"I'm afraid that will not be possible," said the inspector, "not until the case is over. And, in any case, I don't think it would be wise." Griff protested. Apart from his mum, there was no one else who cared for him at all. At least Tabs had been kind to him, even though he didn't deserve it.

"If I were you, Green, I would forget all about that girl." Then the inspector remembered Tabitha's final words. "She did ask me to give you a message, though. She wants to thank you for looking after her doll which she is delighted to get back. Not that that was your intention, I expect."

"Thanks," uttered Griff. "Thanks."

"The best thing for you and her is for you to get her out of your mind," said the DI. "And now you're making me behave like some sort of ruddy social worker. I don't know what the world's coming to... Take him away," he barked at the constable by the door.

"Thank you," said his lawyer.

"Don't thank me. I just hope your client makes a full – and I mean *full* – statement."

10

Mary pulled up outside the house. They had elected to go to church with her and had just got home after a lively Palm Sunday service. She handed Cindy the house keys and suggested she go in and put the kettle on while she put the car away.

On the way in, Tabs mused, "I reckon God actually loves us."

"Yeah. I were watching you in the church. You truly believe in him, don't you? It's because of the Thomases and Danielle, isn't it?"

"Yes and no, Mum. Basically, I've known God was there for a long time. I didn't know it was God, though. I met him when I went into the woods, but I didn't know it was God as such. But today, I have just properly taken it in, he's there when things die just as much as when new things grow. When I saw a dead tree it made me sad, but now I see that God hasn't stopped loving. He makes a new one grow. There's much more to life than we can guess."

"Tabitha, as I keep saying, you're a deep one."

"That's it. It's deep; much deeper than we can imagine. And all the way it's full of love... Mum, stop staring at me like that. Here, put the kettle on." Cindy didn't move, so Tabs took the kettle and filled it with water. She knew that, yet again, a nice cup of tea was called for. Not a china cup this time, but a proper mug.

Spring was really taking hold of the weather now. The daffodils had come to an end and in the woods, the bluebells were showing their intent. The scents and sounds of spring were all around the cottage. Tabitha took turns tending the garden, mowing, digging, trimming and, best of all, planting. Mary showed her how. Tabs discovered she enjoyed working in a garden every bit as much as sitting in it.

"I had no idea that gardens needed so much attention. The fairies don't do the hard work."

"Sadly," agreed Mary. "The magic of childhood is delightful

but doesn't all last forever."

"No. But there is a wonder all the same. I gave up believing in fairies a long time ago, but not the miracles of Nature. It's still brilliant that these tiny seeds we just planted will turn into radishes and lettuces and things. That's kinda cool."

On Easter day, Tabitha and Ashol decided to go to church wearing their long skirts. Her mother had meticulously repaired the one Mary had given Tabs in the shop, but now she was officially presented with the colourful one she first discovered in the garden, and so she was delighted at Ashol's suggestion that they should wear them that special morning. She felt beautiful and must have looked it too, as she noticed heads turn and smile at her, not just in church but in the street.

After church, they all went back for Easter lunch with the Thomases. They ate stewed meat in gravy with fried potatoes and sliced cabbage in the South Sudanese style. Cindy, however, could not take to the dish containing offal that Mrs Thomas never failed to serve up for special occasions. Tabitha had tried, but as someone more inclined to being vegetarian, she had quickly politely declined.

There was joy over the Easter holidays but there was also tension in the air at the Thomases. Ashol may have been content that her father was preparing to go to Juba because he was so excited about it but that didn't prevent her and Deng from being apprehensive. It was all right him saying it was home but he had not been there for years and he had become accustomed to being in Yorkshire. Ashol had never lived there. In Juba, apparently, you couldn't take water supplies for granted, and certainly not electricity. The health facilities were primitive and it was very expensive too. Tabs was conscious that since Mr Thomas's announcement, a slight sense of gloom had permeated his household despite his obvious excitement at going back to his native land.

"You don't want your Dad to go, do you?" Tabitha asked as they threw themselves on the bed in Ashol's room after they had finished the washing up.

"Oh, I do want him to go. It's what he's always wanted."

"But you're worried?"

"Yeah, a bit."

"What about you? Do you want to go? When he's got settled."

"Well, yeah. Sort of."

"You don't belong there like your mum and dad, though, do you? You've been here since you were born. And, like, who do you know over there?"

"No one. Only we've got family. Mum has three sisters and a brother, and Dad has cousins. Then there is my grandma."

"But when you go it's, like, forever, isn't it?"

"Well, yeah. They want me to finish my GCSEs first. Then I could go straight into a foundation year at a university in Juba."

"What would you study there?"

"Don't know, yet. Something that will lead to a job that will help the country grow."

"Like Deng wanting to be a doctor?"

"Not a doctor; that's *his* plan. Mine will be different. Deng may have to do medicine here, in Britain. But that won't be until he's finished his A levels."

"But your dad's going soon. That'll mean he'll be there a long time before the rest of you."

"I know. That's the worst of it. Mum would like for us to go out for Christmas, but we wouldn't be able to afford it on just what Mum earns at the care home. Dad considered staying here until we had finished our exams but he wants to take the opportunity of getting a good job and a home ready for us. When he goes over he'll stay with his brother until he can get a place of his own. He's going to apply for a job with the government. He has the qualifications and experience."

***

When the police caught up with the perpetrators of the assault on 49 Ings Views in a dawn raid in a less salubrious part of Leeds, the language uttered by the gang members was not that found in a standard English dictionary. The protestations of innocence were mixed with colourful expressions of outrage.

DI Gillespie had no need to reveal Gareth Green as the source of his information. Searches of the gang's various addresses had uncovered more than sufficient evidence to implicate them. In fact, they let out Griff's name themselves as someone interested in getting people to do a job on a house he knew – although it wasn't them, was it? It did not take long to obtain defiant admissions, however, even though their lawyers carefully vetted the statements and demanded a plea of not guilty.

Griff pleaded guilty and was granted bail pending sentencing, unlike those protesting their innocence who were deemed a danger to the public. Gareth was only fifteen, but the other three were older – two seventeen-year-olds and one, who at twenty-one, had already served a prison sentence in an adult prison.

After the arrest, Cindy and Tabitha were anxious to get back to normal. Fred had organised a second repair gang and a rota of men to sleep over every night. It had been a real commitment but they had all believed Tabitha and Cindy were worth it.

***

Spring turned into summer early; May turned out to be exceptionally warm. In the woods, Tabitha explored deeper – even up to the edges of the meadow that separated the woodland from the formal gardens that surrounded The Park. She revelled in the crevices and holes in the trees and along the banks and hollows that told of secret beasties not often seen by the casual passer-by. Along the sunny grass pathways winding through the trees, she breathed in the sweet air laden with the scent of a large variety of wildflowers, which punctuated the lively greens of early summer with pink, blue, white, and yellow. She was learning some of their names now. Not that that mattered in the way she enjoyed them, except that it enabled her to find out more about them – she had bought a second-hand book of British wildflowers from Friends of Africa. The bluebells which had dominated the clearings and the areas of coppiced hazel were coming to an end but their green leaves and seed-laden stems continued to crowd up against swathes of pungent wild garlic.

Among the December snowfall Tabs had discovered a couple

of frozen ponds. In the early spring they had been full of lively tadpoles and now in May, brightly coloured damsel flies flitted around the green reeds on their margins. The delicate, pink herb robert was to take her fancy one day, and the next, in the more open places, the fleshy comfrey with its purple flowers that attracted so many bees.

Tabs knew where some of the bees came from. There was a collection of hives on the edge of the lawn belonging to the big house. Apparently, the bees ranged all over Millheaton and beyond. These woods might seem to be just the product of Nature, but they were managed. The paths, the clearings, the ponds, the coppiced areas and the bees were not all there by chance – the area was a managed conservation area and open only to the people who lived at The Park, which included the Old Lodge. Residents of The Park and its gatehouse were not permitted to own cats, and dogs were not allowed to be off-lead anywhere in the grounds and not at all in the woods. As a result, a person walking through them would see much more than the human beings that were frequently accompanied by inquisitive canines.

Very occasionally, Tabitha met another human being. Although she became familiar to others, she rarely spoke. A polite smile sufficed because they, too, were there for the peace. Peace from human beings but not quiet. The woods in May were far from silent. In the heart of the deciduous woodland in spring, the birdsong was enormous, especially at dawn. Songbirds were competing over their mates and their territory but, to the human ear, in the sweetest and most melodious ways.

***

June was a busy month. Three momentous things all happened within days of each other. First were the exams – vital ones especially for Deng. Secondly, it was also the month of Garang Thomas' departure for Juba. And, thirdly, it was when Gareth Green and his associates went to court.

Griff was heavily fined and only received a suspended sentence on the condition that he left the area completely and never re-entered the estate. The others who had pleaded not guilty had been referred to Crown Court and, in view of the nature of their crime, they were not granted bail. Griff hoped he would never see them again and he was only too pleased for a fresh start somewhere where no one knew him. The Johnsons were told that he had got a job as a builders' labourer down south in the London area. Tabitha was happy. Gross had got his second chance and he was also out of her life for good. She felt she had done the right thing. Everyone, including the neighbours, was relieved that the others had been properly detained. It would be months before their case would be heard.

The news from South Sudan was not good. The rival factions were threatening to take up arms again and there was news of fresh atrocities. Mrs Thomas was worried; she was very concerned that her husband should not go back.

"The time is not right," she pleaded, "the situation is too volatile."

But her husband was not to be deflected. "Juba will be safe," he insisted. "The troubles are not in the city. Besides, I have my ticket. If I cancel now, we will lose all that money. And I've already handed in my notice to the council. You will see, there will not be another war. I know it."

Mama Sarah was not convinced but she knew that if it was a question of safety, there would never be a right time.

***

On 12th June, Mary drove Mr and Mrs Thomas to Heathrow airport. No one could imagine the two of them apart. Deng and Ashol were to remain in Millheaton with Tabs and her mum, so they could go to school to do their exams. It was difficult for Deng as he had a religious studies GCSE paper to sit the very day of his father's flight but the complexities of Kant, the British Empiricists and John Stuart Mill served very successfully to take his mind off the fact that when he got home his father was not going to be there. Unlike his mother and sister, he had no misgivings about his father returning to South Sudan. It was time. Ashol was content to know that she and Deng were going to sleep over that night with Tabitha. Her mum and Mary were not due to get back until around midnight.

Tabitha and Ashol had already decided on the GCSEs they were going to study the following academic year and were to spend lessons with the members of staff who would be teaching them. English, maths and science were compulsory but they had selected a further six options. Some subjects selected themselves because they were their favourites. Tabitha went for geography – with Jack Frost – religious studies and French – to the great delight of Mlle Gaudet who was having huge difficulty attracting anyone to take her A-level course. Mr Smith applied pressure on Tabitha and Ashol to study German too but failed.

"*Was hat zwei Enden?*" asked Ashol. Tabs knew the answer – a sausage. It was a tricky question which needed the right gender and plural forms. Mr Smith used it to help his top set remember them.

"*Ein Wurst,*" replied Tabitha.

"*Nein.* You and me studying German." laughed Ashol. Poor Mr Smith.

They had to select at least one art or design subject and Tabitha jumped at textiles and illustration. Ashol wasn't so sure but eventually opted for the same. She was tempted by graphic design but when she saw that some of the less desirable boys were headed in that direction she decided to stay with Tabitha.

***

Two days later they got a text from Juba. Mr Thomas had made it safely and was staying with a member of the family in Gudele on the western outskirts of the city. The hunt for a job was going to begin the next day, he told them. It was a borrowed phone but he would look for a SIM card of his own and tell them the number.

That was the last they heard from him until 9th July, Independence Day.

What they later discovered was that Mr Thomas had been surprised at just how hot he felt it was, and dusty. The house he was living in was called a *tukul* – a home-made house constructed out of wood, mud and thatch, rather like the iron-age round houses which people had lived in in Britain when the Romans came. There was no piped water or electricity. In fact, only a year before, the area had been virgin bush. The suburb was growing without much proper planning and people just built houses on the next spare piece of land within walking distance of a bore hole.

It became clear that work had not been easy to find but Mr Thomas had felt that his qualifications and experience would stand him in good stead and he would soon get a good job and be able to move into a permanent house in a better suburb nearer to the city centre.

11

For those who enjoy learning, July and August can be frustrating. Children who like school can find the summer holidays long and a bit tedious. However, for the teenagers it can be an opportunity to get busy reading in preparation for GCSE and A levels. Deng had looked up the curriculum on the internet and the recommended books and was trying to spend the time he would have spent in school in his bedroom in an attempt to read and learn the language of science.

Tabs admired his commitment. "You're so clever. I wish I had your brains."

"I'm not clever. I'm just reading stuff other people have found out about. And you're good too. Just read stuff and you can learn anything."

"For some of us, it comes easier than others, Deng," said Ashol, "and we've got Shakespeare – *Macbeth*," she added with a tone of mock horror.

"Shakespeare's hard, I know. It gets easier though. I didn't do *Macbeth*. What's it about?"

"I picked up a copy in Friends of Africa," murmured Tabitha rummaging through her bag. She pulled out a second-hand paperback that was satisfyingly thin. They opened it at Act 1, Scene 1. "It begins with three witches in thunder and rain."

They crowded around the book as Tabitha held it up.
"When shall we three meet again
In thunder, lightning, or in rain?"
read Ashol.

"I've heard that bit done before," said Deng. "I think you have to read it like an evil witch." And he read the lines again sounding as evil as he could. The girls applauded. "We have an actor among us," said Ashol. "Sir Deng Thomas."

Tabitha's face lit up. "*I* know. Let's take a witch each. Deng, you can be first witch, I'll do the second and Ashol, you can do the third."

"Yeah, let's," agreed Ashol. They made Deng do his lines and Tabs was a natural as she followed up with:

"When the hurly-burly's done,
When the battle's lost and won..."
"That will be ... ear ... the set of sun," came in Ashol, "What's an ear got to do with it?"
"'*Ere*'not '*ear*'," said Deng. "I think it means 'when'."
"Why didn't Shakespeare write 'when' then?"
"Because he's Shakespeare... and he lived four hundred years ago. What Miss Wright told us was not to worry about words we didn't know but just to keep going. Apparently, Shakespeare invented thousands of new words, so even in his day lots of people wouldn't have understood everything. Let's start again."

They took it from the top and this time threw themselves into it with confident enthusiasm, coming to a crescendo as they chorused:
"Fair is foul, and foul is fair:
Hover through the fog and filthy air."
And Tabs put in a convincing cackle just as her mother appeared. Cindy froze, baffled.
"Shakespeare, Mum," said Tabs in her normal voice.
"Sounds like the Devil's at work."
"Exactly. That's *exactly* what it's meant to be. The story's about how evil can take over people ... er, I think..." she added, less confidently.
"But good wins out in the end. Doesn't it?" asked Ashol.
"I expect so... It's a 'tragedy' though, so I guess most characters have to get killed off... '*Fair is foul, and foul is fair: Hover through the fog and filthy air.*'," reprised Tabs.

By the end of the day, Tabitha and Ashol were halfway through Act Three and Deng was reading about the discoveries of Michael Faraday and the relationship between electricity and magnetism. Their teachers would have been proud of them had they known what they were up to. But *they* were probably relaxing on their well-earned break somewhere in southern Spain or the Greek islands, or hiking up Skiddaw, or whatever teachers like to do to recover their sanity when they are set free for a few weeks before getting ready for the new term.

His teachers would not, however, have been proud of Gareth

Green as he stood before magistrates in London. The papers and TV commentators were all suggesting reasons why evil had broken out on the streets of the capital and other cities, as gangs set about burning and looting. Whatever the motives of some, for many it was simply about taking a break from the deadly round of unemployed leisure without the wherewithal to get away. Lacking initiative, they failed to find the sense of satisfaction that comes with achieving anything – except perhaps a scowl from the more successful in their district, or a look of fear from those they intimidated. Mostly, they were resentful and bored.

Such was the case for Griff. Although he had got a summer job it was as a builder's labourer, which was hard work in sun and rain, did not have the same esteem as the skilled craftsmen for whom he laboured, and was paid considerably less. Such graft was not something he was used to anyway, and after a fortnight he was, as he put it, "knackered". His job and accommodation had been found for him by a combination of government Young Offenders' Teams and charitable institutions. Tabitha's belief in him, and his genuine contrition, had weighed in his favour but contrition didn't stop him from being lazy. His life lacked any real sense of direction and in London he had a distinct shortage of friends. Griff's life was hard, dull, dry and lonely.

So with nothing better to do, he took up with a lad of his own age in a neighbouring flat who had spent most of the last two years suspended from school. Friday was payday and on a Friday and Saturday evenings, they took up the habit of wandering through the streets looking for places they could buy alcohol and hang around with groups of similarly aimless young people.

Thus it was that they found themselves in the high street on that fated Saturday evening in August. When the rioting began, some of the young folk kept to the side but others took advantage of the chaos, smashed shop windows and started looting. Gareth followed them. His brain was turned off by alcohol, he felt the buzz of excitement and he just followed the mob and looked for something to steal. He stepped over the broken glass of a plate glass window of an electrical store and picked up the nearest box in front of him, which turned out to contain a curling wand worth £25, although Griff was unaware of what he had taken.

He still did not know what it was he had when he was arrested with it a quarter of an hour later.

**

Results day loomed. The euphoria of the end of the exams and the termination of school was replaced with anxiety. It was especially nervous for Deng who needed a good result in his sciences to begin the A levels which would take him into medicine.

The dreaded morning came and Deng made his way to the school alone. He was worried. He hadn't come away from the exams with the reaction that some had done, declaring them to be a 'push-over'. He knew some of it with them was just bravado, but there would be no secrets this morning.

He encountered his fellow students gathering in clusters in the yard. They were not all there. Some had decided they had gone as far as they wanted and the lucky ones had already found jobs. Others were looking for them. Some were on holiday or had vacation work and a few did not want to be seen; they would get their results by other means. But Deng and the group he waited with were all anxious to secure their places on their A-level courses. Deng had opted for maths, physics, chemistry and biology and he needed a good pass – at least a '7' – in maths and the sciences to confirm his place on the course.

The doors opened and the teenagers filed in. The results were all in sealed envelopes in alphabetical order of surname. Deng pushed his way to the table marked 'T' and found his, then, buffeted by a group of bouncing girls squealing with delight, he squeezed into a corner and tore it open. Before he could read anything, a couple of others came up to him demanding, "What you got, Deng?"

"Dunno yet..." They gave him room while he read, silently, "English – '9', English Literature – '8', Maths – '6', Physics – '6', Chemistry – '6', Biology – '7', French – '9', Geography – '7', History – '9', Religious Studies – '9', Graphic Design – '7'." He read them out to his impatient friends.

"Wow, Deng. Four nines. That's fantastic. *Four nines!* Amazing."

"Yeah. Thanks. What have you got?" They were all content with their own collection of results. They had achieved their aims but none of them came up to Deng's level – none of them had four nines and an eight. They thumped him on the back. "Going back home? Walk to the corner?"

"Nah. I've got to talk to the head of sixth form. See you."

Deng was gutted; he had failed. Sure, he had got a six or above in every subject. He had achieved twelve good GCSEs, but a six in maths and science was not going to get him on his chosen A-level course. And without that, his dreams of being a doctor would come to an end. He stood quietly in thought for a moment before he noticed the head of sixth form making his way across. "Come, Deng, I think we need to talk." He led him off to a desk on the side.

"You know what I am going to say to you, Deng, don't you?"

"Yeah, I can't do maths and the sciences."

"I would not put it so negatively, Deng. You are very talented. You should develop your undoubted strengths. There are only three others in the school who have got four or more nines."

"Natalie Smith?"

"You must ask Natalie that. We're talking about you, Deng. Mr Kendall was disappointed you hadn't chosen to do English, and Mademoiselle Gaudet would exclaim with French passion if you carried on your French. There is a place for you to do A levels in all your subjects in which you have achieved a nine and, miracle upon miracle, they all fit the timetable. So, what do you say?"

Deng had entered the building that morning hoping to be a scientist and left it half an hour later signed up for languages and humanities. By the time he was halfway home, the weight of trying to excel where his talents did not necessarily lie was lifting from his shoulders. If he couldn't be a doctor that was not his fault. He had done his best, but God hadn't given him the brain for that. In truth, he had known it for some time but had refused to admit it to himself or anyone. Yet it had appeared God had given him something else, and if these results were to be believed, in abundant measure.

Tabitha and Ashol were waiting for him impatiently on the

corner. They wanted to see him approach and try and read in his demeanour what had transpired. The way he came gave no direct clue because they encountered a very thoughtful Deng, but not a dispirited one.

"So, how'd it go?" demanded Ashol.

"OK," said Deng rather laconically.

"What does that mean?" insisted Tabitha.

Deng explained what he had signed up for. "I don't know what Dad would say. He would be disappointed that I can't go on to be a doctor. I hope I have made the right decision. I'd better phone Mum."

Mama Sarah was indeed disappointed. She couldn't hide it. All they had ever talked about was Deng going to be a doctor. When they arrived back at the Thomases, there was a sad air in the room that Tabitha did not think was fair.

"Mrs Thomas," she eventually said, gently, "Deng has done better than nearly everyone in the school. He's got four nines. He's clever in languages and history and you must be very proud of his achievements in religious studies."

"Yes. Praise the Lord. Father would approve of that."

"Mr Gambel – the head of Sixth Form – said I should work to my strengths. And Mr Kendall was there and very happy that I was going to join his English group... and Mademoiselle Gaudet came up and said, *"Félicitations, Deng. Je suis très contente. Mes pieds ont commencé à danser sans toucher le sol."*

"What's that mean?" asked Tabitha. "Your accent's brilliant. You sound just like her."

"She congratulated me and said she was very happy and that her feet had started to dance without touching the floor. I think she likes me."

Hearing Deng actually speak French broke the spell for his mother. She was impressed. Parents are often surprised by their kids' talents – gifts they have not revealed before. Mama Sarah was a touch happier.

"But if not a doctor, where will this take you, Deng?" she asked.

"I dunno yet, Mum. I'll have to see about it. I don't have to make up my mind just yet."

"Could you be a lawyer or an engineer?"

"Not an engineer, Mum. That's maths and science again."

"But a lawyer, yes?"

"Yes. I suppose so."

"Good. I will tell your father you are going to be a lawyer."

"Mum," protested Ashol, "it's too soon. He hasn't decided yet. We need to pray about it."

Deng reached out and touched Ashol's hand before she said anything more and he said calmly,

"Yes. It is one of the possibilities, Mum. There must be others to explore, and I'll ask God what He wants."

"Good. I am happy. Come here and let me kiss you."

Deng looked down at his mother as he took her in his arms.

Later that evening before she went to bed, Tabitha prayed hard that God would lead Deng into something in which he could be fulfilled. This was the longest prayer she had so far made. Talking to God was beginning to become a habit with her, although she couldn't get into the traditional routine of praying at the same time every day, something that she thought being a Christian demanded. But when Deng told her that he never prayed like that – and he had *always* believed in God and had grown up praying, hadn't he? – she felt all right about telling God what she wanted to say when she felt like it. Deng said that these days, it was all right to do your own thing – so long as you didn't forget God was there. She gathered that Mary told God about everything as she went.

"He's my Friend – no one else comes close to Him, so he gets what I'm thinking as I go and sometimes," she had said, "he even gets the rough side of my tongue, and I then have to say sorry."

As she prayed, Tabitha was somehow aware that God was listening, and that He would look after Deng. Then she added, "What about me, Lord?" But she knew what the answer to that prayer would be – wait and see. That was OK. That was the problem Deng had had, she thought. He and his family had made up their minds too soon. She was not going to do the same. She would follow her strengths, whatever they turned out to be. *I'll never be as clever as Deng,* she mused, *but there will be something good*

I can do... I guess.

The weeks that remained before the beginning of term raced by. Deng put aside maths and science and began reading Shakespeare and the other set books. The French was challenging – Molière was a cultural mystery. Many of the words were not in Deng's dictionary. He was struggling with it but Tabitha felt that at least something had been lifted from his shoulders. All he needed now was his father's blessing, which he knew would depend upon his choice of profession. His father would want him to have a good job that could be used to advance the cause of South Sudan. A lawyer qualified. If he couldn't be a doctor, his father would probably want him to sit in an important air-conditioned office in a large leather chair behind a shiny desk doing something 'important'. Deng, himself, decided to allow the suggestion of law studies to prevail while, secretly, keeping all his options open. He hoped God would direct him when the time to make a decision came, just as He had, he felt, over the choice of A-level subjects.

12

The first day in the sixth form was a new experience with its concentration on depth rather than breadth. Deng had only three free periods, which some of the students devoted to sports. He had never enjoyed sport because he was useless at ball games, but Mr Gambel impressed upon them the importance of physical fitness.

Deng was inveigled into doing cross-country, which, it turned out, was a good choice because his long legs ensured he was never last even when he jogged it. Besides, it took him out into some neighbouring fields which smelled lovely as the last of the hay was being harvested. He had never given much thought to the English countryside before but as the term went on, he found a fascination in the change from late summer to early winter.

His choice of subjects all had a majority of girls in the classes. But on the plus side, it was a relief not to have to put up with some of the disruptive elements that had now gratefully left and were making the most of their freedom in the wider world, for good or otherwise. Deng found himself among the ablest students in all his subjects. The work was, however, intense and stretched him, but he enjoyed that.

In two of his subjects, he came across someone new to the school. He was an English Pakistani called Ibrahim whose family had moved from Batley over the summer to manage a convenience store on Beck Ings. It may have been because Deng was the only other non-white in the class that Ibrahim moved to associate with him. Or maybe because of the predominance of girls. He lacked a sister and, perhaps also, owing to his Muslim background, Ibrahim was awkward when it came to girls. Deng, however, was quite comfortable with them – after all, he was always in female company at home, so he was used to it. In French he liked to partner with Natalie Smith because she was pretty good at the conversational stuff, so he didn't immediately warm to Ibrahim's particular attention.

"I wish Ibrahim wouldn't keep following me around," he complained to Ashol and Tabs after a week. "I don't like it. He's a

Muslim."

"So?" demanded Tabitha.

"Arabs are Muslims. In South Sudan, they used us as slaves for centuries. Then in the civil war, they brought in foreign Muslim fighters – the Mujahedin – who did many bad things. And they expelled all the missionaries and compelled Christian children to become Muslims. I don't like them."

"Are all Muslims or Arabs like that?" questioned Tabs.

"Well, no. I suppose not."

"Either way?"

"... What are you getting at?"

"You being prejudiced – just because some are of a particular religion or country doesn't make them bad. And Ibrahim hasn't got nothing to do with the ones that made your ancestors slaves, has he?"

"OK. I suppose you're right. There are black Muslims in South Sudan. They are OK. But Ibrahim is not like them – he's from Pakistan."

"I thought he was from Batley?" smiled Tabitha.

"Well, yeah. But his family are Pakistani."

"But he was born here? – in England?"

"Well, yes."

"So if he was born here, he's British, like Tabs," put in Ashol.

"Well, I suppose so."

"I never thought you were racist, Deng,"

"Well, no, of course not. It's just the history..."

"Oh quit it, Deng. Some Dinkas have done some pretty awful things to other tribes but we're not like them. Ibrahim is himself and can't help where his parents were born or whatever some people claiming to be Muslims have done."

"Yeah. Sorry. It's just so easy—"

"Yeah. But we have to stop doing it. Everybody has to stop doing it."

Deng looked suitably admonished.

"I think he's just lonely," said Tabs. "He needs a friend."

Deng was silent for a moment and then said, "He says he wants to play cricket for Yorkshire. He's in a Saturday team somewhere. And his family want him to be a lawyer."

"Sounds familiar," laughed Tabitha.

"Then invite him round for tea," said Ashol.

Mama Sarah was very unsure. What would her husband say to a Pakistani Muslim coming to their house? Nevertheless, she felt for this isolated young man surrounded by white girls; she knew a lot about being on the outside. And in any case, it was Ashol's idea and she was so keen – so long as she didn't get keen on a Muslim boy being more than an acquaintance. In the end, Mama Sarah decided that less harm would be done by complying, and so Ibrahim was invited back one day after school. Tabitha was invited too.

He turned out to be a very quiet sort of young man and very anxious to please. His family were keen to make friends in the area; it was not just about doing good business. They had occasionally attended the mosque but of late preferred to do their Friday prayers by themselves. His parents were pleased he was invited because they wanted him to make friends locally. One of the things that had decided them to move to Millheaton was that there were fewer Pakistanis in the town and their son would have an opportunity to meet with people who were from different backgrounds to his. Their tendency to have a closed community did not allow the children to learn English as well as they might. In truth, they were also worried about their son being radicalised, but they didn't talk about that.

Ibrahim was quite bright and was keen to study English and saw studying Shakespeare a privilege. Unlike Deng, he had studied Macbeth for his GCSEs and was quickly drawn into conversation with Ashol and Tabitha. Mama Sarah sighed and retreated to the kitchen. She couldn't follow one word of their discussions which seemed to centre on a young king from Scotland who died tragically after having seen a ghost many centuries ago. Why the children had to learn about that she couldn't imagine, but it seemed to have engaged their minds in a positive way.

Ibrahim enjoyed the sweet things Mrs Thomas provided, saying that they bore some similarity with what he had eaten at his cousin's in Manchester. As he left, he invited not only Deng but Ashol and Tabitha to his house above the shop the following week. Tabitha was surprised that he included the sister and her friend. She rather liked the idea of seeing behind the shop, though, which she had frequented since she was a little girl.

Her way to school took Tabitha past the shop and, to her surprise, the following day, Ibrahim appeared and offered to walk with her to the school. He proved to be a very interesting young man who had some fascinating ideas. He was keen to go into law and was learning some Latin to help him.

The day after, he waited to walk with her again. She wondered about this, but it had the benefit of helping to fend off the new generation of 'Gareth Greens' who frequented the area around the shops, threatening to torment her.

That same evening, she and the Thomases went up to the flat above the convenience store for tea. Ibrahim had a younger brother who didn't pay much attention to them but his parents were very pleased they had come. His mother had made some absolutely delicious sweetmeats which they ate with hot sweet tea. Around the walls were pictures of Pakistani cricket heroes in action and some ancient photographs of old people which Tabs decided must be the ancestors.

They asked Deng if he had been born in Millheaton, so he explained the troubles his family had encountered in South Sudan. They were more than sympathetic. Their own family had been driven out of Amritsar at the partition of India and Pakistan in 1947.

"The family never really settled in Lahore," explained Ibrahim's father. "That's why we came to Yorkshire, famous for its cricket. There is much trouble in Pakistan – people should not have to fight or flee because of the powerful."

"Will you go back – to Pakistan, I mean?" asked Deng.

"No. We belong here now. What about you?"

"We plan to return to Juba. Our father is there now getting re-established. When he calls for us, we will go."

"But not until you've finished your education, Deng," put in Ashol.

"No. That will take some years."

"A long time without your father?"

"Yeah. It is."

"And what about you, Tabitha?"

"Oh, me? Dad comes from Nigeria but lives in Leeds. I never thought of going to Nigeria. West Yorkshire is home for my mum and, I guess, my dad too."

"So you're English through and through?"

"Yep."

"And you support England at cricket?"

"No, not really. I'm not interested in cricket."

"Well. Perhaps you will learn to support Pakistan."

"Doubt I could get excited about cricket."

"You never know... Ah, my wife has some more cakes. Come try these."

Tabitha was sure she had put weight on that evening. The need to burn calories may be why they played so much cricket in Pakistan.

The next day, Ibrahim walked her to school again. And the day after that.

On that third day, Deng seemed to be in a funny sort of mood. They were sitting in the shade of the big oak tree in the school grounds eating their lunch. Ibrahim was with them as usual. After the bell rang, they got up and began walking back to the sixth-form centre. Deng hung back and Tabs fell in beside him.

"What's wrong, Deng?" she whispered when they were out of earshot of the others.

"You fancy him?"

"Who?"

"Ibrahim' of course."

"No. Why?... Hey, Deng, you aren't jealous, are you?" Tabs giggled.

"Course not. It's not like that with us, is it?"

They had reached the steps and Tabitha had to get back to her class in the opposite direction and no more conversation was possible.

After school, Tabs saw Deng and Ashol heading off in somewhat of a hurry. Ibrahim found her and offered to walk with her but she declined. She had to go to the town, she explained. She walked into Millheaton town centre and went straight to Friends of Africa.

"Mary. Can I talk to you?"

"Course you can. What's up?"

"It's Deng. He's not himself."

"Let's put the kettle on. Sit down. Mum know where you are?"

"Gone shopping. She won't be back till six."

While Mary was putting the kettle on she texted Bill. He arrived to mind the shop as if he had just popped out and had come back. For him, nothing was too much trouble for this lass – she had gone through so much.

Tea made, Mary sat Tabs down. "Now then, tell me about it."

"Well. Deng's gone all peculiar. He's acting funny. I don't know if it has anything to do with it but he asked me at lunchtime if I was keen on Ibrahim. I told him no and asked him if he was jealous. But he said not because it wasn't like that between us, was it? I don't know if it's about Ibrahim or something else. It might just be that he's missing his dad."

"I'm sure he's missing his dad. But you think Ibrahim has something to do with it. Tell me about him."

Tabitha told her all about Deng's new friend and their home visits and how he had met her outside the shop and walked to school with her.

"But I don't fancy him or anything like that. I hardly know him. He's so kinda 'mysterious'. And he certainly hasn't... hasn't..." Tabs hesitated over the words to use.

"Made any advances," supplied Mary.

"Yeah. Nothing like that. I reckon he's lonely. He just needs a friend... friends."

"And you live near his home."

"Well, I pass on the way to school. Do you reckon I should just ignore him?"

"Certainly not. Ibrahim has done nothing inappropriate. But you might suggest you don't walk in together every day – to avoid too much gossip. But you mustn't avoid him altogether, that would be definitely unkind. Yet you should talk frankly to Deng.

241

You must make it clear that you are just being friendly to Ibrahim and he hasn't suggested that it is more than that."

"Why does Deng take on so? He's behaving, like, he's jealous but it can't be that."

"Oh, he is."

"You reckon? But he's not my boyfriend or anything. It's not like that. He said so."

"Isn't it?"

"No. I haven't kissed him or anything – held his hand... much. It just isn't like that."

"Yet Deng is behaving oddly because Ibrahim is paying you attention. Tabitha, Deng has been sweet on you for a long time. OK, he might not be ready to get... romantic... but that doesn't mean he wants to share you with another boy."

"He has been very protective, but I put that down to his father telling him to look after his mum and sister and that included me."

"I'm sure that is part of it... but it's much more than that. Even if he doesn't realise it, yet. And you like him, don't you?"

"You mean fancy him?"

"Yes... Would you be jealous if he took a girlfriend?" Tabs went quiet. Did she fancy him? Like, did she want more than just being friends? She hadn't thought about it. Having a boyfriend wasn't something she had thought about much. *But if Deng started favouring another girl... Well, yes. I would be jealous, I guess.*

Mary read Tabs' thoughts. "I think you need to talk to Deng... really talk to him."

"But I could just ignore Ibrahim." That was a far less challenging proposition.

"But that wouldn't be fair on a lonely boy, would it? And it might mean Deng rejecting Ibrahim as a new friend too. And it won't solve the problem, either – he'll still be jealous every time a likely lad gives you a glance. And a good-looking girl like you will attract many such glances. No, Tabitha, you're going to have to take him aside and have a heart-to-heart."

"I wouldn't know how to start... And I'm not attractive, by the way."

"Tabitha, I might be prejudiced, and I'm not a boy, but I think

I am safe in saying you have what it takes to turn a head or two. And as for knowing where to start, before you knew me, what did you do when you wanted to work something out?"

"Before I knew you? I would go to your garden and talk to the fairies. But there aren't any fairies, are there?"

"The garden is still there. And even if you don't believe in fairies, it's a good place to talk to someone."

"You mean God?"

"Yes, he'll be there but I was thinking of the particular someone you need to talk to."

"Deng? Take Deng to the garden? Would that be OK? Really?"

"You've never asked my permission to visit the garden. In fact, it's as much yours as it is mine. You can use it as you please."

"Thanks, Mary. You're brilliant."

"I know."

"What would I ever do without you?"

"Without me? You'd make out. But I intend to stick around a bit longer, so you won't have to. Now drink up your tea, and get yourself home before your mum comes back from the shops."

Tabitha woke up the next morning with a plan. She went to school by a different route so as to avoid going by Ibrahim's shop. When she got to the school she went straight to the sixth-form centre and found Deng.

"Deng, tomorrow's Saturday. What have you got planned?"

"A pile of coursework. Why, what's up?"

"I want you to walk out with me, in the afternoon. Without Ashol."

"But..."

"Just say yes."

"Well, OK."

"Two o'clock. By the roundabout at the bottom of Beck Ings."

"But what about Ashol? She'll wonder why not her."

"Leave that to me. She'll be OK about it."

"What's this about?"

"I'll tell you tomorrow."

"Well, OK. Two o'clock."

Tabitha Whatsapped Ashol and told her the plan. Ashol thought it was cool. Deng had been a misery ever since someone told him she was walking to school with Ibrahim, she explained. He wouldn't listen to her when she had tried to persuade him not to read anything into it.

On Saturday, Tabitha found Deng waiting for her. He had been there a full ten minutes in case she was early because he didn't believe a gentleman should keep a lady waiting. If he had known the hours his father was being kept waiting for people in South Sudan, he would have been shocked. There, it was the custom to arrive late to preserve your dignity. But Deng was British in his ways, not African.

Deng's heart leapt as he saw Tabs approach down the hill and cross the bridge over the beck. She was wearing her long colourful skirt. He liked it. Why did she have to look so pretty? What was she doing? He mustn't feel attracted to her; he mustn't have anything distract him from his purpose of studying to return to South Sudan. If Ibrahim fancied her and she liked him, what did that matter? So long as she was happy...

"Hi," said Tabitha, brightly. She was nervous but she tried to hide it. "I want to show you something." She took his hand and led him out onto the Puddleham Road. She didn't let go.

"Deng, I am taking you to a place which has been very special to me since I was eight. Only a few people know about it. It's the garden behind Mary's house. It has a gate into the woods. You will be the only person I have ever shared it with."

"The only person. Not even your mum? Not even Mary?"

"They have never been with me there. Mary lets me be alone – has done for years – but I didn't know that until recently."

"So why are you taking *me* there?"

"To tell you that you are important to me and that you must stop being jealous. It was my truly special secret place that I have not shared with anyone else."

Deng stopped.

"You don't have to do this, Tabitha. I am sorry I was jealous of Ibrahim. It was so stupid and out of order."

"I'm glad you see that," smiled Tabitha, "but I *want* to share this place with you." She propelled him forward. "I found it when I was eight, but I didn't know it was Mary's until last March. I used to sneak in and chill. At first – don't laugh – I thought it was looked after by fairies. I don't believe in fairies now but I do believe in the wonderful power of Nature, and you and your family helped me see God behind it and in it all. That's another reason why it's precious. I visited this place to be alone with Nature and I knew that I was blessed. I could never put it into words. It's a kind of 'thin' place."

"A thin place?"

"Where the real stuff you can't see seems to get very near the surface."

"I think I know what you mean. I have heard about such places. I think a Christian would say, 'where the eternal breaks through into the world' – the numinous. We did something about it in RS. But don't you have to be a saint or someone special to sense it?"

"Since I can, apparently not," she laughed. "But you have to concentrate and wait. If we don't listen and look and feel, we will miss lots of things."

When they reached the Old Lodge, Tabitha led him round to the side gate.

"In here and turn right. Go quietly."

"Doesn't Mary know you're coming?"

"Yes and no. I just come and go and pretend she's not inside the house. That's a different world.

Now when we're inside I don't want you to say anything, just listen."

Through the door, Tabs led him into the little garden. It had seemed much bigger when Tabitha had first encountered it. Deng towered over the nymph, even on her plinth. She balanced there abashed, clutching at her falling garments as the new arrival spotted her. He slowly took everything in: the nymph, the hedges, the wall with its gate, the tall trees beyond them and the fine grass already dry in the early autumn sunshine. And then Tabitha, herself. She had settled on the grass her knees drawn to the side and her skirt spread out around her. His heart raced – he was seeing her as if for the first time. She was incredibly beautiful – more beautiful than ever. And they were in her place. He had always admired her, but now he knew that he had only ever perceived a fraction of her. At that moment, he understood that beauty came from the soul and transformed the features – and that beauty is timeless. So many human beings never get to understand that, spending a lot of money and time on trying to enhance their appearance, while, in truth, to be beautiful, they only need to connect with the eternal Beauty. Tabitha had done so in abundance. Deng sat beside her.

What Tabs saw was Deng lost in a sort of dream. Whatever impact this place was having on him it was profound. She was sure he could see things as deep if not deeper than she could.

They sat perhaps five minutes like this before she took Deng by the hand again and led him to the little gate that opened into the wood. The key was in the padlock waiting for them. Tabitha opened the gate and they stepped out onto the little path which wound its way among the trees. The beginnings of autumn were all around them. Some of the leaves had already turned golden. Giant spiders' webs barred their path in places, and toadstools, large and small, sprang up around the mossy stumps and fallen branches. The whole place was full of living things; the air resonated with the rich sound of birdsong and the buzz of insects.

They walked through the wood to a clearing where the grass was bright green. The patches in the shade were still wet with dew. As they stood together in dappled sunlight, Tabitha turned to Deng. Without saying a word – they hadn't spoken from the time they had entered the garden – their eyes met and then Deng gathered her in his strong arms and she melted into him. She had not planned this part. But it felt just the right thing to happen. They held together for fully two minutes and then he released his arms and once more their eyes connected, and each saw themselves reflected in the other. Somehow their lips met, just for a few seconds, and then Tabitha hugged this magnificent boy to herself again, and he enveloped her. Tears streamed down his face.

It was Tabitha who broke the silence.

"Deng. You must believe me. I didn't plan this bit. I just

wanted you to see that I..."

"I know you didn't. But in the presence of God, surrounded by Nature, things can happen."

"You think this is what God wants?"

"I have just become certain of it. Tabitha, up until a quarter of an hour ago, I was resisting thinking of you as anything more than a special friend. Once, I thought I was destined to be a doctor in South Sudan, and you wouldn't have fitted into that. But now that's all finished. I am to be a student of the Arts. And I have been forced to admit to myself that I have been resisting God in many things. Denying the way I felt about you deep down was wrong."

It was now Tabitha who felt she was falling out of control. They must be sensible.

"But you're only seventeen and I shan't be sixteen until next week." There was concern in her voice – she was afraid for him. "We've years of education to go, Deng. You mustn't be distracted—"

"And we shall not be distracted if we are honest about our feelings. We must take one day at a time. And this day, I believe, has been God-given."

Tabitha was not quite so sure of the God part but she was willing to accept that it was 'meant to be' as her mum often said.

"Do you believe God has a plan for everything?" she asked.

"Absolutely. But it has to keep changing minute by minute because hardly anyone listens well enough to Him to follow it and he has to keep revising it."

They traced their way back to the gate, this time with Deng's arm around Tabitha's waist.

As they reached the little garden, Mary stood back from the window. She had witnessed them arrive and watched them leave in silence, and now return entwined. A tear flowed down her cheek. "Bless them, Lord. Bless them. There is so much that can harm them. May nothing destroy this beauty. Lord, they are so young, and this world so wicked."

In the days that followed, Deng welcomed Ibrahim into their little circle. Unlike some of the students claiming to be an item, Deng and Tabitha did not go around hand in hand all the time, or sneaking around the back of the bike sheds for all to see. But when people referred to Deng as her boyfriend, Tabitha did not deny it as she had done previously. Let them think what they want, she decided. They probably wouldn't understand. She wasn't sure she did, but just that it all felt so right.

"All work out?" whispered Mary the next time they met in church.

"Yes. Brilliant. Thanks, Mary."

"I'm glad for you. I hope you will both feel free to visit the fairies any time."

"We will, Mary, we will."

248

13

When Gareth Green's case was eventually heard, Tabs had had her sixteenth birthday. It made her feel like she should be grown up. There were things she could now do in law that proclaimed the fact. Not that they made any impact on her; nothing changed in practice – her mum didn't begin treating her any differently.

Being sixteen, however, did change things for Griff. As he stood before the bench, his record was invoked and he found himself serving a custodial sentence in a Young Offender Institution. As Tabitha and her friends returned to the school after the autumn half term, it was being gossiped around. Gareth's mother was telephoning a former friend who was keeping Beck Ings informed at every opportunity.

Tabs was saddened. She avoided what she imagined to be her mother's implied "told you so" whenever the subject came up. She felt let down. There was no getting away from the fact that she had been over-optimistic, even if she denied that to herself. *It weren't that I thought he were going to make anything of himself but I just wanted to give him the chance,* she told herself. But, secretly in her heart, she was still sure the young man was not a hopeless case, that he was not 'just that way out' with no hope of redemption.

"What's wrong Tabitha?" inquired Mr Frost after a lesson on rivers one sunny day.

"Nothing."

"What part of 'nothing' is making you look like you've been told that chocolate has been declared a class A drug?"

"Nothing really. It's just this news about Gareth Green."

"Ah. The young man's done it this time, I believe. You persuaded the police to go easy on him. Quite an achievement. And now he's got himself banged up anyway."

"It's not that I like him. He's gross."

"So why be so down?"

"I guess I just thought he was getting better, that's all."

249

"Can a leopard change his spots?"

"You don't think there is hope for people that have got life wrong, then? My mum says some people are that way out, sometimes. There's no hope for them and no point in bothering about them."

"Oh, there is always hope, Tabitha. That's what keeps us teachers going. You and people like you are the kind of success that makes teaching feel worthwhile. A couple of years ago, for example, you didn't believe in yourself and your capabilities but just look at you, now. But one can't win them all. Sometimes you have to allow yourself to be defeated. Gareth Green is a tough challenge."

"But I had thought Griff was sorry for what he had done. I believed him."

"He might have been. But that doesn't mean he has any idea of how to go about living a better life."

"But he could study."

"He could. But you are considerably brighter than Gareth. He wouldn't find it as rewarding as you do. And he hasn't found the friends to encourage him as you have, either. It's not easy for him."

"No. I suppose not. So do you think he is going to spend his whole life in prison?"

"That's up to him. It's tough for him but it's not impossible for him to get his act together. It's never too late. We have to be patient with people like Gareth."

"And never give up on them?"

"Never give up on them. No one should give up on anyone... You believe in God, don't you?"

Tabitha had gotten used to saying she went to church but put like that demanded an admission of faith. She thought about it before she replied.

"Ye-ah."

"Well, does God give up on us?"

"I guess not."

"You know the Lost Sheep parable. There is more rejoicing in heaven when a lost sheep comes back into the flock than over the ninety-nine that never did anything wrong?"

"Yes. But some other parables finish with God sending them to hell," replied Tabitha.

"Only at the final judgement. In the end, when they know the score if people persist in choosing evil over good, then God has no choice."

"But Griff isn't evil, is he?"

"No. But he has done some pretty evil things, Tabitha."

"Yeah. But what if he were sorry?"

"God will forgive him."

"And this latest thing. He didn't know what he was doing, did he?"

"Perhaps not. But it is everyone's job to make sure they know what they are doing, isn't it?"

"Guess so... So what will happen to him?"

"That's up to him. If he's a wise boy, he will take advantage of all the things the young offenders' place offers, including the education."

"Can I write to him?"

"That may be possible if you want to. But think about it first, Tabitha. Really hard. And don't do it without talking to your mum. If you want to write, consider carefully how Gareth might take it. And remember it's easier to start something than to back out."

"If you were me, would you write?"

"No."

"Why not?"

"Because I would have too much to do and it'd be hard to keep up with the commitment. Now's the time for you to get on with your life, Miss Johnson. I believe Mr Kendall wants an essay on Lady Macbeth by next Friday."

"Yes... *She* changed. She wanted 'clean hands'."

"Exactly. And she started off a lot more evil than our friend, Green. At least he hasn't contemplated murder, as far as we know."

Tabs got to thinking, then said, "Shakespeare isn't just about people a long time ago, is he?"

"Bingo. By George, she's got it. Mr Kendall will be delighted. Now, be off with you, I've got a pile of marking to do."

"Thanks, Mr Frost."

"Don't mention it. It looks like chocolate has been reprieved. The sun's come out. Get off with you."

Tabitha skipped away.

That, thought Mr Frost to himself, *is what makes teaching so good. I must remember to pray for Gareth Green ... and for the poor sucker who has to teach him and the folk of his ilk in the detention centres.*

"I think you're going too far, Tabitha," stated her mother, firmly. I'm not sure you should get any more involved in Gareth Green than you are. You've already done more than enough to help him."

"I agree with your mother," added Mary, "whatever would you have to say to him?"

"I'd tell him straight. I'd tell him that if he wants to be happy in this world, he's got to be good, obey the law and help other people."

"And do you think he'll take that? You would sound like the judge."

"But that's why I want to do it. I'm *not* a judge. *I'd* say it because I just want him to be happy. It might mean more coming from me than some posh guy in a wig. *I* don't *have* to write to him."

Mary nodded. "Tabitha's got a point. The judge is paid to say it – getting a letter from another young person would be different."

Cindy defended her ground. "And he might think Tabitha's got a thing for him and that would be awful..." and then with a sense of foreboding, added, "You don't, do you?" Tabs pulled a disgusted face. "I can't understand you, Tabitha. Perhaps you don't fancy him, but he might get that impression. He's going to tell everyone in the place he's got a letter from a girlfriend. It's too risky."

"Very risky," echoed Mary.

Tabitha saw that she wasn't going to get anywhere and decided to abandon the idea, at least for the time being. But somehow she could not put it out of her mind. People change.

Macbeth and his lady found they were haunted by their crime to the point of madness and suicide. It was not too late for Griff, but it could be if he thought all the world was against him. If he just got a letter from her to say she, at least, hadn't given up on him...

Huddled against a wall under the low roof of the cave was a boy – small and thin, a waif – not the strident bully Gross Griff but the ghost of him. He was frightened, trapped in the dark. But although she could see him, Tabitha, herself, was no longer trapped; behind her was an opening to the daylight. But the waif cowered in his corner – he couldn't see either her or the opening. The streaks of sunlight were invisible to him. Then something within his darkness made him realise she was there and he got up and staggered about, reaching out, calling her name, seeking her. Her first instinct was to back away but a wave of pity, or care – she didn't know quite which – prevented her and she remained; he had no power to hurt her. She knew what it was like to be trapped in that cave.

Tabs shuddered and half woke up and in her mind, as she lay there she could sense Griff calling out to her. Then the sun rose above the horizon and streamed through a gap in her curtains. The dream had changed in recent months; she may have still begun in a cave but now there was a way out into the sunlight. She could no longer describe it as a nightmare. If only Griff could see it, too.

Tabs couldn't give up on Griff because she believed she was perhaps one of the few who could make a real difference. He might listen to her. She had to give him a second chance. After all, how many chances did God give people? God kept giving them chances right up until they died and even, perhaps, beyond when they saw God face to face.

She found herself asking God what he wanted her to do. Mum and Mary were right, it was risky. But Mr Frost had given her a clue. How would Griff take it? If she said it straight, if she said it how it was, he was not going to see her as a potential girlfriend, was he? He'd have to be pretty thick to do that and Griff had more up top than he gave the impression of having, sometimes. He had had enough nous to be the boss bully, hadn't he? She agonised over it, and the prospect of bringing it up with her mum again.

As soon as she had an opportunity, Tabs talked to Deng and Ashol.

"Well, I wouldn't," said Ashol straight away. "Where on Earth did you get the idea of writing to Griff?"

"I don't know, it just came into my head."

Deng didn't say much. He admired Tabitha for her courage. Perhaps Griff was worth it, but he wasn't sure.

"Isn't everyone worth a second chance? After all, God gives people lots of chances."

"Yes, but you have to think how to give that chance," replied Deng, "If the wood is rotten, you don't help by putting on good new paint, you just waste the paint."

"Is that from the Bible too?"

"No, that's from me."

"The Wisdom of Deng, chapter two, verse one," smiled Ashol. "There is a Jesus parable though, about not throwing pearls in front of pigs. Same idea. Maybe Griff's too far gone to put so much effort into it. Is he worth it?"

"But that's it. What I feel is that I don't actually think Griff's that rotten."

"You used to call him Gross," reminded Ashol.

"I know, and perhaps he was, but people can change."

"It may be that you've changed more than he has."

"Maybe. But I still think I have to give it a go."

"Put the muck around the tree one more time." This was Deng.

"What?" laughed Tabitha and Ashol together.

"That's the Bible. It's another parable. Jesus told about a man who had a fig tree that didn't bear fruit. He said he would dig in more dung one more year. After that, if it still didn't bear fruit at least they had tried."

"So that's another parable where God says he's not giving up on people. You see it over and over again in what Jesus says. These parables keep coming. But how do I know what to do about Griff? How do I decide whether to write to him or not?"

Almost at the same time as she asked the question, Tabitha

answered it for herself. The garden, the wood. *I must go into the wood where it is quiet and listen.*

It's perhaps in the woods that a person is most aware of the changing of the seasons. As Tabs closed the gate to the garden behind her, she noticed that the leaves of the trees had now taken on their rich autumn colours. The dying leaves of the various species each have a different colour. Why was the autumn so beautiful? What purpose did these glorious colours serve other than to be beautiful?

The ground had regained the softness that it had lost over the summer months and was quite muddy in places. Tabs found a sunny spot in the small clearing and sat on a fallen log. Some of it had crumbled away since she had first found it. Little insects came and went, exploring burrows in the rotting bark, and around the log where it rested on the ground, multi-coloured fungi erupted in clusters. Tabitha studied one by her foot, a group of steep-sided, cream-coloured caps on slender off-white stems. A naturalist would have been able to name these, as they would the bird singing above her, but, as usual, Tabitha didn't know what they were called. No matter; you only need words when you want to talk to others about something, and Tabitha had no intention of sharing this experience with anyone in words. Today, she had come just to listen.

As she sat, she remembered the last time she was here with Deng. But she put that out of her mind and tried to imagine what Griff would do when – if – he got her letter. How many letters would he be used to getting? His Mum would write of course, but who else? His erstwhile chums had long forgotten about him. And in any case, they were not going to try and write a letter, were they? They lacked the ability, and even had they had it, it was not something which would even cross their minds – out of sight, out of mind. As soon as Griff had gone, they had reformed their gangs and new leaders had emerged. Life had moved on and Griff was history. Perhaps that was why he had wanted to be such a big noise when he was around, he feared being forgotten. Being ignored for him would be as bad as – if not worse than – humiliation. It was the same with a girl in Tabs' year, Mandy

Waters; it was because she was afraid of being ignored – allowed to slip into the background – that she wore such ridiculous clothes and so much bling. Mandy wanted to turn heads, she wanted the boys to ogle her and the other girls to feel themselves dull in her shadow – the alternative was to be overlooked, and then, perhaps, just disappear. Mandy had bullied Tabs at one point but Tabs had learned that if you said hi to her, she was a different girl. She'd then latch on a bit. It was in Year 8 that Tabs realised she was all bravado on the outside but scared underneath.

Perhaps it was the same with Griff – scared of disappearing. If he was, what would he do? He could be planning to become the most notorious criminal on the planet and get into all the papers – just to remind the people of Beck Ings that he was still out there more notorious than ever. But if she wrote to him he would know that he was *not* forgotten and that someone, who had been important enough for him to pick on, had recognised some goodness in him. Mr Frost might be right, he might not know how to begin to be good. It was much easier for him to be gross – he had had years of practice – but how do you become good while being scared of disappearing? At that moment, Tabs knew that, despite all the advice from adults and friends, she had to write.

Then she thought about herself, and her own situation. Somehow she didn't need to worry about being noticed, she knew she was wanted, and she knew she was loved. She was not desperate for recognition. That was it about these woods. It wasn't just her mother, or her father, or Mary, or Deng, or Ashol. They were only part of it. Out here, she felt surrounded by love. "You love me." She whispered softly to the trees and as she did so, she became aware of the presence of something much greater than them. The Spirit of all Life seemed to fill her heart. She was loved, loved by the Source of all creation, and forever. There were no words to express this. She stood and closed her eyes, listening. Her mind, and her heart, went back to Griff. If only *he* could know he mattered to the Spirit of Life.

Tabs visualised him looking at the envelope saying, "What she want to write to me for?" Would he be angry? No. Getting a letter – a personal letter – from someone he didn't expect –

probably the last person he expected to get a letter from – would mean he hadn't been totally forgotten in Beck Ings. He might get letters from people whose job it was to care: probation officers, teachers, vicars, his mother – but he would be very surprised to get one from her. He would be intrigued just to look at the envelope. It occurred to her that when he saw who it was from, he might think she was writing him a hate letter. She must make sure from the very first words that that was not her intention. But what should she put?

As Tabitha's mind explored the various things she could say, she realised she had properly made up her mind. She would compose a letter and present it to her mother and Mary. What the letter actually contained was, in part, negotiable – but she was resolved to write. A gust of wind blew across the tops of the trees and large golden brown leaves from a sycamore floated down and landed on her head and shoulder. She picked one out of her hair and studied it. "I hope I am as beautiful as you when I come to the end of my life," she thought. In that moment she knew that to the One who had created her, despite her imperfections, she was indeed beautiful and always would be.

14

Tabitha left it a couple of days until a bright Sunday afternoon which, nevertheless, threatened a shower. As she walked home she could see the wood on the Puddleham Road and, above it, a fine clear rainbow. It was time to write.

She found it surprisingly easy in the end; she knew what she wanted to say. She finished the final draft and looked for an occasion on which to set it before her mother and Mary together. The opportunity arose when she got in from school the next day and found her Mum and Mary sitting down to a cup of tea.

"Mum, I've been thinking hard about writing to Griff. I've decided I have to. I'm going to do it."

"But, Tabitha—" Cindy protested. She had thought that with Mary as her ally, she had prevailed and her daughter had given the idea up.

"No, Mum. I've got to do it. Griff needs to get a letter from someone he doesn't expect to write to him. Look, I've done a draft of what I thought I would write. What do you think?" Tabitha opened her laptop and read.

Hi,

You might be surprised to get a letter from me, but I am writing because I believe that there is a bit of good in you. The police and judges and people will be telling you you're bad. And, Griff, you have done bad things, lots of them. You were a bully at school and a real pain but, somewhere inside you, I reckon there is something good.

I don't want you to think I like you. I don't. I don't want you to get that idea, and I don't want to see you again. I just think someone needs to tell you that you can be happy if you work on the bit of goodness that's inside you.

Griff, if you want to be happy you've got to do these three things.

1. Work hard at all the stuff they want to teach you in the detention centre. Even if you think the teachers are idiots.

2. Talk to God. And not just once but lots of times. And say thank you for every good thing you've got because there's bound to be some.
3. Do something for someone else. Help people. Then you will find real friends.
I know some people will think you're stupid if you do these things. Let them. They want you to be bad so they can be bad, too. But you're better than they are.
I am praying for you.
Your friend,
Tabitha Johnson.

There was silence in the room for what seemed an age. Her mother sat completely still, her mug suspended in her right hand. Tabs could hear the clock on the mantelpiece ticking, and a robin singing in the garden, then the clunk as her mother put her mug down.

"You have made up your mind, haven't you?" sighed Cindy.

"You believe this lad's got a chance?" said Mary.

"I do. I really do."

"Well, you'd better send it then," stated her mother, firmly.

"Just like it is?"

"Just like it is. There is no way he's going to read anything into that. You've always been able to say what's what. Just so long as you don't think he's going to do any of those things, because he won't."

"He might do some of them."

"That's my Tabitha. Not giving up on anyone. But don't let him break your heart."

"Oh, he won't do that. He isn't *that* good." Tabitha grinned. And Mary smiled, and a tear appeared in Cindy's eye.

"The lad who's going to win that heart's going to have to be truly special," commented Mary.

"My heart is not on the market – too many more important things to do than muck around courting, or whatever you called it in your day."

"Quite right," said Mary. Even if her mother didn't, she knew where Tabitha's heart was lodged. And she knew it was safe.

Tabs copied the letter out and put it into an envelope. But now she needed to know the address and she hadn't any idea where Griff was. She was going to have to bring someone else into the secret. She shared her decision with Ashol and Deng.

"Wow," exclaimed Ashol. You're brave.

"No. He's inside. He's safe there."

"But what if he writes back? What if he thinks you secretly have the hots for him?"

"He's not that stupid. If someone liked him like that, they wouldn't say what I write. And he's had plenty of evidence down the years that I think he's gross. Let him write. He doesn't scare me."

"Nothing ventured... You are just brave. I wouldn't dare write to him – especially if he had trashed my house."

"But that's the point. He didn't mean to. Well, not in the end..."

Ashol took a breath to argue but before she could get a word out, Tabs added, "I really believe that. The more I think about it, the more I know it. And neither you nor anyone else is going to convince me otherwise."

"Perhaps Dad's old office could find the address," said Deng. "We could ask at the Council?"

Mr Thomas had not worked in an office that dealt with that kind of thing, but his former boss, recognising the good intentions of the young people and anxious to help the Thomas family, said he would make inquiries. He asked around and eventually came up with the address of the YOI Griff was in.

"The vicar suggests you write to the chaplain," reported Cindy.

"You told the vicar?"

"In confidence. It won't go any further. He can email the chaplain and go from there."

"OK."

"Have a word with Rev. Mike."

Tabs gave a copy of the letter to her mum who passed it to

the vicar. He made contact with the chaplain who gave him an address for Griff. He knew Gareth and would be pleased he had a caring friend on the outside. It appeared the lad was a bit of a loner, which, in the circumstances wasn't such a bad thing.

Tabitha sent off her letter and said a prayer.

***

"Love, love me do. You know I love you." It was Tabitha's latest ringtone. She had decided on Beatles music even though her friends told her it was meant for OAPs. "But, I like it," she protested. Of course, Tabitha Johnson was always happy to be different. This was 'retro-Tabitha.' It was Danielle. A voice call was not her usual method of communication.

"Hi."

"Hi, Tabs. Dad says he's got a letter here for you from Gareth Green."

"He wrote back?"

"Didn't you expect him to?"

"Well, like, not really."

"Well, he has."

"What's he say?"

"No idea. The letter is addressed to you. Dad hasn't opened it."

"OK. I'll come down for it."

"When? We're all out this evening."

"But you're there now. Can I come now, on my way home? I'm still at school."

"Fine. We'll be out after five, though."

Tabitha went straight there. She was kind of excited about getting a letter from Griff. *That's, like, stupid,* she told herself. *Why should she get worked up about a letter from Gross Griff?* But try as she might to control it, her heart beat a little faster as she took the letter from the vicar. He wasn't fooled by her forced nonchalance.

"Hope it says what you want it to. The chaplain added a note to say Gareth appreciated your letter and he had given this to him to pass on."

Tabitha waited to open it until she got home. It wasn't a long letter, but that wasn't surprising. It must have taken Griff some time to put together the few sentences – if you could call them that. She read:

"Hi Tabs,
Cool to get your letter Im sory for doin bad fings to you. Thanks for finkin about me. I wil goto chapel Rev eres grate dude. Wil you do sommut for me can you send me a bibel. And I dont no where me mam is she had to leave the house becos shes got no money now Im in ere. She hasnt bin to see me. Can you find er for me.
Yours fiend,
Gareth Green."

Tabitha didn't know how to react. She had promised that she was not going to write to him again, but now he wanted a Bible. And his mother. Whatever was she going to do? Could she just ignore this? No one, whatever they had done – good or evil – should be out of contact with their mum, should they? Surely that was wrong, for her as well as for him. She was reluctant to approach Cindy, but she was going to have to – she just had to act. The more she thought about it, though, the happier she was. Griff definitely seemed to have reacted positively.

Her mum, as Tabitha predicted, was not happy. Cindy was acutely aware that the world can be a dangerous place, and modern communications make it feel more dangerous than ever. She was worried.

"I told you it wouldn't end there," she sighed.

"It can end any time I want it to," stated Tabitha. She didn't have to respond to Griff. In any case, where was she going to get a Bible, and what sort and at what cost? "But, don't you see, he's at least telling me he's trying to be good." She read the first bit of the letter out loud. "I think he means it – that bit about being sorry."

"Well all right, but you're not going to enter into a regular correspondence with a boy in prison?"

262

"Young Offender Institute."

"Same thing."

"But a Bible couldn't do him no harm, could it?"

"Maybe not, but he can get one from the chaplain there, I'm sure."

"I suppose so. But it will only be borrowed. It's not the same as having your own."

"But do you have to buy it?"

"I can ask Mary if there's a second-hand one in the shop?"

"I hope Mary is of the same opinion as I am about this, Tabitha, I want you to end it here."

"But, Mum." But when her mum was using this tone, Tabitha knew there was no point in arguing.

Probably because Cindy felt she needed an ally, it was she who raised the subject with Mary. Mary knew exactly where to get a Bible suitable for Griff. If someone asked for a Bible, she instinctively felt he should not be denied. Judging from his spelling, it needed to be one in fairly straightforward modern English. That would not be an easy task. I think *The Good News Bible* might work for him. Even then..."

"*The Good News Bible*. What's that?" Cindy protested. Mary was assuming Tabs should comply with his request.

"*The Good News Bible* has been written to appeal especially to young people."

"But does Tabitha have to send it?"

"Well, no. But we should not deny someone a Bible... And I don't think we can ignore the bit about his mum either, can we?"

Cindy hadn't thought about it from the point of view of his mother. "I suppose not."

"Don't worry, Cindy. He's inside a YOI and there's our vicar and a chaplain in between."

"Well, OK. But it makes me feel nervous."

"And rightly so. But Tabitha is a sensible young woman."

"A young woman now, is she?"

"OK, not quite. But I think you can insist that she acts like one in this instance."

Later that evening, Cindy and Mary told Tabitha what they had discussed.

"Wicked," exclaimed Tabitha.

"But you have to act in a very grown-up way about this, Tabitha," emphasised Cindy.

"Of course, I will."

"I mean it, Tabitha. I don't want you to get carried away with this just because you have a kind heart."

"I know, Mum. I won't."

"I'll get two Bibles, one for you and one for Griff," interjected Mary.

"No, you won't. I've got to pay for this," demanded Tabitha.

"What with?" said Mary, flatly. "You're not flush with money, are you? And you help in the shop for nothing... And besides, who am I going to share my fortune with if not you? I'm afraid you're going to have to put up with an old lady who has the desire to support you, you know."

"But I can't—"

"Yes, you can. As we keep saying, life doesn't share things out evenly. If people are going to give to even it up, others are going to have to put up with receiving. In any case, I just want to help you help Griff. What you're doing is making a difference. But I think we should ask Mike to send this so that Griff doesn't get the idea that you bought it for him. That would be wrong. It has to come from him with your blessing."

"OK. You win. But one day it'll be my turn to help you."

"You've been doing that for a long time, lass."

"Thanks. And I think your idea of the vicar is a good one. It'll make mum happier, too." Cindy breathed an assent. "What about Mrs Green though? How do we find her?"

"Let me have a chat with Mike about that, too."

The vicar got the whole story from the YOI chaplain. Apparently, Mrs Green had left the flat she shared with Griff when the landlord repossessed it. She had told Gareth she had gone to the Borough Council in London but they couldn't help her because she hadn't lived in the borough for more than six months. Gareth thought she had gone back to Yorkshire but she hadn't been to see him and she hadn't put an address on her letters. The postmark of her last letter was West Yorks.

Mike thought she might have been referred back to the local authorities for housing in West Yorkshire. If so, she could be anywhere – Leeds, Bradford, Wakefield, Huddersfield, Halifax...

"They'll know at the Housing Department," said Mike. "But I doubt they'll tell me. I can try but—"

"If she's in West Yorkshire, Cat Sowers'll know."

"You mean..."

"There's nowt Cat don't know and if she don't yet, it'll not be long before she does. I'll take myself to Beattie's. What I do for you, Tabitha. I need my head testing."

"Thanks, Mum." Tabs recalled her conversation with Jack Frost. Griff was proving to be hard work to a whole lot of people and it was she who had started it.

It took a fortnight but Cat delivered. All Cindy had to do was let out that she'd heard Griff's mother was back in the area and Cat couldn't wait to get the lowdown. The thought that Cindy Johnson knew more than she did was galling. Eventually, she gathered Mrs Green was in a single room in a lodging house in Heckmondwike. It seemed that owing to a health condition, West Yorkshire County Council had put a roof over her head but nothing more.

"Heckmondwike? But does she know anyone in Heckmondwike?" wondered Tabitha.

"From what I remember of her," added Cindy, "she never was one for neighbouring. Saw her once at the bingo but she never came again. I doubt she's got anyone who would miss her on Beck Ings."

"I gather she was well known at the church Jumble Sales," volunteered Mike.

"But for buying, not helping," said Mary. "You make friends by helping. I guess Gareth was all she had."

"And now he's in prison down south and she's stuck in a strange town where she knows no one," sighed Tabitha.

"Tabitha Chapeltown," said her mother forcibly. "You're not going to try and help Mrs Green, too."

"But she's lonely, Mum. She hasn't got anyone."

"But she's not your responsibility," insisted Cindy. She turned to Mike. "What about the vicar in Heckmondwike?"

"I thought you might say that," he said. "The trouble is vicars are busy people. I'm reluctant to—"

"Mum, you can't get Mike to do any more."

"The church could be involved though," stated Mary. "The vicar doesn't have to do everything. I know someone who runs a charity shop in Heckmondwike. We exchange stuff. Let me go and see her and we'll see if the local church has a visiting team."

"Great," exclaimed Tabitha. "Cool. Can I come with you?"

"I don't think we are going to be able to keep you out of this one, are we?" laughed Mary. "Gareth Green has struck a vein of gold just by leading a load of thugs into your house and looking sad through the eye holes of a balaclava. The Lord works in mysterious ways."

The trip to Mary's friend in Heckmondwike was a fascinating one for Tabitha. Mrs Hollingsworth had got her shop set up with all sorts of interesting knick-knacks. She had a good display of DVDs, but far fewer books than Mary. It turned out that Mary traded stuff with her. The films, ashtrays and colourful glass things – animals, vases, paper-weights and even marbles – were in much greater demand in Heckmondwike, whereas the books, being a speciality of Friends of Africa, turned over much quicker in Millheaton. 'Tit for tat,' Mary called it. Mrs Hollingsworth was a regular at St James in Church Street and a member of the Mothers' Union.

"One of our MU objects," she explained to Tabs, "is to help families in adversity. I think Mrs Green certainly comes into that category. Let me try and see if I can find anything out about her." She seemed almost enthusiastic about it. "I enjoy helping people," she added. "Especially where Mary's concerned. If it wasn't for Mary, we might not have gotten established here in the way that we have done. Having a speciality is the clue because people come from all over if they think you always have something new in their line."

She went on to tell them, over a cup of tea out the back, that Syd her assistant was a real whizz on eBay. That very same gentleman was looking after the customers as they chatted. He had been widowed a couple of years ago. He and his wife hadn't had any children and at seventy-five he found himself very lonely. He used to drop in just to pass the time of day because he liked Mrs Hollingsworth's glassware. Sometimes he brought things in to sell.

"Then, last year," continued Mrs Hollingsworth, "he discovered eBay and sold a few things on it and he asked if he could try and sell some stuff for me. In no time he had cleared out nearly all my dead stock. It's not rubbish to the person who wants it, but finding that person has always been difficult; eBay has made it easier. But, I tell you one thing, it's time-consuming doing things on the computer. He loves it, though; it has given him a new lease on life. Now with him and swapping with Mary here, I can move nearly everything I get given."

It didn't take long for Mrs Hollingsworth to find Mrs Green. She had to explain how she knew about her, of course, and so, very soon, Tabitha got another letter. This time from Mrs Green via Mary thanking her for her concern and telling her that they'd all got Gareth wrong. He was a good boy who had been easily led.

Tabs disagreed with her on that point. For most of the time she had known him, Griff had been the one doing the leading. But she was content to believe that behind it all, there might be a better boy who was learning his lesson in the wider world.

"I wonder if Mrs Green has made any new friends?" mused Tabs. Her mother had given up arguing with her – she always seemed to lose these days.

"So you're going to be her friend now, I suppose?"

"No. She's old, Mum."

"She's my age."

"Exactly."

Her mother gave her a mock scowl.

"No. I just wondered if there is someone from Heckmondwike who also needs a friend?"

"Have you anyone in mind?... You're not thinking of Syd?"

"Syd? Oh no, Mum. He's *really* old. No, just ladies her age in Heckmondwike?"

But she was second. Mrs Hollingsworth had already invited Mrs Green to an evening slide show of the vicar's trip to the Holy Land, a Mothers' Union afternoon tea and the scouts' bingo. She had turned them all down; she was 'not a mixer,' she explained. "Then come to tea at my house – just me," said Mrs Hollingsworth in her blunt Yorkshire way. And she did.

Before long, new friends had seen that Mrs Green got a ticket south to see Gareth. During that visit, she told Gareth that it was Tabitha and her friend Mary who had helped to "turn things around" for her.

15

Tabs had barely got in from school when her phone beeped a text. It was from an unknown number. *Who could this be from? Who's this who knows my number?* She opened it and read in capitals: BE CAREFUL! YUV BEEN TOLD. It had an attached image. Tabs almost dropped the phone. Her screen bore an image of a hangman game. There were spaces for two words with some of it filled in – it was clearly her name TA_ _T_A   J_ _N_ O N. The game was almost lost – only the figure remained to be completed.

What the hell? What should I do with this? I can't show this to my mum; it'll panic her. It's just some stupid prank. Tabs deleted the message and blacklisted the number. But the 'you've been told' resonated with the words of the leader of the attacks. It couldn't be him but it could be one of his cronies on the outside. *Nah. This is, like, what some stupid kid would do. Best to just ignore it. Forget it.*

As she looked at it, the phone sprang to life. "Love, love me do, you..." To her relief, it was Danielle Buckley.

"Hi, Danielle."

"Hi, Tabs. Thought I'd call rather than Whatsapp."

"Getting, like, a habit. Old fashioned."

"Yeah. But it's kinda important and I wouldn't want you to think I was joking... Would you like to go to America?"

"You ... what? ... where?"

"America. You know that boy Adele went to stay with last summer – you know the one who was here at Christmas?"

"Yeah. Can't remember his name. Red or something."

"Clint."

"Yeah. I knew it was something you only got called in America. So, he wants *me* to go to America?"

"Not just you. His church is inviting 'a bunch of kids' – they mean us teenagers – to stay with some of them in August next year, and then they would come to us the year after. A kind of exchange. It won't cost you anything. We'll raise the money for the airfare through doing stuff at church."

"Well yeah. I suppose so. Sounds cool?" *California. That's like in your dreams, girl.*

"Yeah. Dad says you should be one of those who go because you do so much for other people. Then there are Deng and Ashol because they've been coming to church, like, forever, and me, and Adele, of course, because she's been already."

"That makes five."

"Then we're asking the Biggs twins, Dave and Andy. They're thinking about it but they're not sure yet... We won't be staying all together in one house; we'll be with different families..."

"What about Ashol and Deng? I guess, though, with their dad in South Sudan, they might have to go there in the holidays."

"They're cool. Deng says their dad won't have enough money for them all to join him by next summer. They said they'd go if you did. You seem to be important. So it's a yes, then?"

"Hang on, Danielle, I'll have to ask Mum. She's here. Just a minute."

Tabitha called out of her bedroom. "Mum, I can go to America next summer, can't I?"

"America? What's all this about? Whose—"

"With the young people from church. It's Danielle. She's going. Church will get the money."

"Well, I suppose—" began Cindy, doubtfully.

"Mum's cool," said Tabitha, hurriedly.

"Whose paying?" yelled her mum, coming into the room.

"Mum says whose paying?" She put Danielle on speakerphone.

"We'll do some fundraising ... sponsored swim or something."

"We don't have money, Danielle," chipped in Cindy.

No problem. This isn't for rich kids."

"OK?" Tabs looked at her mum. Cindy nodded. If anyone had offered her a trip to America when she was sixteen, she would have bitten their hand off.

"OK," she confirmed with Danielle.

"Cool. I'll text the Thomases right now. Bye."

Tabs put down her phone. Wow. America. Where'd he say he lived? Santa somewhere. Santa ... Santa Barbara. That was it. She was sure that was it. She found her atlas. She knew it was by the sea. On the Pacific Ocean, she had heard Clint say. She traced the coastline with her finger. Yes, there was a Santa Barbara along the coast from Los Angeles in California. It looked cool – and a long way.

"Yes," said Rev Mike to Cindy the following Sunday. "I thought Tabitha would make a good ambassador for us. We'll have some fundraising events in spring. She'll be quite safe. They are all to stay at the homes of church young people of the same age."

How different things are from just twelve months ago, mused Cindy to herself.

"Hello. What are you doing at Christmas, this year, Cindy?" It was Mary coming across holding a less-than-dainty church mug of tea.

"Oh, hello. Hadn't given it a thought. Until last year we never had much choice."

"How about you all come to me this year? I mean you, Tabitha and the Thomases. This year they will be feeling the absence of Garang. As you know, I have three bedrooms. If you don't mind sleeping in a second bed in my room, the girls can have the spare room, Sarah the box room, and Deng can be downstairs in the living room. That way, I reckon I can get us all in."

"That would be nice, Mary. Tab would love it. But we don't have to stay over, we can go home to sleep."

"You can if you want to, but it was great having people to fill up my little house when yours wasn't available. I thought we could do it 'just for fun' this time."

"Well, OK. Thank you. We don't need to ask Tabitha; I know what she would say."

"Then let's go and ask the Thomases."

Mrs Thomas agreed readily enough. The past few months had been rather traumatic and she was glad not to have to be at home – a home in which there would be an empty chair at Christmas. No one sat in Garang's chair; no meal had been the same since he left.

The young people were told the plan. They were, of course, delighted. Cindy offered to bake a Christmas cake and Mama Sarah said she would get a tree. Mary already had some tree decorations to put on it. Deng went to work on adapting and decorating a wooden box to act as a crib and Mary produced a book of patterns for a knitted nativity set which she had got from Mrs Hollingsworth.

Ashol and Tabitha each chose a character to start knitting; Cindy had a lot of odd ends that came in useful. They had soon knitted Mary, Joseph, two shepherds and three wise men. Mary had contributed a sheep and a donkey while Mrs Thomas crocheted a little baby Jesus just the right size to fit into the tiny manger Deng had made to go into his model stable.

***

About three weeks before Christmas, Deng asked Tabitha if they could visit the garden and the wood.

"Sure. Any special reason?"

"Yeah. I want to think, work something out."

"Of course. You can just go, you know. Any time. We don't have to go together. Mary's cool about you going there."

"I know. But it's your place. And I want to go with you. It's not right without you. You belong there. You're part of the place. And, anyway, I want to kinda bounce some ideas off you."

"When do you want to go?"

"Saturday?"

"Fine. I'll meet you on the corner at ten."

"Better make it eleven, then I can get an assignment done before we go."

"OK. Eleven o'clock, it is."

Tabs spent the rest of the week feeling on edge. This was serious for Deng. They had kissed, hadn't they? She hadn't intended it. She was quite content to just have him as her 'boyfriend' the way they were. She wasn't looking for anything more intense.

On Saturday, Deng was waiting for her.

"Finished your assignment?" Tabs asked. He nodded. They walked hand-in-hand towards the Puddleham Road.

"Oui, mademoiselle. Je viens de lire la dernière chapitre d' Eugénie Grandet par Balzac."

272

"Well, I hope it didn't bite. What's 'bal-zack'?"

"Honoré de Balzac. He's a French nineteenth-century novelist who decided to write a different novel about every level of society."

"Every level? Sounds like an enormous task?"

"Don't think he got through his whole list. *Eugénie Grandet* is upper class society. Mademoiselle Gaudet reckons that a lot of it is a bit tedious. But we have to do it."

"Have you read it all in French?"

"Well, some of it. I have in English. I've got time to plough through more of the French before the exam. The trouble is that there are so many nineteenth-century words that aren't in my dictionary. Looking them up on the 'translate' app doesn't always work, either."

Tabitha had already ordered a very big French-English dictionary for him for Christmas, so she hoped he wouldn't get around to getting one himself before then.

"Anyway," he said, "I've done the French assignment that Mademoiselle Gaudet set us to be in by the beginning of next term. Now I have to concentrate on English, history and RS. But there is something else that I need to settle; that's why I want to go to the garden and the wood."

Deng took a plastic sheet from his bag, laid it on the garden seat and beckoned Tabitha to sit beside him. He put his arm around her shoulders, leaned down and kissed her. Tabitha froze but she didn't resist. She wasn't sure where this was leading.

"So what's on your mind?" she asked.

"Well, you know that I was meant to be a doctor..."

"But, I thought you had decided that you... that you had changed your mind? You're not doing the right subjects. You're going to be a lawyer, instead."

"That's what I want to talk about." Tabs uncoiled inside.

"I can't be a doctor. There's no way. The funny thing is that I don't mind that much. The truth is that it was never my idea; it was never something I wanted to do – just thought that that was how it was going to be."

"Your parents wanted that for you."

"Yes. For them and South Sudan."

"But it's not what you wanted and you're not going to, so what's the problem?"

"Well, in our family you've always got to know what you want to be. I mean, you can't just say I will decide next August when the results come out."

"Why not? That makes sense. You're only in first year sixth."

"I know but not with Dad and Mum. You have to know."

"Anyway, I thought that was decided. You were talking about being a lawyer."

"*They* are. But there is no way I want to be a lawyer. It was Mum's idea, again. 'If you can't be a doctor, you'll be a lawyer.' No discussion... So, the problem is that the longer I let this idea go, the more established it will be – just like the doctor thing – and I will have all that explaining to do over again. But this time it will be worse because – and this is what makes it really bad, I won't be able to blame exam results... well, I hope not. It will just be me being... being..."

"Awkward?"

"Well, kind of. My dad would say, 'You don't change canoes mid-stream. You risk being got by the crocodiles.' I can hear him saying it, even if he's not here. And that makes it worse because I can't argue with him. Not that I have thought of arguing with him – not up till now. That sounds so disloyal, doesn't it?"

"No, I don't think it does. I argue with my mum all the time but I still respect her. She wouldn't have thought about some of the choices I have to make because it'd never occur to her that there is a choice; school was different for her. But I get what your dad says. Canoes stand for careers. He's saying it's better to choose your canoe before you paddle out onto the river?"

"You've got it. And if I'm not going to be a lawyer, I've got to choose another canoe... now. Will you help me choose my canoe?"

"But I don't know anything about your possible canoes – what's out there for you? Especially about what it's like in South Sudan."

"But you know me. The thing is that up till now it's been about what I could do in South Sudan. That's the question. I should choose to pursue a career that I can use over there. But what if I stayed here? I can then decide on something I can do here. If it appeals to Dad and Mum."

"And *not* go to live in South Sudan?" Tabs' heart missed a beat.

"The thing is, I don't necessarily have to go there to help the country. I could do stuff for the country from outside as part of the diaspora."

"Diaspora? You'll have to explain, Deng."

"The diaspora means South Sudanese abroad. There are a lot of South Sudanese who live abroad. They still help their country – especially now that internet connections are getting stronger and you can work away from home... But, up to now, that's not been my parents' idea."

Deng stood up and took Tabs' hand and he led her to the little gate and into the woods. They leapt over the puddles and avoided the worst of the mud until they reached the little clearing. The ferns on its margins were golden brown but the grass was tall and lush. A light rain began to fall and Deng pulled out a folding umbrella from the pocket of his wax jacket. Tabitha laughed.

"You act so grown-up," she said. "Not like a teenager at all."

"No, I suppose not. It's just that I have always had to think about things a lot. I wish I didn't."

"But now you're going to tell me that you have an idea for what you might do. What canoes there are for you to choose from."

"You'll tell me the truth? I mean if you think it's stupid?"

"I'd never tell you anything but the truth of what I think ... but it'll be *only* what I think. I don't know much; I might be wrong. And I might, like, be prejudiced."

"You don't want us to go to South Sudan?"

"Of course not. I mean not for me. You're the best friends I've ever had and I don't want to lose you. But I do understand... I think."

Deng smiled. He didn't want to lose her, either. He hesitated.

"So, let me tell you what's on my mind. You... you know what Ashol said about me being ordained – being a vicar?" Tabs nodded. "At first, I thought it was a silly idea. In South Sudan pastors mostly don't come from outside the village; they are

275

chosen by their congregations, and they are not short of people wanting to be ordained. And, besides, ordained ministers have to properly understand what it's like in a place and you can't do that properly unless you grew up there, so it wouldn't work for me to do that there. But if I were to stay in England, there are lots of places where I could work. They need vicars, here, don't they? And the Sudanese diaspora needs ministers... So what do you think? Can you see me like Rev Mike?"

Tabs stood completely still for about five seconds. Deng looked at her anxiously. "Yeah, it's a silly idea, isn't it? I—" Tabitha put her finger to his lips.

"Hush. Don't rush along. Let my little brain catch up. This is serious stuff, Deng. How sure are you? How much do you know about other canoes that might be waiting for you if you're going to stay in England?"

"Well, I ... I am doing the right subjects."

There was a pause in which they both stood in silence, him waiting on her. If he couldn't answer the question to his own satisfaction, how could she? But after a minute of reflection, listening to the sounds of the woods, she continued. "Let me say first that you would make a brilliant vicar. But how many vicars decide what they are going to be aged sixteen? It's just as bad as the lawyer thing if you are making your mind up too early. You feel you need to launch a canoe now because of what your mum and dad think. But, honestly, you don't have to. You don't have to decide until next year if you want to go to college when you're eighteen – and lots of people take a gap year anyway, don't they?"

"I know. But it's different for me."

"Is it? What would be harder – to tell your parents you'll make up your mind when you think it's right, even if they don't like you saying it, or to tell them something when you're only sixteen when you might change your mind again? The idea of being a lawyer is only that, isn't it? An idea. You haven't launched your canoe. You've another year before you have to think about applying for lawyer training or whatever they do. But if you say you want to be a vicar, it'll be like putting the canoe into the water right now if you tell everyone at the church – at school even – and then it'll be hard to change your mind, even if you haven't paddled out very far. People will get excited for you and not just your parents. So you have to be really sure."

"I know."

"And you *can't* be sure yet – *shouldn't* – because you're sixteen and haven't been thinking about it long enough."

"Well, actually, it's been longer than you think, but I just dismissed the idea because of the doctor thing and going to South Sudan and all that. The thing is that I've got to the stage where I have to do something. I know I have to talk to someone. And I wanted to talk to you first."

"Thanks. I'm flattered, Deng. So, I don't think you being a vicar is a silly idea at all. You have a deep faith, you've grown up with the Bible and you care about people. You're a brilliant listener. You're kind and gentle, and you've got guts. I reckon you could paddle that canoe bravely and defeat the crocodiles."

"You think so?"

"I do. But just because you could be good at something doesn't mean you *should* do it. I don't think when someone is sixteen they should set off in a canoe like that at all. Unless you want to leave school and do an apprenticeship, you don't need to risk the crocs. Not at sixteen. I'd say, steer clear of the river for now."

"Yeah. That's like true for *other people* in Year 12 but not for *me*. *I* have to say something. That's the point. And I can't let this lawyer idea go on, either."

"No, I guess you can't. So tell your mum and dad that. And when they say, 'What then?' say, 'I'll tell you when I'm ready.' You're choosing the vicar thing now to stop the lawyer thing. That's not a good reason."

"But they won't like that." Deng's peace was evaporating fast. "I can't just—"

Tabs stood her ground. "You can if it's the right thing to do. I've just told you you've got guts, Deng. If your parents knew you were trying to do the right thing, they would understand. They love you."

"I guess, but it's so complicated." Deng put his head in his hands and Tabs encircled him with her arms. He knew she was right but she didn't get the whole picture. "Thank you, Tabs.

277

Thank you for your wisdom."

"Wise? I'm not that. I've no idea what I want to do with my life."

"You have a whole load of canoes to choose from still. No need to rush. Your mum is not wanting to tell her relatives anywhere. That's why it's complicated. That's the hardest part – even if I can get Mum and Dad to support the idea of waiting, it'll not go down well there. Everyone's supposed to be on a career track and my parents will get heavily criticised if I'm not on one."

"So, let the relatives in South Sudan think you're going to be a lawyer, for now. Your mum and dad needn't say anything until you actually get into your canoe, until you're paddling on the river." A broad smile spread across Deng's face. That might work. His dad only needed to share the minimum. After all, how much did he know about *his* cousins' career plans?"

"Yeah. You *are* wise, Tabs."

"No. Not me. It's this wood. It always says, 'Slow down. Listen. Wait.'"

"God's time."

"And God's got forever, I guess."

"You know, I think I could persuade Dad and Mum if I said that. I will tell them God wants me to wait. And I'm sure he does." Deng grew excited. "I—" Tabs put a finger to his lips.

"Hush. No more words, just listen." They stood as still as they could and listened to the sounds of the wood. Then she turned her face up towards his and kissed him gently on the lips. This could be for forever after all. She leaned into him and put her arm around him. She didn't wish the kissing to end. When they parted, she put her finger on his lips again and took his hand. It was time to move on in silence.

Deng lifted his foot. Squelch. They had stood in the same spot too long and had begun to sink in. He stifled a man-sized snort as he made a second squelch. Now, the silence was quite broken. Tabs grinned. They were kids again. She made an even noisier drawn-out deliberate *splluuurt*.

"Don't be rude."

"You do have a dirty mind, Deng. No. Can't imagine you as a vicar." She laughed. "They don't think those sorts of things."

"Don't they? You don't know Rev Mike."

"I can imagine. Especially if Danielle's anything to go by."

They extracted themselves from the mud making as many varieties of squelch as they could and began to plod back to the garden gate.

"Are you looking forward to going to America?"

"Yeah. Brilliant. I still haven't taken it in yet. It feels too good to be true. Do you like the idea?"

"Yes. But only if you're there. It wouldn't feel right without you."

And their cheeks came together again in the cool damp air. The trees slumbered and pretended to ignore them – they weren't ready yet for the spring. Only the holly trees seemed undeterred by the winter rain as they reached out their shiny rich green leaves and red berries to announce that Christmas was around the corner.

16

"I hope it snows like last year," said Ashol. "The cottage will be wonderful in the snow – just like in the Christmas cards."

But Christmas Eve came and it wasn't to be. Ashol complained about it. "You can't have everything," said Mary. "In all my time, I don't think I have ever seen snow like last year on Christmas Day."

"'Spose not. But there's no harm in asking."

"It'll be cold enough to have the fire going all day though, so you can fill up the log bucket for me before you get changed to go to church."

"Yippee, midnight communion. I just love midnight communion."

"It's OK when you're young. I'll just join you for the service tomorrow."

"The show and tell service."

"Show and tell?... Oh you mean when the vicar asks you what you got in your stocking – so to speak."

"You must show what I'm going to give you," said Tabs.

"A present. For me?"

"Of course."

"So what will I be showing?"

"You'll have to wait and see."

"The fourth fruit of the Spirit."

"Uh? You what?"

"Patience. You know, love, joy, peace, patience... Galatians chapter five, verse twenty-two"

"Yes, patience." Tabs giggled at Mary's propensity for saying exactly where her quote came from. "'Patience is a virtue' – my mum, chapter six, verse four. So you'll have to wait."

Each was filled with delights that Christmas. The older folk enjoyed watching the young ones and the young ones revelled in each other and their presents. Tabitha's gift for Deng was definitely the heaviest one under the tree, and his present for her was easily the lightest. Deng received an absolutely enormous French-English dictionary. He spent a lot of time during the days of Christmas coming out with the most esoteric French words and expressions.

"Apparently," he said, "*poser le lapin*', 'to give someone the rabbit' means not to show up on a date."

"Oh, how sweet," said Ashol who would much prefer a new pet rabbit than a date with a boy.

"I don't suppose it means you get a real rabbit. It's just an expression."

"Sounds like a pretty mean thing to do," thought Tabs.

"Yeah, I suppose. Especially if you don't actually get a rabbit," agreed Ashol.

Tabs' gift from Deng was a silver bracelet with forget-me-not stems and flowers traced around it.

"I love it!" She slipped it over her left hand and clasped it. "Thank you, Deng." She leaned over and kissed him on the cheek as everyone crowded in to admire it. "Can I show it in church?"

"Well if you want." Deng felt both pleased and a bit embarrassed. "But—"

"Oh. Everyone knows about you two," blurted out Ashol. "They've known for months."

"Known what?" asked Tabs.

"That you two are in love and a real item."

"Ashol," reprimanded her mother.

"Can't be months," said Tabitha, uneasily.

"Oh, yes. Ages."

"It *has* been quite noticeable that you are fond of each other," said Mary. "Long before you acknowledged it yourselves of course. That's the general way of it. So it won't come as a surprise to anyone in the church that Deng has given you a delightful present."

"Now you can open yours," said Tabs, eager to change the subject. She rummaged under the tree until she found a flat rectangular gift.

"Mine?" smiled Mary. She held it and weighed it in her hand. If it was a book, it was a heavy one.

"Open it," ordered Ashol with impatience. Mary carefully removed the wrapping and uncovered a glazed frame. Under the glass was a carefully arranged cluster of dried flowers, grasses and small leaves. It was beautiful."

"I can draw a bit," said Tabs, "but nature is far more beautiful than pictures. I just put different bits of it together."

Mary came quite near to shedding a tear. "This is very lovely, Tabitha. I shall treasure it. I'll put it up over there by the front door so everyone sees it as they come in."

"But you've got to take it to church first," ordered Ashol. That was something Mary would be very pleased to do; it would be the first time she had joined in the "show and tell".

Christmas proved to be a great success at Mary's. They stayed three whole nights before going home which meant that Cindy was not alone with Tabs away with her father on Boxing Day – she had reverted to spending the day after Christmas with her dad's family. New Year's Eve in downtown Leeds had not appealed. Then, finally, Cindy invited Mary for tea at number 49 the day after that.

Tucking into yet more Christmas cake and some of the special tea Cindy liked that Tabs had given her for Christmas, Mary said she had had a wonderful time over the last few days, and that the old year had been a year to remember, especially for all the new friends she had made.

"I was wondering if in the new year..." she continued. "Tabitha, I was wondering whether, now you know that it isn't the fairies that tend the little garden, I could hand over to you and Deng some of the heavier jobs. The hedge-clipping, and so on. I'm not so keen on the step ladder these days."

"Sure," agreed Tabs, "Deng could reach without a step-ladder."

"That had occurred to me."

"We were only saying the other day that we would like to help but we didn't want to ask because we didn't want to take anything away from you."

"That's sweet of you, but I keep telling you, Tabitha, that the garden needs you to complete it – and now Deng too."

"When do we need to start?"

"Oh. Not yet. Not before the spring. I won't cut the grass until late March at the earliest."

***

On the third day of January, there was another text from a second unknown number – a different number but the same person. This the message was: "U R DEAD!" The attached image was a photo of the same hangman game only attached to the scaffold was a person with a filled-in face – black with long hair.

Tabitha couldn't deny her fear. She felt her knees wobble and she felt like she needed the loo. When she got inside the bathroom she locked the door and held onto the sink to steady herself and there she was in the mirror – the same mirror that less than a year ago had been decorated with obscene images and threats. Tabs threw up.

Don't be a wimp. It's a sick prank. Don't let it get to you. Before the evil attacks, she would not have given it a second thought. Stupid kids posted all sorts of horrid stuff online. They watched loads of violent stuff on the tele, staying up well past the nine o'clock watershed even in primary school. She thought who might want to have a go at her? *Lots of people, I guess. Rosie's got, like, bitchy because I've left her set and wouldn't go halves with her on a vape. Perhaps I shouldn't have said she shouldn't do it herself, even if it was lemonade pop flavour. She were right to tell me not to be a 'holy Joanne'. Dean Prentice's making out with Amy, and I told her not to be an idiot and risk getting herself pregnant. And then there's all that stuff around me and Deng and them that have a problem with Ibrahim. It could be any of them, couldn't it. It doesn't have to be that gang or their friends. I should just forget it. Or, maybe... what if... Oh, what should I do?*

Reluctantly, Tabs decided she'd better report it to her teachers and if she was going to do that at school, her mum needed to know, too.

***

On that same day, Mary left the shop to Bill and crossed the road to Lumbley, Lumbley and Short, the local solicitors. She had an appointment with Mr Lumbley, Senior, who had been her solicitor since he was Mr Lumbley, Junior.

"What can I do for you, Miss Macey? Not thinking of moving into one of the new flats in town for senior citizens are you?"

"Goodness me no. My cottage is getting filled up with people coming on a regular basis. I couldn't consider downsizing."

"Some people do it to get a bit of well-earned peace, Miss Macey, but you seem to thrive on being busy."

"That is true Mr Lumbley. No, I am not moving house, and I intend to remain active for a few more good years, but at my age, you never know, so I have decided to make a new will." She took a seat in front of Mr Lumbley's desk.

"As you know, I never married and have no children. My nearest relatives are cousins who live in Lancashire. I've only seen them once in the last ten years and probably no more than ten times in my life. I want to leave all my money and treasures to Friends of Africa but I want Cindy and Tabitha Johnson to have the Old Lodge when I leave this life for my heavenly one – unless, of course, it has to be sold beforehand to keep me in a care home."

"You are not related to the Johnsons?"

"Not at all. But I have no close family. No one will contest this. And I can't think of anyone more deserving. They are the closest people I have had since I lost my parents. You know I have been sharing Tabitha's company since she was a little girl seeking the fairies in my garden. Part of her growing up has been in my garden. Only a few weeks ago I told her it is our garden. I don't want some stranger to have it – not the garden, nor my house."

"I think we can draw up a will on these lines, Miss Macey. Now, who would you like to act as executor?"

"Could you do that, Mr Lumbley? I wouldn't want anyone to know what my will contains until I've gone."

"Of course, Miss Macey. Wills are usually best kept secret."

***

As predicted, Cindy took the text extremely seriously. The first thing she did was call DI Gillespie. Tabs was called into the station and was interviewed with her mum there.

"Have you had any other similar texts?"

Tabs had to admit this was the second. "I got one, like, about six weeks ago. It was the same picture although no one was hung. It said to be careful and I had been warned."

"So you kept that one to yourself? Why doesn't that surprise me, Tabitha?"

"I thought it was, like, someone just larking about."

Her mum was furious.

"Mum, kids do pranks all the time. I just thought it was, like, another one of them. And I still think it's someone from school. It doesn't have to have anything to do with the trashing of the flat."

"You may be right," said the inspector, "but I'm going to make some inquiries. See if we can find out whose number this is. In the meantime, watch and listen and tell me straight away if you get another of these texts."

"Is that it?" Cindy was not satisfied.

"I've told you we'll look into it, Cindy. There are no specific threats. But feel free to contact us anytime if anything comes up."

"Thanks," said Tabs. "Come on, Mum. It'll be OK."

"Will it?"

Tabs didn't respond – she had resolved to do a bit of investigation of her own, beginning with Rosie Peters.

17

This new year was a big one for the young people. The teachers were predicting good grades for Tabitha in her GCSEs if she carried on working hard, and she would try not to let them down.

During her first lunchtime, Tabs went in search of Rosie Peters but bumped into a rather rough-looking Amy Lane. She had cut her hair shorter but it still looked like it hadn't been brushed for a week and there was a greasy-looking stain on her skirt.

"Hi, Amy." Tabs was going to ask her where Rosie might be found but thought she would take advantage of the opportunity to begin with her. "You haven't been sending, like, texts, have you?"

"Texts. You? What sort of texts."

Wouldn't you like to know?

"You would know if you had sent them."

"Nah. Why would I do that? You've turned into a swat and it's all about you and that tall dark, what's his name, Bongo? Is he good in bed?"

"Deng. His name is Deng. And it's not like that. Not that it's any business what I do with my boyfriends."

"So how's that different between me and Dean? 'Idiot' is the word you used."

"Yeah. I gues, I shouldn't have said that. I just didn't want you to get hurt." Amy shrugged. "Anyway, I was looking for Rosie Peters. I thought she'd be around here."

"Haven't you heard? Rosie's not coming back to school. She's left."

"Wow. What about her GCSEs?"

"What about 'em? What she need GCSEs for? She's already sixteen. They can't make her stay at school."

"No. Guess not."

"I wouldn't, either, if my stupid birthday wasn't until July."

"Well... er... thanks. See you around."

"Not if I see you first." Amy stomped off revealing a tear in her dusty black tights.

Amy, you're in a bad place. Guess if I believe in God, I should pray for you but that would like make me feel like I think I'm better than you. But I'm not. I'm just lucky with things. Even if people are sending me stupid texts. Anyway, I guess I can rule out Rosie and Amy.

Now Tabitha had a hard-working boyfriend who also needed to study, it suited them both to give each other the encouragement to work as well as play. Sometimes, if they felt a little lonely, they would sit together at the same table, books out, pens scratching and computers rattling, lost in whatever task was to be accomplished. Occasionally, Tabs would get Deng to help with the French, or simply borrow his big dictionary. He would gently help with some clues to the other subjects but, for the most part, they concentrated on their own work.

With Deng and Tabs so close, Ashol sometimes found herself at a loose end, so she would go and sit with Mary in the shop whom she judged, rightly, needed company.

Cindy took a bus to Heckmondwike and went to see Gloria Green. She enjoyed the lady heaping praises on her daughter. Gareth was apparently now out of detention and was working in a furniture-making place to the southwest of London somewhere. "A proper apprentice," affirmed his mother.

***

February half-term was upon them in no time. Tabitha had arranged to help Mary in Friends of Africa. Cindy came round to the shop with a letter she had just received from Gloria Green. It contained a photocopy of an article in the Alderstone Gazette, Hampshire, dated Monday, 14th February. The headline ran: "MY HANDSOME HERO." There followed a picture of Griff with a sheepish smile on his face sitting beside an old lady in a hospital bed. Her face was badly bruised but she was looking up at him with smiling eyes. He was holding her hand. Alongside the picture, the report continued.

Florence Gumbridge (81) was rescued on Thursday last from her burning flat by teenager, Gareth Green (16).

Mrs Gumbridge told reporters that she had been asleep in her ground floor flat early last Thursday morning when she awoke to the sound of her smoke alarm."At first," she said, "I just thought it had gone wrong, but when I got up I found smoke coming out from the living room. The curtains were ablaze." Mrs Gumbridge quickly decided to abandon the flat but fell in the hallway. "I hit my head and must have knocked myself out," she explained, as she showed off cuts and bruises to her head and face.

Green was passing her flat on the way to work at Frimpton's, the furniture makers. "I heard a smoke alarm going off and saw smoke coming out of a downstairs window," he explained. "The upstairs neighbours came out saying an old lady may still be inside. I just took my tools and used them to break open the front door. Inside it was full of smoke. I learned somewhere that you should try and keep under the smoke, so I got down and crawled around. Luckily, Mrs Gumbridge was in the hallway and it did not take me long to find her. She was on the floor." Green dragged her out of the front door. Minutes later there was an explosion and the building was engulfed in flame.

The residents of the other three flats in the block have been found temporary accommodation by the council. No one else was hurt in the blaze.

A spokesman for the Alderstone fire brigade told the Gazette that if Green had not acted as quickly as he had, Mrs Gumbridge would probably have died from the smoke and heat. By the time the fire brigade arrived, the building was well alight. The spokesman refused to speculate on the cause of the fire which would be fully investigated.

Gareth Green was born in Yorkshire and is currently working at Frimpton's as a joinery apprentice. The firm's owner, Frederick Frimpton (56), the third generation of renowned furniture makers, described Green as a talented and hard-working young man."We are proud to have Gareth on the staff; he is a caring young man with a bright future. It doesn't *surprise me that he acted so quickly. Mrs Gumbridge is fortunate that he was passing just when she needed him."* added Mr Frimpton – a sentiment echoed by the lady herself. *"I shall remember him as my handsome hero,"* she smiled through her bruises.

After work, Gareth is a volunteer with the St Oswald's "Kidz Club" which runs special activities for children after school and at weekends. "Gareth is a great asset to our community," commented the Revd Elizabeth Simpson, the rector of Alderstone.*"He is always looking for opportunities to help other people, especially children. But now he has done something for a member of the older generation too. I think he has made quite an impression there."*

Gareth Green has never had a grandmother that he can remember. He told reporters, "Someone once said to me that if you want real friends then you have to help other people. I have tried to do that, and it works." He said he would *definitely go and see Mrs Gumbridge again when her flat was repaired. "I might be able to do a few jobs for her,"* he explained.

Tabs passed the sheet on to Mary who read it carefully, twice through.

"I wonder who told him to help other people?" she smiled.

"I'm glad he's so happy," murmured Tabs, "I knew he was good. Look at the way the old lady is looking at him. I bet hardly anyone ever looked at him with so much love when he was here. I'm happy for him."

"So," exclaimed Mary, "our frog turns into a 'handsome prince'."

"Seems like it," said Tabs, "Except he in't handsome. He's still a bit gross. I hope he finds a girl who can stand him and who will help draw out his best side. I don't know who, though. You wouldn't find me kissing him. Ugh."

"Quite right, you've done your bit. Time to leave him to the folk down south," said her mother, strongly. Cindy found it difficult to give up worrying about what Tabitha would do next.

She had, of late, taken to worrying about what she would get up to in California in the summer. She had seen some LA teenagers on the TV careering around in convertibles. California was so far away, and the Hollywood films made it out to be full of dangerous people, and then there were the earthquakes. Weren't they all waiting for the big one that should strike at any moment?

The shop door jangled and admitted the vicar followed by a blast of cold air.

"Good morning Mike, what can we do for you?"

"A touch of African heat. I come for some African relief."

"Ha, ha," mocked Mary. "Put the kettle on, Tabitha."

"Actually it's Tabitha I was hoping to find." He rummaged in his shopping bag and pulled out a chunky parcel. "This came for you this morning."

Tabitha examined a brown paper-covered package. It was postmarked 'North East Hampshire'.

"I can guess who it's from," smiled Rev. Mike.

"Griff," muttered Tabs.

"Indeed."

"Well, open it then," enthused Mary.

Tabs carefully removed the brown paper. Inside was a shoe box sealed with sellotape. Mary found a paper knife and Tabs slit the tape and lifted the lid. A whiff of beeswax emanated from it. Inside, nestled among balls of newspaper, was a beautiful wooden box with the letters, "TABITHA" inlaid on the lid. Tabitha lifted the box from its packaging. It was finely crafted in walnut with dovetailed corners. The lid was fitted with a small brass clasp which opened at Tabs' touch and beneath the lid was a little card on which was written:

To Tabs. Im no good wiv words but I can make fings in wood I just want to say thanks. Your fiend, Griff.

Tabitha smiled. *No longer a fiend, Griff. You were once certainly, but now I will have you as a friend if you carry on being so nice. Thank you, God, for beginning to make him new like you have me,* she said in her heart.

Her mother, Mary, Rev Mike and Bill all gazed at the box and marvelled.

"I never imagined he would be able to turn out something

like that," murmured Cindy. "I just thought he were a hopeless cause. His mum would be suited."

"I don't want to sound a bit... well, how I shall put it, a bit guarded," warned Rev Mike. "Perhaps I shouldn't be but I'm still nervous. I've got a bit of experience here. Two swallows don't make a summer, as they say. I don't want you to think the job is done, Tabitha."

"I know. I won't count my chickens... or swallows... I was only just saying he is still rather ..." She hesitated.

"Gross you said," contributed Cindy, emphatically.

"Yeah, Mum. But at least he has proved to us that he is not just 'that way out' with no hope. He needed a chance to see he could be different."

"Indeed. He has. And it is all down to you, Tabitha," affirmed the vicar. "You're an inspiration to us all never to give up on anyone. I was just reflecting on the passage in Revelation 21 when God promises to make 'all things new'. It refers to the End of Time, the Last Trump, but God keeps renewing things even in this age. I think—"

"... I think I'm putting the kettle on," interrupted Mary with a smile and, turning to Tabs, warned, "Careful you don't get quoted in one of Mike's sermons..."

"Now, would I do that?"

"Yes," they all chorused.

18

A few days later, all thought of Gareth Green was eclipsed when an unexpected thing happened. Mr Thomas suddenly turned up at Heathrow. Mama Sarah got a call from the airport; he was in the terminal without any money and there was no way he could go anywhere, let alone Yorkshire.

The poor lady was both excited and worried all at the same time. She didn't know whether she was coming or going; she was 'all of a dither', as Cindy would say. Why had Garang arrived in Britain without any warning?

Seeing her mum confused as to what to do, Ashol decided to take matters into her own hands. She texted Tabitha and they both went straight round to see Mary. Before Mrs Thomas knew what was happening, she was in Mary's car heading down the M1.

Four and a half hours later, they found Garang Thomas in a short-sleeved shirt, shivering, tired and hungry huddled on a bench in the arrivals lounge with a battered-looking shopping bag. They were both shocked. Mary was surprised he hadn't been taken away as a vagrant. He was thinner than his wife had ever seen him. He looked haggard and was completely exhausted. Gradually, over an all-day breakfast with copious pots of hot sweet tea, it emerged that he had travelled overnight and had had nothing to eat or drink all day.

They bundled him into Mary's small car and she drove them into Hayes to buy some warm clothes. They found a shop that sold outdoor wear and fitted him out from head to toe. Neither he nor his wife raised any objection as Mary paid a large bill on her credit card. Mama Sarah was too worried and desperate while Garang was on the point of collapse.

Mary texted Ashol that all was well. However, it became abundantly clear to her that Garang needed to sleep before travelling back to Millheaton; she didn't feel like driving all the way back to Yorkshire that same day in any case, so she checked them all into a cheap hotel nearby. In the warm, after eating a few more mouthfuls, Mr Thomas began to drop off in a chair. His wife took him to the bed where he slept for fourteen hours, just waking up a couple of times for a trip to the bathroom and more tea.

Over the next few hours, as they drove slowly home to the north, Garang Thomas began to tell his story. They soon learned that he hadn't told them everything in his phone calls – he said he didn't want to depress them and, if the truth be told, he was less than proud of himself. Shame matters a lot in South Sudanese culture. And it was expensive on the phone just for the five minutes it lasted, so he kept his news good. On the days he had bought a phone card to ring the UK, he had barely eaten but he hadn't told them that, either. Garang's self-esteem was very battered. It would take weeks for him to tell everything. But the sheer joy of his wife at having him back went a long way to restoring his faith in himself, and in humanity. He rejoiced in his good fortune that he had a wife who genuinely loved him – something, he had observed, that was not so common even among those who were married.

When Mary drew up outside the house in Millheaton, Ashol flew out of the door and literally pulled her dad out of the car. She couldn't contain her excitement. The tears streamed down Garang's face as he caught his daughter up in his arms. Tabitha was there too. She was clearly happy that this family were all together again, and Mr Thomas gave her a hug as well. As she opened the front door and sat him in father's chair, Mama Sarah was overcome with joy. She bubbled and fussed and Deng was more talkative than he'd ever been.

Garang wept. "You know, I have missed you all so very much." He was home. Home is with those who love you whether it's in the country you grew up in or somewhere else in the world.

In Juba, it had soon become evident to him – he came to explain in the days of his recovery – that getting a job near to where his brother lived was next to impossible. He had the qualifications and the experience but he had not been around for so long and a local track record with a reference was almost essential for getting a government job. And it didn't help that he didn't know anyone of real influence in the administration, either. He had soon discovered that he was just one among many looking for government jobs; it seemed that all the world wanted to work for the government because it bore a reasonably good and mostly reliable – if not guaranteed – salary and plenty of status.

Working for an aid agency – a non-governmental organisation – had been his next choice and he was eventually taken on by a relief agency as a junior clerk but it was situated in Hai Malakal in the centre of the city, many miles from Gudele where he was living with his brother's family. It took the best part of an hour and a half travelling on overcrowded minibuses to get to and from his office and it cost him a large chunk of his pay. Then when he began work, his brother expected him to contribute to the family budget and at the end of the week, he was left with little to put into savings to get a house of his own. And there was no way he could have ever afforded to rent in Hai Malakal.

His brother was pleased to see him at first, but his hospitality had limits, as had Garang's pride.

Garang had tried to be frugal and careful. He had rarely bought food at lunchtime, putting aside as much money as he could to find a house somewhere to bring his family to when the time was right. It wasn't easy; he had been forced to use some of it for medicines when he had collapsed with a bad case of malaria and typhoid but he had refused to accept defeat.

In the end, though, it had not been the poverty, the lack of suitable work, the disillusionment or the primitive conditions that had persuaded him to return. At the end of January, a cousin had come to him with a very wide grin on his face. He explained that he had pulled off a magnificent coup that would solve all Garang's problems. He had negotiated a marriage to none less than the clan chief. The cousin had rendered the chief a service sometime in the past and was able to call in his credit. He had bargained him up to an impressive one hundred and twenty cows for Ashol. A marriage to a foreign-born educated girl would give the chief added status, and it would pay back the favour. He was not short of bovine wealth, so it was an attractive move. In his culture, cows can only be used to secure wives – tradition wouldn't allow him to sell them or exchange them for anything else. This was an unusually high price but he could afford it. Ashol would be highly honoured to have been worth so much.

The only condition was that Ashol travelled to Juba at all possible speed. Aware that Mr Thomas had not got the wherewithal to pay for her travel, the chief had even offered to pay the fare himself.

This deal would give the clan, including Garang Thomas and his family, a great deal of status as well as the wealth of much-needed cows. Apart from setting the Thomases up, these could be used to help buy wives for the sons of the wider family. And association with the chief would be a definite asset in getting Mr Thomas a better job and a place nearer the centre of the city. On top of all that, reminded the cousin, Ashol was guaranteed a comfortable life in a block-built house with an iron roof together with two other older wives. She would not have to cook and bring up children in a tukul made of mud and thatch like most women. Everyone was a winner. This would mark a turning point in Garang's fortunes – it would re-establish him in Juba. He had arrived.

That night Garang was in turmoil. He loved his country with the sounds and scents of home that even then were wafting through the windows in his brother's house. He had treasured all those memories of a free and happy childhood playing in the dust or the mud depending on the season – no long cold winter nights. He had longed for it for many years and now he was back. But it was not going to work. In this arrangement, Ashol could open the door to all the things his parents had dreamed for him when he was young – wealth, status, decent housing, the best food guaranteed for them all – Sarah and Deng as well as Ashol.

But Ashol knew nothing but Yorkshire. She was British through and through – she'd never lived in South Sudan and she'd probably never heard of bride price. He didn't have to guess at her reaction – or that of the other girls among whom she had grown up. He thought of Tabitha Johnson and her tendency to be outspoken – not disrespectful of him but, nevertheless, not 'backwards at coming forward' as her mother would put it. An arranged marriage such as this might make good sense in a South Sudan context, but in West Yorkshire people would be aghast. At fifteen, Ashol was still a child – marriage at her age would be illegal in Britain. She would be under her parents' care until she was eighteen. Marriage for her was not something they had ever contemplated; they had brought their daughter up in the West and they had taken on Western expectations.

From that moment, Garang knew he could never bring his daughter to South Sudan – the thought of her, at the tender age of fifteen, marrying a middle-aged man his own age with two wives already was abhorrent even to him. The chief would have no intention of allowing her to continue her education – year eleven was more than enough if she was going to respect him as her lord and master. His cousin had said she should travel immediately, so there would be no question of waiting until after she had sat for her GCSEs. And as for living in a concrete house with an iron roof, it was no match for a substantial house in Millheaton with piped water and 24/7 electricity guaranteed. And in Britain, she had the potential of going on to university. His cousin was full of the prospect of greater status, but status of that kind had no meaning for Ashol or Deng. This was the turning point – it hadn't, he now realised, for him, either. It might have done once but no longer – his values had changed even if his heart remained South Sudanese, he had become British in so many ways – especially when it came to marriage.

The plans of his fellow clansmen forced Garang's hand. He had no choice. The negotiations could not be reopened and turning down the offer was inconceivable – impossible. His family were all so excited about the future. He could not even play for time – the deal was virtually sealed and delivered. You did not say no to the chief.

Garang did not tell them he was leaving; they may have prevented it. Two days later he packed a small bag with a single change of clothes and the dollars and British passport he had sewn into his pillow, and instead of turning up for work, he had taken a bus to the airline office in Juba town and had bought a ticket to London via Addis Ababa.

Now there was no going back. His family and the hopeful chief would be very angry; his gift of wealth and status had been spurned. If he returned at all to South Sudan, it would have to be with Ashol, and he simply could not do that. He had been sad to leave; it was his home country. But his longing for his family had now completely overwhelmed everything else and he had few regrets as he boarded the plane.

***

It turned out that Mr Thomas's boss at the council offices hadn't actually accepted his resignation but had rather put him in for extended compassionate leave. The boss said that his skill and dedication should not be lost – and he secretly always believed he would be back before a year had passed.

In the following weeks, Garang was able to talk more about the positive things about South Sudan. The new vibrancy of the city of Juba – a stark contrast to the days when it was occupied by the Sudan Armed Forces. In those days, people disappeared if they dared to say anything contrary to the military regime. Then there was the unbelievable experience of Independence Day, a day no one ever dared thought could happen, which still lingered in the memory despite all the violence since. "Juba," explained Mr Thomas, "is an enormous building site. The buildings are going up four, five and six stories and more but the rents commanded by the most central locations are too big. Investors are falling over themselves to develop every square inch of land they can lay their hands on."

He went on to report that the churches on Sunday were full to overflowing. Many new churches were being built and others were building extensions as the city grew. "And there are so many excited and exciting young people all neatly and colourfully dressed, unlike some of the sad-looking depressed youngsters you see around here."

"But in all of this, you still couldn't make it work, Dad," said Deng.

"It's a young person's country. I can't start at the bottom and work myself up. I'm too old."

"Old. You're not old." protested Ashol.

Garang smiled. "Thank you, daughter. Not here, perhaps, but in Juba most of the population are under thirty-five."

"And we don't have connections. Not ones with high status," reminded Mama Sarah.

"But you could have gained status if I had married that chief?"

"Yes daughter but the price was too high, wouldn't you agree?"

"Ab-so-bloomi-lutely. The thought of it makes me sick."

"So you see, I could have had it all but I love my Ashol too much. All I ask is, when the time comes, you marry a fine upstanding loving young man."

"What if I said, I was not going to get married at all."

"Let's not get too far ahead of ourselves," interposed Mama Sarah. "For now, you have to concentrate on your studies."

"No problem. Absolutely."

Garang laughed "You like that word, Ashol. You have British ways. And I hadn't realised how British I had become, either."

"How do you mean, British, Dad? You're not like anyone else's dad around here."

"No, but I like 10 o'clock to be 10 a.m. and not 11.30 a.m. and I do not expect to budget for bribes to get what I need from officials."

"And not wanting your daughter to be given in marriage at the age of fifteen to someone she'd never met," added Deng.

"Especially that."

Ashol pulled a face. "Apparently, I'm worth all of one hundred and twenty cows. Cheap at the price. Mooo."

"You shouldn't mock, daughter. Many of your cousins are doing just that. Even aged fourteen and for far fewer cows."

"Sorry, Dad. Thanks. Thanks for giving up your dream to live again in South Sudan to save me."

"I'm glad to hear you say that, but it was just a matter of time anyway. I think I would have gotten sick even with you all looking after me. No, even if it hadn't been for that, I think I would still have come back. But I'm glad I went."

"I'm glad you went too," added Mama Sarah, "but even more glad you came back. Can I allow myself to feel at home here now, in Millheaton?"

"Yes, wife, you can."

On the Sunday following, the people at church all crowded around Mr Thomas and rejoiced in his safe return.

"This experience has made me realise that my home is here... among you. I love my country and I am happy to have been back, but now I see I belong here after all these years. I haven't forgotten South Sudan, and I never will, but the place has moved on and it has mostly forgotten me. It has never known Deng and Ashol; this is their home." His declaration was followed by a cheer.

That afternoon, Tabs, Ashol and Deng found themselves together away from the adults. Tabs asked Deng what he felt about not returning to the country of his birth.

"After I have been to university, I would still like to go to South Sudan for a visit. I shall not plan to stay. I shall wait on God and see what he wants me to do."

"I'd love to see South Sudan. Can I come and visit while you're there?" asked Tabs.

"Yeah," grimaced Ashol. "And then Deng can sell you for hundreds of cows and be rich and influential."

"Get lost."

"No one is ever going to give any cows for me. I'm not going to marry before I'm thirty and only then for love... And you won't get me anywhere near South Sudan; I might get kidnapped by that chief. He already has two wives. How many more does he want?"

"As many as his wealth of cows will allow him," answered Deng. "It's all about status. If you're important, you should have the wives to prove it. Unless, of course, you are a Christian pastor, then you can only have one."

"How very sad for them."

"On the contrary. They can marry for love and have status

too. But it doesn't stop them from being poor of course..."

Ashol grabbed her opportunity. "I've been telling you. You should be ordained. You'd make a great pastor – and not because it will make you important. What do you reckon, Tabs?"

"Oh, he'd be brilliant. The ladies would flock to his church all in a swoon but he wouldn't be able to marry any of them because he hasn't a cow to his name," she teased.

Deng had a ready repost. "And that would be because my family haven't got any cows for my sister. That's how it works."

Ashol picked up a cushion and threw it at him. Tabs joined in.

"I now know why the Bible says you should only have one wife," said Deng, fending off flying cushions. "Females can gang up on you and, before you know it, they'll have you do anything they please. One is more than enough."

"No pressure," giggled Ashol. "... Rev. Deng – it has a nice ring to it, though." Deng retrieved a cushion and hurled it at her.

19

Term ended – the final teaching term of Year 11. GCSEs would be upon them in less than six weeks.

Kids were mentally all over the place. Parents and teachers alike were constantly reminding them of how important these exams were. It was, like, now or never and if you didn't perform your world would come to a sad end. Some kids had already given up, of course – whatever their ability, they had decided they were not going to succeed – but Tabs was not among them. She might have been at one time but now she was determined to make a good showing.

What Tabs needed most was an Easter holiday without distractions. Ashol was the same. Having her father home was cool and she could now think like any other student about a future in Britain, which made the GCSEs feel even more relevant. They agreed on WhatsApp communication only. The rest of the time would be spent revising. They had worked out a revision timetable together so each of them would be doing the same things at the same time. That way if either of them got stuck, they could ask the other.

The first Tuesday of the holiday was history day. At nine-thirty, Tabs got down to revising the rise of the Nazi party in Germany. She planned to take notes on her notes and then notes from a revision study guide, then read some model answers and finally write a timed answer to a question from a past paper. Her teachers would be pleased.

Around ten o'clock, however, the plan fell apart. DI Gillespie called. Cindy was out at her cleaning job but Tabitha beckoned him in. He looked concerned.

"What's up, inspector?"

"Is your mum at home?"

"No sorry. She's at work."

The policeman took in a mature sixteen-year-old almost as tall as he was and decided she should hear what he had to say.

"I wish this were a social call but I have to say I am coming

301

with a warning. The gang who trashed this flat are now back out and about. They were angry and resentful when we apprehended them. There was no remorse – their only regret was being made to pay for their crime. It turns out their leader is not an ordinary criminal but a thug in an extreme right-wing racist group which is being tracked by MI5."

"That's awful. Poor Griff getting mixed up with all that."

"That's my Tabitha Johnson, always thinking about the poor unfortunates. I agree with you, he was a victim too. But it's not him I'm concerned about here but you and your mother. We're worried they might decide the job of driving you out of your flat should be completed."

"What? Come back and do it again?"

"Yes."

"I've got exams in a month."

"Bad timing, then. But we think it is best that you ask the council for a transfer to another property."

"But it in't just about this particular flat, is it? It's personal."

"That's why we're recommending you move to another area. It needn't be outside West Yorkshire but far enough away for them to leave you alone."

"But... When?"

"Right away."

"No way. I'm not going anywhere until I've sat my exams."

"I understand how you must feel. But you need to take this seriously, Tabitha. I wouldn't have come if I didn't think an attack highly likely. Talk to your mum about it. When will she be back?"

"She'll be home after she finishes at three."

"Talk to her. Tell her what I've said and that I'll call tomorrow morning."

The DI got up and made for the door.

"I told you, I in't going nowhere."

"I get that. But talk to your mum. OK?"

Tabs reported the inspector's visit using as many neutral tones as she could muster but Cindy was not fooled. She knew a lot more about the world than her daughter – bright as she was. She was horrified. She dreaded what they might do next – Tabs was so vulnerable. Even Scotland felt too close.

Tabs remonstrated, desperate to follow her revision programme undisturbed. This was all wrong. But no amount of shouting about her GCSEs was going to make her mother change her mind. She told her that she could always take them later – this was far more important. There was no way she was going to risk her Tabitha after the police had advised them to move. The risk was not a small one if Inspector Gillespie had called round himself.

Tabs gave up complaining and decided to wait until the next day and hope the policeman had better news. Deep down she was scared but she refused to admit it to herself and got on with the revision. But she couldn't concentrate. The carefully planned programme was in tatters. Her mind kept wandering off, imagining that Nazis were still alive and active in Yorkshire and there was another modern-day Hitler somewhere calling the shots. Ridiculous. But the thought wouldn't go away – not even Harry Potter managed to overcome evil just through his positive thinking. A clever courageous hero he may have been but he still needed his spells. And this gang were real – actual live evil human beings. They weren't like wizarding-world boggarts which could be defied by shouting 'Ridiculous!' at them – they had manhandled her and had tied her and her mum up with tape and threatened that that was not all that they could do.

She was too upset even to share this with Ashol. *It's not fair on her to disturb her revision too.* In truth, she didn't want to talk about it.

That night the dreaded dream returned in full force. The light that had been growing brighter at the end of the cave was now blocked by three masked hulks armed with crowbars, yelling at her that she "'Ad bin warned. Now she were for it." As the lead thug stepped forward, Tabs woke with sweat streaming down her face. She wept. This time, instead of telling herself that this was just a stupid dream, the truth of the real threat forced itself into her waking world.

The morning revision was Macbeth; it was impossible. The evil was so real. For some kids, history and Shakespeare were stories of other worlds long past; Tabs was learning early that they were not.

A half past ten DI Gillespie called. Cindy let him in. He repeated all that he had said. At least Tabitha had told her everything – Cindy had feared she had got only some of the facts he had shared because Tabs had been so adamant about playing them down.

"Would Scotland be far enough?"

"We hadn't considered going that far. Why? Have you relatives there?"

"No. Just think it would be a good start."

"Mum, they don't even do the same exams, there." Tabs stormed out into her bedroom.

"It doesn't have to be outside West Yorkshire." The inspector was sympathetic. "It's your decision. But I have done my duty and reported what we consider to be the risk. If you need any help persuading the council to rehouse you urgently, we would be pleased to put in a word."

"Thank you. I must apologise for my daughter."

"She's a right to be angry, Mrs Johnson. Let me know what you decide."

In one foul blow Tabs' world had been turned on its head – again. She had come to regard the coming exams as absolutely central to everything. Now that was no longer the case. She was soon to learn a French word from Mademoiselle Gaudet that few GCSE students came across – *bouleveser*, to turn things upside down. And Mary talked about upset apple carts.

Cindy and Tabitha came to a compromise. It wasn't difficult; Tabs was scared and didn't put up much of a fight. They would apply for an emergency transfer within West Yorkshire. It might cost a bomb but she promised to pay for a taxi to get Tabitha to Beckside for each and every exam. After all, she had put a few quid aside for education, hadn't she? She hadn't envisaged it being used so early but it was there. Tabs hugged her mum.

"I'm sorry I was cross. I wasn't angry with you. Honest."

"I know, lass. You have a right to be angry. I am, too. It's the way the world is – evil things will always be there and we have to deal with them. You can stand your ground or you can retreat to safety."

"Fight or flight."

"You what?"

"It's what all animals and people do. They can stand and fight or they can run away. I hate the idea of running away but, I guess, sometimes you have to. You don't stick around if there is a tiger on the loose."

"You're right. But things could be much worse. Some people don't have kind police inspectors on their side wanting to protect them."

Tabs called Ashol but would not let her come round. Deng was determined to but she told him she was OK and she needed to get on with her revision; their agreement to leave each other to it still stood. She would see him on Saturday afternoon and cut the grass for Mary as they had arranged. In the meantime, she promised she would give them updates as and when things started to happen. Deng said he would pray for her and her mum and she knew he would. That would be the first thing he would think of doing and she resolved to try it too. Rev Mike had said to tell it to God like it was. You didn't have to be polite to God and worry about the words or anything.

That night God got his ear bent from all three of them.

When she got in at half past three on Friday afternoon, Cindy phoned the council housing department. She was answered by a curt voice. The office closed at four on a Friday but, although it wasn't quite that, nothing could be done this side of the weekend. She was requested to call again on Monday morning. Cindy was worried now. It was clear that 'emergency' meant something far more laid back at the council offices than she had imagined. It was going to take time to get rehoused. The perpetrators of their horrific attack were already out there but the housing department wasn't an emergency service unless someone was actually on the streets, it seemed.

In desperation, Cindy turned to Mary. She needed to talk to someone.

"I'm sorry to put all this on you, Mary, but I didn't know who else to talk to right now. The thing is, I'm so worried for Tabitha. If it was just about me I would brave it out. But I'm at work four days a week and Tabitha is on her own in the flat now that school's finished. She's not going anywhere because she's got this revision bug that keeps her revising all day and she won't go out."

"She's a diligent young lady. I'm so glad you feel you can come to me, Cindy. So we need a strategy."

"You and your strategies. I love them. Keeps a person in control."

"Precisely. It always helps to define our objectives. Now, our number one objective is to keep Tabitha safe, right?"

"Absolutely."

"Number two is to make sure she is not distracted from her school work. Agreed?"

"She's angry about this coming up now. These GCSEs are too important, if you ask me."

"Maybe. But we're not going to be able to change the lass's mind about that, are we? Anyway, if someone is motivated to work, that must be a good thing. The world will always need a person like her.

"Now I would suggest that while you're out, she should come to the shop to study. She'll be safe here and can be left alone to do her thing. And in the evening, she can come to the cottage – she's even got the garden on hand there, so she can talk to the birds and trees as she likes doing."

"I think I can persuade her to do that. Thanks, Mary."

"Then the next thing is to keep you and the flat safe. Why don't I ask Fred if he can fit some extra bolts to your door?"

"But—"

"No buts, Cindy. You know Fred would enjoy doing it."

"I hope we won't be too long in moving... I never thought I'd say that. I were always determined to see things through. But—"

"There's no shame in staying safe."

"I hate it. They'll reckon they've won. Us flitting like that."

"Maybe. But they won't have hurt you and Tabitha. That's what counts. The world's full of refugees and I don't blame any of them for running away."

"South Sudan?"

"The Thomases. There's nothing wrong with fleeing to protect your children."

"And I'll only be exchanging one council flat for another local one... I wish they'd pull their finger out, though. 'Urgent' doesn't seem to be this side of the weekend.

As it turned out, all that Cindy got on the Monday morning was an appointment for the Tuesday after Easter. Nothing was going to happen before then – everything shut down from Good Friday to Easter Monday and urgent meant, 'at the first available opportunity.' That would be an interview – the start of the process.

Cindy was glad when Fred turned up on Sunday afternoon to assess the job. There were no half-measures with him and by the end of Monday, he had attached no less than six bolts to the inside of the door.

"Anyone trying to break that down will make so much racket that they'll hear it in the next street. And it'll take time, too."

"Thanks, Fred. What do I owe you?"

"Another cup of tea."

"Fred—"

"I don't argue with ladies," he smiled.

***

Their timetable for Maundy Thursday morning was maths. At least maths was not about people. There was something solid about maths – it was what it was and couldn't lie or deceive. Tabs found herself actually looking forward to it although it was her least favourite subject.

Cindy was not at work because her client had gone to stay with her son for the long weekend. At half past ten, the doorbell rang. Cindy had closed the bolts and put the chain on. She called through the door.

"Who is it?"

"Inspector Gillespie."

Cindy set about sliding back the bolts. She opened the door a crack to check it was the inspector, then closed it again to release

307

the chain.

"Sorry. Fort Knox," she apologised.

"Glad to see it. I come with some good news for you."

"Come in. What good news?"

"Let's sit down, shall we?"

Tabs heard the inspector and came into the sitting room.

"Put the kettle on, will you, lass?"

The inspector began. "You weren't the first on our gang's list, it seems. They decided to settle a score in Leeds. They raided a house but the chain on their door gave the family time to dial 999 and we had officers there before anyone got hurt. We got 'em red-handed. The gang were caught by surprise and all three of them have been taken into custody. They hadn't reckoned on a CCTV camera, either. This time they will go inside for a long time. So, the good news is that we no longer believe there is any reason for you to move."

"What? I mean, really!" exclaimed Cindy.

"It's highly unlikely that anyone else would bother about you."

Tabs, who had just arrived with a tray set it down and grabbed the unsuspecting inspector in her arms and gave him a huge hug. When the policeman managed to disengage himself he was red in the face. This was not the usual way he was received.

Tabs recollected herself. "Sorry," she blurted.

"Er. No worries. Glad to be the bearer of good news. I hope your exams go well. Do your best. Then in a few years' time, we could do with people like you in the police force... So long as you don't go around hugging the clients, that is... Oh and by the way. We traced that phone number belonging to the hangman text. Forgot to tell you. It belongs to the boyfriend of the mother of one of your friends – Amy Lane. She admitted 'borrowing' his phone and sending you the text. The first text was from her mother's previous partner. So you were right – a stupid and, as far as we're concerned, a time-wasting prank."

Later that night, Tabitha texted Amy Lane. "So, do you want to fess up about the hangman?" *I don't expect to hear back from her. But I want her to know I know.*

The following day, Good Friday, they went to church and sat with the Thomases. As she listened to the sad gruesome story of Jesus being killed by the evil powers of his day, it occurred to Tabs that Christians didn't shy away from horrible things. Jesus faced the cruel evil head on and it killed him. But the thing was that they didn't believe it ended there; this was not the end of the story. Soon they would be singing about Jesus 'conquering the grave' – even death defeated. That was the difference between Macbeth and the story of Jesus. In Macbeth, you can never write off the witches. Fate will have its way – Malcolm and Macduff only win because the fates have decided it. But nothing can stop Jesus from winning. That was why Good Friday was good – he loved so much he couldn't stay killed.

***

During the evening of an Easter Day with Mary at the Johnson's flat – Cindy being determined to invite Mary to hers – Tabs said something quite amazing. It amazed her mum and she also amazed herself.

"Mum, I don't think you should cancel your appointment at the housing office on Tuesday."

"No? You heard the inspector. The danger has passed."

"It's not about that. We don't have to rush now, so it can wait until after the exams but I reckon it wouldn't hurt to get a new start somewhere, anyway – go somewhere different to do my A-levels."

"Not Chapeltown? You know what I said—"

"Nah, Mum. Not Chapeltown. Somewhere *completely* new."

"What about your garden? What about your friends?"

"They'll still be here. I don't mean so far away. And, anyway, the garden's not like it was. It was once big and mysterious but now when I go, I always go through into the woods beyond and that's getting small, too. The world's a big place and I want to explore it."

Cindy was amazed but not for long. If little Tabby had ventured, so would grown-up Tabitha. She had known that all along.

"OK. If that's what you want. I've always been a comer-in on Beck Ings. But now we can afford to be picky if we're not thinking before July. Where'd you fancy?"

"I dunno. Somewhere near the moors?"

"Mytholmroyd. I always fancied that place. It's not industrial like it once was. The mills have closed down. There may be more houses to choose from"

"Is there a sixth-form college or anything?"

"Dunno. You'll have to check that out."

Tabs Googled on her phone. "There was but they've closed it down."

"But kids must go to school somewhere."

"Looks like all Calderdale sixth-formers will have to go to Halifax. How far's that?"

"Not far. Why don't you put that into your phone, too? I don't know why you bother asking me first."

Tabs did as she was asked. "Seven miles. That's nothing. People go much further than that from Millheaton... Yay. Look at these pictures – Midgely Moor. I love it."

"There in't no going back? You're definitely set on flitting?"

"After the GCSEs."

Tabs was amazed at how exciting all this sounded. It didn't *have* to be Mytholmroyd though, did it? The world beckoned.

20

Two days into May, Tabs' phone broke into song: *Love, love me do.* It was Mary.

"Hi Mary," said Tabs brightly. She was glad of the distraction. In a week's time, she would be doing her French oral and she and Deng had been putting in some practice. Deng had been brilliant in giving her tips.

"Hello, Tabitha. I have heard something today I thought you should know and I'm afraid it's not good news."

"Oh?" *Not the gang back again?*

"I went to Heckmondwike this morning to swap some stuff with Mrs Hollingsworth." *So not the gang.* Tabs took a breath. "She told me that last week Gloria Green travelled south. Apparently, Gareth is in some sort of trouble again. She doesn't know what."

Tabitha went cold. She felt a dark wave of sadness sweep over her. There was always something. Did life ever run smooth? She didn't know how to respond; she said nothing.

"Are you still there, Tabitha? You OK?"

"Yes... Y... You don't know what he's supposed to have done?"

"I don't know any of the details, I'm afraid. But I wanted you to know what I know in case anyone says anything."

"Yes, thanks, Mary."

A day later, when Tabs got home feeling good about her French, Mary told her she had learned more details. Apparently, Griff had been engaged in a Saturday night brawl whilst under the influence of alcohol. Had Gareth's weekends been as well looked after as his working days, things might have turned out differently. Now he was on a serious charge of GBH, and the future looked bleak for him. Tabs did not know what to think. She didn't want to face people. She could just hear her mum saying they had known all along that he was not going to change. She had been wrong.

But to her surprise, it didn't happen that way. Her mother just sighed and said, "I can't imagine what Gloria Green must be feeling – she was so hopeful. Oh, Tabitha, you did so much."

Rev Mike's wife at church just came and cuddled her.

"You did all you could," she whispered. "Try not to be too down."

Mike told her that he would include Gareth in the church prayers. Mary looked upset as if Griff were someone who truly mattered to her. Tabitha was amazed at how many people were saddened by the news. Clearly, she was not the only one who cared about Griff – they had bought into her care for him too.

"What you did for Griff has made lots of people aware of him, and they are all gutted," commiserated Danielle. "You must've done some good. He made you that box."

"Yeah. But it didn't last."

"It's hard to be good all the time. Too easy to get into the wrong crowd. He's probably feeling sorry now. You're not going to give up on him, are you." It wasn't a question. Tabs realised Danielle, at least, didn't want her to.

"Thanks. I can't... I can't stop wanting him to make something of himself. But now he's ruined everything, hasn't he? He'll lose his job and probably go to prison for years."

Tabitha had grown up knowing the world could be a tough place. But she had found a way to survive and was on the way to escaping – discovering a new-found freedom. However, it didn't mean it got any easier for the other kids she'd been to school with and it was especially hard for Griff. He had gone around pretending to himself that he owned the estate but out in the wide world, he had hit the buffers. Yet the kind people she had made friends with had not given up on him. Probably because they knew God never did. Tabs hoped that he hadn't given up on himself. But she knew she could do no more – not for now, anyway.

"I... I'm not going to write no more. It wouldn't be right. Not right now. Mary thinks so, too."

"No," agreed Danielle. "I didn't mean you should do that. I agree, you've done your bit. He's probably hoping you never hear about this. But that doesn't mean you're going to stop caring – or praying – are you?"

"You honestly reckon praying will make a difference?"

"Bound too."

"The vicar's daughter has to say that."

"Rubbish. I say what I want to."

"Yeah. Doing things only because it's what your parents want doesn't count for anything. Unless you choose to do it, it's rubbish."

"Yeah, pointless detritus..."

"Garbage."

"Trash."

"Practising for America?" smiled Ashol as she caught the end of the exchange.

"Nah," replied Danielle. "Just seeing how many words we can find for a load of—"

"Enchanting girls. Good to see you all," butted in Rev Mike on his way from group to group. The girls were overtaken by giggles. "What are you laughing about, now?" smiled Mike, "have I said something?"

"Perfect timing, Dad. Nothing to worry about. I'll tell you later. What are you after, calling us enchanting?"

"Well, now you mention it, you could help me get these boxes to Mary's car."

"Creep." Danielle laughed. They each took a cardboard box. They were very heavy.

"Books," explained Rev Mike.

As they staggered out to the car, Danielle whispered to Tabs, "I do believe in prayer... honest."

"I know," said Tabitha. "It's cool."

**

Things were not getting any better in South Sudan or Sudan, and the Thomases were no longer as hopeful as they had been just a few months ago. There was a renewal of tribal conflict and some terrible news where women and children were being bombed and starving and refugees were pouring across the border.

The rest of the world seemed to be in such a mess too; the prayers were long at church. She remembered what Rev Mike had said. "There is no happy-ever-after in this world – but there is

313

always going to be something to rejoice in. God is with us."

On her way home from school, she called into the little garden. The sights, sounds and above all the fragrance of the new spring filled her senses. A year ago her home had been trashed but, out of that, she had found so much love.

With her arms around a cool beech tree, Tabs prayed for Griff, wherever he was. Perhaps one day he would find some kind of life too, some kind of escape from the net his behaviour had woven around him. He was banged up in a cell now, wasn't he? *He was trapped in a nightmare cave for real and his way out seemed even further from the light.*

Tabs thanked God for His patience with the world. "You know all the wrong things we do, all the time. It must make you very, very angry... and sad," she sighed. She never thought she would feel sorry for God. *God is made of spirit so he doesn't have shoulders but if he had, they would have to be very broad... and always there for people to cry on.*

***

Alone in his cell, Gareth Green was coming to terms with what he had done. He had blown it. No one would ever want to know him now, would they? He felt sick, angry and abandoned. The cell was sparsely furnished but on the bed was a small New Testament and Psalms. He picked it up. It fell open at Luke, chapter 15. Gareth began to read aloud to himself.

"Now – the – tax – col... col... lec... collec... tors... collectors *– and – sin – ners – were – all – d... dra... w... drow...* it's too bloody difficult. It's too effing hard," he screamed. "Everyfink. It's not ruddy fair. Nobody cares. God, I hate you. Do you hear? I hate everyfink." He slung the testament across the cell and he banged his head hard on the wall, drawing blood. Then he sank onto the bed scattering drops of blood mixed with tears onto the pillow and sobbed.

That same evening, Mrs Hollingsworth led a prayer meeting in Heckmondwike and they prayed for Griff and Gloria.

At Millheaton Vicarage, it was Danielle's turn to say grace, and she mentioned Griff as she prayed.

Mary wrote a letter to Gloria hoping it would find her soon.

Garang and Sarah Thomas and Ashol remembered him in their family prayers, while Tabitha and Deng kept a quiet vigil in the garden.

But Mrs Gumbridge wrote Gareth a letter.

"I know you are in trouble but you are a good boy. I know it was only the alcohol that made you do it. I hope you don't spend too long in prison because I miss seeing you. I have talked to Mr Frimpton, and he has promised me you can go back to work when you come out."

The following day, Griff's solicitor visited him.

"Hello. Fallen out with God, have we?" he said, picking up the book in the corner of the cell. It was still open at Luke 15.

"Can't read it, can I? It's too bloody difficult."

"Let's see." He read, "Now the tax collectors and sinners were all drawing near to Jesus..."

"Who are they supposed to be? Them tax collectors?"

"The people who were on the outside, those whom respectable society didn't want to know because—"

"They'd done bad things... Like me."

"Precisely."

"But what did they all want with Jesus?"

"He spent time with them. He loved them just as much as the rest. It says here that there is more rejoicing in heaven over one sinner who is sorry for what he had done than the ninety-nine who have never done anything wrong. The parable of the Lost Sheep."

"Do you reckon he thinks about me? I mean God..."

"The Bible says he does. The Bible says he goes on loving everyone – even the ones that have done evil."

"What if I keep doing bad things?"

"It says he'll never give up on loving you, come what may... And it seems that your fellow human beings have not given up on you either. I am pleased to tell you that your employer Jacob Frimpton – who, by the way, is keeping your job open for you – the Rev Elizabeth Simpson and Mrs Janet Watkins, the leader of St

Oswald's Kidz Club, are all going to stand as character witnesses at your hearing. Gareth Green, you're a lucky young man to have so many friends..."

Gareth got a year. It could have been worse. He was told that if he agreed to do remedial English classes, he could have a cell in D wing. D wing was only for those deemed to be on the road to better things. He wanted to be able to read; perhaps this was his chance. Entering the classroom, he was shown to a desk at the front of a small classroom with three others.

"Hi. Don't I know yer?" said a young inmate, in a strong West Yorkshire accent.

Green looked at him, trying to remember where he had seen him.

"Darren Brown. You remember me? I lived on Beck Ings for six months. Went to Beckside Academy."

"Yeah. I remember. Yer the one that done the bingo place. I remember the 'elicopter."

"Yeah. Pigs in the sky. No chance. You a friend of that black kid, Tabitha Johnson, in't ya? She lived underneath us in Ings View. Someone done their place over, I 'ear. Made a real mess."

"Yeah, I 'eard... Tabs Johnson. She's a great one, she is. Goin' places, she is."

"How'd you know? You bin seeing 'er, like?"

"Nah. I haven't been back t'Beck Ings for years. She wrote me a couple of times when I were banged up last time. Told me to behave meself." And he had tried, hadn't he?

"Bit of a cheek. Who does she reckon she is?"

"It weren't like that. I grew up wi 'er. I reckon she just cares how I turn out."

"She fancy you, then?"

"Nah. Not 'er.... I dunno. She's just real clever, that one. Reckon, she'll be sommut important one day, she will."

He would reform – he would. She'd believed in him, once. He could still show her, yet. When he got out and he'd done something good, he'd write and tell her. He hoped it would not be so very long. With good behaviour inside he could be out in six more months.

***

Beattie's Bingo was going through harder times of late but Cat never missed.

"They say..." she held forth to the other ladies on her table as they were waiting to start. "They say that that there Tabitha Johnson's wantin' to stay on at school. She's well-gone sixteen but she don't want to do no work. Apparently, she coulda got a job in Gregg's. They don't pay so bad there but no, not 'er. She's gonna carry on studyin' if they'll let 'er."

"Aye. We 'ad one o' them among our grandchildren. Staying around eatin' and paying nowt."

"'Er mum's reet proud on 'er, they say, but if she were mine, I'd tell 'er to frame 'ersen. Earn 'er keep."

"Yer would an 'all, Cat... Edecation. I ask ya. Lazy lot them students. 'Bout time they put in some proper graft."

Bing-bong. "Welcome all," boomed Beattie's Bingo caller in his dulcet tones. "No sweat 'ere, ladies. All fun. Great prizes terday. Some lucky person's goin' 'ome with a fortune. OK, eyes down... Number 88, two fat ladies... Number 60, grandma's feeling frisky."

Meanwhile, up the road in Beckside Academy, sitting at her lone desk in the gym, Tabitha mopped the sweat from her brow as she prepared to turn over her fourteenth three-hour exam question sheet.

"You may turn over and begin," said the bored-looking invigilator.

The paper wasn't as frightening as she had feared and she breathed out a sigh of relief. *Thank you, Lord.*

That night, Tabitha dreamed she was flying. She was soaring in the clear open air looking down onto the dark opening of the cave that had haunted her for so long. And, somehow, she knew there was now no going back.

The morning brought a text sent sometime in the small hours. It was from Amy Lane.

Tabitha

*"Saw you today. Wanted to say soz. Wot I
did were stupid."*

Tabs responded:

> "It certainly was. Didn't you think how
> my mum would go ballistic after what
> happened to us?"

"Soz."

> "You're forgiven. What's this about
> your mum having a new boyfriend?"

"It stinks."

> "Wanna talk about it?"

"UR busy."

> "Not that busy. We can go to the
> park. Get an ice cream."

"Why? Do you want to be my friend, again?"

> "Never stopped being one. xx."

Bonus Story
A SCHOOL TRIP

The guy who's writing my story don't want to put this bit of it in the book. He says it don't fit in because he's going to begin with the police helicopter, and this story is earlier than that. I think I get it but I'm a determined kind of girl, aren't I? So I'm going to write it myself and tell him he's got to put it in somewhere.

It belongs to the beginning of Year 8. Jack Frost, our head of year, told us that he wanted us to have an outing. At first, I thought he said it was to New York, like in America. Wicked. But he said that he meant Old York, as in half way to Scarborough, so not so cool. But, actually, it turned out, like kinda cool anyway, so that's why I want to write about it. Apart from anything else, it'll be a bit of homework that I can hand in to Mr Kendall, our English teacher. I guess he'll like it - until the end, that is, when he comes into the story, himself. Sorry for the English, Mr Kendall, sir. It don't sound right if I do it posh. No probs. I've taught the school spellchecker my words, too, so it likes them now.

So around my thirteenth birthday - that's 6th October for all you guys who want to give me a social media like (I'm on Instagram and TikTok) -Jack takes us all on a jolly to York on a coach. I say all, Griff were banned. He was going but apparently, he did something that got him grounded. No one knows what it was. We reckon it was, like, just an excuse to get him off the bus - too much of a liability. I was dead pleased when I heard. As you may know by now, Gross has been a pain for years. Anyway, that didn't stop Dean, Gary and Shawn heading for the back seat and chucking out some girls that got there first but Ms King were not having any of it and made them sit near the front by Mr Kendall and Jack while she went near the back with the girls. Me, Rosie and Amy were, like, somewhere in the middle with Miss Chandler, who left soon after. Don't know if we had anything to do with it.

It didn't take us long to get there. No one threw up like normal. That's because we were no longer children, were we? I mean we were all twelve and some of us, like me, already thirteen.

When we get there we stop in this car park near the walls. Jack Frost stands up and says that our visit is not meant, like, to be fun. He goes, "This is your opportunity to learn about the past. York has been an important place for thousands of years. The Romans were here 2000 years ago and some of the things you see, like these walls, were built by them."

We get out and Jack tells us the Romans brought their ships (boats, really - there were a picture of one) all the way up from the sea. He's the geography teacher, so he has to go on about things like 'the lowest bridging point', so we knew it was going to be a wide river with a big bridge and - guess what? - it is. It's quite impressive, actually.

The Romans didn't do stuff by halves, the walls are really high and they must've used a load of bricks - well, rocks - to finish them. They were built to keep the wild native people out. No doubt the people Gross is descended from. Miss Chandler is definitely a Roman, though. That's why she likes French.

You can go on the walls but Ms King wouldn't let us because she doesn't trust the likes of Dean and Gary not to lark about. Me and Rosie and Amy asked if we could go on us own, cause, you know, we'd not leap off, would we? But she said no because we'd get separated and get lost. As if.

So we cross the bridge and we can't move for people. The place were, like, packed with tourists and, basically, me and Rosie kinda got lost, anyway - well, parted from the rest. It weren't our fault. Like, Mr Kendall had just disappeared.

Well, I suppose it were Rosie's fault, too, really. You know what she's like for shops and she can't walk by one without looking at the window displays. We're supposed to be going to the minster, this giant old church that you can't miss, but Rosie don't care if there are shops and here there are lots. I kinda panic for about ten seconds and then Rosie spots this sign which says,

'Shambles Market' and so that's where we go.

Apart from what the Romans built to keep the riffraff out, York is basically for tourists who like oldy worldy stuff, and kids who are into Harry Potter. There's this street that's like been built to look just like Diagon Ally with all the wizardy shops. You can get fitted out for Hogwarts just like Harry and Hermione. If we were in Hogwarts, I would be in Ravenclaw and Gross and his cronies in Slytheryn, of course.

Anyway, we had a great time on us own. It's a good job we didn't have no spend because we'd've spent it all there. In the end, we started to feel hungry. There were some ace food stalls but our pack-up is with the others, so I said we'd better find them. They were all going to the minster and that en't going to be hard to find.

We're going round looking for the way in when we spot them. Well, we actually see Gary and Dean, really. They are climbing on this statue of this Roman guy and Jack is trying to get them down before the cops come.

Then we see Amy and she goes, 'Hi, where'd you two get to?'

'Diagon Ally.'

'Ooh, that sounds good.'

'Yeah. Whoever built this place were a Potter fan.'

'Nah,' goes Rosie, 'It's not about being a fan. It's about the money, innit? When I leave school, I'm going to open a shop.'

'Ms King miss us?' I ask.

'No, don't think so.'

'So what's happening about us dinner?'

'Dunno. Apparently, Mr Kendall were in charge of that and he seems to have got lost.'

Of course, he turns up in the end. After us dinner, we go inside the minster. It's really big. I mean 'really big'

At the end of the day, we all pile back aboard the coach and Jack Frost says he expects us all to write down one thing we've learned from the trip. I mean, I'd learnt loads. What shall I put? I dunno. Something about the Romans, I guess. They were clever guys. They knew York were going to be a great place to make money - enough to build a huge minster - and judging from what we saw, it still is. Rosie's made up her mind she's going get a shop of her own in York one day. I hope she does.

When we get back, I ask Jack Frost why he wants to work as a teacher in Millheaton when there are plenty of things he could do to make money in places like York. He says that there are many things more important in life than making money and looking after kids is one of them. I'm glad he does. I mean, where would I be without people like him?

ACKNOWLEDGEMENTS

Tabitha began a long time ago. The teenage characters that feature in this story all exist in reality but none of them is based on a single individual – they sum up a lifetime's experience of working with young people going back to my own teenage years. So, if you've had me helping in your youth group, this is your story, so thank you. You are far too many to name – all of you are precious and different, coming from different parts of the world, not only West Yorkshire.

This book is dedicated to those who teach our teenagers. A lot of people do not realise that to survive in a secondary school, teachers have to have a deep commitment and love for the young people they encounter there. For the most part, it isn't the young people that make the job hard but the huge time commitment outside the classroom to ensure that the system works. Most of us only see the tip of the iceberg, so I thank the teachers as well as the youngsters who have inspired this work.

I wish to thank my beta readers, Mary Cookson, John Lynch, Jo Ullah and others, both adult and teenage, who have given their precious time to grapple with this at the various stages of its development. Also Pip Lovell, Anne Hewett, Kirstie Smith, Abi Gray and Remigio Raphael for helping with the young contributors. I am once again grateful to Anna Hewett-Rakthanee – still a teenager herself – for taking the trouble to get to know Tabitha and producing a beautiful cover design.

And finally, I am indebted to the great people of West Yorkshire with all their varied histories and cultural diversity. Without them, Britain – nay the world – would be the poorer. I may have grown up in Northamptonshire, studied in London and Canterbury, and taught in a secondary school in Papua New Guinea but I had still much to learn when I arrived in West Yorkshire. It was there that I met my wife who gets the final thanks – without her, as with all my writing, this book would never have been completed.